PHAEDRA

Titles available in this series

Greek Translations

Anna

published by Livanis 2011

PHAEDRA

Beryl Darby

JACH

ISBN 978-1-9997176-3-6

Printed and bound in the UK by
Berforts South West Ltd
Enterprise House,B52 Wrest Park, Silsoe,
Bedfordshire MK45 4HS

First published in the UK in 2018 by

JACH Publishing
92 Upper North Street, Brighton, East Sussex, England BN1 3FJ

website: www.beryldarbybooks.com

In memory of Anne Marie Aubrier –
such a delightful and interesting lady.

1910

Eleni and Maria had grown up together. There were three months between their birthdays, Eleni being the elder. They lived four houses apart in the village, Maria's father having the taverna and Eleni's father running the general store. Having been inseparable friends for years they were now no longer speaking to each other.

As soon as they were able to walk one would arrive at the other's house and spend the remainder of the day playing together. As they grew older their games involved catch, running up and down the dirt track that was the main road into the village until they were out of breath; giggling they would return to a house for a drink of cold water and decide upon their next activity.

In the small gardens behind the cottages the owners kept chickens and grew vegetables. From when they were first able to undertake small tasks they would be sent to the compost heap with the vegetable waste and expected to look for any eggs that had been laid and tell their mother the location.

Once they were considered by their mothers to be old enough to help with the household chores and begin to learn how to look after a house their playtime was curtailed. Each morning they would be expected to watch whilst their mother made the meal she planned for her family that evening, or made cheese or tsatziki once the milk had been delivered. Each girl was expected to be able to make up the salad to accompany whatever her mother

7

cooked each day. After a week of observation and instruction each was allowed to try to make the bread.

Turning the dough was hard work and neither girl was strong enough to complete the task unaided. Once the loaves had been prepared and shaped she would walk with her mother to the baker and ask him to place it in his oven, handing over the few lepta he charged for the service. Once the baked bread had cooled they would wait whilst their mother sliced it and help to pack it into the wooden barrel which would keep it fresh for the week or longer. Any bread left from the previous week would be sprinkled with water and baked hard over the open fire to make rusks and they would be in trouble if they allowed them to burn.

Neither girl complained. It was part of their education to learn how to cook, preserve food and make an appetising meal, often from very little. In between the cookery lessons they would be shown how to polish the wooden dresser, clean the windows so there were no smears left behind, check for cobwebs in the corners and generally make sure the house was clean and presentable if an unexpected caller should arrive.

Maria did not know who this caller would be. Occasionally Eleni's mother would arrive and the two women would send the girls outside whilst they talked. Maria's mother was getting fatter and Maria confided in Eleni that her mother must be having another baby. From her pallet in the corner of the room she could clearly hear what took place between her parents in their large bed, although the curtains were drawn around.

Although their mornings were taken up with the household chores, during the afternoon they were expected to sit and learn from their mothers how to weave cloth and blankets on the loom that stood at the side of the room. Finally each would be released from their mother's watchful eye and they would rush to meet up and spend the remainder of the day together. If either had made biscuits that morning they were allowed to take one for the other to sample and give her opinion.

The days passed monotonously, the only break in their routine was when Maria's mother gave birth to a healthy boy, attended by Despina, and Maria was expected to look after the house, tend to her mother's needs and have a meal prepared for her father each evening. She would lie down on her pallet each night so tired that she fell asleep immediately and only stirred when her father shook her by the shoulder in the morning and told her it was time she was up.

Each Sunday they would accompany their parents to church, sitting with their mothers whilst the men sat across on the other side of the aisle. They would sit beside each other, rolling their eyes when a neighbour arrived with her head uncovered and have to rush back home to collect her headscarf, watching old Manolis struggle in on his crutches, giggling when they heard him snoring during the service.

They sat demurely in church, covertly watching the boys, who had been scrubbed clean in the bath tub the previous night and given a clean shirt to wear, although they often had no shoes. Afterwards they would compare notes, deciding who had the nicest eyes, the curliest hair, who was tallest; and they knew the boys were watching them in the same way. Which girl had the prettiest hair, the largest eyes, the longest legs and which one was beginning to blossom into a woman?

The village was affluent compared with many in the region. The men would work their fields, growing melons, cucumber, courgettes, onions, garlic, tomatoes, beans and barley. Their wives and their children were expected to join them on a Friday to help with the arduous work of harvesting the crops ready for the men to take to market the following day.

Each week the men would drive their donkey into the nearest town, their carts loaded with produce. One of the bare foot boys would follow them collecting dung that the donkey would deposit as they travelled along the dirt road. This would be taken back to their farm and used as manure.

At night the girls would watch their fathers count the money they had taken during the day, but the amount meant little to either of them. Neither of them could count past ten and they could only write their names with difficulty. The boys would attend the Church where the Priest would give them a rudimentary knowledge of reading, writing and numeracy, but this was not considered necessary for the girls who would be responsible for running a house and bringing up a family.

Not all the villagers were farmers. Two had herds of goats and sheep that were rounded up and milked each day; the milk being placed in churns and strapped to their donkeys to be taken through the village and sold to the women to enable them to make cheese and tzatziki. Their oldest boys would accompany them to help with rounding up the animals. These boys would have boots, similar to their fathers, to protect them from the thorny scrub, their younger brothers having to wait until the boots were too small for their siblings so they could inherit them and have some warmth and protection during the winter months. When the animals were sheared the wool was taken back to their houses where their wives would wash, card and spin the wool into yarn before selling it to the women in the village to dye into a colour of their choice.

The forge was always busy, having three men working there, and a steady stream of customers would arrive from the outlying areas to have their donkey's hooves trimmed and new shoes fitted. They would also make or repair the farmers' forks, spades and hoes along with sharpening their shears and scythes and the scissors the women used. The metal grills that were placed over the window openings were also made and fitted by them, along with the hinges for the doors and their metal bar locks.

Panayiotis and his father called themselves carpenters, although they would do almost any job that was required of them. They would repair a shutter or door, make simple furniture, replace a tile on a roof, rebuild a wall or dig a grave in the churchyard whenever required.

The baker rose early to light his fire so the oven would be at the correct temperature when the women began to arrive with their dough or a meal they were unable to cook over their open fires. The metal implements he used to place the bread on whilst it baked and the long metal pole that was used to extract it safely from the intense heat needed continual repair and renewal by the blacksmiths. The butcher sold the surplus rabbits that the men shot and also doubled as a surgeon and dentist in an emergency. His ministrations were adequate for minor injuries, but no one wanted to be cut open by him if they could avoid the trauma.

Everyone, even Maria and Eleni's father, had olive trees along with a few apple, orange, lemon and pomegranate trees and it would be a communal effort by the villagers when the fruit was ready for harvesting. When the barley had been cut the winnowing would take place. Even the youngest child could be placed in the chair and guide the donkey around the threshing area to remove the seed from the stalks. The grain would be collected and placed in large baskets before being tossed into the air by the older children to remove the chaff.

There were a number of wells in the village and each day the women could be seen carrying heavy buckets back to their homes. Water was precious and used sparingly; the same small bowl being used by everyone to wash their hands and face until it was so discoloured that it was taken outside and given to a plant. Once a week a tin bath would be placed in the kitchen area, a meagre amount of water heated and each member of the family would take their turn to sit in it and wash their body. The man, being the head of the household, was always the first to take advantage of the facility and once again the dirty water would be taken outside and poured onto the dry soil around a plant.

The toilet was outside in a specific area where the chickens would roam and peck at the waste keeping the grass relatively clean and the odour at bay. Some, more self conscious than others, had placed a low wall to screen the area from the house and give a modicum of privacy, but when out in the fields or orchards any area was used when the need arose.

On the hill towards the end of the village there were bee hives, tended diligently by old Manolis who would struggle across the uneven ground on his crutches to remove the honey. This he sold to Eleni's father who in turn would sell it to the villagers to use as a sweetener. Manolis was rarely stung by his bees, but the other villagers gave the hives a wide berth and never attempted to steal honey for themselves.

During the mild evenings the women would sit outside their houses, often gathering in small groups to chat whilst they sewed, knit or crocheted, the children left to their own devices, whilst the men spent their evenings in the local taverna owned by Maria's father. There the men would sit, sometimes playing dominoes or back gammon, drinking the cheap village wine or the raki that Maria's father distilled in an outhouse.

Once it was too cold to sit outside the women would stay in their own homes, rarely visiting a neighbour, but the men continued with their routine of visiting the taverna each evening whatever the weather. The only time the women had a respite from their continual round of household chores or field work was on a Sunday when everyone donned their most respectable clothes and went to Church. They would listen intently to the sermon delivered by the village priest, kiss the religious icons and return to their homes, grateful for the two hours of rest they had experienced before the routine of the week recommenced.

Village life was arduous and mundane, the monotony only broken by Easter, Christmas, a Name Day or the occasional wedding, birth or Christening ceremony. No one complained; they knew no other way of life and provided there was enough food to feed the family and everyone was healthy they asked for nothing more. The one time there was an unexpected occurrence was when a cart was driven through the village carrying an old woman. Eleni and Maria stood with the other villagers shouting abuse and jeering whilst the boys threw stones at the unfortunate leprosy sufferer.

The doctor would visit once a month, unless there was a severe illness or accident when a man would be dispatched on a donkey to the town asking him to visit immediately. Other minor injuries or accidents, along with childbirth were dealt with by Despina. She prided herself that she had never lost a baby or its mother. The only excitement was when the pedlar appeared and the women would inspect his wares, selecting skeins of silk thread in various colours for their embroidery or taking the opportunity to renew a broken jug or cooking pot.

As the girls grew older they no longer played games but gathered together in small groups to talk whilst the boys would show off their prowess at football and try to attract the attention of a girl who had caught their eye. Some days they would walk as far as the big house on the corner before taking a path that led through the fields and watch the men, stripped to the waist, working in a field, their wives working equally as hard beside them.

Both girls would eye the men's naked chests and admire their rippling muscles, but most of them were already married and the younger ones betrothed

'Did you know that Anna is getting married next year?' asked Maria.

Eleni nodded. 'I knew she was betrothed to a boy from the next village last year. Have they set a date yet?'

'Not that I've heard. We could ask her.'

Eleni wrinkled her nose. 'I'm not sure I want to get married.'

Maria looked at her friend in surprise. 'You have to get married.'

'Why?'

'Well, it's expected of you. Besides what else would you do?'

'I don't know, but I don't want to have to spend my days working out in the fields.'

'You might not marry a farmer.'

Eleni gave Maria a scathing look. 'Who else is there to marry? The boys who help their fathers with the sheep and goats are too young and the men at the forge only have daughters.'

'Your father might decide someone from another village is suitable for you.'

'I don't want to marry someone I only meet on a couple of occasions before my wedding day. Suppose I disliked him?'

Maria shrugged. 'Even if you married a boy from our village you might find you don't like him. He might have bad breath or hit you if his meal was not ready when he wanted it.'

Eleni lowered her voice. 'I've heard that Manolis the bee keeper used to beat his wife until she took an axe and broke both his legs. That's why he's on crutches now.'

'His wife has been dead for years.'

Eleni nodded sagely. 'Once he was able to move around again he hit her over the head with the same axe. He claimed it was an accident and he didn't see her standing behind him.'

'I don't believe you. You're making it up.'

Eleni shrugged. 'I'm only telling you what I've heard.'

Maria leaned towards her friend. 'I've heard that when you're married you're expected to make lots of babies. My Mamma says once you become used to – you know – it isn't so bad.'

'Suppose you don't like – you know – and don't want babies?' frowned Eleni.

'That's when your husband would probably beat you. Do you know who you will marry?'

Eleni shook her head. 'I just hope my Pappa won't want me to marry one of my cousins. There are three of them that my father could choose from.'

'Have you met them?'

'Once.'

'Did you like one of them more than the others?' asked Maria eagerly. 'Could you suggest that your father betrothed you to him?'

'They are all older than me. One was very good looking, but

he hardly spoke and when he did I had a job to understand him. His father said he was very deaf and it made the words difficult for him to say.'

'Why is he deaf?' asked Maria curiously.

'I don't know.'

'What about the other two?'

'One has funny eyes and I wasn't sure if he was looking at me or somewhere else. The youngest one walks with a limp and stutters badly.'

Maria rolled her eyes. 'I think their mother must have had the Evil Eye put on her when she was expecting them. I don't think your father will consider the deaf one or the one with funny eyes as a suitor for you. He wouldn't want to have grandchildren with defects,' said Maria positively. 'He'll probably choose the other one with the limp and the stutter.'

Eleni shrugged. 'I hope not. I certainly wouldn't want – you know – with any one of them. The thought makes me feel ill. Pappa hasn't mentioned any one of them particularly to me so I'm hoping they may already be promised to someone else.'

'Of course, when I do get married I will insist that I have a house of my own,' said Maria imperiously with a shake of her head. 'I am not going to move into his parents' house and have to do as his mother tells me all the time.'

'He could move into yours.'

Maria shook her head. 'There's really not enough space. My brother and I have beds on the wall beneath the window, my parents have their bed on the opposite side and my mother has her loom on the far wall. There's no space for another bed.'

'What about the outhouse where your father keeps his still?'

'He wouldn't give that space up. How would he make the raki for his customers?'

'I was thinking your brother could move out there. His bed would not take up a lot of space.'

'Have you ever seen how big the outhouse is? The only way you could fit a bed in there would be to have half your mattress outside. I'm just thankful that my father doesn't keep sheep or goats or they would be in our living room during the winter. Think how dirty and smelly that would be and they might climb on you during the night.'

'At least you would be kept warm.'

Maria gave her friend a withering look. 'I'd rather have an extra blanket.'

Eleni nodded. In that respect she certainly agreed with her friend. 'Have you noticed Elias's moustache?' she asked, indicating the young man who was standing some distance away sporting a fuzz of hair on his upper lip.

Maria giggled. 'He's very proud of it. He keeps touching it with his fingers. If he isn't careful he'll wear it away.'

'Do you think he has a hairy chest like my father?'

'Go and ask him.' suggested Maria mischievously.

Eleni looked at her in horror. 'You can. I wouldn't dare.'

'We can look for him in the fields tomorrow. If he has his shirt off we'll know if he has a hairy chest.'

Elias knew the girls were discussing him. Neither girl was bad looking and he had that strange feeling in his loins as he gazed at them. He had experienced it a good deal recently and was aware that there was only one way to dispel the discomfort. He slunk back to his house and hid behind the low stone wall in the garden, hoping neither his mother or father would come out and discover him relieving himself.

Eleni considered Maria's words about a possible suitor and decided she would approach her mother, although she knew it would be her father who finally told her who her future husband was to be. If her mother told her it was to be the cousin who was deaf or the one with the funny eyes she would ask her mother to intercede on her behalf.

'Mamma, I've heard that Anna is getting married next year.'

Despina nodded. 'It's a good match. His father has a large olive grove.'

'Is that why her father decided she should marry him?'

'Probably.'

'Who has the largest olive grove in this village?'

'Babbis I think. Your father would know.'

'So I could marry one of his sons.'

'You're more likely to be betrothed to one of your cousins.'

Eleni screwed up her face. 'I don't like any of them.'

'It won't be up to you to say if you like him or not. Your father will decide if he is suitable.'

'Suppose I refuse?'

'You can't disobey your father,' said Despina firmly.

'I wouldn't want to leave the village. I'd rather stay here. There must be a local boy I could marry.'

Despina looked at her daughter suspiciously. 'Who do you have in mind?'

Eleni shrugged. 'No one in particular. Elias is nice looking and so is Panayiotis, Mattias is too young for me and the other older boys are already promised to someone.'

'There's more to a man than his looks. You're still too young to be thinking of marriage anyway. Let me look at that embroidery. Are your stitches straight?'

Despina took the piece of cloth into her hands and scrutinised the line of leaves that Eleni had embroidered. If the girl was thinking about marriage it was time to speak to Yiorgo about a suitor for her and it was unlikely that he would consider one of the village boys as her future husband.

Elias knew both girls were watching him and commenting on his appearance. His moustache was thickening and he was beginning to encourage the ends to curl upwards. Elias wondered if he would be able to persuade either girl to meet him in the orchard one evening and if she would allow him to investigate beneath her bodice or even better, beneath her skirt. It was annoying that they always seemed to be together.

Eleni had a strange fluttering feeling in her stomach. Her father had announced that they were going to visit his brother and family in the next village after Church on Sunday. That meant meeting her cousins again and could mean that her father was nearing a decision as to which one was suitable for her to be betrothed to. She would avoid the one who was deaf and the other who could not look straight at her and see if the youngest one was more attractive, despite his limp and his stutter.

Upon arriving at their house she saw the three young men were present, still wearing the clean clothes they had donned for Church that morning. Her father and his brother disappeared to the taverna whilst her mother and Olga sat outside talking over glasses of lemonade and freshly baked biscuits. Eleni sat there decorously as the three young men hesitated to make conversation with her, shuffling their feet self consciously. She sipped at her lemonade and tried not to drop any biscuit crumbs onto her skirt.

'So, Eleni,' her aunt finally looked at her, 'Your Mamma tells me that you are a very accomplished young lady.'

Eleni blushed. 'I have tried hard to learn from my Mamma.'

Olga nodded. 'As every girl should. It is so important once you are married to be able to please your husband's palate and keep his clothes in good repair along with your other duties.'

Eleni blushed more deeply and nodded.

'I would have liked one of mine to have been a girl, but it was not to be,' continued Olga, 'Now I am thankful I only had boys so I did not have to make sure they knew how to cook and sew. Their father has taught them how to look after the land. I make sure there is a substantial meal waiting for them each evening and that their shirts are clean for Sunday when we go to Church. The good Father has complimented me on many occasions on how clean and well behaved they are.'

'I'm sure they are a credit to you,' murmured Eleni.

She did not like her third cousin any more than the other two. The way he looked at her made her feel uncomfortable. Sitting in the garden listening to her mother and Aunt Olga talk, her aunt extolling the virtues of her three sons, was extremely boring.

'My Alexandros, my first born, he's a joy. He tries so hard with his speech, but because he cannot hear the words we speak clearly he cannot always say them. We are all patient with him and he has improved considerably from when he was a small boy and could only make noises. We took him to the doctor, but he said there was nothing he could do and we would gradually understand what Alexandros was trying to say. He was right, of course, and if we are really at a loss to his meaning Alexandros draws a picture or points and we do the same when we have been unable to make him understand.' She patted Alexandros's hand and he smiled, understanding that whatever his mother had been saying about him was complimentary.

'I've no complaints about my other two. They're all good boys. Up in the fields with their father whatever the weather and never a complaint from any of them. They're always willing to help with any of the heavy work and collect the water from the well for me each morning. All three are mild mannered and good tempered. There is never a cross word between them.'

'Are any of them betrothed?' asked Despina and Eleni crossed her fingers surreptitiously.

Olga shook her head. 'Not yet. We've considered some of the local girls over the years, but one from a different village might be more suitable. We have heard rumours that a couple who live here are quite free with their favours.' Olga shook he head. 'How do they expect to make good marriages if they allow the boys to take advantage of them? Besides, you could never be sure of their behaviour once they were married. They could conveniently forget their vows when another man caught their eye. I would never let any of my boys marry a girl of dubious character.'

'We keep a strict eye on Eleni,' Despina assured her sister in law. 'She has an unblemished reputation.'

Eleni felt her face go hot and from the corner of her eye she could see the youngest of her cousins looking at her speculatively.

'I'm sure you do, and you must bring her to visit us more often. She should get to know her cousins better. I understand that she's a little shy at the moment, but give her time and I'm sure she will enjoy their company.'

Eleni sat silently in the cart as they drove home to their village. She did not like any of her cousins and shuddered inwardly at the thought of being married to any one of them. Upon arriving at their house she climbed out of the cart and began to walk along the road.

'Where are you off to?' called Despina.

'I'm going to meet Maria.'

Despina shook her head. 'Not tonight. I need some help with the chores that were not done this afternoon and your father will want his supper.'

Elias saw Maria standing a short way down the road and for once she was alone.

'Where's Eleni?' he asked.

'She's gone to visit her relatives. I've been waiting here hoping she would be back soon.'

'She could be gone for hours yet. You know what it's like when families start to talk together.'

Maria sighed. 'I suppose so. I might as well go back home.'

'You could always walk down to the orchard with me. You'd still be able to see them coming down the road.'

Maria felt both flattered and a little excited. Elias was asking her to walk with him. That must mean he liked her.

'I do like your moustache, Elias. It makes you look so handsome and grown up.'

Elias smiled with pleasure and twirled one of the ends. 'I am fortunate that it has grown quickly.' He moved his hand to his chin and stroked the darkening hair growth. 'I think I will grow a beard as well.'

'If you grow a beard won't that detract from your moustache?'

Elias shrugged. 'I can always shave the beard off.' He pushed open the gate leading into the orchard and waited for Maria to pass through. 'Come on,' he said as she hesitated. 'We can sit under the trees and eat some apricots. You'll be able to hear the donkey and cart coming.'

'I shouldn't really be alone with you,' demurred Maria. 'My Pappa would be cross.'

'There's no need for your Pappa to know. We'll go in amongst the trees where we can't be seen from the road.' Elias took her hand and Maria felt a tingle go through her body.

Elias looked at the apricot trees critically. 'Some of the fruit looks ripe and ready to eat.' He released Maria's hand and reached up to the branches, testing each fruit before he picked it and placed it in the pocket of Maria's apron.

'That should be plenty,' said Maria. 'If we eat too many we'll feel ill tomorrow.'

Elias grinned at her. 'I'm never ill. Come on, let's sit here.'

Maria sat demurely beside him and handed him an apricot. In two bites he had demolished it and began to rummage in her apron pocket for another, managing to touch between her legs and feeling her give an involuntary little jerk. As soon as he had eaten the second one his hand went back into her apron and Maria held his wrist.

'I'll pass you one.'

'I'd rather get it out for myself. You know you are the most beautiful girl in the village and every time I see you I want you for my wife.'

Maria blushed. 'You'd have to ask my Pappa.'

Whilst Maria held Elias's wrist he placed his other hand inside her apron pocket, but he was not searching for an apricot. Maria gave a gasp.

'Elias, you shouldn't touch me there until we are married.'

'I want to touch you there. I want to touch you all over. It could be years before your father would agree to us getting married.

21

There's no harm in touching or looking,' he added. 'I'd like you to touch me.'

Maria placed a hand tentatively on Elias's chest. Elias lifted it and kissed her palm. 'You have beautiful soft hands. Put it there.' he placed her hand on his trousers between his legs and she could feel his hard erection beneath the cotton.

'No, Elias, we shouldn't.' Maria withdrew her hand.

Elias drew a deep, shuddering breath. 'That felt so good. Let me touch you again.'

Maria shook her head. 'If I let you I know what will happen.'

'Wouldn't you like it to happen?'

'It isn't a question of what I would like,' replied Maria primly.

'At least undo your bodice and let me touch you.'

Maria hesitated and Elias took that for her acquiescence. He knelt beside her and undid the laces on her bodice, pushing his hands beneath her blouse and cupping her breasts.

'They're bigger than I thought,' he said, massaging her breasts gently. 'You shouldn't lace your bodice so tightly. You're keeping them all squashed up. If it was looser you could show them off properly.'

'I don't think my father would approve if I flaunted myself.'

Elias pushed her blouse up further and placed a hand over each of her breasts. 'I wish I could take these home with me.'

'Don't be silly, Elias,' giggled Maria.

'I'm not being silly. I would have one in each pocket and spend all day touching them. When I went to bed at night I would place them on my pillow and kiss them until I fell asleep.' He bent his head and began to kiss Maria's breasts, running his tongue over her nipples and feeling them harden. 'I can't wait to be married to you, Maria.'

Maria did not answer, the sensation Elias was creating in her as he kissed and fondled her was making her head swim and she thought she might faint. Abruptly he pulled away from her.

'I have to do something. I'll be back in a minute.'

Maria looked after him puzzled as he disappeared further into the trees. She pulled down her blouse, tucked it into her skirt and re-laced her bodice. She was loath to get up and leave the orchard, but how long was she supposed to wait for Elias to return? She took an apricot from her pocket, her fingers sticky from the juice of those that had been crushed by Elias's grasping hands, and bit into it slowly. If he had not returned by the time she had consumed two fruits she would go home.

As she took a bite from the second Elias reappeared, looking a little embarrassed. 'I'm sorry. I couldn't contain myself any longer.'

Maria shrugged. 'There's no shame in needing a pee urgently.'

Elias looked at her with a slightly bemused expression. That was not what he had disappeared for. 'Are there any apricots left?' he asked, delving into her apron pocket and allowing his hand full rein between her legs.

Maria wriggled against him, enjoying the sensations he was creating in her. 'Stop it, Elias. I really should go now. I'm sure Eleni will be home any minute and she'll wonder where I am.'

'Don't tell her you've been with me.'

'Why not?'

'She might tell your Mamma and she might stop us from meeting again.'

'I'm sure she wouldn't.'

'I'm sure she would.'

'I mean I'm sure Eleni wouldn't tell my Mamma.'

'It's still better to keep it to ourselves. Meet me here again next week. Make an excuse to Eleni so you come alone. I want to be with you, not her.'

'You really do want to marry me, Elias?'

'Of course. I wouldn't want to meet you again otherwise.'

'Oh, Elias.' Maria kissed his lips and ran her hands across his broad shoulders. 'I do love you.' Her earlier aversion to being married was completely dispelled after experiencing Elias's attention.

'I'm pleased about that. I wouldn't want an unwilling wife. You go on home and I'll follow later.'

'You're not going to walk me home?'

'It's better that we're not seen together until your father has given his approval. Meet me here next Sunday. Promise?'

Maria nodded happily. 'I'll be waiting for you.'

'What is that mess on your apron?' asked Anastasia as Maria entered the house.

Maria looked down guiltily. 'I picked some apricots. One of them squashed in my pocket,'

'You shouldn't be up in the orchard on your own.'

Maria was about to say that she was with Elias then thought better of it. Her mother would be even more disapproving if she knew her daughter had been up in the orchard with a young man from the village and no one chaperoning them.

'I was passing the time whilst waiting for Eleni. I'll wash my apron, Mamma and be more careful in future.'

Eleni sought out Maria the following evening. 'I'm sure my Pappa is going to insist I marry one of my horrible cousins,' she said, close to tears.

'They could be nice men, despite their unfortunate afflictions.'

'According to my mother we are going to visit them regularly, every other Sunday and she has also invited them to come and visit us. I will be so embarrassed if the villagers see me with them.'

Maria tried to hide her joy at the news. If Eleni was visiting her cousins there would be no reason why she couldn't meet Elias on a Sunday evening. 'Unless anyone stops and speaks to you no one will notice their problems.'

'They'll see that Nikos, the youngest, one has a limp even if he doesn't speak to anyone.'

Maria shrugged. 'That's nothing. Many men walk with a limp.'

'The old men, not the young ones. What did you do with yourself yesterday evening?'

Maria looked down at her skirt, her face reddening. 'I waited around for you to come back and picked some apricots. One of them squashed in my pocket and my Mamma was cross because it was my best apron. She made me wash it out immediately.'

'Has the stain gone?'

'I think so. If it hasn't I'll have to make myself a new apron and use that one as a rag.'

'Shall we go up to the orchard and pick some apricots now?'

Maria shook her head, 'I don't think it would be a good idea for me to eat some more today and if I made a mess of this apron my Mamma would be really cross and probably forbid me to go up there again to pick fruit.' Maria did not want to go to the orchard with Eleni; that had become a special place for her and Elias.

The girls talked desultorily, Maria's head was filled with thoughts of Elias and Eleni was thoroughly depressed about a future visit to her cousins.

Eleni gave a deep sigh. 'At least we won't have to go again this coming weekend. We'll be able to meet as usual in the evening.'

'Of course.' Maria had not considered that Eleni would expect to meet her on the Sunday evening when she had promised to meet Elias. She would have to think up some excuse when the time came. 'Forget about your cousins. Shall we walk down the road and see if the other girls are around?'

As they made their way towards the forge Elias was walking towards them. 'Good evening, Maria and Eleni.'

'Good evening, Elias,' they chorused back and he continued on his way.

'Now if my Pappa said I was to marry Elias I would not be unhappy,' observed Eleni. 'He is so good looking.'

Maria gave a secret smile. She was the one betrothed to Elias.

After the church service on Sunday Eleni took Maria's arm. 'I'll meet you this evening.'

Maria shook her head. 'Not tonight. I have awful stomach ache. I want to stay at home quietly. I may even lie down for a while.'

Eleni nodded sympathetically. She knew how uncomfortable

she felt each month. 'I'll see you tomorrow. You'll probably feel better by then.'

'I expect so,' agreed Maria. She was sure that after she had spent some time with Elias she would feel considerably better. Each time she thought about their impending assignation her heart gave a flutter.

Maria waited until they had eaten their evening meal and she had washed the dishes for her mother before she slipped out of the door. She was thankful that she did not have to pass Eleni's house to get to the orchard. Eleni would have been bound to see her and ask if her stomach was now well enough for them to spend the evening together.

There was no sign of Elias and Maria walked into the orchard until she stopped beside the tree that she believed she and Elias had sat beneath the previous week. She looked around anxiously. Would Elias actually come? She blushed at the memory of her allowing him to unlace her bodice and lift her blouse. She should have refused. Having had his way he was probably not interested in her any more, despite having told her at the time that he wanted to marry her.

Maria could hear someone moving towards her and she spun round, relieved when she saw it was Elias.

'You gave me quite a fright,' she said.

'I thought it better to enter the orchard further down and make sure there was no one else around.' He held out his arms to Maria and she entered them happily. He kissed her lips hungrily. 'You've no idea how difficult it has been for me to wait a whole week to be with you again. You are all I've thought about.'

'Oh, Elias, I've been thinking about you too.'

'Did you tell Eleni?'

Maria shook her head. 'You told me not to.'

'Good, we don't want her to be here with us when we are enjoying private things. Sit down; the ground is quite dry.'

Elias pushed her away from him gently and she sank to the ground where Elias joined her. He took her hand in his.

'I couldn't believe how beautiful you were last week. Undo your bodice and let me look at you again.'

Without hesitation Maria complied. As she hoped Elias did more than look at her breasts. He stroked them, cupped them, kissed them and bit at them gently whilst Maria made small noises of pleasure. She was not sure quite how it happened but Elias had his hand up her skirt and was investigating her most private place of all with his fingers whilst he continued to kiss and fondle her.

'Elias, you mustn't.'

'I want to and I know you want me to touch you. I don't want to feel you through your skirt. I want to touch your skin and soft hair.'

Maria felt powerless. She knew she should resist, but he was making her feel so good inside. She revelled in his intimate investigation and felt quite breathless. When he finally pushed his trousers apart and thrust himself inside her she gave a little cry then gave herself up to the sensations he was creating and moved rhythmically with him, She was floating, her head was spinning and she clutched Elias's broad shoulders as if she was drowning. There was an incredible moment when something inside her seemed to explode and then she felt Elias go limp.

He was breathing hard as he smiled down at her and stroked her cheek. 'That was really good. Was it good for you as well?'

Maria could hardly speak. 'Yes,' she murmured. 'Do it again.'

'I can't for a while, but we can continue to enjoy ourselves.' Elias turned his attention back to Maria's breasts, whilst she lay there longing for him to be able to take her again.

Both Maria and Eleni were counting down the days until Sunday but for different reasons. Maria could not wait to spend some time in the orchard with Elias and repeat the wonderful experience she had had the previous week and Eleni was dreading that she would be taken to meet her cousins again.

'Pappa has said we're not going visiting this afternoon.' she whispered to Maria as they left the church together. We'll be able to meet up this evening,'

Maria shook her head, 'I'd rather not. It's a bad week for me.'

'I thought that was last week,' frowned Eleni.

'No, I just had stomach ache then. It must have been something I'd eaten.' Maria wondered what excuse she could make the following week if Eleni was not visiting her relatives.

Eleni felt despondent when her father announced they were visiting her cousins again. 'I don't know what to say to them,' she protested. 'Why don't you and Mamma go and I'll stay here?'

Her father shook his head. 'It is a good opportunity for you to get to know everyone better. You'll soon find you have things in common to talk about. We should have made the effort to meet up more often when you were all younger.'

Eleni shook her head, but knew she could not disobey or argue too vehemently with her father. He would disappear to the taverna with his brother, spending the time drinking and laughing, whilst she would be left sitting uncomfortably with her aunt and the three young men.

She sipped at the lemonade she had been given and nibbled at a biscuit trying to avoid looking at any of her cousins, although she knew they were all scrutinizing her appearance. She was quite relieved when Nikos made a suggestion.

'M-m-mamma, as P-p-pappa and Uncle are at the t-t-taverna would Aunt D-d-despina and Eleni be interested in w-w-walking around the village? I w-w-would be happy to accompany you,' smiled Nikos.

Olga nodded. 'You can all walk with us. We can go to the Church. I'm sure you would be interested to go inside, Despina. We have some very fine icons and I take my turn with the other ladies to polish the candlesticks and other fitments each week. Even on my death bed I would rise and complete that duty.'

Eleni held her tongue. She had been brought up to attend Church every week, the only exception being when she had suffered a severe bout of tonsillitis and could not lift her head from the pillow. She did not think her aunt's action would be appreciated if she spread illness amongst the villagers. She decided she did not really like her Aunt Olga very much and if she was forced to marry one of her sons she would certainly refuse to live under the same roof as her aunt.

The icons were no different from the ones in the church at Kastelli. Trying to look interested she trailed around beside her mother whilst her Aunt Olga kissed every icon and related the history of every Saint. As they moved slowly around the church she felt Nikos surreptitiously touching her bottom and she glared at him. He smiled back and as he finally held the door open for them to leave he actually dared to pinch her buttocks.

The colour rushed to her face and she wished fervently that her father would reappear and announce that it was time to leave. Once they were home she would complain to her mother about the behaviour of the young man and plead with her not to have to make any more visits.

'Mamma, can I talk to you about our visit this afternoon?'

'Not now. Your father has something to tell you.'

Eleni bent her head. That could only mean that her father had made his decision about her future husband. Obediently she followed her mother into the living room and sat on the stool waiting for her father to finish stabling the donkey.

He entered rubbing his hands together. 'Well, that was a good visit. I'm sure Olga made you very welcome.'

'Yes, Pappa.'

'How are you getting on with your cousins? They're good, hard working boys.'

'I'm sure they are.' Eleni looked down at her hands. She was gripping them so tightly that the knuckles were white.

'My brother and I had a long talk and we think that Alexandros would be the most suitable one for you to marry.'

Eleni looked up in horror. 'That's the oldest one, isn't it?'

'That's right. Alexandros,'

'I don't want to marry him, Pappa. I can't understand what he says.'

'You'll soon get to understand him. His family have no problem. They will all help you until you have become familiar with his speech.'

Eleni shook her head. 'I don't want to get married and I certainly do not want to have to go to live with Aunt Olga.'

'You'll get used to the idea. It won't be for a while yet anyway. We'll make a betrothal announcement at the beginning of the next year and you can be married at the end of the summer when there is less work for them to do on their farm.'

Eleni sat there stunned. 'So soon?' she managed to utter.

'It's about the right amount of time. You'll have a year, near enough, to finish making your wedding clothes and I'll have some money saved up so the villagers can have a few barrels of wine with the wedding meal. It will be quite an occasion.'

Eleni felt hot tears on her cheeks. 'Can I go and tell Maria?'

'She'll be envious that you are going to be married before her. I don't know who her father will find for her, she hasn't any suitable cousins.'

'She could marry Alexandros,' said Eleni quickly. 'I wouldn't mind.'

'No,' her father shook his head. 'We've reached an agreement and can't change things now. I could do with something to eat, Despina. I've not been sitting eating biscuits all afternoon, like some people.'

Despina rose immediately. 'I only need to heat up the food I left ready. We can all have a glass of wine with our meal to celebrate the good news. Are you hungry, Eleni?'

Eleni shook her head. She felt sick. 'Not at the moment. I can always have something when I've seen Maria.'

'You ought to eat something and join us in drinking a toast to your future,' chided her mother.

'Let the girl go, she's anxious to tell her friend the good news. Isn't that right, Eleni?' Her father smiled at her benignly.

Eleni nodded dumbly and walked to the door. What was she going to do?

Eleni did not go towards Maria's house but in the opposite direction to where the olive groves were planted. There was unlikely to be anyone around and she needed to be alone. She sat down on a low stone wall and buried her face in her apron, sobbing hard.

'What's wrong?'

She looked up startled and tried to remove the tear stains by rubbing her apron across her face.

'Are you hurt?' Elias was looking down at her compassionately. Eleni shook her head.

'There must be something wrong. You were sobbing as if your heart would break. Have you had bad news? Is someone ill?'

'My father says I have to be married.'

'Well, that's good news, isn't it?'

'My Pappa says I have to marry one of my cousins. I don't like any of them and the one he has chosen for me is deaf. I can't understand a word he says.'

Elias frowned. 'That's unfortunate, but you probably will understand him, given time.'

'They're all horrible and their mother is even worse. She took us to visit the Church and we had to say a prayer when we entered, kiss every single icon, and say another prayer before we left. We were in there for hours.'

Elias stroked his moustache. 'When are you supposed to be getting married? '

'Pappa said we would be betrothed next year and married at the end of the summer. What am I going to do?'

'Suppose you told your Pappa that you had already promised yourself to someone else?'

'He would ignore that.'

'He couldn't ignore it if you were expecting a child.'

'Elias!' Eleni's face flamed.

Elias took her hand. 'Let's go into the olive grove and we can talk about your situation without fear of being interrupted.'

Eleni swung her legs over the wall and Elias caught her as she jumped down. They sat together behind the wall and Elias placed his arm around Eleni's shoulders.

'So, is there anyone in the village that you especially like?'

'I've not thought about any of you in that way.'

'Any young man in the village would be happy to be married to you. I've thought about you a lot, Eleni. You are the loveliest girl in the village. I'd be proud to know that you were going to be my wife.'

'You would?'

Elias nodded. 'You're much too delightful to be married to some deaf cousin who you don't like.'

'I don't think my Pappa will change his mind.'

'Then there's only one thing to do, isn't there?'

'What's that?'

'I told you, tell your father you're promised to someone else and make sure when you do so that you are expecting a child.'

'That doesn't seem right.'

'Can you think of a better idea?'

Eleni shook her head.

'Come here, then.' Elias pulled her to him and kissed her cheek. 'Do you like me, Eleni?'

'Yes.'

'Then show me how much. If you want to tell your father you are promised to me you have to show me that you mean it. I wouldn't want to get my hopes up and then find that you didn't care.'

Elias began to unlace Eleni's bodice and thrust his hand up inside her blouse. He let out a sigh of contentment. 'I've been longing to do that for such a long time. Just looking at you as you walk along the road makes me want you.'

'Really, Elias? Would you really like to be married to me?'

'It would be delightful. We wouldn't have to lie in an olive grove to enjoy each other.'

Eleni gave a little giggle. The sensation she was experiencing as Elias touched her breasts was most enjoyable. He shifted his position slightly and with his free hand began to pull her skirt up above her knees.

'What are you doing? You shouldn't pull my skirt up.'

'I want to look at you and touch you. Wouldn't you like to look at me?'

Eleni hesitated. She had seen her father naked on occasions and never taken very much notice of his body. There was nothing wrong with looking at naked manhood. Elias pulled apart his cotton trousers and Eleni gasped. She had certainly never seen her father like that.

Elias smiled at her. 'You're not going to refuse me now, are you? You can see I'm desperate for you.'

'I'll not refuse to marry you, Elias.'

He pushed her legs apart and knelt over her. 'We'll make a promise, and by the time your father is ready to betroth you to your cousin we'll tell him it's impossible.'

'No, Elias, we mustn't. Suppose I became pregnant?'

'I thought that was what you wanted so you could tell your father you were already promised and couldn't marry your cousin?'

Eleni bit at her lip. 'Let me think about it, Elias.'

'What is there to think about? You know it's the only solution.'

'You wouldn't tell the other boys in the village tomorrow?'

'Certainly not.' Elias knelt across Eleni and pulled her skirt up to her waist. 'I'll be gentle, I promise you.'

Eleni closed her eyes. If this was what was needed to avoid marrying one of her cousins she would succumb to Elias. Even if she did not become pregnant before the announcement of her betrothal, Elias could ask her father for permission to marry her and they could confess that they had lain together.

When Elias finally left her body she could not complain about the experience. He had been gentle and not hurt her as she had anticipated. Unexpected sensations of pleasure and longing had flooded through her and she wondered if that always happened or only on the first occasion.

She smiled timidly up at him. 'Thank you, Elias.'

'I should be thanking you. You are just as delightful as I always imagined.'

'I can't wait to tell Maria that we are secretly betrothed.'

Elias frowned. This was a complication that he had not anticipated. 'That's not a good idea. Keep it to yourself. We don't want word to get back to your father. Tell Maria you are going to be betrothed to your cousin. This will be our special secret.' He kissed her cheek. 'Promise?'

'If you say so, Elias. When will I see you again?'

'You see me every day in the village.'

'No, I mean like this.'

'Come to the olive grove on Wednesday after you've had your meal. I'll be waiting for you.'

'So how was your visit this Sunday?' asked Maria. She was feeling decidedly aggrieved. Elias had not arrived in the orchard as she had expected, although she had waited there for nearly an hour hoping he would turn up.

Eleni shrugged. 'As bad as ever. My father says I am going to be betrothed to the oldest cousin, Alexandros, the one who is deaf.'

'Oh, Eleni. That's awful. What are you going to do about it?'

'I'm trying to think of something.'

'You could run away from home.'

Eleni shook her head. 'Where would I go? ' She sighed. 'I'm sure there has to be a way out. Alexandros may not want to marry me.'

'He'd be a fool to refuse.'

Eleni shrugged again and did not answer. If she was pregnant by the end of the year she was certain that her aunt would not encourage any of her sons to marry her. Her father would have to agree to her marrying Elias instead.

1911

Maria could hardly contain herself. She had watched her body thickening over the previous four months and she was certain now that she was carrying a child, although she had been able to keep the knowledge hidden from her mother. She was sure that Elias would be as delighted as she was when she told him that evening. Her father would not have any excuse to delay their wedding and at last she would be able to tell Eleni.

Eleni had been acting strangely over the previous few months. She had made excuses that she was unable to meet up on a Wednesday evening. At first Maria had accepted the excuses, then became convinced that Eleni was doing it deliberately because she was piqued at Maria's continual refusal to meet her on a Sunday evening and then decided it was unimportant.

Despite the night being cold with snow threatening Maria wrapped herself in her cloak and left her house. Elias was waiting for her, rubbing his hands and stamping his feet.

'It's too cold to be here for very long,' he said as he kissed her.

'It doesn't matter,' Maria smiled broadly. 'Once we're married we won't have to meet in the orchard. I'm pregnant, Elias.'

'Pregnant? Are you sure?'

'Absolutely certain. I didn't have any of the usual woman's signs last month or the one's before. I've been longing to tell you, but I wanted to make quite sure first.'

Elias swallowed down his feeling of dread. He would have to speak to Maria's father. He knew the man would not refuse him to preserve the good name of his daughter, but it was likely to be an acrimonious discussion.

'When would be a good time for me to come to the taverna?'

'You can't talk to him there; people will be around. It's far better that you come to the house once the New Year celebrations have finished. The villagers will have spent all their money and Pappa will be closing early.'

'After Twelfth Night then.' Elias placed his arms around her. 'You really should not be out here on a night like this. You mustn't get a chill.'

Maria giggled up at him. 'Then you must hold me close to you so I stay warm.'

'That's not a good idea. You know the effect you have on me.'

'We could go to the shed again where you store the winter feed for the animals. It will be warm in there.'

'Do you really want to?'

Maria nodded eagerly. 'Of course I do. No one will see us walk through the village together as it's dark.'

'Come on, then. We'd better hurry. I'm becoming more than ready to roll around in the hay with you.'

'I hope you'll be doing more than rolling around,' Maria looked up at him mischievously as they hurried from the orchard hand in hand.

'Now all the celebrations are over we can visit your cousins and make your betrothal to Alexandros official.. We'll go on Sunday after church. I'm sure they'll be waiting anxiously for us.'

Eleni shook her head. 'It isn't possible, Pappa. I'm promised to some one else.'

'You're not promised to anyone without my permission.'

Eleni took a deep breath. The moment had come. 'I'm pregnant.'

'You're what? Tell me I didn't hear right.'

'I'm pregnant, Pappa'

Yiorgo looked his daughter up and down. 'I don't believe you.'

'It's true, Pappa. I'm promised to Elias.'

'Elias? Elias from the village? I arrange a good marriage for you and you behave like the village slut.'

'You wanted to marry me to Alexandros. He's older than me and deaf. What is good about that?' answered Eleni angrily.

'His father has extensive farm land. You would have had an easy life.'

'I don't care how much farm land my uncle has or if I would have had an easy life. If you had listened to me when I said how much I disliked all of them this would not have happened. I only did it because I didn't want to be married to Alexandros.'

'So you had an arrangement? That's worse than if you had some affection for each other.'

'I do care for Elias and he said he wanted to marry me. He said Alexandros would not want to marry me if I was pregnant and I believed him.' Tears were coursing their way down Eleni's cheeks. She wished Elias was there with her to lend his support.

'You stupid girl. You deserve to be sent to Leros.'

'I'd rather go to Leros than be married to any one of those horrible creepy cousins.'

'Have you told Elias that you're pregnant? He may well change his mind when he hears that news.'

'I haven't told him yet. I've not had the opportunity.'

'Well, I'll certainly be having a word with him and his father tomorrow. Be thankful that I haven't taken my belt to you, my girl. You've been brought up to know that such wayward conduct is wrong.'

Yiorgo rose early, determined to speak to Elias's father before he left to go to the fields and see if the frost had damaged any of his late crops. He knocked hard on the door and demanded admittance from the bleary eyed man who had obviously consumed a considerable amount of alcohol the previous night.

Yiorgo pushed his way inside,. 'I want to talk to you and also to Elias. Did you know he had been seeing my daughter and he has made her pregnant?'

'He's been seeing Maria.'

'He's also been seeing my Eleni.' Yiorgo compressed his lips. He was not sure he wanted the young man as a husband for his daughter.

'Are you sure your Eleni is pregnant?'

'She's a truthful girl. Time will tell, but I don't think she has made the story up. What do you have to say, Elias?'

Elias looked up reluctantly. 'It's possible,' he admitted.

'That's settled, then. You'll marry my Eleni.'

Elias shook his head. 'It isn't as simple as that. I've said I'll marry Maria. We met with her father last night.'

'Well you'll have to tell him you can't marry her after all,' said Yiorgo triumphantly.

'Maria is also pregnant,' muttered Elias.

'What?' Elias's father looked at his son in disbelief. 'Is this true, Elias? Have you made two girls pregnant at the same time?'

Elias shrugged. 'They're both lovely girls.'

'They were, until you took advantage of them.'

'I didn't mean to make them pregnant,' said Elias truculently.

'You stupid boy. What made you think that they wouldn't become pregnant? You've lived on a farm all your life and watched the animals mating and the subsequent outcome.'

Yiorgo clenched his fists. 'If you were my son I'd thrash you to within an inch of your life.'

'Well he's not your son. I'll deal with him and it wouldn't hurt if you installed some morals into your daughter. It takes two, remember.'

'Your son must have forced her. She would never have submitted to him willingly.'

Elias gave a slight smirk. 'I didn't force either of them. They were both more than willing.'

Yiorgo longed to hit Elias but he knew Andreas would come to his son's defence and he could not take them both on in a fist fight.

'I'm going to speak to Maria's father. He may not be so happy for you to marry his daughter when he hears about your philandering.' Yiorgo stamped out of the cottage, slamming the door behind him.

Andreas turned to his son and shook his head. 'You have been totally irresponsible. What got into you? Surely one girl was enough.'

'Eleni asked me to make her pregnant so she would not have to marry her cousin.'

'She asked you! Then the girl's a trollop. Best you stick to the arrangement we made last night and you marry Maria. No running off to visit Eleni on the sly.'

'I'll want to see my child.'

'You'll see it every day in the village. To make two girls pregnant at the same time is nothing to be proud of, Elias.'

Elias held his head in his hands; he was not sure which girl he preferred – Maria who was full of mischief and thoroughly enjoyed his lovemaking or Eleni who had only accepted him in the first place to avoid having to marry her cousin, but who was now a willing participant.

'I suppose it will have to be Maria, provided her father is still agreeable,' said Elias finally.

'Then Maria it must be. Forget Eleni and don't see her again however tempted you may be.'

Elias nodded. How was he going to keep the knowledge from Maria that he was also fathering a child with Eleni? The truth was bound to get out eventually and he could end up with neither girl and just a bad name in the village.

Yiorgo hammered on the door of the taverna until Anastasia finally opened it to him. 'We're not open yet, Yiorgo.'

'I need to see Manolis and I need to see him now.'

'He's only just up,' protested Anastasia. 'We were late last night. We stayed up celebrating as Maria is betrothed.'

'I know,' growled Yiorgo. 'That's what I need to see him about. I'll wait in the taverna until he comes.'

Anastasia shrugged. 'I'll tell him.' She was not expecting Manolis to be pleased to have an early morning visit from his neighbour. After the amount of wine he had consumed the previous evening he had slept heavily, snoring loudly, and complained about his head when he finally awoke.

Yiorgo sat at a table, running his worry beads between his fingers whilst he waited for Manolis to appear. If the man did not know his daughter was pregnant he might be persuaded to cancel the betrothal that Elias claimed had been sealed the previous evening.

Manolis was still suffering from the excessive amount of alcohol he had consumed the previous night when he sat down at the table opposite Yiorgo. He had planned to stay in his bed for the remainder of the morning to recover.

'What is so urgent that you had to see me immediately?' He leaned his head on his hand, wishing the pounding would stop.

'I understand that Elias came to see you last night.'

Manolis nodded and winced as an arc of pain shot up into his head. 'They may have done wrong, but he's prepared to put that right by marrying her.'

'He can't right two wrongs.'

'What do you mean?'

'He's made my Eleni pregnant also.'

'What! You mean he's been seeing both of them?'

'Must have been. On the sly. I didn't give him permission to court my Eleni.'

Manolis groaned. He wished he could think straight. 'Are you sure it was Elias who made your daughter pregnant?'

'I've just come from him and his father. He admitted he'd been seeing both the girls.'

Manolis frowned. 'He can't marry both – which one is it going to be?'

'If you tell him you're no longer willing for him to marry Maria then he'll have to marry Eleni.'

Manolis shook his head, again regretting the reaction it gave him. 'I'll not do that. My girl is not only pregnant but she's over the moon to be marrying Elias.'

'How do you think my daughter is going to feel?' asked Yiorgo angrily.

'The same as my daughter would if I now forbade the marriage. I'm sorry about your Eleni, but I'm not prepared to refuse my daughter.'

Yiorgo banged his fist on the table, making Manolis wince and clutch his head. 'You have to. She says that Elias loves her.'

'He told my Maria that he loved her and I've agreed to their betrothal and an early marriage. Things have to stand as they are, Yiorgo.'

'What about my Eleni?'

'It's not my fault if he fooled around with both the girls and they believed all he said. A man will tell a girl what he thinks she wants to hear when he needs to get his way with her.'

'He's irresponsible. He'll probably have any number of other girls once he's married to your Maria.'

'Then that's my problem to sort out.'

'He won't be allowed near my Eleni, that's for sure.' Yiorgo rose. He felt close to angry tears of impotence. He had hoped Manolis would be so disillusioned about Elias that he would be willing to cancel the betrothal. Now it was going to be his daughter who was going to be disgraced before the villagers.

Yiorgo left the door to the general store locked. He could not deal with customers yet. He went into the kitchen where Eleni was washing the dishes.

'I've something to say to you, my girl. Dry your hands and come into the living room.'

Dutifully Eleni followed her father into the family room and sat on her stool at the table. By the look on her father's face he was not going to tell her the news she hoped for.

'Did you know that Elias was seeing Maria?' he asked.

Eleni looked at him, puzzled. 'She never said anything to me.'

'I've spoken to him, his father and Maria's father. He became officially betrothed to Maria yesterday evening.'

Eleni's face blanched. 'He can't have done. He said he wanted to marry me.'

'More fool you to believe anything he said. Maria's pregnant,' continued Yiorgo relentlessly. 'He's been seeing both of you and no doubt telling you both that he's in love with you and wants to marry you.'

'I don't believe it,' whispered Eleni. 'How could he?' No wonder he had asked her to promise not to tell Maria that he was seeing her. No doubt he had asked Maria for the same promise.

'I'll talk to my brother. There's a chance that Alexandros will still accept you.'

'No, Pappa. I told you that was the only reason I went with Elias. I know Uncle Mikaelis is your brother, but I do not like him, his wife or any of my cousins. I will kill myself rather than marry Alexandros or either of his brothers.'

'Don't be so dramatic, girl. You'll do no such thing.'

'I will. I swear I will.'

Eleni threw herself onto her pallet sobbing and Despina looked between her husband and daughter. She had never known Eleni defy her father in any way until now.

'Leave it, Yiorgo. The poor girl has had a shock. You go and open up the store and I'll talk some sense into her.'

Despina sat on the pallet and took Eleni in her arms. 'Are you sure you're pregnant, Eleni? You didn't just tell your father that because you don't want to marry Alexandros?'

'I'll not marry Alexandros or either of his brothers even if they were still willing to have me. I'm sure I am pregnant, Mamma, and I'm sorry. I didn't mean to bring disgrace on the family. I truly believed Elias when he said he would like to marry me.'

Despina shook her head. 'Your father says Maria is also pregnant by him. You're better off without him. Who knows how long he will stay with her before another girl catches his eye?'

'I didn't know he was seeing Maria. She didn't tell me. I thought she was my friend. I'll never forgive her.'

'You two will have to sort that problem out between you. Now, how far are you?'

'I've missed two courses and my next one should be any day.'

'I can give you some medicine but it could be too late now to do anything to prevent the event. We can but hope that nature takes over and your reputation can be restored before it becomes village gossip.'

'I don't care if it does,' replied Eleni defiantly. 'You can throw me out and I'll go to a different village and beg. I'll tell them I became pregnant deliberately because Pappa was going to force me into an impossible marriage.'

'We'll not throw you out, Eleni. Your father is cross and upset at the moment, so am I, but we'll not turn you out of your home.'

'How could either of you expect me to marry a man I cannot talk to and who cannot talk back to me? The noises he makes when he tries to speak frighten me.'

'He's a kind and gentle soul.'

'He's still deaf. There's something wrong with all of them. I hated having to go and visit them; listening to Aunt Olga telling me how good they all were and knowing they were looking at me as if I was a donkey they were going to buy at market. Would I be good for breeding or just as a working animal? Well, now they'll know; I'm good for nothing.'

Despina stroked her daughter's hair. 'Your father should have spoken to you and listened to your objections before he went ahead with agreeing a betrothal.'

'He was set on the idea. Whatever I had said would have made no difference. Elias said that Pappa would only allow me to marry someone else if I was already pregnant.'

Despina sighed. Elias had a lot to answer for, putting that idea into Eleni's head so he could have his way with her.

Maria could not wait to tell Eleni her good news. As soon as her mother released her from the daily chores she hurried down to the general store.

'What do you want?' asked Yiorgo.

'I wanted to see Eleni, to tell her my news.'

'She doesn't want to hear it. Go back home, you wanton hussy.'

Maria looked at Yiorgo with tears in her eyes. 'Elias and I are going to be married. I'm sure Eleni will be happy for me.'

'Eleni already knows. Get yourself back home where you belong.'

Maria looked at Eleni's father in disbelief. He had never spoken to her unkindly before. Who had already told Eleni she was getting married?

Maria tossed her head and walked out of the general store. Had Elias seen Eleni when he was on his way to work that morning or had it been her father who had told Yiorgo? She knew Eleni's father had paid an early morning call at the taverna and by the rough tone of their voices they were in the midst of an argument. Maybe Eleni's father had been unable to pay his bill. If her father had told Yiorgo her good news he must have passed it on to Eleni. Eleni was obviously jealous that Maria was to be married before her.

She walked along the road to the fields where she knew Elias would be working. He looked up in surprise when she called to him and he saw her waiting for him at the edge of the field. He wiped his brow with his arm and ran his hands down his trousers.

'This is an unexpected surprise,' he smiled as he approached.

'Did you see Eleni when you were coming to work this morning?' asked Maria.

Elias shook his head.

'I don't know what's wrong,' said Maria miserably. 'I went to the general store to tell her our good news and her father said she already knew and didn't want to see me. I thought she would be happy for me.'

'I expect she's just feeling a bit upset.'

'Why should she be upset? She's going to be betrothed to her cousin any day now.'

'We'll see if that comes about. She doesn't like him at all and was hoping she could persuade her father to allow her to marry me.'

'You? Why would she expect you to marry her?'

'Who knows what you young girls think? I'm sure she'll get over it. Now, give me a quick kiss and then I must get back to work.'

'Is a kiss all you want?'

Elias grinned at her. 'No, you know it isn't, but we can't be seen enjoying ourselves in the middle of the field during the day. I'll meet you this evening.'

Maria's eyes sparkled and she lifted her face up to Elias.

The wedding ceremony between Maria and Elias had taken place at the beginning of February. As the couple left the church, hand in hand, Eleni stepped forwards. This was the moment she had been waiting for.

She stood in front of them and spoke quietly, although her words were full of venom.

'I curse you, Maria and Elias, and any offspring you may have.'

Maria paled and clutched tightly at Elias's hand as Eleni walked away. 'Can she really curse us, Elias?'

'Of course not,' answered Elias firmly as he crossed himself. 'Take no notice of her. I've told you, she's jealous because you're marrying me.'

He turned and looked after Eleni's retreating figure. She did not look pregnant. Had she made the story up in the hope that he would marry her?

All three fathers had been too ashamed of Elias's two timing and deception to mention it to anyone and as yet the villagers were not aware that Eleni was pregnant. They were mildly surprised that Maria was to be the first of the girls to marry as she was the younger and even more surprised that neither Eleni nor her parents attended the customary feast that was held in the square later.

'What did you say to Maria and Elias?' asked Despina.

'I told them what they deserved to hear,' answered Eleni.

'You cannot bear a grudge for ever. The fault was partly yours.'

'Had Elias told me he was seeing Maria I would not have listened to his suggestions. I'm pleased now that I haven't married him. I would never be able to trust him to be faithful to me.'

'Your father could speak to Mikaelis again. If Alexandros will not accept you maybe one of his brothers would be willing.'

Eleni gave her mother a scathing glance. 'I thought I had made it quite clear that I will never marry any of my cousins. In Aunt Olga's eyes I am a loose woman and she would certainly not consider me suitable for one of her boys.'

Despina sighed. She had hoped that once Eleni had overcome her disappointment that Elias was not prepared to marry her she would be willing to marry Alexandros, or even Lucas or Nikos. If the marriage had taken place promptly the child could have been declared premature. The villagers would smile and know that the marriage had been consummated before the wedding ceremony, but think none the worse of her. Once she had given birth to a baby without a husband her reputation would be in shreds and it was unlikely any local man would ask for her hand.

'If only we had some relatives you could go and stay with. You could return in about a year and claim to be a widow.'

'The only relatives we have are Uncle Mikaelis and Aunt Olga and I am certainly not prepared to go and stay with them. I imagine Aunt Olga is telling all her friends what a lucky escape her Alexandros had from me.'

'I don't think your father has told them why the betrothal did not take place.'

Eleni laughed bitterly. 'So what did he say? That I did not want to marry Alexandros? At least that is the truth. If he had believed me in the first place this would not have happened.'

'You cannot blame your father.'

'I blame him for not listening to me. All he could think of was the amount of land that Uncle Mikaelis owns.'

'He is a wealthy man compared with us.'

Eleni shrugged. 'I don't care about wealth. I could have been the richest woman in the whole of Crete, but I would never have been happy married to Alexandros. Imagine what it would have been like if I had given birth to a baby who was deaf like him and unable to speak properly? He would be considered to be the village imbecile. That would be more degrading to me than having a child with no known father.'

'You're not planning to tell the villagers that Elias is the father?'

'What would be the point? He's married to Maria now and they wouldn't believe me. Let them speculate and gossip. I don't care. I just want to have the child and get on with my life.'

If Eleni saw Maria as she went to the baker or to collect the water she would turn her back and walk in the opposite direction, even returning to her house on occasions so she would not have to acknowledge her erstwhile friend. The medicine her mother had given her had not had the desired effect. Eleni had let her skirt out, but she was still not noticeably pregnant, unlike Maria who strutted proudly down the village street, her stomach pushed out as far as possible. Eleni was seething with resentment. That Elias should have been two faced and declared his love for her when it was obviously untrue was bad enough, but to make her friend pregnant at the same time was unforgivable.

The weather became unseasonably warm and Eleni stayed inside the house away from the prying eyes of the villagers as it was becoming evident now that she was carrying a child. The heat was already troubling her, making her feet and ankles swell uncomfortably and her mother no longer expected her to collect the water or take the dough to the baker. Despina made excuses to the villagers who remarked that they had not seen Eleni around, one time claiming that she had strained her back so could not manage the heavy buckets from the well, another time she said Eleni had twisted her ankle and walking even a short distance was painful for her. Despina knew the truth would come out eventually, but she wanted to delay the gossip for as long as possible.

Maria longed to know why Eleni was keeping to her house, but a lingering sense of loyalty to her old friend stopped her from asking the villagers for information. If Eleni's predicament was as she suspected she would have loved to have known who was the father. Was it one of her cousins who had finally persuaded her that he was not as objectionable as she thought? If that was the case she was surprised that a betrothal had not been announced. Whenever she broached the subject with Elias he would brush her speculation aside and say he did not indulge in gossip like an old woman.

The day seemed even hotter than usual to Eleni. She placed a wet rag on her forehead and then went outside to pick a cucumber. She would cut that and place some on her forehead and it would withdraw some of the heat from her body. As she bent to cut the vegetable she was seized with a gripping pain in her stomach and she gasped in surprise and agony. Taking a deep breath she picked up the cucumber and walked back into the house.

'What's wrong?' asked Despina.

Eleni shook her head miserably. 'I don't know. I've never had a pain like this before.'

Despina looked at Eleni with concern. Surely it was too soon for the baby?

'Lay down for a while and you'll probably feel better. I expect it was where you bent over to cut the cucumber. Give it to me and I'll cut it and place some on your forehead.'

Eleni lay down on her pallet and gave a groan as another wave of pain hit her.

'Whereabouts is your pain?' asked her mother.

'There. Inside.' Eleni placed a hand on her stomach and gave a gasp of horror. 'Mamma, I'm sorry. I've wet my pallet.'

Despina looked at Eleni and shook her head. 'The baby is coming. Don't worry about your pallet.'

'It can't be. I'm sure it isn't time yet.'

'Babies come when they are ready. I'll get some cloths and start heating some water. You're sure it's early?'

'Positive.'

Despina frowned. In that case her daughter could have a serious problem. The baby might not be strong enough yet to endure the trauma of being passed through the birth canal and would be unable to help itself.

'Have you felt it moving?'

Eleni shook her head.

'I'll tell you father to go for the doctor. Try to relax and take a deep breath between the pains.'

Despina hurried into the general store and confronted Yiorgo. 'Shut the shop, Yiorgo. You have to go to town and ask the doctor to come back here with you. Eleni's started her labour.'

Yiorgo looked at his wife in surprise. Childbirth was a natural thing and Despina was quite capable of dealing with it. There was no need to ask the doctor to attend. 'What's the problem, then?'

'It's too soon. There's something not right. The poor girl is in agony and she says the baby hasn't been moving. Go on, Yiorgo.' Despina lowered her voice. 'I think it could be dead. Only a doctor can deal with that problem.'

'The doctor may not be in the town. He may have gone to one of the villages.'

'Then ask around; find out where he is and insist that he comes here with you immediately,' answered Despina impatiently.

'He'll have to be paid.'

'Take some money with you. Pay him whatever he asks, but hurry up and go looking for him. I'll sit with Eleni and do what I can until he arrives.'

Despina sat beside her daughter, sponging her forehead, rubbing her stomach intermittently with raki to help alleviate the pain and holding her hand. Each time a pain overtook her Eleni gasped and clutched her mother's hand so tightly she made her wince and Despina longed for her husband to return with the doctor.

It was mid afternoon when Yiorgo finally returned accompanied by Doctor Kandakis. He frowned when he saw Eleni.

'How long has she been like this?'

'She began to complain this morning. She bent over to cut a cucumber and her pains started.'

Whilst he was talking the doctor took a stethoscope from his bag and placed it on Eleni's stomach, moving it around and listening intently. 'I can't hear a heart beat. How far gone is she?'

'She thought it should born in July. What can you do?'

'I'm sure the child is dead and I will have to pull it out. I cannot guarantee the outcome but if it stays inside it will decay and set up an infection. That will be fatal.'

Despina wrung her hands. 'Just help my daughter.'

Yiorgo disappeared into his shop. He had done as his wife had asked of him and he had no wish to be present when his daughter's private parts would be exposed or watch the procedure the doctor would undertake.

From his bag Doctor Kandakis removed a small jar of chloroform and a rag along with a large and vicious looking pair of forceps. 'I need to wash my hands.'

Hurriedly Despina produced a bowl of water that she had been heating anticipating having to wash a new born baby. He rolled up his sleeves and dabbled his hands in the bowl before wiping them on the towel that Despina held ready for him.

He poured a few drops of chloroform onto the rag and held it beneath Eleni's nose. 'Hold that there for me,' he instructed Despina, 'but turn your head away so you don't start breathing it in.'

The doctor knew there was little chance of the woman being affected but he did not want her to watch what he was about to do to her daughter. Ideally the girl should have been in the hospital where the baby could have been cut out by a surgeon.

Doctor Kandakis pushed Eleni's legs apart and squinted at her. She was hardly dilated. A sure sign that the child was dead. He rolled his sleeves up higher and inserted two fingers into Eleni, then a further two until he was able to place his whole hand inside her. He could feel the baby's head, but was unable to get a grip on the slippery skull. With his free hand he picked up the forceps and began to probe gently until he felt the forceps had made a purchase on the head. Gently he pulled the head towards Eleni's cervical opening. If by any chance the child was still alive he did not want to cause damage to the brain.

Kneeling, so that he was able to see exactly what he was doing the doctor pulled again with the forceps and then grasped the back of the head with his hand and began to ease it forwards. Once the head was free the rest of the body slid out easily. The head was too large in proportion to the small body; the umbilical cord was twisted around its neck and the baby he withdrew was blue and lifeless.

Doctor Kandakis gave a sigh of relief. You could not give a dead child brain damage. He laid the body on the towel he had wiped his hands on and turned his attention to expelling the placenta, finally satisfied that he had done all he could, he wrapped the child and the placenta in the towel and straightened up.

'You can remove the rag from your daughter's nose. I need to wash my hands again and then there is nothing more I can do. I have removed the dead child along with the placenta. Hopefully no infection will occur now. You can wash her and make her comfortable. Keep a close eye on her for the next few days and if her temperature rises take her to the hospital.'

'The baby?'

The doctor shook his head. 'It is dead. Had she carried full term it would have been unlikely to have survived. It was not fully formed. I suggest you dispose of it before she sees it. Mothers often get strange ideas if their child is born dead and want to keep it, hoping they will see some signs of life.'

'Thank you, doctor. How long will it be before my daughter recovers?'

Doctor Kandakis shrugged. 'I cannot say. Much depends upon her general health. I would say a month at the outside. If I speak to your husband will he have the money for my bill?'

Despina nodded. 'I'm sure he has. We're very grateful to you for coming out.'

The doctor replaced the forceps and chloroform in his bag and walked through to the shop where Yiorgo was waiting anxiously for him.

'My daughter?' he asked.

'I've done all I can. Her recovery is in the hands of God now.'

Yiorgo crossed himself fervently and opened the box where he kept his daily shop takings. 'Tell me how much I owe you.'

'Three drachmas,' answered Doctor Kandakis, knowing the man was unlikely to argue about the cost and Yiorgo began to take coins out of the box and placed them on the counter.

'You're probably quicker than me. Take whatever is owing.'

Swiftly the doctor counted out three drachmas in lepta and Yiorgo watched in horror as he was left with only seven lepta. The shop had been closed all day and he rarely took more than seven drachmas a week. He would have no money to buy any further supplies of coffee or rice from the town this week.

Having bade Doctor Kandakis farewell and thanked him yet

again for visiting Yiorgo entered the back room. Despina placed her finger on her lips and signalled to him to go into the garden with her.

'What are we going to do, Yiorgo? The doctor has left the body with us.'

'I'll speak to Panayiotis and ask him to dig a grave. I'll have to ask if I can pay him next week.'

Despina shook her head. 'You can't do that or the whole village will know she was pregnant.'

'It was becoming obvious,' remarked Yiorgo. 'Besides, Manolis, Elias and his father know.'

'We'll say she made a mistake and had an internal obstruction. You can burn her pallet and,' Despina hesitated, 'the baby with it. That way no one will know there was a child. They might speculate and gossip but they'll have no proof.'

'Are you sure that's right?'

'Doctor Kandakis said it was unlikely to have survived even if she had carried full term. It's not really a baby, it's a 'thing'.'

'Maybe she can marry Alexandros after all.'

Despina shook her head. 'Eleni meant it when she said she would kill herself rather than marry any one of them. Leave it be. Go and cut some grass whilst I hem up a new pallet for her. She can't be left lying on that one when I've washed her.'

Word had spread around the village that the doctor had been called to attend to Eleni and she was gravely ill, perhaps dying. Yiorgo told his customers when they enquired that his daughter had been suffering from an obstruction that had required removal. They speculated on the nature of the obstruction but it could not have been a still birth as Panayiotis had not been asked to dig a grave. Even a child that did not live was always given a decent burial.

'What do you think was wrong with her?' Maria asked Elias.

Elias shrugged. 'How would I know? I'm not a doctor.' If Eleni had been pregnant he hoped she had miscarried and his dalliance with her would not be discovered by Maria.

Eleni lay on her pallet attended continually by her mother. For two days she hardly stirred and Despina was seriously concerned that her daughter was not going to recover. If she died she would hold Elias accountable and blacken his name throughout the village. Finally Eleni opened her eyes.

'The baby?' she asked.

Despina shook her head. 'Don't worry about that at the moment. Concentrate on getting your strength back. I've made some broth. If I help you to sit up could you drink a little?'

Wearily Eleni nodded. She was relieved that she was no longer experiencing the excruciating pain, but she felt sore, bruised and incredibly weary. Dutifully she sipped at the broth that her mother held to her mouth, then sank back on her pallet and closed her eyes.

Strange visions and memories came back to her; an unknown man bending over her; a sickly sweet smell and the feeling that she was being ripped apart inside. She was sure she remembered her mother washing her gently and then her father and mother lifting her from her pallet, lying on their bed and then being placed back on her pallet again. Where was her baby?

Eleni forced herself to open her eyes again and look around the room. She could see no sign of a baby anywhere.

'Mamma, where's the baby?'

Despina took Eleni's hand. 'There is no baby, Eleni. The poor little mite has died inside you.'

'No baby?' Relief and horror fought for supremacy in Eleni's mind. She had cursed all Elias's offspring. He had been the father of the child she had carried and in cursing him she had effectively cursed her own child. She wondered if the same fate would overtake Maria. Her one consolation was that if Maria lost her child she would have to go through the same agony she had endured.

'Can I see it?'

Despina shook her head. She could not tell her daughter that the body had been burnt. 'The doctor took it away with him.'

Eleni considered the information dispassionately. She had not formed any sort of bond with her unborn child. She was sure if she had married Elias she would have felt very differently and been distraught that she had miscarried.

'You won't make me marry Alexandros, will you? I don't want to marry anyone. I never want to have a baby again.'

'No one will make you marry anyone.' Despina thought it unlikely that any man would be willing to marry her daughter if the truth was ever discovered. 'You just lie there and rest.'

Doctor Kandakis had declared himself satisfied with Eleni when he visited two weeks after her stillbirth.

'You have healed well. You have no temperature so there is no infection. You should still have a certain amount of rest each day for the next two or three weeks. When you feel able, do not do too much at any one time. Pace yourself. Your body will tell you when it is time to rest.' The doctor cleared his throat. 'Of course, the circumstances around your pregnancy are not my concern, but I do have to warn you. It would be most unwise of you to become pregnant again. There is no guarantee that you would not miscarry in the same unfortunate way and it might not be possible to remedy the situation so successfully.'

Eleni listened to his advice. She had no intention of ever becoming pregnant again, although she was convinced that if Elias was not the father the baby would have been full term and healthy. She had brought misfortune on herself by cursing him, but hoped her ill wishing would also affect him and Maria.

Eleni finally rose from her pallet, thin and pale. She would take the dough to the baker each day and eventually was strong enough to collect a bucket of water from the well, but unless she was sent on an errand by her mother she avoided setting foot in the village and declared that she was not strong enough yet to help the villagers when they harvested their vegetables or fruit. She no longer spent her evenings gossiping with the other young girls or sitting outside during the summer months with her mother and talking to the neighbours.

She was always prepared to clean or cook whilst her mother sat at the weaving loom. Once Despina relinquished her place Eleni would take over and even when it became dark she would continue to work by the light of an oil lamp. On a Sunday she would attend church dutifully with her mother but once the service was over she hurried back to the house, not wishing to stop and speak with anyone.

Her Aunt Olga had visited and once over her initial surprise Eleni determined to make her position quite clear.

'I was very ill. The doctor could not guarantee I would survive.'

'What was wrong?' asked Olga curiously.

'I'm not exactly sure. I began to feel very ill and the doctor had to be asked to visit me. He said I had an internal obstruction that would kill me if it was not removed swiftly.'

'But you are well now?'

Eleni smiled sadly. 'I am probably as well as I will ever be. I have to rest each day and I must not lift anything heavy or do strenuous work.'

'I thought you collected the water for your mother each day?'

'Only half a bucket in the morning. I have been told that I must not help with the winnowing or picking fruit from the trees.'

'Surely in a year or so your body will have recovered sufficiently for you to live an ordinary life?'

Eleni shrugged. 'It's possible or I could end up a virtual invalid needing my mother to care for me. Of course, marriage and child bearing are absolutely out of the question now. The doctor has said that I should never try to carry a child. It could be fatal to me. Even if I did get married I would not be able to look after a husband and a house the way I would like or that would be expected of me.'

'How sad,' observed Olga. She had been disappointed that Eleni's father had withdrawn his daughter from the marriage arrangement, but now she was thankful. She would not want any of her sons married to such a sickly girl.

Maria insisted that she was not prepared to move into the house Elias shared with his father.

'It's no way to start a marriage with another person in the bedroom listening and seeing all we do.' Maria slid her hand down the inside of Elias's leg, feeling his instant reaction to her touch. 'I need to be in a house of my own with you.'

Elias persuaded his father to rent the empty cottage at the end of the village. Maria did not seem to have any problems whilst pregnant and joined Elias and his father each Friday to pick the crops ready for market the following day. Panayiotis had been commissioned to make a cradle and Maria and her mother had spent all their free time making shawls, blankets and nightdresses ready for the arrival. When it became obvious that the baby was due any day Elias insisted she stay in the house.

'I don't want my first child born in a field,' he said firmly. 'You are to stay at home and rest. Your mother can sit with you and send for Despina when the time arrives.'

Anastasia had stitched a spare pallet cover and also prevailed upon Elias to clear an area where it could be placed for Maria's confinement. It would be foolish to soil their bedding. Now it stood ready, along with a collection of towels and clean rags.

Maria was beginning to feel increasingly nervous. Would she spend days in pain, as some women had been known to suffer, before her baby was born? Would the child be perfectly formed? The curse that Eleni had placed on her and Elias on their wedding day was now haunting her.

Elias was also concerned, but he had no intention of mentioning his fears to anyone. He kept trying to convince himself that both he and Maria were fit and healthy and the curse Eleni had put on them was done through spite and would not be effective.

When the time came Maria gave birth easily. Elias had sent for Maria's mother when her pains first started and Anastasia sat beside her daughter, offering her advice and encouragement until

Despina arrived. By early evening a perfectly formed, healthy girl had been born and she had been named Phaedra after Elias's long dead mother.

Once Maria's obligatory days of confinement to her house were over she carried her baby proudly around the village. Phaedra was a beautiful little girl and Maria now believed that Elias was right. Eleni's curse had been nothing more than spite as she had not been able to marry Elias.

Eleni would glare balefully at the mother and child from a distance. The little girl might be perfect at the moment but who was to say how she would develop? She could suffer a severe bout of measles and develop pneumonia, or chicken pox and be so scarred that she would not want to show her face. Every so often one of these ailments would affect the village, the germs probably brought back from the weekly visits to the market in town by the farmers. It was also possible that the blame could be laid at the door of a pedlar or even the doctor when he paid his monthly visit.

1912 - 1924

When Phaedra was almost a year old and Maria told Elias she was pregnant again he was delighted. He had proved his manhood originally by becoming a father, and another child would confirm his virility. The men of the village held you in higher esteem the more children you fathered, although the women felt sorry for the poor mothers who were never free from a baby at their breast and a toddler clutching at their skirt.

To Elias and Maria's delight their second child was a boy and he was called Mikaelis after Maria's grandfather. Once again Eleni did not attend the feast that was arranged for the villagers to celebrate the child's safe arrival into the world. The only gift she was prepared to give the new born was another curse and hope this time it would be effective.

Maria conceived easily over the following years, but no sooner had she told her husband and mother the news than she miscarried. Finally she carried a child the full term but it was a weak little boy, born with a cleft pallet and unable to feed from his mother. Three days later Panayiotis was asked to dig a small grave. Eleni murmured 'How sad' when Despina told her the news and turned away so her mother would not see the pleased smile on her face.

Eleni's mother and Anastasia were on friendly terms again and her father patronised the taverna regularly. None of them ever mentioned Eleni's claim that Elias had made her pregnant at the same time as Maria. Only Despina and Yiorgo knew that she had spoken truly.

Elias visited the taverna rarely and always made sure that Yiorgo was not there when he arrived. If he saw him sitting by the bar he would slip back out of the door and return home. He was happy with Maria and doted on the two children he had. He gave thanks for them each Sunday and always added a special prayer of gratefulness that he had chosen Maria rather than Eleni.

Despina was concerned. It was more than eight years now since Eleni lost her child, but she still appeared traumatized by the event. She was unwilling to meet people and had taken to walking alone in the hills most afternoons, even when it was cold and windy. The only thing that prevented her daily outings was rain and then she would sit in the house at the weaving loom for hours on end.

Yiorgo was also concerned. His daughter should have recovered from her unfortunate experience by now and be married. He would have to look around for someone suitable when he visited the town to stock up on supplies for his shop. He had finally accepted that there was no possibility of her marrying any one of her cousins, but there could be a young man in the town who Eleni would find to her liking.

When the winter months gave way to spring Eleni was relieved to be able to return to her walks on the hills at the back of the village. She needed to get out of the confines of the house, but still had no wish to mingle with the locals. From her walks up in the hills Eleni found a certain amount of tranquillity. She would not suddenly see Maria rounding a corner with Phaedra and Mikaelis, or come face to face with Elias as he returned from the fields. She would be free from her mother's concerned looks and her father's veiled hints that she should be married by now.

She discovered hollows in the ground where she could lie and look up at the sky, watching any clouds that scudded across to mar the perfect unbroken blue. If there was a chill wind blowing or she became too hot she would sit just inside one of the small caves she had discovered. They were no more than a cleft in the hillside, but gave her a modicum of shelter as she watched the insects in the grass or a bird pecking at berries for food. Other days she would sit a respectful distance from Manolis's bee hives and watch the insects hurrying in and out, or look down on the fields where the men were working. When she became bored with sitting and doing nothing she would walk further round the hill away from her village to where she could see the small cluster of houses in the distance that were their nearest neighbours.

There the scrubby grass and thistles grew more luxuriantly along with gorse bushes and small trees. Even the caves seemed larger and she peered inside them curiously. She had sat and watched from a safe distance and never saw any animal go in or out, so provided she did not venture towards the back she should encounter nothing worse than a spider or a few bats if she went inside.

As it became colder upon the hills and summer drew to a close Eleni began to sit inside one of the larger caves. Being able to sit inside the rocky shelter meant the wind passed by the entrance and she was relatively warm. After some days of using one particular cave to avoid the wind she began to consider it her own little domain and felt safe there.

The villagers tended to avoid Eleni now and not try to engage her in conversation. Whatever illness she had suffered had evidently turned her mind and they crossed themselves when she passed them by. They were sympathetic towards Despina and Yiorgo; it could not be easy having a daughter, once healthy and lively, who had changed into a recluse and appeared to live in her own world.

The years passed almost unnoticed by Eleni. One day was the same as any other. Whenever she saw Phaedra and Mikaelis playing together outside their house a feeling of bitterness and impotence overtook her. Elias deserved a punishment for his seduction of her and Maria also for not telling her friend of her own relationship with Elias. They were supposed to be friends; sharing secrets and confiding in each other. The fact that she had been as much to blame as Maria did not enter her mind.

Eleni knew how the villagers regarded her and she did not care about their opinion. She wished heartily that she had not been so foolish as to listen to Elias's suggestion to avoid marriage to Alexandros, although she was still relieved that she had not been forced to marry her cousin. The visits from her aunt had become less frequent as Eleni continually assured her she was still far from strong and despaired of ever being really well again. Physically she had recovered completely, but even she realised that her mind was slightly deranged due to her obsession with the curse she had laid on Elias and Maria. Each day she woke up hoping that she would hear that some unfortunate accident had happened to their children and neither had survived.

Maria looked at her daughter critically. 'Where have you been?'

'Outside with Mikaelis. He was playing football and I played knuckle bones with Anna.'

'Nowhere else? You haven't been up to the orchards or the olive groves?'

'No, Mamma. You have always said we're not to go to either place unless you or Pappa are with us.'

Maria took Phaedra's chin in her hands and tilted her face to one side. 'Something has bitten you.'

Phaedra put up her hand and touched her face. 'I can't feel anything.'

'It doesn't hurt?'

'Not a bit. I expect it will be gone by tomorrow.' Phaedra was totally unconcerned.

Maria nodded. Her daughter was probably right. At her age a spot would suddenly appear for no reason and if left alone would disappear without a trace. 'Don't scratch it,' warned Maria. 'If you get dirt in it you'll have a nasty place that could leave a scar.'

Phaedra nodded. Her mother was making so much fuss about a pimple.

To Maria's consternation the small red spot seemed to grow larger during the next few days and then left a white mark behind when the redness disappeared. Another spot developed closer to her daughter's eyebrow and followed the same course. Phaedra complained that she had a headache, but insisted that the spot did not hurt at all when she touched it.

Maria was puzzled. Mikaelis and Phaedra were always together and Mikaelis had no sign of any insect bites or spots. It was hardly the kind of ailment you could refer to the doctor. As the summer became warmer Phaedra's skin took on a healthy tan, but the two white spots showed up more clearly against her brown skin and she often said her head hurt inside. Maria's remedy was to keep her daughter inside the house when the sun was at full strength, but it seemed to make no difference to Phaedra's bouts of head pain and the two patches of white skin had now become one large area. spreading from her hair line down to her ear on the left side of her face.

When Phaedra's grandfather met Phaedra and Mikaelis walking along the village street he looked at her face critically. 'What have you done to your face?'

Phaedra touched her cheek with her hand. 'Mamma thinks an insect bit me a week or so ago but it doesn't hurt.'

'Does your cheek feel sore?'

'Not at all.'

Andreas nodded. He was sure he knew what was wrong with his granddaughter's skin and must make the family aware of the problem. 'Is your father at home?'

Phaedra nodded. 'Mamma has heated some water so he can have a bath so we have been sent out to play.'

'I'll call on him later when he's had a chance to wash and dress himself.' Whilst he waited a decent amount of time he would call in on Manolis and have a glass of raki and buy a small bottle to take away with him.

When Andreas arrived at the house Maria was busy baling out the water from the galvanised tub so she would be able to lift it and empty the remaining water into the garden. Her face was flushed and her skirt damp whilst Elias was sitting with a towel across his legs and a broad smile on his face. Andreas knew exactly why the children had been sent out to play.

'I'm sorry to interrupt but I'd like you to get dressed and come outside with me, Elias. I need to speak to you.'

Elias looked at his father in surprise. What did his father need to say to him that could not be spoken of in front of his wife? Had Eleni threatened to tell Maria that she had also been pregnant with his child? He would deny it, of course. Once married to Maria he had been waiting for Eleni to give birth before he rekindled his earlier relationship with her, planning to tell her that he had been forced to marry Maria when he really preferred her. It could have been amusing to have two women to enjoy, but she began to act so strangely that he had abandoned the idea.

During his visits to the town with his father on market day he had made the acquaintance of a local girl and she had finally agreed to let him have his way with her. She would smile at him and lick her lips and Elias would immediately feel himself stirring. Making an excuse to his father he would hurry away and he and the girl would hide behind a door pleasing each other as long as they dared before straightening their clothing and parting with a promise to meet again the following week. The fact that someone could open the door at any minute and they would be discovered only added to their frenzy for satisfaction.

'What's wrong?' asked Elias as he pulled his shirt over his head. He hoped his father had not found out that he had been dallying with the girl in the town.

'Finish dressing and come into the garden.' Andreas placed the bottle of raki beside the sink and picked up the almost empty bath. 'I'll empty this for you, Maria.'

'Will you stay for supper?' asked Maria.

'Not tonight, but thank you for the offer. Keep that bottle of raki safe until Elias has spoken to you.'

Elias pulled on his trousers, placed his feet into his boots, shrugged in puzzlement to Maria and followed his father out into the garden behind the house.

'What do you need to speak to me about?'

'I saw Phaedra and Mikaelis in the village.'

Elias nodded. 'We sent them out to play. Phaedra's getting a bit big to see her father taking a bath.'

'What's wrong with the girl's face? Have you asked the doctor to look at her?'

Elias shook his head. 'She's fine. It's just a mark on her face where she was bitten by something.'

'I hope you're right, but I think it could be worse than an insect bite. It has definitely become larger during the summer.'

'It only looks larger because it isn't tanned like the rest of her face.'

Andreas shook his head. 'I'm not a doctor but it could be the start of leprosy. If it is you're all at risk.'

Elias looked at his father in shocked amazement. 'It can't be. How would you know?'

'I've seen it develop before. There was a man in the village many years ago. Started the same way. Just a white patch that grew larger, then cracked and nodules began to form.'

'Phaedra doesn't have any cracks. It's just some white skin. No one in the village has noticed or mentioned her face.'

'I've noticed and soon others will. I won't be the only person in the village to know the first signs of leprosy. If she is sick you'll be run out of the village.'

Elias crossed himself. 'What can we do?'

'Have you tried rubbing her face with raki? If it is just an infection from an insect bite the raki will clear it up. I've left a bottle in your kitchen. If that doesn't work ask the doctor for his opinion and if it is confirmed she'll have to go to a leprosarium for treatment. The other alternative is to hide her up in one of the caves and see what develops. If it clears up or is no worse in six months you'll know it was nothing and she can return home.'

'She can't live in a cave!' Elias swallowed. 'She's my daughter. I can't just abandon her.'

'I'm not suggesting you abandon her. She can have a pallet up there and you or Mikaelis can take her fresh water each day. You have to think of yourself, along with Maria and Mikaelis. If she stays at home you could all become infected. The germs are less likely to spread in the open air. I'll not be happy to visit you in your home whilst she's there, and I won't want you working too close to me in the fields.'

'It would be dark and lonely in a cave.'

'You can take her an oil lamp. Explain to her that it will only be for a short amount of time.'

'What will I tell the villagers? They're bound to notice that she isn't around.'

'Say she has gone to stay with relatives or has decided to become a nun and has gone to experience a life of seclusion. Once you know she is well she can return home and no one will think anything of her time away.'

Elias shook his head in despair. 'I'll have to talk to Maria. I'll see what she says.'

Andreas nodded. 'You must do what you think fit, but for your own sakes get her out of your house.'

Elias watched as his father walked dejectedly away up the road. Surely his father could not be right. He would look closely at Phaedra's face before he spoke to Maria.

Elias held Phaedra's chin in his hands and tipped her face towards the light coming in through the window. The white patch did seem larger than he remembered from some days ago, but was he imagining it?

'Does your face hurt at all, Phaedra?'

Phaedra frowned. 'No, why should it?'

''Not where you had the insect bite?'

Phaedra rubbed her face beside her eye and shook her head. 'I can't feel it at all.'

'Let me touch it and tell me if you can feel me.' Elias placed on finger on the white area and pressed gently.

'No, I told you, Pappa. I can't feel it.'

'And you don't feel ill?'

'I've had some headaches lately, but Mamma says that is probably from the sun and she has made me stay inside. She's been teaching me how to weave on the loom.'

Elias nodded. 'That's a good girl. Just do as your Mamma says.' He looked at the white area of skin again. Could he see a slight crack in the skin at her hair line or was that his imagination? He must talk to Maria. His father's idea that the girl spent some time away from them to see if anything developed was a sensible idea.

'Maria, come outside. I need to talk to you.'

'I'm cooking, Elias.'

'That can wait. This is more important.'

With a sigh Maria removed the pot from over the fire and took it out to the kitchen. 'What's so important?' she asked impatiently as she went out to the garden, wiping her hands on her apron.

'My father was here a short while ago.'

'I know. He emptied the bath tub for me. I was surprised he didn't stay for supper.'

'He had a good reason.'

'Why? Is he ill? He's never refused my cooking before.'

Elias shook his head. 'It's Phaedra.'

'Phaedra?' Andreas had always doted on his granddaughter.

'Listen, Maria, my father is concerned. He says the white mark on her face could be a leprous infection.'

'Leprosy?' Maria's face paled. 'It can't be. Where would she have caught that? There's no one in the village who is suffering.'

'I don't know how or where you catch it. Make her take all her clothes off and look at the rest of her body.'

'What now? Before we eat supper?'

'I can't eat anything until I know that she's healthy.'

Maria gave a shrug and called Phaedra to her in the kitchen. 'The white mark on your face looks a little larger. Have you any white marks elsewhere?'

'I don't think so, Mamma.'

'Take off all your clothes and let me look at you.'

Phaedra lifted her blouse above her head and Maria tried not to show her horror. There was another white patch of skin that extended from beneath Phaedra's shoulder blade to the centre of her back.

'It's alright, Phaedra, you can put your blouse back on and ask your Pappa to come back into the kitchen.'

'Elias,' Maria spoke in a whisper, 'there's a large white patch on her back.'

Elias crossed himself, praying that his daughter was not sick. 'My Pappa said she could try bathing her face in raki. He also made a suggestion. I don't think you will like it, but it could be for the best.'

'What are you talking about?'

'If we asked the doctor to make a diagnosis he would probably take her away and she could be in a leprosarium for years waiting for the results of tests. By that time she certainly would have contracted the disease by being surrounded by other sufferers. He suggested we sent her to live up in one of the caves for a few months to see if anything developed. If the white patch hasn't grown larger or gone away in that time she can come back home without a problem.'

'Elias!' Maria felt her head reeling and she clutched at her husband's arm. 'She's only a child. She can't be sent out into the hills to look after herself.'

'I'm not suggesting that. There are a number of caves nearby. I'll find one that is suitable and sweep it out. She can have a pallet up there and an oil lamp for at night. Every day Mikaelis or I can take her fresh water and you can send her up food and clean clothes.'

'When it becomes cold she'll freeze to death.'

'I hope she'll be home before the winter, but she'll be sheltered from the elements in a cave. A couple of extra blankets and she should be warm enough.'

'Suppose she refuses to go?'

'She has to go, Maria. Until we know whether she is infectious or not we are all at risk.'

Tears began to course their way down Maria's cheeks. 'It's not right, Elias. I can't.'

'You have to, Maria. Mikaelis could become infected as well as you and I. Speak to her tonight and I'll look for somewhere suitable for her to live tomorrow. The sooner she is out of the house and you can clean it thoroughly the better. She'll come to no harm. I'll go up and stay on the hillside with her for the first few nights and she'll soon become used to living up there.'

Maria wiped her eyes on her apron. How was she going to tell her daughter that she had to go and live in a cave up on the hill?

Supper was eaten silently and afterwards Maria called her daughter back into the kitchen area.

'I have something very important to talk to you about and I need you to be sensible and grown up.'

Phaedra's eyes widened and she looked at her mother fearfully. Was her father ill?

'The mark on your face has become larger and you have another similar mark on your back. We don't know the cause but your grandfather is worried that it could be some sort of contagious skin infection. He has left a bottle of raki with us for you to dab on your face to try to clear it.'

'Why don't you ask the doctor to have a look the next time he is in the village?'

'That is part of the problem. If we ask the doctor he probably will not know and he'll want to take you away for tests. They could take weeks or months before they were completed.'

'Where would he take me?'

'I'm not sure, but it could be the big hospital in Heraklion.' Maria hurried on. 'Your Pappa and I have talked about it and decided that before we speak to the doctor we want to give you the chance to become properly well again. Pappa is going to find a suitable cave up on the hill and you will go up there to live for a few weeks. If your face looks better then you can return home and there will be no need to speak to the doctor. Even if the patch on your back is still there no one will see it.'

'A cave? Up on the hill?' Phaedra could not believe her mother's words. 'Are you and Pappa coming with me?'

Maria shook her head. 'We can't. We have to stay here. Your Pappa has his work and I have to look after Mikaelis.'

'But what will I do up there all day on my own?'

'You can have your crochet and embroidery with you and we will visit you. Every day either your Pappa or Mikaelis will bring you up some fresh water. If you want anything else you will only have to tell them and they can bring it up the next day.'

'You mean I'm to stay up there all the time? Every day? What about at night when it's dark?'

'Your Pappa is going to make sure the cave is clean and you will have an oil lamp. He'll show you how to fill it and light it. For the first few nights your Pappa will stay up there with you. Once you realise there is nothing to be frightened about it will be like living in your own little home.'

'I'd rather stay here.' Phaedra's lip trembled. 'I want to do some more weaving on the loom.'

'Of course you would and we would like you to stay here with us. If we spoke to the doctor and he took you away goodness knows when we would ever see you again. It's far better that you stay close by where we can continue to look after you.'

'What will I tell my friends?'

'Nothing. You keep it a secret between us. We won't want anyone to know you are living up there.'

'Suppose my face doesn't get better?'

'I'm sure it will within a few weeks. Put the raki on as your grandfather suggested.'

'But suppose it doesn't? Suppose the white patch gets bigger?'

'Then we would have to speak to the doctor. No need for you to worry about that at the moment.'

Phaedra turned away. She rarely looked at herself in the square of mirror that hung beside the sink in the kitchen. Now she stood on tiptoe and looked at her face. She had no idea the white patch was so large. She measured it with her fingers. From the top of her ear it spread down onto her cheek and up above her eyebrow into her hair line. She touched it gingerly; there was no pain so there could not be anything very wrong.

The only person who slept well that night was Mikaelis who had no idea of the plans afoot for his sister. Elias rose early and walked to the end of the village where the uncultivated scrub land began. He climbed the hill, knowing he was out of sight of any of the villagers unless one decided he needed to go to the next village by way of the cart track. Even if they did Elias would hear the donkey's hooves and once sitting down he would be unlikely to be seen.

He visited a number of caves until he decided he had found one that would be suitable. The entrance was reasonably narrow and then it widened out into a fairly spacious area behind. Phaedra would be able to have her pallet there, away from any draughts, and there was also space enough for two or three boxes. She would be able to keep her food in one, her clothes in another and store her extra blankets in the third.

Elias hurried back to his house. He would return with a brush to ensure that the area was clean and he could leave that up there so Phaedra could sweep out any debris that might blow in. At the same time he would pack up a box containing an oil lamp, some old cups and plates along with eating utensils and a spare blanket. There would be more than enough to carry when Phaedra moved up there.

Early each morning Elias carried more items up to the cave. Maria was busy washing all Phaedra's clothes along with weaving an extra blanket. Phaedra sat and watched the activity impassively. This could not be happening. She was being banished from her home.

'We'll go up tomorrow,' announced Elias finally. 'We'll leave early and go as a family. If anyone asks where we are going we will say to visit relatives in a nearby village and Phaedra is proposing to stay with them for a while. Remember, Mikaelis, you do not say anything different to anyone, not even your closest friend.'

Mikaelis nodded. He was not sure what all the secrecy was about. His pallet had been moved as far away from Phaedra as possible and he had been forbidden to touch her or any of her belongings.

'How long will Phaedra be away?' he asked.

'We're not sure, probably just a few weeks. The fresh air will help to clear the white mark from her face. You'll be able to go and visit her and take her up some water.'

'Will she have to stay in the cave all day?'

Elias shook his head. 'She can go wherever she pleases out on the hill provided she does not walk back towards the village where she could be seen.'

Silently the little family trudged along the cart track away from the village until Elias finally left the path and began to climb the hill. Once behind some gorse bushes he led the way to the cave he had selected..

'This is the cave where Phaedra will stay for a short while,' he said to Mikaelis. 'No one from the village will see you up here, but make sure you do not make a regular pathway by continually turning off the road at the same place.'

Phaedra hung back as she saw the cave. It looked dark and forbidding to her.

'Go inside and take a look, Phaedra,' urged her father. 'I've swept it clean and placed your pallet a little further in where it widens out. The boxes for your belongings and food are there, along with the oil lamp and spare oil. I'll check the wick regularly and trim it or renew it and show you how you can do that for yourself.'

'Come in with me, Pappa. It will be dark in there. I won't be able to see anything without the lamp.' She reached out to him tentatively with her hand, but he did not take it.

'Very well. Maria, you and Mikaelis sit outside.' He placed the pallet he had carried up on the ground outside. He would use that to sleep on when he stayed on the hillside for the first few nights until Phaedra was used to staying up in the cave alone.

He smiled at his daughter. 'You'll soon be used to sleeping and living here on your own. At one time girls of your age were considered old enough to be married. They would be sent to live in another village with a family they had never met before. Often they would never see their parents again. We want to be able to see you every day.'

Elias strode confidently into the cave and waited for his eyes to become accustomed to the interior darkness. He lit the lamp and stood it on one of the boxes. It dispelled the darkness, but it felt cold and dank after being outside in the warm sunshine. Phaedra shivered.

'Do I have to sleep in here?'

'Whilst the weather is good you can sleep outside if you want. Just take your pallet back inside each morning. Look around and tell me if there is anything else you think you want me to bring up for you.'

Phaedra glanced around. She was not sure what her father and mother had packed into the boxes for her. She shrugged. 'I can't think of anything at the moment. Can we go back outside?'

'I'll leave the lamp alight. When you go to sleep turn it down very low. That way the oil will last until the morning and you'll be able to take it outside to refill it. The spare bottles are over there. Don't waste it.'

Phaedra nodded dutifully. She would certainly not waste it. She did not want to be in the cave in total darkness.

Maria tried to smile cheerfully as her husband and daughter emerged. She indicated the basket that say beside her.

'I've brought you up some fresh bread, a large cheese, hard boiled eggs, some tomatoes, cucumber and plenty of olives. If you store the food in a box where it's cool it will keep. Your father brought you up a box of rusks and they should last you for quite a while. Mikaelis will bring you up some fresh water tomorrow morning.'

'Can he stay up here with me?'

'For a while each day. That means you will have someone to talk to in the mornings and in the afternoon you can go for a walk or sit and sew or crochet. It will be no different from when you were at home.'

Phaedra looked at her mother doubtfully. She thought it was going to be very different living in a cave without her family around her.

Although Phaedra knew her father was outside she hardly slept. Each time there was a rustle in the grass she sat bolt upright expecting to see a snake or animal entering the cave. Her heart beating wildly she would lie back down and close her eyes, willing herself to go to sleep. Finally she gave up and sat with a pillow behind her back so she could watch the entrance to the cave.

As the sun rose she could see the sky lightening through the mouth of the cave and she breathed a sigh of relief. Nothing had eaten her during the night. She pulled on her boots, unwilling to step onto the cold earth floor in bare feet. Cautiously she looked out of the cave entrance and saw her father rolling up his pallet.

'Did you sleep well?' he asked.

Phaedra shook her head. 'I was frightened. I kept hearing noises.'

'So did I,' he smiled. 'They're nothing to worry about. Probably a mouse moving through the grass hoping not to be spotted by an owl or just the breeze making the leaves on the trees rustle. I'll leave my pallet rolled up beneath this gorse bush. That way it will be here when I come back this evening. Before I go I'll put some more oil into your lamp. Keep it turned down low whilst you are not inside. No point in wasting good oil.'

'What am I going to do with myself after you've gone Pappa?'

'Make sure you put some raki on your face when you've had a wash. Don't waste the water. Save it to wash your hands in later. Put your pallet out to air as it's a fine sunny day. You could put your boots out as well. It won't hurt to walk around on the grass barefoot..'

'I don't want to get a thorn in my foot.'

'I'll ask Mikaelis to bring up your summer shoes.'

'And my night shoes. My feet were cold last night.'

Elias nodded. It was still mild at night, but maybe Phaedra already needed an extra blanket in the cave where the sun did not penetrate. He would bring one with him when he returned to spend the night on the hillside.

When her father no longer slept up outside the cave Phaedra was frightened, particularly if the sky was overcast and there was no moonlight to dispel the darkness. She was used to having her pallet against the wall in the living room. Mikaelis had a pallet below hers and they slept toe to toe; whilst her parents' large bed was on the other wall. Without the sound of people breathing, muttering or snoring the silence in the cave was oppressive and she frequently cried herself to sleep.

Each day she swabbed her face with raki and would ask her brother or father if the white mark was disappearing. When Maria came she would scrutinize Phaedra's face carefully but could see no sign that the whiteness was any less, despite her fervent prayers each Sunday.

The summer came to an end and Phaedra was becoming accustomed to her solitary existence. She no longer cried bitter tears every night when she lay on her pallet. Either Mikaelis or her father arrived each day and brought her fresh water and more food as necessary. She preferred it when Mikaelis completed the errand as he would stay, talking and laughing with her, whereas her father was always in a hurry to return to his work in the fields.

Every Saturday the whole family trudged up to visit her. They had told the inquisitive villagers that Phaedra was staying with relatives in another village and they were visiting her each week. They hoped that her services could soon be dispensed with and she would return home. No one questioned the veracity of their statement. It was customary to go and stay with relatives to help them through a crisis.

Elias only stayed long enough in the morning to give Phaedra her water and clean clothes before he hurried back to the fields. Mikaelis would arrive during the afternoon and would stay with his sister until the light began to fade. He thought it was an exciting adventure to live in a cave and wished he was allowed to do the same. As the days grew shorter Phaedra was condemned to spending many a lonely hour sitting inside the cave to keep warm. The oil lamp, unless she turned it up fully, did not give her enough light to sit and sew. She was reluctant to do this for more than a short while each day as she did not want to end up in darkness having used up all the precious oil.

It was a miserable existence and she asked her father continually if there was any sign of improvement in the white patch on her face.

Elias had shaken his head. 'Give it time.' He did not tell her that she had some nodules developing, although Phaedra was well aware of the bumps she could feel above her eyebrow and on her forehead. Finally Elias was forced to tell his daughter that she was suffering from leprosy.

'Why don't you ask the doctor for some medicine for me?'

'There is no medicine. If we spoke to the doctor he would take you far away and we would never see you again. It's better that you stay hidden here and we look after you.'

'If I came home, Pappa, I could stay in the house and never go out so no one would know I was there.'

Elias shook his head. 'You cannot be inside with other people. It's safe enough for us to visit you here in the open air. The germs will blow away. If we were all together again the germs would be contained in the room and we would all end up infected.'

'So how did I become infected?'

'We don't know. No one knows how it starts. Once someone has it they have to be kept away from everyone else who is healthy. You wouldn't want to give it to Mikaelis or your mother, now, would you?'

'Of course not, but I hate having to live up here on my own. It's going to be so cold during the winter.'

'I'll bring you up an oil stove and plenty more oil. That will keep you warm. You're better off than many. I've seen one or two when I've been in the town with your grandfather and they have to live on the streets and had to beg for their food until they are reported to the authorities and taken away.'

'Where do they go?'

'To a leprosarium somewhere.'

'Would they get treatment there and recover?'

'I've told you, Phaedra; there is no treatment. This is not like having a cold where you will be better by the end of the week. If you were in a leprosarium it would be like a prison.'

After her father left that day Phaedra shed despairing tears. She had to accept that she would spend the remainder of her life living in a cave on the hillside and being looked after by her parents.

Eleni decided she must take advantage of the remaining fine days before the winter set in to go walking on the hills. It would not be long before she would be forced to sit inside bent over her embroidery or spending weary hours at the weaving frame. Once it began to rain it would be unsafe to walk up the hill as she could slip on the mud and twist an ankle, being forced to lay there until her father alerted the villagers and they came searching for her. She would have to content herself with walking along the cart track if she wanted to go out.

She walked along, her head bent, inconsequential thoughts in her mind, wrapped in her cloak to keep the cold wind at bay as the clouds scudded across the sky. She shivered. Tomorrow she would walk further around the hill and sit in her cave where she would be comfortably out of the wind for a while.

Phaedra sat just inside the mouth of the cave, wrapped in her cloak. The oil heater that her father had brought up for her kept the interior reasonably warm, but it was dark and depressing sitting inside on her pallet. She wished her father would hurry up and visit her. Mikaelis had only stayed a short while that morning when he brought a fresh loaf and a small churn of milk. She had drunk the milk gratefully. It made a change from the water that was usually the only way to quench her thirst, but she would have loved a hot meal made by her mother.

Her brother had then hurried back to the fields where he was expected to help his father and grandfather gather in as many of their crops as possible before the inevitable rains began. When that happened the men stayed home from the fields, congregating in Manolis's taverna and complaining that many of their crops would be ruined and they and their families would starve that winter.

The wind was blowing more keenly than ever the following day and Eleni battled against it, her head bent as she walked over the uneven ground. Until now the sheltered hollows had been sufficient to settle into if the wind blew, but today it was too vigorous to be comfortable sitting in one. Once sheltered a little by the clumps of gorse the walking became easier and she raised her head to see how close she was to the shelter of her cave where she would be able to get some respite from the wind and be able to sit for a while. She was about to walk towards the opening when she saw someone sitting outside the cave she had come to consider her own refuge.

Quietly she retreated to the shelter of the gorse bushes and watched. Who was this person? Were they just having a rest, sheltering from the wind, before continuing on their way? Eleni's eyes narrowed as she saw Elias appear from the far side of the hill. What was he doing there? Did he have an assignation with the person at the cave? Was he cheating on Maria? The thought of that possibility gave her a feeling of immense satisfaction.

He sat down on the ground outside and placed various items on the ground. The cloaked figure rose and Eleni could see now that it was a woman. She took whatever had been placed on the grass into the cave and returned to sit beside Elias. They were having a conversation, but Eleni was too far away to hear what was being said.

Eleni waited and watched. The pair sat a distance apart and made no attempt to touch each other even when Elias rose to leave. The woman looked up at him and said something to which he replied with a nod and a smile. Eleni did not dare to move. She did not want Elias to see her up there watching him. She waited until he was out of her sight down the hill before she left the gorse bushes that had been hiding her and hurried along the rough track. Tomorrow she would return and find out if the woman was there again and if Elias visited her.

The rain that fell over night and in the morning of the following day prevented Eleni from venturing up onto the hill. She had to content herself with walking along the cart track which was muddy and unpleasant due to the rain that had fallen earlier. She wondered idly how long it would take her to walk to the next village although she was not likely to find it any different from her own. She would not consider that today, but when the spring arrived it could be an interesting diversion to her mundane routine.

As she raised her head she saw to her consternation that Elias was hurrying in her direction.

Very deliberately Eleni turned and began to walk back the way she had come. The only reason Elias would have to be so far out from the village was if he had been up on the hill to meet the woman in the cave. He must be besotted by her to have walked up there when it would be like walking on glass where the undergrowth would be slick with the falling rain. As soon as the weather improved Eleni determined that she would go up and hide behind the gorse patch and see if the woman was still there and if Elias visited her again.

For two days Eleni was frustrated. As she had started to climb the hill she could feel her boots slipping and sliding beneath her. She would be foolish to venture further up until the ground was dryer. She walked slowly along the track and was almost at the end house when she saw Elias walking towards her and turn into his cottage. She gave a thin smile. If she saw him up at the cave again she she was going to spread the word in the village that he was cheating on his wife.

Saturday dawned fine and Eleni was anxious to get out of the house. 'I've prepared all the vegetables and added two chicken wings. I'll leave the pot simmering on the fire. Don't forget it's there, Mamma. Take a break from your weaving occasionally and check it. It wouldn't do for it to boil dry.'

'What's your hurry?'

Eleni smiled. 'It's a fine day and I want to go for my walk on the hill. I hate just walking through the village on the cart track and soon that will be the only option that I have. '

'Make sure you are well wrapped up. It could be cold up there.'

'I'll be plenty warm enough climbing up. If I find it too cold I will come home.'

'Are you meeting someone?'

Eleni looked at her mother in surprise and shook her head. 'No, I'm certainly not meeting anyone. I just enjoy being up there on my own. I watch the birds and if I sit quietly they come quite close to me. I'll be home before dark. The birds will have gone to roost by then so there would be no point in staying up there any longer just to see the stars appear.'

Eleni took her time climbing the hill and walking along to the gorse bushes. There was no immediate rush. Elias was unlikely to visit the woman until late in the afternoon. Once she had seen him arrive she would return home. She had no wish to hang around and see what transpired between them.

As she reached the patch of gorse she could hear low voices. Cautiously she peered through the spiny branches. Sitting on the ground in front of the cave was Maria, Elias and Mikaelis, a short distance away sat the woman. The family were well wrapped up and appeared relaxed and enjoying each others company. The truth dawned on Eleni. The woman living in the cave was Phaedra. The story the villagers had been told about her visiting and staying with relatives was fictitious.

Eleni drew in her breath. Why was the girl living up there and not at home with her family? There could only be two explanations; the girl was pregnant and they wished to hide the fact, or the girl had contracted the dreaded leprosy disease and she was no longer welcome to live at home with her family.

Keeping behind the gorse bushes Eleni retraced her steps until she had rounded the hill and knew she could no longer be seen. This was retribution indeed for Elias's duplicity. It may have taken some years for her curse to be effective, but there was no way it could be lifted now however hard the family prayed in church each Sunday for the girl to recover.

Deep in thought Eleni walked back down the hill and into her home. She would not be able to walk that way again and take advantage of the shelter of the cave. Any one of Phaedra's family could appear at any time and even if Phaedra left the cave would be contaminated. She felt unreasonably annoyed. Why did they have to choose her particular cave to hide the girl in?

Her mother was still sitting at the weaving loom and a savoury smell of chicken and vegetables greeted her. She walked over to the fire and wrapping her hand in her cloak she lifted the lid off the pot. To her relief she saw that her mother had added more liquor and there was no sign that their supper was boiling dry.

'You're back earlier than I expected,' remarked Despina.

'It was too cold to stay up there any longer.' Eleni hung her cloak behind the door. 'I'll see what the weather is like tomorrow. If I walk in a different direction the wind may not be so cold.'

Despina nodded. She was busy counting the threads of the pattern she was weaving and did not want to make an error.

'Mamma, when did Doctor Kandakis last visit the village?'

Despina stopped her counting. 'Why? What is wrong with you?'

'Nothing. I just don't remember seeing him around for weeks now.'

'I expect you were up on the hill the last time he came. No one in the village needed him except Maria. She's expecting again but appears well so he didn't stay long.' Despina clicked her tongue in annoyance. She had lost count of her threads to answer an unimportant question.

'When is he coming again?'

'How would I know? When he sees fit, no doubt.'

Eleni sat on the stool near the fire. She would only take a quick walk up the hill each day, just to check that Phaedra was still inhabiting the cave, until the doctor visited the village again. She would be looking out for him and when he arrived she would ask if she could speak to him confidentially. He would know if it was permissible for a leprosy sufferer to live in a cave close to the village. If he said it was not a problem she would spread the word amongst the villagers and Elias and Maria would soon find they had to leave the area and live elsewhere. If one member of the family was contaminated it was possible that everyone else was also and no one would want them around.

Eleni took a shorter route up to where she could see the cave entrance, but often there was no sign of Phaedra. She dared not go and peer into the entrance as she did not want Phaedra to tell her father that her hiding place had been discovered. Nor could she stay behind the gorse bushes for too long due to the cold wind that now blew steadily most days and her fear of missing the doctor when he visited their village.

October 1924

Each time Eleni heard a donkey trotting down the cart track past their house she would look out hoping it would be Doctor Kandakis, but it was over two weeks before her vigilance was rewarded. She waited until he had entered the house, asked after her health and then turned to her mother asking if there was anyone in the village who needed his attention. She slipped outside and stood a short distance up the road. From there she would be able to see when he left to continue on to the next village and she could easily catch up with him as the donkey ambled on its way.

As the doctor rode slowly up the cart track she hurried towards him and placed a hand on the donkey's rein.

'May I have a quick word with you, please?'

Doctor Kandakis frowned. 'Why didn't you speak to me when I was in the house? You assured me you were well.'

'It is not about me. I believe there is a woman suffering from leprosy who is living in a cave up on the hill.'

'Are you sure she is sick?'

'I have never been close enough to her to find out for sure, but looking at her from a distance I feel certain she is a sufferer. Is it right that she should live so close to the village if she is sick?'

'If she is leprous she should certainly not be living here. If I arrange for a cart to be sent for her. Can you show the attendants where she is?'

Eleni nodded. 'I can wait outside the village and as soon as I see them coming I can show them where the cave is situated.'

'I'll tell them to look out for you. She can then be brought to me in the town and I can assess her. If she is just a hermit she can be released to go on her way when I have examined her provided she has no illness. Who else knows she is up there?'

'I have no idea. I only spotted her by chance when I was out walking. It would be a great relief to me to know that she had been moved elsewhere. I would not want to suddenly come across her and risk being infected.'

'She could be just a harmless old recluse and you would have nothing to worry about. Best avoid her, though, she could be deranged.'

'Thank you, doctor. You have put my mind at rest and I'll avoid going up near that area until I know she has been taken away.'

Smiling with delight Eleni returned to her house. She would now walk to the end of the village every day until she saw the cart travelling along the track. She would stop the men and indicate the location of the cave. Once they began to climb the hill she would return to the village and wait for the cart and the girl to travel back through the village. She knew everyone would be curious to see the occupant and jeer at them and she wanted to see Maria and Elias's reaction when they saw their daughter being taken away.

It was almost a week before the cart trundled through the village and Eleni had begun to think the doctor had forgotten. She stopped the cart and asked the men to follow the track towards the next village.

'Go slowly and give me time to climb the hill. I'll not go right up to the cave. Once I'm close to it I'll wave to you and then leave you to go about your business.'

Eleni began to climb the hill as rapidly as possible. Once she could see the cave entrance she stopped. Phaedra was sitting outside and someone was with her. Eleni screwed up her eyes.

The figure did not look large enough for Elias, but it could be Mikaelis.

She waved frantically to the men and was pleased when she saw three of them begin to walk up the rough ground whilst a fourth stayed and held the donkey's head. Eleni promptly disappeared behind the gorse bushes and virtually ran back down the hill to her house.

Mikaelis saw the men coming and looked at Phaedra in terror. 'Get inside the cave and hide,' he ordered. 'I'll tell them I've been living up here.'

Phaedra realised that the men were actually looking for her and she obeyed her younger brother without question. She went back into the recess that held her pallet and blew out the oil lamp. They would not be able to see her in the darkness and once they realised there was nothing wrong with Mikaelis they would go away and leave her alone.

She cringed fearfully against the wall as she heard the men talking to Mikaelis.

'Where's the woman?' one asked roughly.

'What woman? I'm the only person around up here.'

'We've been told there's a woman living up here and she's leprous.'

'That's nonsense. There's no one else around.'

'There must have been a mistake made, then. Wrapped in your cloak you could be taken for a woman.' The man eyed Mikaelis up and down and turned to his companion. 'We'll take him back to the doctor for an examination. I suspect he's lying.'

'I'm not lying. I'm telling you the truth. There's nothing wrong with me.'

The man ignored Mikaelis's protests. 'Collect your belongings. You're coming with us.'

Mikaelis cast a panicked glance towards the cave. 'There's nothing in there that I want. I was just spending the afternoon up on the hill.'

The second man caught hold of Mikaelis's arm and held him firmly. 'I don't advise you to start running away. We'll catch up with you and not be so gentle the next time.' He cuffed Mikaelis on his ear, making the boy's ears ring.

'I'll have a quick look inside,' said the first man. 'Could be any number hiding out up here thinking they wouldn't be found.'

'There's no one in there,' called Mikaelis, hoping desperately the man would believe him. 'Take me to the doctor if you want. He'll confirm there's nothing wrong with me.'

'Then you've nothing to worry about except a long walk back from the town.'

To Mikaelis's horror the man took a candle from his pocket and lit it in the shelter of the cave, shielding it with his hand from the draught.

'Got you,' Mikaelis heard him say and Phaedra was being dragged out.

The man who had hold of Mikaelis hit him again and this time the boy lost consciousness and slumped to the ground.

'Hold onto the girl whilst I have a look inside and see if there's anyone else.'

'There is no one,' insisted Phaedra. 'I've been living up here alone.'

'Who's that then?' The man pointed to the inert body on the ground.

'He's my brother. He'd brought me up some food. There's nothing wrong with him.'

'That will be up to the doctor to decide. Get any possessions you want with you and we'll be off.'

'I want everything.'

With a sigh the man opened the boxes and began to throw Phaedra's belongings onto the blanket on her pallet. He pulled the opposite edges together and tied them firmly.

'Where are you taking me?' asked Phaedra fearfully.

'To the town to see the doctor. Hurry up. We haven't time to stand here gossiping with you. Bring your pallet.'

Phaedra rolled up her pallet and picked up her spare blanket. She was wearing her cloak and boots and most of her meagre belongings were now bundled up in the other blanket. She had no idea if there was anything else she needed to take with her. If the doctor said she needed hospitalization Mikaelis could come back and tell her parents and they would bring her anything else she asked for.

The man who had hit Mikaelis lifted him up and slung him over his shoulder whilst another took hold of Phaedra's arm and began to drag her down the hill, followed by the third man carrying the blanket that contained her belongings. Slipping and stumbling, Phaedra had no choice but to accompany them, her pallet and spare blanket dragging on the ground.

Unceremoniously Phaedra was lifted up into the cart, her bundle thrown in and Mikaelis placed on the flat bottom. Mikaelis's ankles were tied together and so were Phaedra's.

'Just in case you get some idea that you can jump out and run away,' remarked the man grimly. 'You won't get far with your ankles tied.'

Tears were running freely down Phaedra's face as she helped Mikaelis up onto the wooden seat beside her. She should have thought to bring a rag with her and a bottle of water. She could at least have tended to Mikaelis's bruises and seen if he was badly hurt. She placed her arm around him and pulled him close to her, enabling his head to lie on her shoulder.

As they drove through the village the men stopped working in the fields and hurried over to the roadside to see who was being taken away and the women craned their necks around the doorways and crossed themselves. Elias went rigid with horror. In the cart were both his daughter and his son. He must tell Maria and hope that the shock would not cause her to miscarry their latest child. This time they were praying that the infant would be healthy and strong enough to survive.

He ran down the road towards their cottage and met Maria who was already striding towards the village. She had tears streaming down her face and she was shaking with rage.

'Where is she? It's her doing. I know it is. I'll make her regret it.'

'Maria, stay calm. Think of the baby,' pleaded Elias.

'What about my other babies? They've been taken away. She must have found out that Phaedra was up in the cave. I hate her,' Maria shouted back at her husband hysterically.

Maria reached Eleni's house where the woman was standing outside, a malicious smile on her face.

'This is your doing, Eleni.'

'My curse has come, Maria. You will never see your children again,' she said triumphantly.

Maria flew at Eleni, tearing her headscarf off and grabbing her hair. 'You're wicked; evil. You should be run out of the village.'

Eleni was momentarily stunned by the physical attack and then she began to fight back. The two women grappled on the ground, kicking and punching each other, tearing at each other's clothes and scratching their faces.

'Maria, stop. Please, Maria.' Elias tried ineffectively to pull his wife away. 'Think of the baby.'

'Another child to lay the curse on.' Eleni punched Maria in the stomach and Maria gasped for breath. She took Eleni's head between her hands and slammed it down on the ground. Eleni's eyes rolled and she seemed to make an effort to get up before lying motionless.

'Maria, you've really hurt her. Get up now. Fighting with Eleni will not bring the children back home.'

Maria drew a shuddering breath and allowed Elias to help her to her feet. 'I hope I've killed her,' she shouted.

Despina hurried over to where Eleni laid motionless. 'You had no reason to attack my daughter. The whole village is a witness to you starting the fight.'

The villagers had gathered around to watch the two women brawling and heard Maria's words. They crossed themselves.

Women did not fight like wild cats in the street inflicting bodily harm on each other.

Yiorgo picked up the limp body of his daughter and carried her inside their house. Despina immediately began to bathe Eleni's head with cold water.

'What happened?' asked Yiorgo. 'I was in the shop and the next thing I knew there was this commotion going on outside. What made Maria pick a fight with our Eleni?'

'Maria's children have been taken away. She blames Eleni.'

'You mean they were in the cart? Are they sick?'

'They must be. The cart wouldn't have come for them otherwise.'

'I thought their daughter was staying with relatives.'

'That's what they told us. Don't just stand there, Yiorgo. Ride into town and bring the doctor back here. Eleni is seriously hurt.'

Elias hurried his sobbing wife back to their house. 'Maria, what came over you? You really have hurt Eleni.'

Maria looked at her husband, wild eyed with grief. 'She cursed our children. Our poor Phaedra has been afflicted and now she and Mikaelis have been taken away. We'll never see either of them again.'

'We could be mistaken about Phaedra. Once the doctor has examined her he could decide she is suffering from some other skin ailment. We know there is nothing wrong with Mikaelis so he'll be back soon enough. He'll be able to tell us where Phaedra is if she is hospitalized. We'll be able to go and see her.'

Maria shook her head. She knew Elias was trying his best to comfort her and give her some hope, but she could not believe the words he said.

The door to their cottage opened and Elias looked up anxiously. Was this Eleni's father come to take revenge for the assault on his daughter? Instead his own father stood there looking grim.

'Get your belongings together. I've brought my donkey and cart down.'

'What for?'

'You can't stay here. The villagers will assume you are diseased as well as Phaedra. Go now before they drive you away with only whatever you can carry in your arms.'

'Where can we go?' Elias looked at his father in distress and puzzlement.

'Anywhere. Despina and Yiorgo will seek revenge for the attack on their daughter. They'll rouse the villagers up and you could end up being stoned if you're still here tomorrow. Start gathering up what you need. The sooner you leave the better.'

'Are you coming with us?'

Andreas shook his head. 'I'll tell people you stole my donkey and cart to make your getaway. Someone needs to be here for Mikaelis when he returns. I'll look after him.'

'This is all Eleni's fault. She cursed us. If she hadn't done that Maria would never have hit her.'

'Elias, the fault was yours originally. Had you not made Eleni pregnant at the same time as Maria she would have had no reason to curse you.'

Maria stood there as if stunned. 'What do you mean? Did you make Eleni pregnant?'

'Don't be silly,' answered Elias swiftly. 'You know she's never had a child.' He glared at his father. It was true; he was the cause of the enmity between the two women. Sullenly he stripped the blankets from their bed and bundled them up.

'Don't just stand there. Collect everything from the kitchen,' he ordered Maria. 'We need to take as much as possible to our new home – wherever that might be.'

Each village the cart trundled through drew people out to see who was being taken away. They jeered and threw stones at Phaedra and she bent over Mikaelis to shield him from the onslaught. Finally the cart descended a hill and the buildings of Aghios Nikolaos came into sight. In the distance Phaedra could see an expanse of blue that she could only imagine was the sea. It seemed to go on for ever. Never having been out of her village before she had no idea where she was or where she was being taken.

Eventually the cart stopped and one man alighted and knocked on the door of a house and waited for the doctor to appear.

'We've brought the woman you told us about and found a boy there with her. We've brought him along as well.'

Doctor Kandakis nodded and looked at Phaedra who gazed back fearfully, whilst Mikaelis stirred and tried to lift his head.

'It's obvious. She should have been brought in long ago.'

'What about the boy? Shouldn't you examine him?'

Doctor Kandakis shook his head. 'Bound to be sick also. No reason to be hiding out up there with the woman otherwise. Tell me your names,' he ordered Phaedra.

'My brother is not sick. The men hit him. Please let him return home.'

'Your names,' barked Doctor Kandakis.

'I'm Phaedra and my brother is Mikaelis.'

'Take them down to the port and get one of the boatmen to take them over.'

Phaedra followed the exchange of words. 'Please let my brother stay here. He isn't sick.'

Doctor Kandakis ignored her and went back inside his house, shutting the door firmly.

The men in charge of the cart did not argue with the doctor. They were paid well to carry out the unpleasant job of finding and bringing any lepers who were reported to be hiding in caves up in the hills to the doctor but they were always pleased to pass their passengers on to a boatman.

The cart continued down to the small harbour and Phaedra tried again 'Please let my brother get off and shelter somewhere until he recovers,' begged Phaedra. 'Truly he isn't sick.'

'We only do as the doctor says.'

Helplessly Phaedra sat in the cart and watched as various

fishermen approached offering to make the journey across the water for which they knew they would be well paid.

'Put them on my deck,' said one. 'I've the largest boat with the biggest sails. I can get them there before night fall. Yiorgo can come with me to take an oar.'

Phaedra's ankles were untied and she was led over to the boat. She was tempted to run and see if she could hide somewhere but she could not leave Mikaelis alone at the mercy of these men. She was pushed up the gang plank, her pallet and the blanket containing her possessions thrown up after her and Mikaelis was once again slung over the shoulder of one of the men and carried up. He sank down on the deck beside her, still hardly conscious.

She cradled Mikaelis in her arms. The motion of the boat was making her feel ill and she was petrified. Where were they being taken?

Yiorgo arrived at the doctor's house and stressed the urgency of his mission. 'My daughter, she's been knocked unconscious. Please come and help her.'

Doctor Kandakis shook his head. 'There's no point in me going back with you if she's unconscious. Despina can look after her. You'll just have to wait for her to open her eyes. How did it happen? Did she fall from a height?'

'There was an incident in the village. The cart came for a girl who had been hiding out up on the hill. Her mother blamed my daughter and attacked her.'

'Yes, your daughter said she thought there was an old woman hiding out up there. I found out it was a girl and there was a boy living there with her. They're on their way to the island now. Tomorrow I'll send the cart for the parents. They'll have to be tested as they are probably carrying the germs and will be sent off to join their offspring. I'm sure someone in the village will be able to identify them.'

Yiorgo turned away. Were Maria and Elias also suffering from leprosy? If so they were certainly not welcome in the village.

When Yiorgo returned home he found Eleni was still unconscious and there was a sense of impending menace in the air. The men were gathered together in small groups muttering and casting glances in the direction of Manolis's taverna.

Despina looked up anxiously when her husband returned. 'Is the doctor coming?'

Yiorgo shook his head. 'He said he could do no more for her than you can.'

'She hasn't stirred, Yiorgo.'

'Give her time. It can take quite a while to recover from a bang on the head.'

'Did you hear what Maria said? She said she hoped she'd killed Eleni.'

'I'm sure you must have misheard. She probably said she hoped she *hadn't* killed Eleni.'

'I know what I heard,' muttered Despina.

'I'll go up there tomorrow and sort things out with them.'

Maria was still snivelling and clutching at her stomach as Elias loaded up the cart. He continually looked warily down the road to the centre of the village. It was most likely that the villagers would wait until it was dark, hoping to take them by surprise, before driving them from their house.

'Are you going up to collect everything from the cave?' asked Maria as she wiped her eyes yet again on her apron.

'There's no time for that and it wouldn't be sensible. Phaedra's possessions would be contaminated by now. Better to leave them and get away from the village as soon as possible.'

'Where will we go?'

Elias shrugged. 'I don't know. We'll just follow the cart track. It leads to the next village and probably goes on to another.'

'Where will we live?'

'I don't know the answer to that either,' answered Elias shortly. 'We may have to stay in a convenient cave ourselves for a while until I've found some work and we have enough money to pay rent for a cottage. Move yourself, woman.' He was dreading that Maria would recover herself sufficiently to start questioning him about the accusation his father had made.

Maria sensed that her husband was becoming impatient with her questions. She was distraught that her two children had been taken away and certainly did not want their next child to be born in the fields.

The journey out around the headland seemed to go on for hours and the light was beginning to fade when the fishermen lowered the sails and began to row through an inlet and finally moored at a small jetty.

Phaedra lifted her head. She could see a village nestling below the hills across the water. It should be possible to walk there on the spit of land that jutted out and joined the area where they were being put ashore. She and Mikaelis would walk over there the following day and hide in the hills before finding their way back to their own village. With this comforting thought in mind she did not resist as a short plank was stretched from the boat to the stone jetty and she was told to go ashore, her belongings thrown over to her once she was on firm ground.

Mikaelis, although still not fully conscious realised he was being sent to a leprosarium along with his sister.

'I'm not ill. Let me go. Take me back.'

As the fisherman pushed him towards the plank he struggled and lost his balance, falling over into the water.

'Mikaelis!' screamed Phaedra. She knelt down on the jetty and held out her hand in the vain hope that he could reach her and she would be able to pull him out.

Mikaelis clutched at the boat and the fisherman used an oar to push him away. The sea was too deep for Mikaelis to stand with his head above the water and Phaedra watched as he sank down out of sight, his arms flailing.

'Help him. Help him,' she called frantically.

Without a second glance the fisherman pulled up the plank and took to the oars with his companion, rowing away from the jetty leaving Mikaelis floundering in the sea.

Their arrival had not gone unnoticed and people had made their way down towards the jetty. Phaedra looked at them; some had facial disfigurements and others had limbs that were crippled and useless. Phaedra shuddered. This was her ultimate fate.

A woman, leaning heavily on a stick, stepped forwards.

'What happened?' she asked. 'Where's the man who was with you?'

With a shaking hand Phaedra pointed to the sea where Mikaelis had disappeared. 'The fisherman, he pushed him under. He's my brother. Can anyone find him and bring him ashore?'

The woman shook her head. 'There's no one here who could do that.'

'What can I do?' asked Phaedra desperately. 'He's only a boy.'

'There's nothing you can do. You have to accept that these things happen. He won't be the first to have drowned.'

A tear rolled down Phaedra's face and she stifled a sob. 'I must go and look for him.' She walked along the jetty, peering down into the water and calling Mikaelis's name.

'You're unlikely to find him. He could be anywhere. Once he was under the water the currents would start to take him.'

'Then he may have been washed ashore somewhere, possibly injured and needing help.'

'Don't get your hopes up. If he has been washed up he would have been battered against the rocks.'

'Can you take me to the hospital, please? Maybe there's a doctor there who could help?'

Ariadne looked at Phaedra with something like amusement. 'There's no doctor here.'

'I thought I was being taken to a hospital.'

'This is the hospital. What were you expecting? A building with beds and people to look after you? Here we look after ourselves. Why do you think you were told to bring your pallet and blanket with you? Without those you would have spent the night lying on the ground in the cold.'

'No hospital?'

Ariadne shook her head as Phaedra looked at her in disbelief. 'Follow me and we'll see if we can find you some shelter for the night.'

'She can come and share my mattress,' offered a man leering at Phaedra.

'Go away, Nikos. She's no more than a child. She doesn't want you men pestering her.' Ariadne waved her stick at him.

'Can you carry your belongings? You'll need somewhere to stay the night.'

'Where can I go?'

Ariadne considered. 'I suppose we can make a space for you and we'll look for a shelter for you tomorrow. Have you eaten? I don't want you keeping me awake all night with your stomach rumbling.'

Phaedra shook her head. Food was the furthest thing from her mind.

'I've bit of bread left that you can have.'

Ariadne led Phaedra up the ramp to the main pathway on the island. Curious eyes were on her, making her feel uneasy. Tomorrow she would definitely walk along to the village she had seen and hide up in the hills. Then she would have to find her way back to her own village and tell her parents that Mikaelis had drowned. She did not want to dwell on the awful event. It was just possible that the current Ariadne had spoken of had washed him up on the shore and he was lying there now recovering. She must look for him first the following day before she thought of walking to the village.

Phaedra placed her spare blanket around her shoulders, rolled her pallet and held it beneath one arm and struggled to carry the blanket containing her belongs as she followed Ariadne into a dark, ramshackle building a short distance away from the path.

'Wait until your eyes become accustomed to the lack of light. You don't want to fall over anyone. They won't take kindly to you landing on top of them.'

'Is this where you live?' she asked Ariadne timidly.

Ariadne nodded. 'What were you expecting? A room of your own?'

'I thought you would live in a cottage like I used to.'

'Now that would be a luxury. Move over, Dimitra, and tell Maria to do the same. We have a guest for the night. Go over by the wall, girl, and I'll sleep this side of you. No one will be able to bother you without climbing over me. What's your name?'

'Phaedra.'

'I'm Ariadne. Sit down there and I'll give you a bite to eat. Then we'll bed down.' Ariadne moved her own mattress closer to the woman she had called Dimitra giving Phaedra sufficient space to lay her pallet down.

'Don't you have an oil lamp?' asked Phaedra.

'Not often and we save it should someone need attention during the night.'

'I can't really see what I'm doing and I could have some food in my blanket.'

'Then look for it tomorrow.'

Phaedra ate the stale piece of bread that Ariadne handed to her. She had thought that living in a cave was a hardship, but at least she had eaten fresh food every day, had an oil lamp and plenty of space to lay her pallet.

Phaedra hardly slept; the sounds of the other occupants continually intruded upon her and she was haunted by the memory of Mikaelis falling into the sea. Silent tears ran down her face. She was so close to Ariadne that she could hear every breath the woman took and dared not move her own cramped limbs for fear of disturbing her. Ariadne had no such scruples, kicking Phaedra every so often as she shifted her position until she sat up on her mattress and yawned widely.

'Are you awake? If you want something to eat we need to get down to the port now and see if there's anything left. You may have to wait until the boats have been.'

Phaedra did not understand – why would there be nothing left? Food was the last thing on her mind. 'I must look for my brother.'

Ariadne shook her head sadly. 'I fear you'll be wasting your time.'

Phaedra set her mouth in a determined line. 'I have to look. He would go looking for me if I had fallen overboard. If I find him would someone be able to help me to bring him back here? I wouldn't be able to manage on my own.'

'If you find him.' replied Ariadne dubiously. 'I expect one of the men will be willing to help. You ought to come down and see if there's a bit of food you can get inside yourself first.'

'Where are the shops?'

'There are no shops.' Ariadne seemed amused by Phaedra's ignorance. 'Here you just go and help yourself to whatever supplies are available in the storeroom. Don't be greedy and take more than you'll be able to eat in the day. It only goes stale or mouldy.' Ariadne picked up her stick and a jug that stood close to her bed and hauled herself to her feet.

'What about my belongings? Should I bring them?'

'They'll be safe enough here. Dimitra, listen, the pallet and whatever is tied in that blanket belongs to Phaedra. Make sure no one touches them whilst we're gone.'

Obediently Phaedra followed Ariadne along the footpath where she turned down towards the port. Phaedra immediately began to look anxiously for any sign of Mikaelis. There was activity in the village across the sea.

She pointed to the boats that were preparing to set off. 'Do you think they've found Mikaelis?'

Ariadne shook her head. 'They're bringing us a supply of

100

water for today and some food. I'm sorry about your brother, but there's little chance that he would have survived even if he was able to swim. The currents are strong and generally sweep everything out to the sea.'

'I do wish he hadn't been with me when the men came,' said Phaedra miserably. 'There's nothing wrong with him. My poor mother will be devastated when I tell her.'

'How are you going to do that?' asked Ariadne.

'I thought I would follow the path round and make my way into the hills over there. I'm not sure which direction I have to go in to reach my village but I'm sure I'll find my way.'

Ariadne looked at Phaedra in amazement. 'You thought you could walk over to the hills? Don't you realise you're on an island?'

'An island?'

'Yes, the sea is all around us. There's no way you can reach the hills over there or the village for that matter. The only way to get across is by boat.'

'Do you think one of the fishermen would take me?'

Ariadne looked at Phaedra scornfully. 'They'll not come near us and they certainly wouldn't let you on their boat. We ought to look in the storeroom and see what food there is before some of the others are up and around looking for something to eat. When the boats arrive we have to keep off the quayside until they've finished unloading so we don't infect them.'

Phaedra followed Ariadne into the dark, cavernous building. On the ground stood boxes and crates, some of them with the remains of mouldy vegetables in the bottom. Ariadne began to rummage amongst the boxes and held up half a loaf, two squashed tomatoes and a handful of olives.

'Better than nothing. We'll come back down later when the new supplies have arrived. At least we should have some fresh bread then and there might even be a bit of meat. I'll show you where the drinking water is.'

Phaedra walked beside Ariadne down the path which gradually widened out to become a small square. Set into the wall was a drinking fountain and a queue of people were waiting to fill their jugs or cups. The men and women looked incuriously at Phaedra; she was just another person who had been sent to join them on the island.

Ariadne filled her jug from the water fountain and the two women moved to one side. 'Have a drink, but leave some for me. I don't want to have to queue up again.'

'I have a jug. You should have said and I could have brought it here with me.'

'It's better that your belongings stay tied up in that blanket until you have somewhere permanent to live.'

Phaedra handed the hug back to Ariadne. 'Thank you. I'm going to look for Mikaelis now.'

Ariadne frowned. 'Where are you planning to look?'

'I'll go down to the beach beside the jetty and walk all around the island.'

'You can't do that. A short distance along from the jetty the fortress walls go down to the rocks.'

Phaedra looked at Ariadne in despair. 'He could be lying round there. I have to look.'

'Once you've made sure he's not on the beach here go back up to the top of the ramp and walk along by the fortress walls. You can look over or through them and see the area below. You can't get lost. When you reach the tunnel go through and you'll find yourself back in the square.'

Ariadne shook her head sadly as Phaedra walked away. There was no chance that she would find her brother alive even if he had been washed up into the rocks.

Having scoured the beach area in both directions Phaedra climbed back up the steps to the fortress walls and began to make her way along the dirt path beside them, continually looking over or through the openings to see if there was any sign of Mikaelis below. She shuddered as she saw the rocks with the sea sucking at them greedily. Even had Mikaelis not drowned he would in all probability have been dashed to death.

As Phaedra reached the end of the path to where it curved around to the other side of the island she was able to appreciate that the hills she had thought were just a short distance away were in fact across quite a large expanse of water.

'Don't go too close,' a voice warned her. 'The walls may not be safe. You don't want to end up on the rocks below.'

Phaedra peered over the section of wall at the drop to the sea and shuddered. She would certainly be careful. The rocks here looked even more dangerous than those she had seen earlier and there was certainly no way to get down to them.

A girl appeared from a small watch tower and looked at her suspiciously. 'You're new. You'd better be careful that you don't fall over.'

Phaedra took a step back.

'What are you looking for?'

'My brother.'

'Well he's not likely to be down there. He's probably with the men.'

Phaedra shook her head. 'He was pushed into the water by the boatmen and I couldn't reach him. I was hoping he might be washed up on a beach and needed some help. I'm going all around the island looking for any sign of him.'

'When did this happen?'

'We were brought here yesterday afternoon and Ariadne said it was too dark to go and look for him then.'

'You're not likely to find him. He will have been swept away by the current either out to sea or across to the mainland.'

Tears filled Phaedra's eyes. 'That's what Ariadne said, but I still have to look. If he is lying somewhere injured he'll be relying on me to help him.'

'I'll come with you. The other side of the island is even more dangerous in places than here, although its even less likely that he would be washed ashore there.'

'Would you be able to let me have a drink of water, please?'

'Why didn't you bring some with you?'

'I shared Ariadne's jug. My belongings are still packed up until I have somewhere to stay.'

'Wait there.' Flora retreated inside a small watch tower and returned bearing a jug that was half full. 'Don't drink it all in one go. We may need some a bit later and we can't get any more until we reach the square.' She held out her hand and Phaedra dutifully returned the container to her.

Together they walked back up to where the path began to round the tip of the island. A bastion for the Venetian fort had been built jutting out onto the sea with a watch tower at each end that could be reached by a catwalk that ran around the perimeter wall.

'How do I get around there?' asked Phaedra.

'Do you think you could climb over the wall and manage to walk along the cat walk?' asked Flora.

'I can try.'

Phaedra sat on the wall and swung her legs over. Testing the ground carefully with every step she took she walked a short distance along the cat walk. Looking down at the sea a wave of giddiness overtook her. She was far higher up than she had realised and the sea was sucking and pounding at the foundations of the fortress way below; the movement of the waves making her nauseas.

Clutching onto the crenulations on the wall she edged carefully back to where Flora was waiting and breathed a sigh of relief when she reached her. The wall was deeper that side and it was difficult to scramble back onto it and let herself down onto the path where she felt safe.

'I can't walk along there. I'm frightened I will fall over. The sea keeps moving.'

'Of course it does. You'll get used to it.'

'I've never seen the sea before. I lived in a village in the country.'

'On a farm?' asked Flora curiously.

'No, my father worked on my grandfather's farm, but we had a cottage in the village. I wish I could go home,' she ended miserably.

'We all wish that, but we have to accept that we are here for the rest of our lives,' answered Flora.

'Which house do you live in?' asked Phaedra. She could not see any buildings in the area and Flora seemed to have appeared from nowhere when she had called her.

'I live in the watch tower. Come on if you want to walk around to the tunnel. There's no point in standing here feeling sorry for yourself.'

They walked as close to the Venetian walls as possible looking at the rocks down below until they came to another small beach area and Phaedra hurried forward towards the sea anxiously.

'There's no sign of him.' She wiped away the tears that were dribbling down her face with her sleeve. 'What am I going to do?'

'There's nothing you can do. You've looked for him and not seen any sign. We may as well go back to the square.'

Phaedra went towards the tunnel entrance but Flora called to her. 'Not that way. We'll go back the way we came.'

'Ariadne said that the tunnel led through to the square.'

Flora nodded. 'It does, but it isn't a good idea to use it. The men sit in there and will call out to you and try to catch your skirt. You certainly don't want to wander in there amongst them by yourself. A few are fit enough to hold on to you and the others would enjoy knowing you couldn't get away. Before you knew it they'd be like a pack of dogs tearing at you.'

Phaedra shuddered. 'I'll definitely not go through there. Are all the men on the island like them?'

'No, there are some decent ones who won't touch you. There are also the women up on the hillside where the men can go so they don't need to attack every woman they see. What they want is available.'

Phaedra nodded although she was unsure what Flora was talking about. 'Is there anywhere I can live? Ariadne allowed me to stay in her house with the other women last night, but it's terribly crowded.'

'Ariadne is kind and well meaning. You'll have to look around for yourself and see if you can find anywhere habitable.'

Ariadne had stayed sitting on a block of stone in the square when Phaedra left her. She was looking for Antonius. As she saw him finally arrive she stood up and approached him as he took his place in the queue at the water fountain.

'Do you know of a house that would have a space for a young girl who arrived yesterday?' she asked.

The old man shook his head. 'I've not walked around the island for a while now. As far as I know all the habitable places already have occupants. There may be a space in one of the tunnels or the church.'

'That's not a suitable solution. She's no more than a child. You know what will happen to her if she's in a tunnel or the church with the men. She needs to be in a house like mine where there are other women who can keep an eye on her.'

'Then you will have to speak to them. I'm too old and tired now to go tramping all over the island and talking to people. If they had done as I suggested years ago we wouldn't have this problem now.'

'I'm sure you tried your best,' Ariadne soothed the old man. 'I'll ask around.'

Ariadne hobbled from one dilapidated building to another and asked the women who were occupying the house if they could accommodate an extra person. She was continually met with a shake of the head and told to ask elsewhere; they already had more than enough bodies crowded into their area.

'Can I stay living in your house for a while?' asked Phaedra when Ariadne told her she had been unable to find anyone willing to take an extra person. 'I'm willing to look around and ask people if I can shelter with them.'

Ariadne frowned. 'I couldn't find anywhere for you so I suppose you'll have to stay in my house with the other women. It's not ideal. There are already too many of us for comfort and as soon as someone dies there will be a scramble to take her place. Even during the day you have to step over people if you want to go outside.'

'Doesn't anyone go out to work?'

'What work? There's nothing to do over here. We sit around and wait for the boats to bring supplies and when we've eaten we sit around until nightfall and go to sleep. The men who are able break up the wooden boxes that our food comes in so we can have a fire to cook over and we wash our clothes sometimes. Some of the men play cards but there's nothing else for anyone to do.'

'What about a bath? I've only been able to have a wash for months and I used to have a bath each week.'

'You can wash in the sea. It's not painful if you don't have open sores.'

'I don't like the sea. It keeps moving and makes a noise.'

Ariadne snorted in amusement. 'Of course it does. During the winter when the wind blows strongly it becomes far noisier with the waves crashing against the rocks and drawing the shingle back. You'll get used to it.'

'When does the doctor visit you?'

'Doctor?' Ariadne gave a wry laugh. 'He calls himself a doctor. He comes to the quay side and dumps some tablets ashore and leaves. He never actually comes on the island and examines anyone.'

Phaedra began to feel even more unhappy and depressed. Tears began to run down her face. She had not enjoyed living in a cave on the hillside but at least there she had been given light and warmth along with the fresh food sent up by her mother. This island was infinitely worse than anything she could have imagined. She rubbed at her eyes with her sleeve.

'I don't want to be here,' she sobbed. 'I want to go home and see my Mamma and Pappa. They'll be worried about me and expecting Mikaelis to go to the village and tell them which leprosarium the doctor sent me to. They'll never be able to find me here and Mikaelis isn't able to tell them.'

Ariadne placed an arm around the girl's shoulders. 'It isn't so bad here when you get used to it. Provided the boatmen can come over we have plenty of food. It's miserable when it rains, but then it's pretty miserable anywhere when that happens. Maybe Ritsa would be willing to go around the houses again. She might have more luck than me. I can't walk around any more. My legs are hurting too much. Standing there crying is not going to help you.'

Phaedra sniffed and rubbed her sleeve across her face. It was true, standing there feeling wretched and crying to go back home was useless.

Phaedra accompanied Ariadne back to her house and was introduced to Ritsa. She had the same white mark on her face as Phaedra, but some of the nodules that had developed had subsequently cracked and scabbed over. Phaedra felt both frightened and revolted; this was how she would look in a few years' time. Together they went from house to house again speaking to the current occupants and asking if they would be able to have one more person staying in the house with them. Everyone refused although many of the men who heard Phaedra's request offered to share their mattress with her.

Ritsa had scowled at them. 'She's a little girl. Not old enough for what you have in mind.'

By the time they had visited everyone Phaedra was exhausted and wanted nothing more than to lie down and sleep. 'I can't walk around any more; I'm just too tired. I've already walked all round the island with Flora and I didn't sleep well last night. I'm grateful to you, but I'll just sit down here and come back down to the house in the square when I've rested.'

'You can come and sit beside me,' called a voice and Phaedra looked up startled.

Ritsa smiled. 'You'll be safe enough up there with Kyriakos. I'll try to think of somewhere for you. If I start to pester people they might have a change of heart and decide you can join them.'

Phaedra looked at the man who had called to her. 'How do I get up there?' she asked.

'Use the steps.' Ritsa pointed to the short flight of concrete steps lower down the path. Feeling foolish Phaedra climbed them and walked along to where the man sat propped against a wall. A length of wood stretched on one side giving him a windbreak and another smaller piece was fixed to it. He no longer had any feet and one leg looked considerably shorter than the other.

'I'm Kyriakos,' he informed her. 'I'm known as Kyriakos the legless for obvious reasons. Come and sit beside me. When did you arrive?'

Phaedra sat down on the patch of concrete beside the helpless man. 'I was brought over yesterday.'

'Where did they find you?'

'I was up in the hills behind my village. I was living in a cave.'

'Don't you have any parents?'

Phaedra nodded. 'I lived with them until they became concerned about my face; then they found a cave where I could live.'

'That must have been very lonely up there on your own.'

Phaedra shrugged. 'Either my Pappa or my brother came every day with some food for me. At the weekend my Mamma would come with them.'

'Do they know where you are now?'

Phaedra shook her head and her tears began to flow again. 'No one knows where I am.'

'So you're all alone?'

Phaedra nodded. 'Mikaelis was going to go back and tell my

parents what had happened so they could come and find me. That's not possible now.'

Kyriakos looked at her sympathetically. 'Even if your parents had found out where you were they could have done nothing. The only people allowed to set foot on this island are those suffering from leprosy. The boatmen dump our food and water on the jetty, every so often we're told to collect up our rubbish and place it down on the beach for a boat to collect, but we're not allowed to have anything to do with anyone from the mainland.'

'I thought I was going to a hospital where I would have treatment and be made well again.'

'There is no treatment. You have to accept that once you are afflicted you're an outcast. No one wants to have you around for fear that you will contaminate them. Even the doctor refuses to come onto the island and treat us as human beings.'

Phaedra shifted uncomfortably on the hard concrete. 'What am I going to do?' she asked sadly.

'There's nothing you can do. You will have to make the best of it over here the same as the rest of us.'

'I haven't even got anywhere to shelter permanently. Ariadne has said I can stay in her house until I can find somewhere else.' Phaedra shuddered. 'She said that when someone died there was always someone wanting to take their place in a house. Do people often die?'

Kyriakos nodded. 'It happens. We all have to go sometime.'

'Where do you live?'

Kyriakos chuckled. 'I live here.'

Phaedra looked at the uncomfortable slab of concrete, the wooden windbreak and the ruined houses that she could see lower down by the Venetian walls.

'What do you do when it rains or gets too cold to sit outside?'

'I ask some of the fitter men to carry me to the tunnel for shelter.'

'Why don't they take you into their house?'

Kyriakos shook his head. 'There's no space anywhere. Even the tunnels and church are overcrowded.' He picked up his water jug and drained the contents. 'I'll ask the next person who passes to get me a refill from the fountain.'

'I thought the fishermen brought over barrels of water. Why don't people use that instead of queuing up at the fountain?'

Kyriakos nodded. 'Provided the weather is good the boatmen bring some every day. If everyone took their drinking water from the barrels there would never be enough to wash your face and hands, rinse your plate and cooking pots, let alone having an occasional bath or washing your clothes. As it is there's never as much as we'd like.'

'Where did you live before …..?' Phaedra's voice tailed off and she indicated the man's legs.

'Down there and round the corner.' Kyriakos waved towards the Venetian walls.

'Did your house have a roof?'

'Over about half of it.'

'Is anyone living there now?'

'I've no idea. The rest of the roof could have fallen in or the walls collapsed for all I know or care.'

'Can I go down and have a look?'

'Who's going to stop you?'

Phaedra managed to smile at the man. 'I'll go and see if there's any of it left that would be suitable as a shelter. If there is may I stay there?'

Kyriakos shrugged. 'I'm not likely to be using it again.'

Phaedra rose from the concrete, rubbing her buttocks where they felt numb from the hard surface. She walked to the edge of the patch of concrete and looked down to a dirt path. To get to it she would have to scramble down some crumbling steps beside a large concrete tunnel.

'What's this?' she asked.

'A Venetian water tunnel. Be careful. There are openings every so often where you can put a bucket down and bring up any water that is in there. It's usually stagnant and smelly. Won't be much at the moment as we've not had very much rain, but you wouldn't want to fall into it. You'd not get out without help.'

Gingerly Phaedra climbed down the few feet to the dirt path. It was sheltered from the wind down there, but there would be no protection against the rain. Moving carefully along the path she came to cluster of derelict buildings that she had not noticed when she had been looking over the Venetian walls. She investigated each one; either the walls were no higher than her waist or shoulder or there was no roof.

In one of them a wooden door lay on the ground where it had fallen from its hinges as the supporting wall had collapsed and part of the roof was still in place, although sagging dangerously. She looked at it speculatively. If she was capable of moving the door she could place it across the side walls that still stood just above the height of her shoulders and it would make a rudimentary roof on the exposed side.

Struggling to lift the heavy door, she finally managed to drag it across to the far wall. She pushed and pulled, panting from her exertions, until she had the door propped against one wall. Not knowing if she would have the strength she pushed the door further and further up until it was balanced precariously on top of the wall. She stood back and looked; the wall seemed sound but she did not want it collapsing onto her.

She then tried the difficult manoeuvre of moving one end over to the side wall and to her horror as she pushed it toppled off and fell out of sight with a thud. Phaedra felt like crying. It had taken all her strength to get the door on the top of the wall and now she had lost it. She sat on the ground and buried her face in her skirt. She was tired and hungry, frustrated and miserable.

'Are you alright?' she heard Kyriakos call. 'I heard something falling.'

Phaedra rose to her feet. 'Yes, I'm fine. It was nothing to worry about,' she called back.

With a deep sigh she decided to go and see if she was able to retrieve the door and try a second time to erect it as a roof. She returned to the dirt road and began to climb up the bank by the side wall of the house. As she reached the top she realised the earth bank rose half as high as the walls and the door was lying behind the back wall. It was far easier now to lift one side of the door on to the back wall and then push it across to the side wall, giving a small sheltered area below. It was better than nothing and she would tell Ariadne that she would move her belongings there and it would be her home temporarily until anywhere more suitable became available. It would also be relatively easy to negotiate the crumbling steps once she had become used to them.

Phaedra returned to where Kyriakos was sitting and smiled at him. 'I don't know if it was your house, but there are some reasonably high walls down there and a piece of a roof. I've managed to place a door across the walls to make a bit more roof. I'm going to live there for a while.'

'You ought to place some large blocks on top of the door. We often get a very high wind. You don't want it blowing down on you in the night.'

'I'll do that tomorrow.' Phaedra was certainly too tired now to think about any more physical exertion. 'Do you think Ritsa will be back soon? I'm hungry and thirsty.'

'Go and get some food from the storeroom and bring something back for me. Take my jug with you and fill that from the drinking fountain at the same time.'

'What would you like to eat?'

'Whatever is available. I'm not fussy.'

Phaedra was surprised, having been told that the boatmen were bringing food over that morning she had expected a plentiful supply, but there was little available. She placed a loaf into her apron pocket along with an onion and a large portion of cheese.

There were some apples, speckled brown and with worm holes, but she took four and hoped Kyriakos would find her choice acceptable.

There was the inevitable queue for the drinking fountain and Phaedra took her place, annoyed when a man pushed ahead of her but not daring to remonstrate. Carrying the full jug carefully she walked back up the road to Kyriakos and mounted the steps. She placed the jug beside him and emptied her apron pocket.

'There wasn't an awful lot in there.'

'I expect people have taken what they wanted to make their evening meal. The left overs are sufficient to stop me from starving.' Kyriakos broke off a large piece of the bread and bit into the onion, spitting out the skin. He held it out to her. 'Do you want some?'

Phaedra shook her head. 'Haven't you got a knife?'

'My teeth are just as good.' He pulled off a piece of the bread he had taken and took another bite of the onion.

Phaedra contented herself with some of the bread and broke off a piece of cheese to eat with it, her fingers leaving dirty marks on the food.

'Weren't there any olives?' asked Kyriakos

'I didn't see any.' She did not admit that she had not investigated every box and jar that was in there. 'Do you think I should go and look for Ritsa?' she asked.

'I doubt if you'd be able to find her. Better to wait until she comes back here for you.'

'I'll feel very embarrassed if she tells me she has found somewhere for me to live.'

'Why?' asked Kyriakos. 'You don't have to tell her you have made a shelter. Just accept whatever is offered. You can always come up here later if you're unhappy living with the other occupants.'

'She's gone to a lot of trouble on my behalf.'

Kyriakos smiled to himself. He doubted that Ritsa had

visited all the houses on the island a second time. Once Phaedra had decided not to accompany her she had probably sat down somewhere and spent the time gossiping.

'Have you any belongings with you?'

Phaedra nodded. 'The men who came for me tipped all my possessions into a blanket and tied it up like a parcel. Ariadne said it would be safe stored in her house until I found somewhere to stay permanently.'

'You're more fortunate than many who arrive here with only the clothes they are wearing. What do you have with you?'

'A spare blanket, two skirts and three blouses, along with some plates, cutlery, a cooking pot and a jug. They didn't bring my oil stove or the lamp my father had given me.'

'Wouldn't have been much use if they had brought them. There's never sufficient oil for the lamps, let alone a heater.'

'How do you keep warm in the winter?'

'Put all your clothes on and wrap yourself in your cloak and blanket. Try not to get too wet when it rains as your clothes will take a long time to dry. You can at least walk around and keep yourself relatively warm.'

'I hope the little shelter I have made will keep the worst of the rain out.'

Kyriakos gave her a sad smile. 'The only places that are truly waterproof are the tunnels and the church. So many people crowd into them when it rains that you can hardly move. What did you do with yourself when you were up in your cave?'

'I had some embroidery and crochet work with me. When I had finished it I used to unpick it and start again. I used to go for a walk each day, but I had to be careful that wherever I went I would not be seen by any of the villagers.' Phaedra frowned. 'One of them must have seen me otherwise the men would not have come for me. My parents had told everyone I was living with a relative in another village.'

Kyriakos shook his head. 'Once you are a leper no one wants

to know you. Your best friend or even your parents will tell the authorities where you're hiding.'

'I'm sure my parents told no one. It had to be one of the villagers. They probably didn't even know it was me up there. I just wish my brother hadn't been there when they came. He wasn't ill and now he's probably dead.'

'Didn't they bring him with you?'

Phaedra nodded. 'He fell into the sea and the fishermen left him to drown. He couldn't touch the ground and I couldn't reach him. I walked all round the island this morning with Flora but there was no sign of him. Ariadne said he had very likely been washed out to sea by the currents or dashed to pieces on the rocks.'

'Even if he had been able to swim he would be no match for the currents around here. People have tried to swim across to the shore. It doesn't look very far, but if the wind is in the wrong direction you just get blown away. No one as far as I know has managed to swim across.'

Phaedra shivered. 'I thought I would be able to walk across to the hills I could see. I didn't realise there was sea all around us. I'd never seen the sea before.'

'Be careful when you go down to the beach for a wash. Don't go out further than the top of your legs. Until you're used to it you'd do better to sit on the edge. You'll be safe enough there.'

'I would like to have a wash,' said Phaedra wistfully. 'I always washed my hands and face each day with the water my father brought up for me. I feel dirty.' She looked at her begrimed hands from where she had lifted the wooden door. 'I used to have a bath each week when I lived at home.'

'You'll become used to being dirty, wet and hungry. No point in dwelling on what used to be. You just have to make the most of whatever you do have.'

Phaedra sat silently beside the crippled man. He was unable to help himself, yet he did not seem unduly despondent; he appeared to have accepted his affliction and disability. She hoped, that given time she would become as stoical.

Ritsa finally returned to say that she had not been able to persuade any of the women to accommodate Phaedra in their already overcrowded houses.

Phaedra shrugged. 'I'm not surprised, but I'm grateful to you. Thanks to Kyriakos I have managed to find a rudimentary shelter that I can use. I'll collect my belongings from Ariadne's house tomorrow and bring them up here '

'Come back with me now. We'll be cooking up a bit of supper and if you want a share you need to be there before it's all gone.'

Phaedra looked at Kyriakos. 'What about you? What will you have for supper?'

Kyriakos held up the remains of the bread and cheese. 'That will keep me going.'

Phaedra followed Ritsa back down into the main square of the village. Outside some of the houses there were small fires with stones surrounding them to keep them contained. On each stood a cooking pot and savoury smells filled the air. Phaedra felt her mouth water. When had she last eaten a hot meal?

'Sit down there,' ordered Ritsa and pointed to spot on the ground. 'You can share my plate. I'll get enough for two.'

'I have a plate in my bundle.'

'By the time you've gone and found that the food will probably have been eaten.'

Ritsa returned with a plate that was heaped with rice, vegetables and a small piece of chicken. Carefully she divided the contents of the plate into half as she sat beside Phaedra.

'Where did all this come from? I didn't see it when I went down to the storeroom for Kyriakos.'

'The boatmen brought it over this morning. Once they have left we go down and gather up whatever we want to make a meal later in the day. It's wise to be down there as soon as possible. Have you got a spoon?'

Phaedra shook her head. ''Not with me, but I have two in my bundle.'

'Then you'll have to use your fingers.'

Phaedra looked at her hands. 'They're dirty.'

'You should have gone and had a wash in the sea.'

'I'm frightened of the sea,' admitted Phaedra. 'I'd never seen it until yesterday.'

'It's safe enough provided you stay on the edge. I'll come down with you when we've eaten and you'll soon get used to it. At least it means there's plenty of water to wash your body and your clothes.'

Despite her dirty hands Phaedra ate hungrily and wished there had been a little more chicken. 'Is there any left?' she asked.

'A bit, maybe. Are you still hungry?'

'I was thinking of Kyriakos. He's only got some bread and cheese. If there's anything left I'm sure he'd appreciate it.'

Ritsa looked at Phaedra in surprise. She had never thought about taking the old man any left over food before. 'I'll have a look.'

Ritsa returned with her plate containing mostly rice, courgette and onion. 'Better than nothing, I suppose. Take it up to him and then come back here. I'll go down to the beach with you. You can show me where you've found to shelter and I can collect my plate from Kyriakos.'

'You won't take the place I've found away from me, will you?'

'I'm probably better off sheltering with Ariadne and the others. If you're worried that you'll find someone else has occupied the space I'll help you bring up your pallet and blanket tonight.'

'I'd be very grateful,' answered Phaedra humbly.

Kyriakos looked at the plate of food in surprise. 'This is an unexpected pleasure. People tend to forget I am sitting up here whilst they are eating.'

'I'll not forget you,' promised Phaedra. 'I'll help myself to twice as much as I need and bring the rest up to you. I'm going down to the sea with Ritsa now and then I'll bring back my belongings. She'll collect her plate from you then.'

Phaedra looked at the sea timidly. 'Take off your boots and tuck up your skirt up between your knees so it doesn't get splashed, then you can bend down and wash your hands and face. You're quite safe provided you only stand on the edge.'

Phaedra obeyed Ritsa's instructions and placed her feet in the water. She drew back rapidly. 'That is so cold.'

'Of course it is, but you'll get used to it. Go on, have your wash or it will be dark before you move your pallet.'

Hurriedly Phaedra placed her hands in the sea and it did not feel quite as cold. She rubbed her hands together and drew up a handful of water and smeared it over her face. She looked at Ritsa. 'Am I clean now?'

'You need to wash your face a few more times. It's still dusty and tear streaked.'

Finally satisfied that she was as clean as possible Phaedra stepped back from the water's edge. 'What do I dry myself on?'

'Use your skirt to dry your feet. You can't put wet feet into your boots. Your hands and face will dry in the air.'

Phaedra took a last look at the sea as it lapped gently against the shingle. 'It isn't as frightening as I thought.'

'Just be careful until you're used to it, even then you shouldn't go out too far. You need to know that if you lost your footing you'd be able to crawl back to the shore.'

'I don't think I will be going in past my ankles.' Phaedra pulled her boots back on her damp feet. 'The shelter I've found is just down from Kyriakos. I think it may be his old house. It will be sufficient for me at the moment, but I would be grateful if you heard of anywhere more suitable for me to live.'

Ritsa nodded. She thought it very unlikely anyone would be willing to take an extra person into their already over crowded rooms and Ariadne had been pleased when she heard that Phaedra had found somewhere else to live.

'I'd like to take Kyriakos up some food every night. He only seems to have bread and cheese otherwise, and I think it could be his old house that I'm going to live in.'

Ritsa scowled, disfiguring her face even further. 'If you want extra food for him you'll have to come with me to carry it back and help with the cooking. There's a limit to the amount Ariadne and I are able to do.'

'Of course I'll help. Do you cook for everyone in your house?'

'There's no one else able to do it. They're either too unsteady on their feet or their hands are too badly crippled to be much use. We'll appreciate your help, but I'll expect it every day in exchange for your meal and one for Kyriakos, not just when the fancy takes you.'

'I'll go down to the storeroom with you tomorrow morning You can tell me what you want and I'll help carry it back and prepare the vegetables.'

Ritsa nodded. It had been worth Ariadne befriending the girl and giving her a place to sleep for a night.

Phaedra collected her blanket of possessions and placed it outside the house. She thanked Dimitra for looking after it for her and returned to collect her pallet and spare blanket. 'Would you be able to help me?' she asked Ritsa. 'I can't manage all of it. If I placed the spare blanket around my shoulders and carried the bundle could you bring my pallet?'

'I suppose so.' Ritsa folded the pallet as best she could and placed her arms around it. 'This is heavier than it looks.'

'That's why I knew I couldn't carry everything. I don't want to leave my belongings out on the path. Someone could take them.'

'Someone probably would. If anything is left lying out on the pathway it is considered unwanted and the first person to see it claims it as their own.'

'Will my possessions be safe in my shelter?'

'They should be. The people here respect each other's dwelling place much as they do on the mainland. You don't break into their house and take something that doesn't belong to you.'

Feeling reassured Phaedra climbed up to where Kyriakos was sitting, the empty plate beside him. 'I enjoyed that. It made a change.'

'I've made an arrangement with Ritsa. I'm going to help her and Ariadne with the cooking so I'll be able to bring you a plate of food every night.'

Carefully Phaedra bumped her bundle down the steps to the dirt track below. By the way it had been manhandled, thrown into the cart, onto the boat and then again out onto the quayside any damage to the contents would already have been done.

'You can throw my pallet down,' she told Ritsa as she removed the blanket from around her shoulders and threw it down to land on her bundle.

'Can I come down and see where you're planning to live?'

'If you want. It might be easier to scramble down the bank from a little higher up than climb down here.'

Very carefully Ritsa slid and slithered down the stony bank. Phaedra waited until she was safely down, then walked along to where she had thrown her belongings. She picked up her bundle and led the way to the rudimentary shelter she had made. Ritsa looked at it critically.

'Where are you going to sleep?'

'Over there under the door that I managed to push up onto the walls. The rest of the roof doesn't look terribly safe and I wouldn't want it to fall on me in the night.'

'I don't know how dry you'll be in here when it rains,' observed Ritsa.

Phaedra shrugged. 'It's better than nothing and I could always go and sit in the storeroom during the day. It's rather dark and miserable in there but at least it's dry.'

'You won't be much help to me if you're sitting in there all the time.'

'Can you think of anything better?'

'You could come and sit in Ariadne's house. We could both sit on my mattress.'

'Do you mean your pallet?'

Ritsa nodded. 'When we've had a number of people arrive from the mainland they send some mattresses over. They're not the same as a pallet as they're covered in rubber. It makes cleaning easier.'

Phaedra was not sure she would be happy lying on a pallet that was covered in rubber. It would be very hot during the summer. 'Will it be alright if I bring up some empty boxes from the storeroom and place my belongings in them? I can't leave them in my blanket as I'm sure to need it when it gets colder.'

'Where will you put those?'

'I'm not sure yet. Maybe at the foot of my pallet to stop the wind blowing in or at the side if the wind is coming from that direction. In the summer I could put them under the roof area and hope it doesn't fall down on them.'

'If it isn't blown down during the winter it will probably be safe enough during the summer. I'll leave you to it and collect my plate from Kyriakos. Don't forget you're helping me tomorrow.'

Phaedra placed her pallet on the ground beneath the door that was balanced on the walls above her and untied the blanket that held her belongings. She only needed a plate and jug and would leave everything else until she had collected some boxes. She looked around despondently at the small area. It was becoming dark and she did not have the comfort of an oil lamp to dispel the gloom and make it more cheerful. She shrugged. She might as well go to bed as there was nothing else to do. Night noises held no fear for her having become used to them whilst sleeping in the cave. Tomorrow, when she had finished helping Ariadne and Ritsa she would look for the girl called Flora again. They were of a similar age and could well become friends.

Phaedra walked up to the watch tower and called to Flora.

'What do you want?' she asked.

'Nothing; just to talk. How long have you lived over here?'

Phaedra asked, taking in the girl's emaciated appearance as she emerged from the tower.

Flora shrugged. 'I was here the summer before this.'

'Do you have a proper meal each day? You look so thin,' observed Phaedra.

'I eat what's available. There's usually some bread, cheese and olives along with the fruit that is sent over.'

'Is that all you eat? That can't be good for you. I've agreed to help Ritsa and Ariadne with the cooking in exchange for a meal for myself and Kyriakos. Why don't you come down and join us? Another person would make little difference.'

Flora looked embarrassed. 'I don't think they would want me around.'

'Why not? Have you fallen out with them?'

Flora shifted uncomfortably. 'Not really. When I first arrived Ariadne was kind to me and let me have a place in her house. I hated it. It was stuffy and smelly. I wasn't used to having people around me all the time and one of the women was dying and groaning continually. Ariadne thought I was referring to her legs when I said it was smelly in the house. I tried to explain how I felt but she didn't seem to understand that my comment wasn't personal. She said if I wasn't happy to live with them I could always find somewhere else to live. I heard her say to one of her friends that she had never come across anyone so fussy and I should be grateful that I had a space in her house. I looked around and found this little tower and said I would look after myself.'

'Not eating properly is not looking after yourself. You ought to have a proper meal every day.'

Flora shrugged. 'I can't build a fire and I don't know how to cook food anyway.'

'Didn't your mother teach you?'

'I don't really remember my mother. One day she was there and the next she had gone and I never saw her again. My sisters kept an eye on me during the day whilst my father was at work and he would collect some cooked food from neighbours most nights. If we were hungry we just ate whatever we could find around the house or go and pick some fruit. When my arm became infected they made me live outside and finally told the doctor and he had me brought here.'

'Please come down and join us. I'm sure Ariadne and Ritsa will be happy to show you how to cook. I'm watching and learning from them. We could learn together.'

'I'm no use to anyone.' Flora held out her arm for Phaedra to see the ulceration that spread from halfway up her forearm to above her elbow.

'I'm sure you could help in some way. You could stir the cooking pots or clean the plates. Ariadne and Ritsa have to take food to those who cannot leave their mattress and some of them are unable to help themselves so they have to be fed. Let me speak to them and ask if you can share our meal in exchange for some help.'

Flora eyed Phaedra doubtfully, tears glistening in her eyes. Since she had left the house where Ariadne and Ritsa sheltered she had avoided their company, going down to the storeroom at night to help herself to anything that was left over and filling her water jug when there were few people around. She was lonely and miserable and a good deal of the time she was hungry.

'Please, let me ask them. You only need to have a meal and then you can return up here if you prefer to be alone. Come down this evening. If they refuse you can share my plate.'

'Do you mean it? If I come down you won't turn me away?'

'Certainly not. I'm sure they will all be friendly towards you if you give them a chance.'

Flora shrugged. She would be no worse off if the women rejected her.

'I'll expect you this evening,' said Phaedra firmly, hoping Ritsa and Ariadne would not object to providing an extra meal.

Flora had arrived and Phaedra insisted that she sat next to her and had a full plate of food. At first she had eaten greedily, her arm curved around the plate as if to hide it from the others. When she had finished she looked up at Phaedra.

'Thank you. I enjoyed that.'

'Thank Ariadne and Ritsa. They did the cooking. I just prepared the vegetables and made sure nothing burnt. That is something you could do each evening.'

'I suppose so,' answered Flora doubtfully.

Ariadne looked at the malnourished girl and felt guilty. As her legs had become more painful she found it difficult to look after the sick women in the house and without Ritsa's help it would have become impossible. Even so, she should have sought out the waif previously and looked after her to the best of her ability, despite the girl's declaration that she was capable of looking after herself.

'If you expect to have a decent meal each day you have to do something in return. Watching the pots to ensure nothing burns could certainly be your job. It would give us the opportunity to wash the bedridden women before they have their supper and you could call us if there's a problem.'

1925 - 1927

Phaedra became accustomed to living in her makeshift house. She had placed some large rocks on top of the door to prevent it from blowing away during a high wind, but she still eyed the roof warily. Each day she had brought up an empty box from the storeroom and piled them beneath the sagging rafters hoping they would give it some additional support. She had collected more empty boxes and placed those across the entrance to give herself some shelter from the weather, leaving just a small opening as a doorway. Inside one of the boxes she had stored her meagre possessions and in the other she placed her spare skirt and blouses along with the shoes she had worn during the summer when in the cave.

The winter months had been difficult. There had been rain for days on end and her woollen cloak was soaked through, giving her no protection at all. The boatmen had not always been able to make the journey across the short stretch of sea to deliver supplies of either water or food and Phaedra, like the other occupants, had gone hungry and used the water from the drinking fountain sparingly. She did not wash for days at a time as when she saw the waves coming in to the small beach she retreated rapidly to the safety of the storeroom.

She began to think herself fortunate to have a small area that she could call her own. A number of the men and women died during the harsh winter due to their illness and the primitive living conditions they were forced to endure. When newcomers first arrived on the island they had to make do with sheltering in one of the tunnels or the church and once a death had been announced there were a number of people who then claimed they were entitled to the vacated space. She had no idea how many people were living on Spinalonga, but there were considerably more people on the island than had lived in her village.

The seasons passed and Phaedra became used to being cold and wet during the winter. Often she was unable to see the mainland due to the low cloud and mist and was unable to watch for the boats to arrive. It was frequently too wet to light a fire to cook food, dry their wet clothes or provide some warmth. During the summer months it was far too hot with little shade provided by the ruined buildings. The days passed monotonously, there was nothing to do each day except watch for the boats bringing them supplies and squabbling with the other women about the food they would cook that day. She realised she was fortunate to have companions to talk with. She had been lonely when she had lived up in the cave on the hills with only her father and brother visiting her each day and her mother once a week. Although Flora left the group of women each evening after their meal she was happy to spend time with Phaedra during the day.

Gradually Phaedra became more familiar with the occupants of the island and could greet them all by name and knew where they lived, but she still avoided the men. For a while she had taken to wearing her bodice laced as tightly as possible beneath her blouse, despite the discomfort it gave her. Finally she realised that it was ineffective in flattening her breasts and she could not prevent them from developing further. During the winter she had walked around with her cloak clutched tightly to her so she could stay relatively warm and disguise her developing body, but now the summer was approaching she would be unable to wear it. This gave her a dilemma. The men were going to realise that she was no longer a child, but had blossomed into a woman. The looks some of them gave her made her frightened. She would be no match for them if they decided to molest her.

Most of the morning she would spend in the company of Ariadne or Ritsa along with the other women who shared Ariadne's house and she felt safe. Once the preparation of the vegetables for the evening meal was completed she would visit Flora in her tower talking with her until they returned together to help Ariadne and Ritsa to cook and serve and then take plates of food into the house for those who were immobile.

Phaedra avoided wandering around the island on her own and asked Ariadne how safe she would be from the unwanted attention of the men.

'I'm frightened that some of the men might approach me and I'd be unable to get away.'

'They probably will try to attract you. Don't give them the opportunity to think you could be interested in them. Ignore them or tell them to go away. Stay close to the square and main path. There are women over here who are willing to accommodate the needs of the men. Just make it quite clear to them that you're not that kind of young woman and they must look elsewhere.'

'Is that why there are some small children here?'

'There are usually one or two born each year. They don't always survive even if they are born free from leprosy. The lack of good nourishing food and insanitary conditions doesn't help them. Even if they do live the authorities come and take them away to an orphanage somewhere on the mainland eventually and the mothers never see them again.'

Phaedra's eyes filled with tears. 'That's terrible. At least my mother did not live with that nightmare hanging over her. She was expecting another baby when Mikaelis and I were taken. I hope that one survived to comfort her. My other brothers and sisters died shortly after they were born.'

'Sure to have. No point in you dwelling on what happened.'

Ariadne's mouth set in a hard line. Her child had been taken away and she had never had another to take his place.

Phaedra sighed and turned away. She would remember Ariadne's advice if any of the men approached her, but she would avoid going through the tunnel where so many of them lived.

The hot summer days were almost as difficult to live with as the cold and wet winter days. There was little shade once Phaedra left the shelter of her house. She no longer wore her boots and went bare foot, the soles of her summer shoes were worn away now. The rough ground that was littered with small stones made walking painful until her skin toughened, but she was concerned that her boots would wear out also if she wore them continually. It was incredibly hot and stuffy in Ariadne's house and once the sun rose it was far too hot to sit with Kyriakos or in Flora's tower.

'Why don't we walk around to the other side of the island?' suggested Flora when they had finished preparations for the meal they would cook later. 'There's usually a breeze round that side.'

'I've only been around there once before when I was with you looking for my brother,' admitted Phaedra. 'I don't want to go through the tunnel with all the men in there. I wouldn't want to be around there and find a group of men had come looking for us.'

Flora shrugged. 'We can walk around on the path and come back the same way. They won't know we're there and we don't need to go near the tunnel. If we go together we should be safe enough.'

'The path isn't very wide and it's such a long way down to the rocks if you fell.'

'Why should you fall? You can walk beside the cliff face and you'll be perfectly safe. I've not heard of anyone falling over and into the sea yet.'

Dubiously Phaedra agreed and although they saw no one it was definitely cooler on that side of the island where a breeze blew in from the sea. They reached the ruined church and sat down beneath the trees.

'Why doesn't anyone live this side?'

'There aren't any houses,' answered Flora simply.

'So why haven't they built some?'

'They didn't build the ones where they live now. They were already here from when the Turks lived on the island. I've heard that Antionis was urging them to build some more or at least repair the houses they were living in but no one took any notice of him. I think he's given up trying now. A lot of the men would not be strong enough to cope with the work involved anyway.'

'So they'll all eventually fall down and no one will have anywhere to live.'

'Probably. Let me know when you are ready to go back.' Flora yawned, lay back on the ground and closed her eyes.

Phaedra found it pleasant sitting beneath the shade of the trees by the church but she did not feel safe enough to emulate Flora. She wished she was not so frightened of the men so that she had the courage to come alone and sit in the peaceful area more often.

Due to the instruction given by Ariadne and Ritsa and helped by Phaedra, Flora was now a proficient cook. She could safely be left in charge of the meal, knowing when to add more seasoning or liquor to the pot whilst Phaedra joined Ritsa in the house and prepared the women who had difficulty in leaving their mattresses or propped up those unable to feed themselves.

Ariadne's legs had become more swollen as the sores erupted and became infected making it difficult for her to walk around. She relied on Phaedra and Ritsa to make the journey to the storeroom each morning and bring back whatever there was available to make a meal in the evening. Between them they were able to carry back sufficient to cater for everyone who lived in Ariadne's house and also Kyriakos and Flora.

It was as they left the storeroom that they saw the boat approaching. Ritsa shaded her eyes.

'I think there are some more people arriving. That's a big boat approaching and it hasn't come from the village over there.'

'Where are they going to live? There's no space in any of the houses.'

Ritsa shrugged. 'I don't know. We ought to get off the jetty whilst they unload them.'

The two women walked to the top of the ramp and watched as men were roughly placed ashore. Their boxes and bags thrown after them.

Ritsa gasped. 'Look; they're all restrained. They must be criminals.'

Without another word they walked back up to Ariadne's house and deposited the food they had with them.

'Keep it inside,' warned Ritsa. 'There's a boatload of criminals arriving and they could well try to steal it.'

Ariadne looked at her in horror. 'We don't want criminals over here. This isn't a penal colony. The only crime any of us has committed is becoming sick. Warn the other houses that they are coming.'

Obediently Ritsa and Phaedra went from house to house around the square telling the occupants that a boat load of criminals was being disembarked. The people began to gather their possessions together, placing them beneath their mattresses or within easy reach. As they walked from the square and past the entrance to the jetty they saw some of the men were being released. They quickened their step. There were more houses further up the path and those people needed to be warned also.

'Kyriakos,' Phaedra hurried up the steps to where the man sat. 'A whole boat load of criminals has been sent to the island. Guard your belongings.'

Kyriakos looked at her in disbelief. 'Criminals? Why would they send criminals here?'

'I don't know, but they were tied up when they arrived.'

'Pass me that length of wood. If they try to take anything from me I'll hit their legs. Just because I can't move around doesn't mean to say that I can't defend myself against robbers.'

'We're warning everyone and then I'll come back to stay with you. They'll be less likely to attack you if they see you're not alone.'

Phaedra returned to the path where Ritsa was standing in the doorway of the church, shouting the news to its occupants.

'Kyriakos has armed himself with a length of wood. As soon as we've told everyone I'll go back and stay with him. He might think he can fight them off, but he wouldn't stand a chance if two or three attacked him.'

Ritsa looked at Phaedra sceptically. What made her think she would be any more successful?

It took them some time to visit every house and impress upon the occupants that the boatload of people they had seen arriving were criminals and then Phaedra realised that no one had warned Flora. Although she insisted on living in the watch tower, and everyone appeared to know her, she only came down to the square to help with the cooking in the evening and would wait for Phaedra to call on her if she wanted her company.

Phaedra hurried along the path to the end of the island until she saw the watch tower.

'Flora, are you there? I need to tell you something important.'

Flora looked out of the low doorway suspiciously. Phaedra related the news of the arrival of a group of men who must be criminals. 'You ought to go down and stay with the women,' Phaedra advised her. 'They would make sure you were safe.'

Flora shook her head. 'I'll stay in my tower. I think it's unlikely they'll come this far up. Once they see there are no more houses up here they'll return to the main area. They'll be too busy looking for somewhere to live to bother about me.'

Phaedra did not feel as confident as Flora appeared to be 'I must go back to Kyriakos now. He's planning to fight off the new arrivals if they try to take anything from him and he couldn't do that alone. Promise me that if one of them does come and try to take your tower that you'll go down to the women and not try to resist. You could get badly hurt.'

When Phaedra returned to where Kyriakos sat she was surprised to see the length of wood lying at his side and he was leaning back with his eyes shut.

He smiled at her. 'Who told you those men were criminals?'

'They all arrived tied up so we thought they must be.'

'You misjudged the poor souls. They had been placed in strait jackets for causing a riot at the hospital in Athens. They're all fellow sufferers and don't mean us any harm.'

'How do you know?' asked Phaedra suspiciously.

'A couple of them came up this way. They assured me we had nothing to fear from them and asked me for some water. One of them went to refill my jug and have a look in the storeroom for some food. He came back and said their belongings were on the quay side and insisted his friend went back down with him to help to move them. They've brought them back up here to me for safety.'

'Where are they now?'

'Another man came with them. They said they were going down to have a wash in the sea and also wash their dirty clothes. They'd found some clean clothes in their bundles. Can you make a bit of extra food tonight? It will show them that we are prepared to be friendly.'

'I suppose so,' Phaedra agreed grudgingly. 'I'll have to go back down and see what's left. There'll probably only be a few vegetables.'

'Better than nothing.'

As Phaedra reached the storeroom she could see the men on the beach and turned into the storeroom quickly, waiting for her eyes to become used to the small amount of light that penetrated through the doorway and the grilled window further up the wall.

As she had anticipated there were only vegetables left, along with some cheese. Quickly she loaded her apron and hurried back to Ariadne.

'Kyriakos has spoken to some of the men who arrived. He says there's nothing to be worried about. They aren't criminals. They've been sent here from the hospital.'

'It was Ritsa who said they were criminals,' said Ariadne accusingly.

'I know. We saw they were restrained and came to the wrong conclusion. Kyriakos has asked if we can make some extra food for them.'

'All of them?' asked Ariadne in horror.

'No, I don't think so, just for the three that he's met. I'll go up and tell Flora she has nothing to fear and say she has to come down and help as usual. I've collected some more vegetables to add to the pot.'

Ariadne sniffed. 'I suppose so. You'd better use a separate cooking pot for those vegetables. We can add a bit of meat and rice to it and then you can carry it up to them and put the food on their plates up there.'

'May I use the basket I take down to the storeroom in the mornings? It would be easier to put everything in there to carry up.'

'Make sure you don't leave it up there with them.'

'I won't,' promised Phaedra. 'I'll wait whilst they eat and bring it back down to you.'

An hour later, carrying the basket containing the cooking pot and some bowls, she returned to the patch of concrete where Kyriakos sat and saw he was playing cards with two men and a third sat with a book in his hands.

'Come and be introduced, Phaedra,' called Kyriakos as she climbed up the steps carrying the basket carefully. 'There's nothing to be frightened about.'

Still Phaedra hung back These men were probably no different from the ones she avoided on the island.

'Phaedra, this is Spiro and Panicos.' Kyriakos indicated the two men who held playing cards in their hands. 'The one with his head in a book is Yannis.'

Yannis looked up and smiled. 'We won't hurt you or try to steal your belongings.'

Phaedra nodded to them and placed a portion of meat and vegetables into each bowl and handed them to the men who ate hungrily.

'That was magnificent,' commented Yannis as he wiped the bowl around with some bread. 'I don't know when I last enjoyed a meal so much.'

'She's a good girl,' smiled Kyriakos, making Phaedra blush. 'She makes sure I have a proper meal each day and does her best with whatever is sent over to us.'

Panicos moved a little closer to Phaedra and she looked at him warily. 'Where do you live?'

'Further up the path.'

'Are there some proper buildings somewhere where you're sheltered from the elements?'

Phaedra shook her head. 'Not really, most of the houses are falling down.'

'So why don't you repair them?'

Phaedra regarded him scornfully. 'You haven't seen the island yet, or the people. I'll take you on a tour tomorrow. That will answer all your questions.' She gathered up the bowls and replaced them in her basket. 'Is there anything you want, Kyriakos?'

'No, these young men can refill my water jug.'

'We ought to see how the others have fared,' said Spiro. 'We can take your jug with us and refill it at the same time. Come on, you two.'

Reluctantly Yannis and Spiro rose to their feet and followed Phaedra as she walked back to the square. She watched them approach the other new arrivals and an argument appeared to be taking place. As she stood there the man called Yannis seemed to be calming them down until they began to disperse in small groups of two or three.

Phaedra returned to the makeshift building she called her home, but sleep eluded. Stealthy footsteps came to her ears and she stiffened. Was it one of the men finally deciding they would molest her or one of the new comers looking for somewhere to sleep? She crept to the doorway of her house. She was certain she could see someone leaning against the wall of the Venetian fort. She swallowed the lump of fear in her throat. If it was one of the new arrivals and he was planning to jump she must stop him.

She climbed up the bank and as quietly as possible she made her way along to where she could see the man standing and apparently talking to himself.

'What are you doing?'

Her voice made the man start and he turned round. 'Who's there?'

'Only me, Phaedra. What are you doing?' she asked again.

'I couldn't sleep. I was cold so I thought I would walk around for a while.'

'It isn't wise to go walking around here until you know the island. A bit further on the path narrows and there's a dangerous drop.'

'No doubt if I'd fallen people would say it was no more than I deserved. It's all my fault that people have been sent here.'

'And is it?'

'I don't know,' Yannis spoke miserably.

'Sit down and tell me. You're Yannis, aren't you.?'

Yannis nodded and sat back against the earthen bank. 'I caused trouble at the hospital. A group of us held the orderlies prisoner and demanded better living conditions. At first they agreed and then it became worse than ever so we tried again. That time they were ready for us. They brought in the army and we were placed in strait jackets and shipped over here. I only wanted to make things better, not worse.'

Phaedra listened as Yannis recounted the deprivations they had suffered and was thankful she had been sent to Spinalonga.

'Why is it worse here?' she asked as Yannis finally lapsed into silence.

'There's nowhere to live. At least at the hospital we were dry when it rained.'

Phaedra shrugged. 'If it rains you just have to go into the tunnel or church the same as everyone else to shelter. You just have to make the best of it.'

'I never thought they'd send us here.'

'What's so bad about being here? You have your belongings and you said I'd given you the best meal you'd eaten in years. You're not confined to a hospital ward and there are no orderlies here to prevent you from doing as you please, but don't go wandering around in the dark again. Go back to your friends.'

Phaedra accompanied Yannis back down to where the three men were soundly asleep. 'I'll see you tomorrow,' she whispered. 'Try to get some sleep. Nothing seems so bad in daylight.'

Obediently Yannis climbed the steps and lay back down. He did feel warmer now. He recognised that he had been foolish to go wandering off alone in the dark. He could have fallen over and hurt himself and no one would have known his whereabouts to come to his aid.

Phaedra waited in the shadows for a while and then climbed back down the bank to the shelter she called her home. She did not want this man to know where she lived.

Phaedra took sufficient coffee from the tin where Ariadne stored their supply. It was the one true luxury everyone enjoyed; a cup of freshly brewed coffee in the morning. She heated the water and added the coffee grounds. It was probably not as strong as the men would like, but it would be better than nothing. The remainder of the day they would have to drink water.

Having delivered her gift to Kyriakos and insisted that he shared with the men Phaedra hurried down to the storeroom. It was doubtful that there would be any decent food left from the previous day, but she did not want the new arrivals to help themselves greedily to the new supplies when the boatmen delivered.

It was not long before Spiro joined her. 'Is there any food?' he asked.

'Not yet. The boatmen will bring the water barrels first from Plaka and then some food. Other boatmen come from another village further round the coast with more food. When you see them near the shore you have to clear the jetty. They won't put anything ashore if they see you there waiting for them. You'd better tell the others who arrived with you. If they start coming down the boatmen will go away and we won't have anything.'

'I'll stay down here and tell anyone who arrives that they have to wait. Will there be enough to go round?'

Phaedra shrugged philosophically. 'Probably not for a few days, then they'll be sent word that more people have arrived. Don't worry, we won't starve.'

'I hope they send some more figs.'

'You just accept whatever they bring and be grateful.'

'Well whatever we have cannot be worse than the food we were given in the hospital.'

'At least you had doctors and medicine.'

Spiro looked at her. 'Whatever gave you that idea? We were given Chaulmoogra tablets each day and they made us feel sick. I never saw any doctor visit the wards where we were.'

'Did the tablets make you better?'

Spiro shrugged. 'Not that I noticed. No one recovered as far as I know but the medicine may have slowed the illness down a bit. Being here in fresh air and with some decent food could make far more difference to us than taking tablets.'

'I don't think my face has become any worse.'

'Then that's a good sign. Here come Yannis and Panicos. I expect they're looking for something to eat.'

'Then they'll have to wait like the rest of us. Good morning, Yannis. You were still fast asleep when I came down here.'

Yannis looked embarrassed. 'I had a bit of a disturbed night. I woke up cold and it took me a while to get warm again.' He hoped Phaedra would not mention his encounter with her. 'I've been talking to Kyriakos. He suggested I spoke to Antionis. Can you show us where he lives, please?'

Phaedra looked doubtfully at Yannis. 'He's old and has become blind. It would be better if only one of you visited him or he might feel threatened.'

'I'll go,' said Yannis, 'And thank you for the coffee. We only ever had water in the hospital. I couldn't believe how wonderful it was to smell and taste it again.'

'I said you were better off here.' remarked Phaedra. 'Come on, treat Antionis gently.'

'Of course I will. I'm not a ruffian despite whatever Spiro has told you about me.'

Phaedra knocked on a door and a sightless man opened it. 'Who is it? What do you want?'

'It's me, Phaedra. One of the hospital men wants to speak to you.' Phaedra took the man's arm and guided him over to where Yannis stood.

Antionis sat down on the ground and Yannis squatted beside him.

'I'll leave you to talk,' said Phaedra. 'Help Antionis back into his house when you've finished. He won't be able to find his way unaided.'

Phaedra and Ritsa collected food from the storeroom and Ritsa plied her with questions regarding the new arrivals.

'The ones I've met seem quite nice. From what they've told me I understand that the hospital conditions were appalling, but they're worried about not having anywhere to shelter. I left one of them talking to Antionis this morning. I've said I'll take them around the island this morning when I've finished helping you and Ariadne. I'll need to take an extra loaf and some more of that meat. Until they've settled in I've said I'll make a meal for them each night.'

'Is Ariadne agreeable to that?'

'It isn't really up to Ariadne. She's no longer able to help with the cooking. I'll still collect the food with you from the storeroom each day and help with the preparation. I don't expect you and Flora to cook for extra people without help. If we need any more vegetables I'll go down and collect them. I'm sure we'll manage.'

Ritsa did not argue. It was becoming more difficult to cook sufficient in one pot for so many people, but to use a second meant having a larger fire and firewood was precious, particularly during the winter when they would sit around the embers and try to keep warm before retiring into their cold houses for the night.

'I'll have to ask the men to break up some more boxes.'

'That could be a job for the new men. If they want a meal they have to provide the firewood.'

When Phaedra finished helping with the preparation of the vegetables she walked up to where Kyriakos was sitting, surprised to find he was alone.

'Where are the men?' she asked.

'Said they were going to walk around and talk to some of the others who came over here with them.'

Phaedra shrugged. She really did not mind what they did; she had only offered to show them the island out of courtesy and after her encounter with Yannis the previous night she thought they should all recognise that to wander around once it was dark could be dangerous.

Flora arrived as the fires to cook the food were being lit.

'Come on,' said Phaedra brusquely. 'You have a job to do, remember. We're cooking for three extra again tonight so we're using two pots. Make sure you give them both a stir every so often. We don't want to find one of them has burnt food in the bottom.

When we've eaten you can go and feed Maria whilst Ariadne feeds Poppi and Ritsa helps Dimitra. I'll clean the dishes before I take the food up to Kyriakos and the men.'

Flora nodded. She hoped she would be capable of feeding the helpless woman. She had not been asked to deal with any of the very sick women before and was grateful that she had not been asked to wash them. One woman in particular had a very nasty sweet and sickly smell to her.

Phaedra was disconcerted when she took a meal up to the men to find that Yannis was obviously unwell.

'What's wrong with him?' she asked Spiro anxiously.

'I don't know,' admitted Spiro. 'He went off on his own this afternoon and when he came back he said he had climbed to the top of the hill and then spoken to Alecos. He has this idea that we should all start building houses.'

'He may have slept in the sun. He's probably done far too much and needs to rest. Can you eat some food, Yannis?'

'No,' Yannis voice was hoarse. 'Drink.'

Phaedra held Kyriakos's water jug whilst Yannis drank before lying back down, shivering violently.

'I'll wash his face and then cover him with Kyriakos's rug. He may have recovered by tomorrow.'

Despite Phaedra's optimism it was three days before Yannis showed signs of recovery. Either Phaedra or Spiro had stayed by his side, washing his face with cold water and giving him frequent drinks until he was able to eat a little of the food she had prepared. She was surprised when she went up on the fourth day to see that Yannis was not there.

'Where has Yannis gone?' she asked Kyriakos.

'Said he was going for a haircut and then he wanted to meet Christos, the builder and get him to talk to Antionis with him. I don't know what he has in mind, but he said he had an idea for extra water and he probably wants to talk to them about it.'

Phaedra shook her head. 'He'll not get any help from Christos.

I hope he'll come back here and rest when he's seen them. Make sure he doesn't fall asleep in the sun. He doesn't want to be ill again.'

'I'm not his keeper.'

'Nor am I,' answered Phaedra, 'But I don't want to be continually acting as his nurse. He must learn to be sensible.'

It was early afternoon before Yannis returned to where Kyriakos sat. He refused to join in a game of cards and sat pretending to read a book, whilst making plans for the following day. He ate the meal that Phaedra brought up for them silently, engrossed in his thoughts.

'Are you feeling better, Yannis?' asked Phaedra. 'You've hardly said a word.'

'I've been too busy enjoying my supper to talk, but I'm certainly feeling cleaner having had a haircut. I gave myself a good wash in the sea before I came back here.'

Phaedra nodded. She knew how much better it felt once you had been able to wash your hair. She saved up water until she had enough to pour over her head and run a comb through her tangles, not daring to immerse her head in the sea.

'Was Christos any help to you?'

'No,' answered Yannis shortly. 'Most people have agreed to store someone's possessions or moved over to make enough room for their mattress at night but he refused. He has a fair sized house and it looks in better repair than most. There are only six of them living there, but according to Yiorgo he was adamant that no one else was going to move in.'

'He's probably worried that if he agrees to one person moving in others will follow.'

'It would only be a short term arrangement. Just until we're organised.'

Phaedra looked at Yannis and did not comment. What was he expecting to organise?

As Phaedra delivered a jug of water to Kyriakos in the morning she looked at Yannis in concern. He was hollow eyed and seemed in a hurry to leave his companions.

'Where are you going?' she asked.

'To be alone,' he replied abruptly.

Spiro shook his head at her. 'Leave him alone. He's going through a bad patch. He'll get over it once he accepts the inevitable.'

Each day Yannis returned tired and dirty from his exertions, but he refused to disclose his activities to his friends. 'I'm just poking around,' he said. 'It passes the time.'

Phaedra stood on the jetty along with most of the other villagers. She was mesmerised. There was a priest talking to them from a boat. He had wanted to know if they had a priest on the island and a doctor. The people had called back to him that they had nothing except the food sent over to them from Plaka or another nearby village each day.

She had seen the priest turn to the boatman and ask him a question. In answer the boatman had shaken his head. The priest looked back at the people who were holding out their hands in supplication to him and asked if they would care to join him in a prayer and receive his blessing. Phaedra realised that she could hardly remember going to church each week and receiving a blessing from the priest. She stood there, her hands clasped before her and her eyes closed, as the priest began to intone a prayer asking for them to be given relief from their suffering and peace in their hearts rather than resentment for their ailment. He finished with a blessing and most of the villagers crossed themselves reverently.

Phaedra felt herself being pushed forwards into the sea by the press of people behind her and the boatman was obviously becoming alarmed. She clutched at the person next to her in panic.

'Please don't push me over. I can't swim.'

'I'll hold you up if that should happen. Don't worry; you're safe enough.'

Phaedra did not feel at all safe, although she was only standing in water that came just above her knees. Abruptly the boat began to move away, but the priest remained standing and calling to them.

'I will come back. I promise you I will return.'

Phaedra remained standing in the sea until the people began to move off the jetty. Once the area became less congested the man who was holding her arm began helping her to the shore.

Once the water was only lapping around her ankles he released her. 'You're quite safe now.' The smile he gave her was more like a grimace, but she forced herself to smile in return and thank him. Now safely back on the shore she wanted to escape from his attentions.

'I must help Ritsa. She won't be able to get the bedridden back to the house without some help.'

The man nodded. He had no wish to detain her. It was far too soon after receiving a blessing from a priest to have carnal thoughts.

'I wonder if he will come again?' he mused. 'Even priests do not always keep their promises.'

Yannis went down to the small beach and washed away as much of the dirt as he could from his hands and face. In the distance he could see a boat drawing steadily out towards the sea and standing in the prow was the figure of a priest. He could only assume that it was Father Theodorakis, the priest from Elounda who was making the journey.

As Yannis returned to the patch of concrete where Kyriakos was sitting he couldn't help noticing that the villagers were clustered together in the street talking animatedly.

'Has something happened?' he asked as he sat down beside Kyriakos and Spiro.

'We had a visit from a priest.'

'Who was he? Where did he come from?'

'I've no idea. He was in a fishing boat and he called out to us, asking how we lived over here.'

'I hope you told him,' said Yannis with a wry smile.

'We did. He said a prayer for us and then gave us all a blessing.'

'I would have liked to have received that,' said Yannis sadly.

'He said he would come again,' Spiro reassured him. 'If you didn't insist on going off on your own every day you would have been around at the time. What are you doing with yourself?'

'You'll see.' Yannis lay back and yawned. He did not want to disclose his activities to anyone until he was satisfied that he had managed to make a building reasonably habitable.

Spiro did not pursue the matter. He would take a walk around the island tomorrow and see for himself what Yannis was doing.

Phaedra sat beside Kyriakos and told him that Yannis had built a small house 'No wonder he's been so tired.' She pointed to Yannis who lay asleep a short distance away. 'I didn't believe it when Spiro told me and insisted that I should go and have a look. Spiro is as proud of the accomplishment as if he had built it himself. He's asking people to help to build some more, or at least repair them.'

Kyriakos chuckled. 'He'll be lucky to find anyone to help. Why should they if Yannis will do it for them?'

'He can't be expected to do everything himself.'

Kyriakos yawned. 'Then why do any of it? No one has asked him.'

'Wouldn't you like to have a house of your own to live in again?' asked Phaedra.

Kyriakos shook his head. 'If I was in a house on my own people would forget about me. At least sitting here I can ask them to bring me water and food as they pass by.'

'I hope Yannis might be willing to make mine a little more weather proof before the winter sets in.'

'He probably will. Oh, here comes Spiro and he has young Flora with him.'

Spiro sat down beside them and smiled at Kyriakos. 'Has Phaedra told you about the house Yannis has built?'

Kyriakos nodded. 'She tells me you've been trying to encourage the other villagers to help to build some more.'

'I have one helper. Flora has offered to bring us up as much water as we need whilst we're working and also some food if we're hungry. It will save us from having to stop work to go up and down. I'm insisting that she keeps her arm wrapped whilst we work. She doesn't want to get any dirt in it and make the infection worse. Have you got an old blouse by any chance, Phaedra?'

'Only the ones I wear, but there could be something in the bundle of clothes that Yannis says belong to his cousin.' Phaedra opened the sack and took out a shirt that was far too large for Yannis. 'I hope he won't mind,' she said as she used her teeth to rip strips off at the hem and handed them to Spiro to use as bandages. 'If Flora is willing to help I am also, but you'll have to tell me what to do.'

1928 - 1929

Although Phaedra had not got over her fear of the sea, at Yannis's request she had sat down on the jetty and begged the boatmen as they drew close enough to hear her for tools or materials to assist with the rebuilding work. Some days Spiro would take her place, but neither of them were as successful as Flora. She would call to the boatmen as they approached, saying that just one nail or screw would be useful, but even better would be a saw, screw driver or hammer and gradually they would bring something to toss ashore to her.

The first time Manolis delivered supplies to the island he was surprised to find a young girl sitting on the jetty.

'Hello,' she called. 'Could you bring us a hammer please?'

'What do you want a hammer for? You can't eat it.'

Flora giggled. 'Don't be silly. Yannis needs it. He's trying to do some repairs and he needs a hammer. We take old nails from lengths of wood and bang them straight with a stone so they can be used again. A hammer would make it so much easier.'

'Hammers cost money. I'll find out how much you will need to pay.'

'We haven't any money.'

'Then you're not likely to get a hammer.'

Feeling uncomfortable about being so abrupt with the girl Manolis rowed away. The other boatmen had become used to Flora requesting items from them and eventually Dimitris succumbed to her entreaties. He bought a hammer and a few nails and tossed them ashore to her. Flora was delighted and thanked him with a broad smile on her face before running up the ramp calling excitedly to Yannis.

Having been successful in procuring a hammer and some nails Flora began to beg the boatmen to bring them a ladder, explaining that it was necessary for them to reach a roof and effect a repair. Manolis, who arrived regularly from Aghios Nikolaos, with extra produce for the islanders, pretended to turn a deaf ear to her entreaties, but he was curious.

'Why don't you ask the government to repair your houses?'

'They don't care how we live. They only send us food and water so they cannot be accused of starving us to death. Sometimes it is too mouldy for us to eat or we have to pick the maggots out.'

Manolis saw tears fill the girl's eyes and he turned away embarrassed. Was he really taking them inedible food and being paid for doing so?

As he walked to the market with his buckets of fish he saw a dirty scrap of ribbon lying on the ground. On impulse he picked it up and stuffed it into his pocket. He approached the various fishermen that he knew and asked if they would be willing to contribute to the purchase of a ladder. They laughed at him and after two hours he had only been given six lepta.

The following day when Manolis delivered goods to the island he threw the piece of ribbon to Flora. 'A present for you.'

Flora picked up the grubby ribbon and looked at it admiringly. 'It's beautiful. Is it really for me?'

Manolis nodded. 'I found it yesterday and thought you might like it.'

'I've never had a present before,' she said wonderingly. 'Thank you.'

Manolis rowed away from the island. The girl said she had never been given a present before and she was as thrilled with the piece of ribbon as if he had given her a necklace of diamonds. He felt guilty. She obviously had very few possessions and never asked for anything for herself; it was always building materials to help with the repair of houses. In another week he should have enough drachmas saved to purchase a ladder.

It became customary for him to take a small gift for her each time he visited. Sometimes it consisted of a few nails, screws or hinges that he had picked up where they had been discarded or dropped accidentally and other times it was a comb for her hair, a length of wool or even a flower. Having thrown the items ashore for her he would moor close by and stay talking to her before making the return journey.

Flora still pleaded continually with the boatmen to bring them a ladder and finally Dimitris arrived and pushed the unwieldy article onto the jetty. Flora rushed off to tell Yannis of her prize and Dimitris watched from a distance as two men lifted it and carried it up through the archway.

When Manolis arrived Flora greeted him with the news. 'We have a ladder. Dimitris brought a ladder over for us.'

'Well that should make your friend Yannis very happy.' Manolis did not admit that he had been instrumental in purchasing the ladder and arranging for it to be brought over. 'Here, I thought you might like these.' He handed her a couple of glass beads.

Flora turned them between her fingers and held them up to the light marvelling at the array of colours that were reflected back at her. She would ask Phaedra to help her to thread them on to the piece of wool Manolis had brought her a few days earlier and then she would be able to wear them as a necklace.

Christos had finally agreed to give Yannis advice regarding building, but on the proviso that his house was repaired first and Yannis felt obliged to comply. The villagers watched Yannis and Spiro in their efforts, no longer ridiculing them but still not offering to help.

Christos had insisted that the shutters be replaced before he would consider that his house was finished and would withstand the winter weather. Having given in to Christos's demands meant that Yannis's house had no shutters and when the first storm blew up it was cold, damp and miserable inside. He and Spiro had carried Kyriakos up to the building where he would at least be sheltered from the worst of the weather and he agreed it was preferable to sheltering in the church or the tunnels.

Yannis sat and shivered. It had been raining and blowing relentlessly for three days. The rain had come through the window openings in his house; his clothes were wet and his mattress damp. No boats had been able to bring supplies to the island and he was as hungry as all the other occupants. He lay back down as close to Kyriakos as possible, hoping to receive some warmth from the man's body and be able to sleep.

The wind died down and Yannis was woken by the sudden silence. He had hoped he might die from starvation and never wake again. He struggled to his feet. He could no longer tolerate living on Spinalonga. He slipped and slithered down the hill to the main road and then down to the Venetian walls. He leaned over, the drop was deep and there were rocks below that were being sucked at greedily by the sea. He looked across the bay and then back down at the rocks where he was contemplating throwing himself, hoping to be fatally injured.

He felt someone take a firm hold on his belt. 'What are you doing, Yannis?'

'I can't.' He sank down onto the ground shivering violently.

'You can't what? You can't face a few days of being cold and hungry? Some of us have faced it for years. It will happen more than once before the winter is over. You just have to get used to it and accept it.'

'I can't.'

'You don't have a choice,' Phaedra answered him curtly. 'When it's warm and you're not hungry you are full of grand ideas about rebuilding and making life better for all of us. You're no different from the others over here. The moment things become difficult you are ready to give in. The winter doesn't last for ever.'

'The house is cold and wet. The rain blew in on everything.'

'You shouldn't have done so much for Christos. He's quite capable of looking after himself. Did he give you any help? No. He just stood and criticised. You should have concentrated on your own house and told him to fix his own shutters.'

'He says I haven't done the work well enough for my house to withstand the winter.'

'Then you'll just have to make more repairs as you go along. Now it's stopped raining you and Spiro could fit a shutter.'

'The rain will still come in through the other window and the door. I let Christos have the wood I had saved for one of my shutters.'

'Then go and find some more. Don't be so defeatist.'

'I'm just so cold and hungry.'

'The boats are on their way. Once they have delivered I'll make you a hot meal. That should make you feel better.'

Although Yannis did feel somewhat warmer after he had eaten the meal that Phaedra had prepared he was still unwell. He lay on his mattress alternately sweating and shivering for a week. Spiro watched over him anxiously and when he declared his intention of going down to the church and speaking to Panicos and the other men from the hospital who were forced to shelter there Spiro was adamant.

'If you go down there you'll probably become chilled again and goodness knows what some of the men are suffering from. You could catch anything. I'll go down and ask Panicos to come up here to speak with you if it's so important.'

When Panicos arrived Yannis pleaded with him to encourage the occupants of the church who were fit enough to help him build weather proof shelters. Panicos listened patiently, then sighed and rose to his feet. 'I'll try, but you can be far more persuasive than me.'

Yannis was still brooding on the conversation when Spiro returned and Yannis asked him about the conditions the men were living in at the church.

Spiro shrugged. 'Probably about as bad as you can imagine.'

'I have to go down there.'

Refusing to listen to Spiro's protests Yannis made his way unsteadily down to the church with Spiro following him. Yannis walked into the church, the smell that greeted him of unwashed humanity, excrement and vomit threatening to overwhelm him. Trying to ignore the fetid atmosphere Yannis harangued the occupants on their living conditions and pleaded with them to help him repair the decrepit buildings where they sheltered during the summer. Unable to stay inside the church any longer Yannis stumbled out of the door and took a deep breath of the fresh air.

Once he had recovered sufficiently he shook his head at Spiro. 'I'm amazed they have survived living in that atmosphere. It's horrendous in there. If we could at least get some of them out and living under better conditions it would help. Come with me and look at the buildings around here and see which would be feasible to tackle.'

Spiro followed in Yannis's wake and between them they finally decided that four needed the least work.

'We'll collect materials from those that are beyond repair and make a start tomorrow if the weather holds.'

Once a house had been completed Yannis arranged for Panicos and three companions to move in and Yannis insisted that the fittest of them should help him and Spiro each day. Although the man had agreed grudgingly he had dutifully arrived at Yannis's house and listened to Yannis's ideas for repairing another. To Yannis's delight two more men appeared with him the following day and between them they managed to complete three more houses over the next weeks.

Once some of the other fitter men realised that if they wished to have somewhere weatherproof to live that was not overcrowded they finally agreed to join the small work force. The men listened to Yannis and he was able to inspire them with his enthusiasm and the fact that he had managed to construct a reasonably weather proof shelter on his own and with help had repaired four other houses finally encouraged them to offer their help.

Having finished preparing the vegetables Phaedra would go down and sit on the jetty with Flora for a short while. Phaedra still found it unnerving watching the small waves wash in and out and would make an excuse to return to the storeroom. If there was some fruit that looked reasonably fresh and was not riddled with worm holes she would select a few pieces and carry them to wherever Yannis was working. She would sit and listen as Yannis gave instructions to the men who were helping him that day. Whenever they took a short break he would continue to talk about his plans and ideas. Phaedra did not always understand, but her respect for the man grew. He harangued and cajoled, but never raised his voice when asking the men for help and was always ready with his praise for their efforts.

With more workers the building work moved faster and more houses were able to be occupied. There were fewer men crowded into the tunnels or church when it was wet and cold; or the sun beat down mercilessly on them. With only three or four people in a house the communal cooking on which they had been so dependent was no longer necessary. They appreciated being able to choose from the produce that had been delivered and decide for themselves on the meal they would eat.

The food was not only more palatable when cooked in small quantities it was also shared out more fairly. Previously if you had been unfortunate enough to have the last serving it often consisted only of rice or pasta; the vegetables and meat already gone.

Although Yannis was pleased with the progress they had made he was adamant that he would not move from the original house that he had constructed into a more weather proof dwelling until everyone on the island had somewhere suitable to live. Phaedra had asked if he could place a roof on her shelter and Yannis had refused.

'The side walls are ready to fall. It really isn't safe for you to be living in here.'

'I've nowhere else to go unless I ask Ariadne if I can move back into her house and I don't want to do that. I'm used to being alone.'

Yannis frowned. 'There's a small house at the top of the main road. We haven't done any work on that yet as it wouldn't be large enough for more than two people. Would you and Flora be willing to share?'

'I could ask Flora. She's used to living alone like me.'

'She needs to move out of the tower. She has to prop half her mattress up against the wall and sleep curled up. That can't be good for her.'

'I'll speak to her this evening and let you know what she says.'

Flora was sitting in her usual position on the jetty when she saw Manolis's boat approaching and waved to him. He raised his hand in return and pointed to his passengers. Flora realised the men in the boat were priests and immediately ran to tell Yannis.

Yannis wiped his begrimed hands down his trousers and followed Flora back down to the jetty where Manolis had now tied up his boat and the two priests were ashore. To Flora's surprise Yannis and the younger man were suddenly in a close embrace and she backed away embarrassed. She looked at the priest and smiled shyly.

'Have you come to stay?'

Father Minos shook his head. 'I've been given permission to visit. I imagine that is Yannis that Andreas was overjoyed to meet. The boy I met years ago has changed and I would not have recognised him. They would probably appreciate some time together to talk. Can you show me to the church and I can hold a service there for those who would like to attend.'

Flora shook her head. 'You can't use the church. Some people who haven't any houses yet still live in there and it isn't very big. I'll take you down to the square.'

As she led the way she called out to everyone that the priest was visiting the island and people began to emerge from their houses and follow them. Father Minos waited until crippled people had been carried as close as possible and placed on the ground. He held up his hands and began to pray, moving between them fearlessly.

Phaedra stood on the fringe of the crowd, pleased that they were in the square and she was in no danger of being pushed into the sea. The responses to the prayers came automatically to her as she strained her ears to hear the words the priest said. As Father Minos gave a final blessing a collective sigh went up from the people and they began to push forward towards him.

Yannis had been standing to one side and now he called to the people, asking them to move away and promising that the priest would talk to all of them. He stood beside Father Minos as the people quietened and began to ask questions and the priest answered as best he could.

Spiro was at Andreas's side and led the way to where Phaedra and Flora were standing so he could introduce them.

Phaedra looked at Andreas curiously. 'Did you know Yannis was here? Is that why you sent him some of your belongings?'

Andreas shook his head. 'I had no idea. I thought he was in hospital in Athens. My bundle of possessions was picked up by mistake and given to him.'

'Poor Yannis, he thought you had contracted the disease. It was something else he blamed himself for,' said Phaedra sadly.

'Yannis has no need to blame himself for anything,' declared Spiro stoutly. 'He has to be thanked for being instrumental in having us sent here. Now we're getting everyone rehoused the conditions here are far better than they ever were in the hospital. We have the freedom to go wherever we wish on the island, fresh air, fresh food; what more could we want?'

Andreas could think of a number of other things that were needed to make their life comfortable.

Spiro turned to Phaedra. 'How about some food for our guests? I'm sure Ariadne will lend you a couple of extra plates and I imagine Yannis and Father Minos want to talk together without an audience.'

'I'm forgetting my manners,' smiled Phaedra. 'We're not used to having guests. Come on, Flora. I hope there is some decent food left in the storeroom.'

Having shared a meal, sitting with Kyriakos on the patch of concrete, Yannis and Spiro took Father Minos and Andreas on a tour of the island, introducing them to the various occupants they met on the way. Although neither priest showed their emotions they were horrified by the pathetic and helpless people that they met, although all declared that their life was so much better since Yannis had arrived.

As they finally said farewell on the quay Father Minos promised that he would petition the authorities and demand that the inhabitants were treated as sick people and not as outcasts. Yannis had smiled at the priest's intensity, but felt doubtful that the authorities would take any notice of him however hard he pleaded on their behalf.

Despite Yannis's scepticism, Manolis began to bring sacks of sand and cement over on his fishing boat. Flora greeted him gleefully each day and rushed off to tell Yannis that help was needed to move the unwieldy sacks. He accompanied her back down to the jetty and as she skipped down beside him she suddenly stopped in consternation.

'I forgot. Manolis asked me to tell you that Anna was waving.'

Yannis pulled Flora to him and kissed her briefly on her forehead. 'That's one of the most wonderful things I've ever heard.' The sacks forgotten, Yannis rushed back up the hill to the fortress walls and looked across at his village. He was disappointed to see no one.

'Who's Anna?' asked Flora who had followed him. 'Is she your girl.'

'No, she's my sister. I used to live over there in that farmhouse.'

'Oh, Yannis. I had no idea. No wonder you were so unhappy when you first arrived.'

'It's still difficult. Some days I can see my family working in the fields. I used to hate the work, but I'd be grateful to be back over there with them and working outside in all weathers now.'

Yannis returned to the jetty and Phaedra looked at him curiously. What had made Yannis kiss Flora and then race up the hill? She felt a pang of both anxiety and jealousy.

'Did you know that Yannis use to live in the village across there?' Flora pointed to the cluster of buildings across the water.

Phaedra shook her head. 'I've never asked him. He told me he was in Heraklion when he was admitted so I had assumed he lived there.'

'I think that's why he won't go anywhere near the jetty when the boatmen are around. He's probably concerned that they'll recognise him.'

'What difference would that make?'

'I expect he's worried about his family; they could be driven out of the village.'

'Whatever for?' asked Phaedra.

'That often happens when someone in the family is confirmed with leprosy. At the time I felt very resentful that my father had taken me to the doctor, but now I realise it was for the best. Had I been found living in the shed my family could have been driven away.'

Phaedra looked at Flora in horror. 'Do you think that will have happened to my parents?'

Flora shrugged. 'How would I know?'

Phaedra pressed her hands to her head. 'I wish I knew if they were safe.'

Each day more items arrived and the people rummaged through the sacks of old clothes and shoes to find something that fitted them or helped themselves to an extra blanket. A crate of bandages had arrived and Spiro took charge, ensuring that no one took more than they needed to change the soiled rags they were using. Once Yannis had moved any building materials that had also been delivered he would hurry up the hill, climb up onto the cat walk of the fortress wall and strain his eyes to see if he could discern Anna waving. Most days she appeared and on other mornings his sister, Maria, was waving, her baby in her arms.

'Be careful, Yannis.' Phaedra stood by his side. 'The wall you're leaning on could give way.'

'I'm quite safe.' Yannis suddenly grabbed Phaedra's arm. 'Look, Anna's waving.'

Frantically Yannis waved back and ordered Phaedra to wave also. Dutifully she raised her hand and waved with him until Anna turned away and began to walk back up the path, a taller figure following her.

'It was Anna and that must have been my Pappa.' Yannis turned to Phaedra beaming.

'Does this mean you'll be leaving us, Yannis?'

'Leaving? What gave you that idea?'

Phaedra shrugged. 'You have family close by and are a friend of the priest. I thought they might arrange for you to return home.'

Yannis shook his head. 'This is my home, Phaedra, now and for the remainder of my life.' He gave a deep sigh. 'I have to accept that.'

Phaedra was comforted by Yannis's assurance that he would be staying on the island. She had been worrying herself for the previous few weeks that he would be able to return to his home and they would once again be left to fend for themselves without his encouragement and support. She realised now how fond she had become of him and she relied upon him to be around. She spent most of the afternoons watching him work and made sure if he needed anything she was there to fetch it for him. He treated her with respect, thanking her for the meal she provided each evening and telling her how good it tasted. She could not envisage life on the island without him now.

'What's happening over there?' asked Phaedra. 'It looks as though someone is putting up a tremendous struggle.'

Yannis's face paled. 'I hope it isn't either of my brothers who are being sent here. Come on, we ought to go down and see who's arrived.' He held Phaedra's hand to help her climb from the cat walk to the rough path below.

To Yannis 's surprise it was not a person who was placed on the jetty but a goat with a label tied to her neck saying that she was for Panicos. Unlike the scrawny animals that had been slaughtered and the carcass they received being little more than skin and bone there was enough flesh on her to make a nourishing meal for a number of people if she was butchered carefully.

'You can't eat her,' said Flora, horrified at the idea. 'She's expecting a kid.'

Yannis turned the label over and read "Panicos. For milk." He smiled at Flora. 'Come on, let's take her up to Panicos. He'll have to be responsible for her. I'm not prepared to be a goatherd.'

When Flora returned from delivering the goat to Panicos Manolis passed her a letter and she looked at it curiously, quite unable to read the name on the envelope.

'It's for Yannis,' explained Manolis. 'It must be important because the priest gave it to me. Can you take it to him? I'll wait here until you return.' He had taken to spending longer and longer each day talking to Flora and was trying to teach her how to count.

Flora nodded and looked again at the envelope. Like most of the other women on the island she could neither read nor write and had a great respect for Yannis who appeared able to do both with ease.

Yannis opened the letter excitedly and read the contents; hardly able to comprehend the news that Andreas sent. He beat his fists in the ground and groaned.

'Is it your Mamma?' asked Phaedra tentatively, realising that he had received bad news.

Yannis shook his head. 'My sister has died.'

Phaedra looked at him in horror. 'How? She waved to you earlier today. She was alright then.'

'Not Anna, my other sister, Maria. I thought it was her waving to me some days with a child in her arms but it must have been Anna. Maria died giving birth to a child. How do women die when they give birth?'

'I don't know. My mother had other babies and they died.' Phaedra shrugged. 'It just happens.'

'Everything "just happens". It isn't fair, Phaedra.'

'Life isn't fair. I was fine living in a cave on the mainland. I wasn't harming anyone and due to me my brother died. If he had not been there with me when they picked me up he would still be alive..' Phaedra spoke bitterly.

'I'm pleased you're here and not living somewhere on the mainland. Everyone on this island has suffered a tragedy of some sort. I need you and your common sense to keep things in perspective.'

'You take everyone's problems to heart and think they are your fault. They're not. You have to learn to shrug and walk away.'

'I wish I could. What makes you so wise, Phaedra?'

Phaedra shrugged, 'I'm not, but when I see everyone relying upon you to do everything and blaming you if things do not always go as they want I feel like screaming at them and telling them to go away and give you some peace.'

'You never turn me away when I bring my problems to you. That means you are a very special and precious friend.' Yannis bent and kissed her, it was meant to be a friendly kiss, but it became more passionate.

Phaedra drew away from him and touched her lips with her finger.

'I'm sorry,' he apologised. 'That became more than friendly.'

'I've never been kissed before,' Phaedra spoke almost in a whisper. 'I've always avoided the men over here. They frighten me.'

'Do I frighten you?' Yannis looked at her in concern.

Phaedra shook her head. 'You're not like most of the other men.'

Yannis slipped his arm around her waist. 'I wouldn't want my favourite girl to be scared of me.'

'I thought your cousin was your favourite girl.'

Yannis shook his head. 'Not any more. I've released her from our betrothal agreement. I hope she'll find a decent man to marry and be happy.'

'I wish I knew how my parents are and if I have any brothers or sisters now,' said Phaedra wistfully. 'Flora said they could have been driven away from the village after my brother and I were taken away. My mother was expecting another baby.'

'It might be possible to find out. How far away from here is your village?'

'I don't know. My father and grandfather used to go to a town each week to sell the farm produce, but I've no idea where it was.'

'What is the name of your village?'

'Kastelli.'

Yannis frowned. He had heard of it but did not know the location. 'How long did it take you to get here?'

Phaedra shrugged. 'It was in the afternoon that the men came and we were brought over here the same day. We arrived just before it became dark.'

'Then your village can't be far away. It's possible that Father Minos or Andreas know where it is. I'm sure one of them would take a message from you or bring you news of them.'

Phaedra shook her head. 'It would mean telling them that Mikaelis was dead.'

'I think they would be grateful to know that you are alive and well.'

'Maybe.'

'Think about it. They could probably find out if your parents were still living there. I wouldn't ask either of them to try to contact your parents if you weren't willing.'

Every day Flora sat on the jetty, asking the boatmen for any building materials they were willing to bring over. Despite having sand and cement a spade was needed to mix it and a trowel for the rendering to be applied to a wall that was constructed of flimsy lengths of timber in-filled with stones.

No sooner did she tell Manolis of their needs than the articles mysteriously appeared. She looked for him eagerly each day and once he had off loaded the goods he had transported from Aghios Nikolaos he would stay talking with her for most of the morning and he had agreed to teach her how to count.

Phaedra saw the rapport between them and felt sad. If they were in a village on the mainland Manolis would have asked to court Flora and by now a wedding date would have been fixed. She also felt slightly envious. Yannis always behaved affectionately towards her, but had never attempted to kiss her again.

1930 - 1931

Whenever Flora saw the young boatman arriving she would run up to where Yannis was working and he would hurry down to inspect the goods that had been brought over.

Yannis stopped at the top of the flight of steps leading to the jetty and looked at the man who stood there looking around hesitantly. He did not look like a new sufferer arriving. He walked towards Yannis, assessing the nodules and sores on his skin as he did so.

'Good morning. I'm Doctor Stavros and I have been asked to come here by the authorities.'

'Why?' asked Yannis suspiciously. 'What do they plan to do with us now?'

'I understand there are some more sufferers due to come over and the authorities want to know if there is sufficient accommodation for them. Would you be willing to show me where you live? After that I could then visit the hospital cases.'

'We are all hospital cases,' replied Yannis grimly.

'Of course. I was referring specifically to those who are bedridden.'

'We'll go this way.' Yannis turned up the path and led the way to where Kyriakos was sitting. 'I suggest you start here.'

Yannis left the doctor examining Kyriakos and returned when he saw the doctor pick up his bag. As Yannis led the way around the island the doctor followed him miserably, expecting at any moment to be taken to the hospital patients. He followed Yannis through the tunnel and into the square where a number of people were sitting or lying around.

'Wouldn't they be better off inside? It can't be comfortable sitting there.'

'All the houses are occupied and there aren't enough anyway.'

'Can't they go into the hospital?'

'The hospital is a ruin.'

Doctor Stavros's head was throbbing. He had expected to find the people living in houses and the most severely afflicted cases in a hospital building where they would be looked after. 'Could we go somewhere and talk for a while.? I'm rather confused. This is not what I expected.'

'What did you expect? A row of beds with clean sheets and dedicated nurses? We have to look after ourselves and each other as best we can.'

'I was only asked to come and compile a report. I have to say how the latest arrivals have settled in and I can requisition some essential supplies. How many of you are living over here?'

'Three or four hundred.'

'As many as that! No wonder there isn't sufficient accommodation.'

'The men are gradually rebuilding but priority is being given to the women and those least able to look after themselves.'

'So where do the others live?'

'Mostly in the church. There are still a few in the tunnel but in another week or so they should be housed somewhere better. Any new arrivals would have to stay in there at first if there was no room in the church..'

'So if you are capable of building your own house you have somewhere to live; if not you are condemned to living in the church or the tunnel we passed through.'

Phaedra had joined them, bringing up bread, cheese, tomatoes and olives from the storeroom to make a rudimentary meal for them. She quickly corrected the doctor.

'Yannis insisted that the first houses were occupied by at least one other person who needed to be looked after. The others had to help him repair the next houses. Those who are in the church now are the most recent arrivals. You could go and talk to them and then visit the houses with Yannis.'

'Where do you get the materials from to rebuild the houses?' asked the doctor curiously. Surely if the authorities could send out building materials they should realise that medicine was equally important.

'Manolis brings them over from Aghios Nikolaos.'

'Yes, but who pays for them?'

Yannis shrugged. 'I don't know. Father Minos visited us and after that the supplies we needed began to arrive. He must have asked the church to donate them.'

Doctor Stavros accompanied Yannis to the church and hurriedly retreated from the foul smelling interior. 'I cannot possibly treat people in there. It's a breeding ground for disease. If they want to see me they will have to come outside. Maybe we could visit some of the people in the houses instead?'

Yannis led the doctor from house to house until finally Doctor Stavros stopped and ran a hand over his head. 'I can't possibly see everyone during this visit.'

'What's the point in you seeing any of them? asked Yannis. 'You'll go away and write your report, and come back next year to ask if we are feeling better.'

'I'll not do that. I will write to the authorities and tell them about the conditions I have found here. I'll also tell them that you need medicines and a doctor over here permanently. A hospital needs to be built so the sick can be properly cared for.'

'I wish you every success, but I cannot see the authorities taking any notice. As far as they are concerned we no longer exist.'

Upon his return to the mainland Doctor Stavros wrote a

long and impassioned plea to the government, but no reply was received.

Doctor Stavros decided he must make an arrangement with Manolis to be taken across to Spinalonga one day each week and the fisherman could return to collect him later in the day. He did not relish the weekly journey as he was unused to the sea and dreaded being caught out on the water if a strong wind suddenly blew up.

Now Doctor Kandakis was no longer the official doctor for the island he also refused to visit the outlying villages. The visits were to become the responsibility of Doctor Stavros. He handed Doctor Stavros a small book containing a list of the various villages and brief notes about any patients he saw regularly.

'If you are delayed it is usually possible to spend the night in one of the villages at a taverna rather than have to return to Aghios Nikolaos.'

'How am I expected to get to the villages?' asked Doctor Stavros.

Doctor Kandakis shrugged. 'You can walk or you can buy my donkey. I'll not have any use for her now.'

'Where would I put a donkey? I live in the town and do not even have a back yard.'

'I can rent her pasture out to you. Let me know your decision or I'll be sending her to the slaughter house next week.'

Doctor Stavros knew the doctor was asking far more for the donkey than he would get at the knacker's yard for her skin and meat, but he felt obliged to accept the offer of the beast and pay rent for the pasture where she was tethered. Walking to the villages was out of the question. Although they were none of them far apart, he would not be able to visit more than two in a day if he was on foot, he would then have to pass through the same villages again the following day to visit the ones that were further away.

He looked at the animal, knowing nothing about donkeys and she seemed placid and amenable.

'How often does she need to be re-shod?'

Doctor Kandakis did not mention that he neglected the donkey's hooves until he noticed that she was having trouble walking. 'Just get her checked out every so often. It depends how far she has had to travel.'

With this scant information Doctor Stavros handed over the amount Doctor Kandakis had demanded and insisted that the saddle and bridle should be included in the price. He would have to ask one of the local farmers where they took their animals when they needed attention.

'Whilst I'm here do you have any information about the people who are who are living on Spinalonga?'

Doctor Kandakis shook his head. 'I don't keep any information about the people who are on Spinalonga. They are all lepers. I have a list of names of those who have been found living locally and taken over there, but I have never been given any details of the ones who have been sent there from any other area.'

'I would be grateful for the list you do have.'

Doctor Kandakis shrugged and passed Doctor Stavros some sheets of paper that were clipped together. The names of the people on the island were unimportant. They were all lepers wherever they may have come from.

Doctor Stavros left the donkey tethered in the field. He sighed. That was another job he would have to do each day, going to the field and ensuring the beast had sufficient food and water. He would probably have to buy fodder for her during the months when there was little grass available and that would be more expense. His head was aching and he wanted to return home and look at the sparse notes Doctor Kandakis had given him.

Doctor Stavros poured a glass of raki and sat at the table, a notebook and pencil at his side. He turned his attention to the notebooks relating to the villagers. There seemed no logical order to the lists; there was no date, often the person was referred to only by their baptismal name along with the name of the village where they lived. It would be necessary to ask each villager for information about themselves and their family. The doctor abandoned his original plan of working from Doctor Kandakis's notes.

Tomorrow he would call at the stationers and purchase a number of notebooks. Each one could have the name of the village on the cover and inside he would make a list of the inhabitants. He could then record the date he had examined or treated a patient and the subsequent outcome.

By the end of the evening the doctor had made a list for himself. He should be able to visit Shisma and the villages en route to Fioretzides. Provided he was able to ascertain the names of all the villagers reasonably quickly he could then return to Aghios Nikolaos via Karterides and Lakkonia.

He would then travel along to Elounda, visiting the various villages on the way and then ride up the hill to Mavrikiano and Pines. From there he would be able to ride down to Pano and Kato Elounda and return to Aghios Nikolaos. There were other outlying villages that he knew he would have to visit, but they could necessitate stopping over night. Before he planned that route he wanted to ensure there would be a convenient taverna in the area to accommodate him.

His visits to the villages were time consuming and often frustrating. He went from house to house to ask the names of the occupants, often finding only the elderly at home or the cottages deserted. He then had to travel out to the surrounding fields and speak to those who were working. He continually had explain that he was their new doctor and would visit them regularly, often having to listen to some who wished to tell him a long history of ailments.

When he returned home he checked the information he had in his new notebooks against the ones that Doctor Kandakis had given him. Very often the same name appeared on a number of occasions in Doctor Kandakis's notes and Doctor Stavros realised he would have to check on his subsequent visit to a village just how many people with the names Maria, Anna, Yiorgo or Yannis actually lived there.

He decided he could no longer put off visiting Skinias, Selles and Vrouhas. Provided he was not stopped by anyone in the other villages that he passed through he should be able to make the journey in one day and be back in Aghios Nikolaos before night fall. In most of them there were no more than twenty adult inhabitants and three or four children making his job relatively easy.

His impending visit to Kastelli would probably mean he needed to stop overnight as it had a far larger population than the villages he had visited previously. He consoled himself that once he had the list of inhabitants of each village up to date he would not have to spend time going from house to house and could revert to his original plan of visiting a number of villages in one day and only having to spend time with anyone who was ill.

Making his way up the hill to Pines the following week his donkey slowed and looked back at him reproachfully. There were mostly small farms in the area, and Doctor Stavros was able to stop and speak to the men and women who were working in the fields. Satisfied that he had recorded as many inhabitants as possible in the area he rode slowly on to Driros which appeared almost deserted. Having spoken to the elderly people he had found sitting outside their houses and ascertaining their names and those of their relatives he moved on towards Kastelli. After only a short distance the doctor realised his donkey was definitely limping and he dismounted. A quick examination of her hooves showed that she had lost one of her shoes. He had no choice but to walk and lead her by the rein until he finally reached Kastelli.

As he walked along the cart track he knocked on each door and no one appeared to be at home. At the last house there was an elderly lady sitting outside and he approached her with a smile.

'Good afternoon. I am Doctor Stavros. I have taken over the duties of Doctor Kandakis. Would you be able to help me, please?'

She cupped her ear with her hand. 'You'll have to speak up. Can't hear a word you're saying.'

Doctor Stavros raised his voice and tried again. The woman shook her head and mumbled something unintelligible before rising and walking back inside the house.

With a despairing sigh Doctor Stavros continued around the corner where he saw a large, well kept house. Surely whoever lived there would be able to help him. He tied his donkey to the railing outside the window and a woman looked out at him with a frown of displeasure. The door was opened and she spoke frostily.

'Please remove your donkey. This is not a hitching post.'

'I apologise for causing you any inconvenience, Madam, but I am hoping you might be able to assist me. My donkey is lame and I wondered if there was a forge in the village where I could take her for some attention.'

'Follow the road down and you'll find it.'

The door was closed before Doctor Stavros had an opportunity to enquire about the occupants. He was relieved to find the forge was only a short distance away and he could see men hard at work inside. They were sweaty and dirty, their naked torsos scarred from the sparks that flew up at them whilst they beat the metal into shape. He tethered the donkey to one of the window rails and stood just inside the door waiting to be noticed. He knew it would be useless to try to make himself heard over the general clamour.

A man nodded to him eventually and indicated they should go outside.

'Can't hear a word in there. What can I do for you?' The man coughed and spat upon the ground.

'I've bought Doctor Kandakis's donkey from him. I don't actually know anything about animals. She began to limp on the way here and I see she has lost one of her shoes.'

'That could be the reason she was limping. The doctor's

not been to us in a long while. He may have visited a smithy elsewhere, of course. Hold her head and I'll take a look.'

Nikos examined the donkey's feet and shook his head as he straightened up, coughing again. 'Her hooves certainly need to be trimmed and all her shoes are loose. She needs new ones. Do you want me to do it?'

'How long will it take? I ought to be back in Aghios Nikolaos tonight.'

'I'll work on her during the afternoon. You've time to go to the taverna. They can probably provide you with a meal. She'll be ready for you in good time for your journey back to Aghios Nikolaos.'

Doctor Stavros gave a sigh of relief. He had envisaged having to make arrangements to stay in the village overnight. He would continue to visit and list some of the inhabitants of Kastelli during the afternoon before visiting the taverna as a meal would be welcome.

'How long have you had that cough?' asked the doctor.

Nikos gave a grin. 'We all have a cough. It comes with the job. The smoke and the heat gets down inside us. Have you got a nose bag for your donkey? If they're busy munching at some food they're more interested in that than what we are doing to their hooves.'

'Doctor Kandakis said I should carry one with me in case we were delayed anywhere.'

'Good idea to have one with you whenever you travel. Hard to explain to a donkey that there's no meal available for her.'

'Is there anyone sick in the village that I ought to visit whilst I'm here?'

'I don't know of anyone except Eleni, of course, but you won't be able to do much for her.' Nikos tapped his head.

'I'll visit her just the same. Could save me from being called out at an inconvenient time. Where will I find her?'

'Her father runs the general store. Walk along the road and

you can't miss it or the taverna. Come back when it suits you. I'll leave her tethered outside when she's ready, but give me or one of the men a call before you ride away. I'll be able to show you what I've done and let you know how much you owe us then.'

'Don't you have a standard price for re-shoeing that I can pay now?'

'Yes, but I don't know how much attention we'll have to give to her hooves and how long that will take.'

Hoping the man was trustworthy Doctor Stavros walked away. First he would return to the big house and see if he could find out the names of the occupants there. As he knocked the woman looked out of the window again and then reluctantly opened the door.

'What do you want? I told you where the forge was situated.'

'I have come to thank you for that. I have left my donkey there for her hooves to have whatever attention is needed. Whilst I wait for her new shoes to be fitted I would be grateful if I could ask you for some information.' As the woman went to shut the door again the doctor continued hurriedly. 'I am your new doctor in this area and I am trying to update the records given to me by Doctor Kandakis.'

The woman looked at him suspiciously. 'What information are you wanting?'

'Just the names of the people who live here and to enquire about their health generally.'

Grudgingly Sofia opened the door wider to admit the doctor. 'You'd better come in and sit down. Dimitra, bring some coffee and biscuits for the doctor.'

'Please. Do not go to any trouble on my behalf. Just a glass of water would be very acceptable.'

'Dimitra,' the woman called again, 'Just water.'

A young woman appeared from the scullery area and placed a glass of water on the table along with a plate of biscuits.

'This is our new doctor,' announced Sofia. 'You'd better tell your mother to expect a visit from him.'

'Is she ill?' asked Doctor Stavros.

'Not that I am aware, but if you are updating your medical records I imagine you will want to visit everyone in the village.'

'Of course. Maybe I could start with yourself, Madam, and the people who live in this house.' Doctor Stavros looked around. If the furniture and china on display was anything to judge by the family were a good deal wealthier than the usual villagers that he called on. If he was ever asked to visit the house he would ask an enormous fee.

'There's my husband and myself, our daughters and Maria's husband. '

'How many daughters?'

'Just Maria and Fotini,' declared Sofia. 'My older daughter is expecting her first child.'

'And she is keeping well? Plenty of rest and good food?'

Sofia nodded.

'Now, if you could give me your husband's name.'

'Alesandros Danniakis. He's a tax collector.'

'And your name, Madam?'

'Sofia.'

Doctor Stavros made the entries into his notebook. 'And your daughters are Maria and Fotini Danniakis?'

'Maria is now known as Maria Roussakis. Her husband, Yiorgo, lives here with us.'

'Well, I think that's all. If I could just have a quick word with your help, Dimitra. If she can tell me her husband's name and where she lives that would be a great help.'

'I can tell you that,' offered Sofia. 'She lives in the house opposite. I could probably tell you where most people live if you have the time.'

'I'd be very grateful. I'm gradually visiting all the villages but I often have to go out to the fields to speak to people. It all takes time,' sighed the doctor. 'I tried to speak to an old lady a short distance up the road, but I don't think she could hear me.'

Sofia smiled. 'That would have been Soula. She's stone deaf. Now the first cottages have Anna and Mikaelis living there.'

Doctor Stavros entered the names into his notebook as Sofia reeled them off to him. It would be necessary at a later date to ascertain exactly which houses they occupied. Finally he thanked Sofia Danniakis and took his leave. He would now visit the woman whose father had the general store, and then the taverna to have a leisurely meal before returning to the forge to collect the donkey. At least he would need nothing more to eat that night; a glass of raki and some olives would be quite sufficient.

Yiorgo looked suspiciously at the stranger who entered his small shop. 'What can I do for you?'

'I'm Doctor Stavros. I have taken over the practice from Doctor Kandakis. I've left my donkey to be re-shod at the forge. The man there said he only knew of one person in the village who was sick. He said that she was the daughter of the owner of the general store. Am I in the right place?'

'There's only one general store in Kastelli.'

'So would it be beneficial if I saw your daughter?'

Yiorgo shrugged.'You can see her, but it will make no difference. Doctor Kandakis said there was no point in him calling any more; waste of his time.'

'I would like to judge that for myself. I would be failing in my duty if I accepted whatever he said about a patient without seeing them for myself.'

'Go next door.' Yiorgo indicated with his thumb. 'My wife will be there and she'll let you in and explain the problem.'

Having knocked loudly so he would be heard over the sound of the loom that was working inside Doctor Stavros waited. As soon as the loom was silent he knocked again more gently and waited until Despina opened the door.

'I'm Doctor Stavros,' he said and explained again that he had taken over from Doctor Kandakis. 'I wondered if it would be convenient to see your daughter. Her name is Eleni I believe.'

Despina shrugged. 'You can see her, but there's nothing you can do for her.' The doctor followed Despina through the doorway and into the living room.

Eleni was propped up on her pallet, her eyes closed.

'Hello, Eleni. I'm Doctor Stavros come to pay you a visit.'

Eleni's eyes opened and rolled around in her head whilst she made indistinguishable noises, every so often a bout of maniacal laughter came from her and she would rock herself backwards and forwards. Doctor Stavros patted her hand and turned back to Despina.

'Was your daughter born disabled like this?'

Despina shook her head. 'She was a perfectly normal young girl until that woman assaulted her.' Despina did not mention that Eleni's behaviour had become strange after her baby had died. That was in the past.

'Why was she assaulted?'

'My Eleni used to enjoy walking on the hills. She told Doctor Kandakis that there was an old woman suffering from leprosy hiding out in a cave up there. It wasn't an old woman, it was the daughter of a couple who lived in the village. Their son was taken away at the same time.'

'How awful for them, but no excuse to inflict such damage on your daughter. Do they know the state she is in?'

'They left the village that same night. They knew they would be turned out and Eleni's father had a score to settle with them. Just as well they did go or my Yiorgo would be in prison now. Maria's father has the taverna and the other grandfather still lives here and farms his land. They stole his donkey and cart when they left. Never thought he would see that again, but three days later he found it parked back outside.'

'What a sad story. Do you know where the children were taken?'

'No idea. Doctor Kandakis should know. Why don't you ask him?'

'I will when I return to town.' Doctor Stavros looked at Eleni again. 'Are you able to understand what she is trying to say?'

'Sometimes, but mostly it is just nonsense.' Despina sighed. 'I worry what will become of her when I'm no longer around to look after her.'

'I'm sure arrangements can be made to ensure her welfare when that day comes. I'll call in again the next time I am this way.'

'What for? There's nothing you can do.'

Doctor Stavros hesitated. 'I may be unable to help your daughter, but I'm sure you could help me. I am trying to compile a list of all the people living in the village. Would you be able to tell me the names of your neighbours and possibly some of the other residents?'

Despina shrugged. 'You'd better sit down. I've lived here all my life so I know most people '

It was more than two hours later that Doctor Stavros walked on down the road to the taverna. Once again he had to explain who he was and then asked if it was possible for him to get a meal of any sort in the establishment.

'We don't have much call here for food. I'll see if my wife has anything suitable.' Manolis opened the door at the back and called to Anastasia. He turned back to the doctor. 'She says she could cook you up a few sausages.'

'I'll be happy with that. Whilst I wait could I have a glass of wine?'

Manolis poured a glass and pushed it across the counter. 'So why are you in our village? I've not heard of anyone who's sick.'

'I've left my donkey at the forge. She needs new shoes. Whilst I wait I might as well have something to eat. I'd also like to arrange to have a room here occasionally where I can spend the night. Kastelli will be one of the villages I pass through regularly on my way to some that are further out. If I am delayed I may not be able to return to Aghios Nikolaos the same day.'

'You'd have to have a corner in our living room.'

'I'm sure that would be suitable for a night.' Doctor Stavros did not relish sharing a room where he would be in close proximity to the other occupants. 'I'd like to become familiar with the people who live here in the village. I understand your name is Manolis. I believe there is another man in the village of the same name.'

'Used to be.'

'Is he no longer living here?'

'Died a couple of years back. He kept bees. His nephew has taken over collecting the honey now.'

Doctor Stavros nodded. This was the information that Despina had given him, but it had been as well to check her veracity.

'Do you have any family?'

'Not now. They moved away.'

'Where did they go?'

Manolis looked at the doctor suspiciously. 'What's it to do with you?'

'Nothing. I was just making conversation.'

'How many sausages do you want?'

'Three would be sufficient.' Doctor Stavros realised that he was not going to elicit any information about the man's daughter who had been accused of injuring Eleni. He lapsed into silence as he drank his wine. Before he returned to Aghios Nikolaos he would call on the village priest and see if he was able to glean more information from him.

The elderly priest shook his head at the enquiry. 'I know Eleni and her family, of course, but I cannot give you any information about the youngsters who were taken away. I've only been in this village for five years. I took over from Father Elias after he died.'

Doctor Stavros consulted a notebook. The name of the priest was there and beside it was written the word "died". There was no indication of his illness or the date of his death but if the current priest was to be believed it had to be at least five years earlier.

'Are you able to tell me the date you arrived here?'

The priest frowned. 'Not exactly. It was a few weeks before Easter.'

Doctor Stavros nodded. 'So if you have been here for five years that would mean you arrived in nineteen twenty six.'

'That sounds about right.' The priest smiled. 'There was so much that needed to be put in order that I took little notice of when I actually arrived. I understood that Father Elias had died suddenly and I was sent here to conduct the burial service and ensure all was in order for the next incumbent. Then the Bishop decided I might as well fill the vacant position, so here I am.'

Doctor Stavros realised he was not going to receive any useful information about the taverna owner's grandchildren. He would speak to Doctor Kandakis when the opportunity arose and see if he could find out more. It was possible that they had been found free from disease and had been sent back to their parents.

Doctor Stavros sat at his table and scrutinized the list of people who had been found hiding out in shepherds' huts or caves and sent to Spinalonga. Without a date for their arrival or the name of the village where they had been found it was going to be an impossible job to bring the records up to date. He cursed Doctor Kandakis for his inefficiency and laziness.

Before he went to the expense of purchasing yet more new notebooks he would call on Doctor Kandakis again and ask if he had any further information about his patients who lived in the villages or on Spinalonga. He would also take the opportunity to ask about the brother and sister who had been removed from Kastelli.

Doctor Kandakis opened his door to him and frowned. 'If you've come to complain about the donkey I don't want to know. You bought her and that's the end of the matter.'

'I've not come about the donkey. I wanted to ask if you had any more notebooks relating to the health of the villagers.'

'I gave you all I had.'

Doctor Stavros nodded. 'I thought that was the case. The most recent entries; can you tell me if they relate to the last few months or the previous year?'

Doctor Kandakis shook his head. 'I'd need to see the patient to remember when I last saw them.'

'Quite. I understand.' Doctor Stavros did not believe the claim that the man's memory would be so good. It was just a further excuse for his laziness to record his visits accurately. 'There is one more thing I would like to ask whilst I'm here. Do you remember a brother and sister who were found up in the hills behind Kastelli?'

Doctor Kandakis shrugged. 'Vaguely.'

'Were they brought to you for a diagnosis?'

'I expect so.'

'Can you recall if they had leprosy?'

'Bound to have. No reason to hide away otherwise.'

'Do you know what happened to them?'

'They would have been sent to the island to join the others.'

'Do you remember their names?'

Doctor Kandakis shook his head. 'They were just two more trying to evade the authorities. I would have got rid of them as quickly as possible. Couldn't risk them infecting me or my premises. I always had a boat standing by to receive them or the men who had collected them would have kept them locked in an outhouse over night and they would have been shipped out the next morning.'

'I believe there may have been some trouble in the village after they were taken away.'

Doctor Kandakis shrugged. 'The villagers may have turned the relatives out of the area. Nothing to do with me.'

'I was thinking of an assault that took place on the woman who reported the youngsters to you.'

'As I said, problems between the villagers is not my business.'

'Even if the woman had been rendered unconscious by the attack?'

'There's nothing you can do if someone is unconscious except wait for them to come round again. No point in visiting.'

'I saw the woman when I was in the village last week. She is an imbecile and being cared for by her mother.'

Doctor Kandakis shrugged. 'No amount of visits or medication from me would have made any difference to her condition. I understand she has been like that for some years now. Now, if there's nothing more I can do for you I really would like to return to my meal. It will be getting cold.'

Doctor Stavros turned away. He had not really expected to glean any information from the doctor, but at least he had tried.

It had been necessary to call at every house in all the villages to enquire about the current occupants and if he received no answer to his knock he visited the general store or taverna to ask where people lived. He was given directions to a number of houses where the occupant had the same baptismal name as the one he had mentioned until he was finally able to feel certain he had found the person listed by Doctor Kandakis. One woman in Shisma looked at him in amazement.

'Didn't you know? My mother in law, Maria, died some years ago.'

Doctor Stavros was embarrassed. 'I am sorry. I only have the list that Doctor Kandakis gave me and he mentioned visiting Maria in this village. Would there be another Maria?'

'At least five other women here share that name.'

'I have located three. Would you be able to tell me where I might find the other two?'

'They're probably in the fields. I believe Yiorgo is at home and his wife is called Maria.'

When Doctor Stavros knocked at the door of the third cottage the door was opened by a young man clutching his arm. He confirmed that his wife's name was Maria, but there was nothing ailing her.

'As you're here would you be able to take a look at my arm?'

'What's wrong with it?'

'If I knew that I wouldn't be asking you,' was the surly reply.

'Take off your shirt. How did you hurt it?'

'Replacing a tile on a roof. The dog chased a cat and ran into the ladder. I ended up on the ground with the ladder and tile on top of me.'

Doctor Stavros looked at the purple bruise that covered the man's upper arm and side. 'Can you lift your arm above your head?'

The man grunted in pain as he tried and Doctor Stavros felt his collar bone. 'I can't make a definite diagnosis without you going to the hospital and having an X-ray but I think you have dislocated your shoulder. I don't think you've broken your collar bone. Do you hurt anywhere else?'

'When I breathe.'

'You have badly bruised ribs. One or more could be cracked.'

'What can you do for me?'

'Very little, I'm afraid. I can try to manipulate your shoulder back into place. If that doesn't work then you will certainly need to go to the hospital.'

'I've no time to go travelling to hospitals.'

Doctor Stavros shrugged. 'It will be painful,' he warned him.

The man nodded and Doctor Stavros placed his hands on the man's shoulder. He pushed one way and pulled the other. The man howled with pain and there was a loud click.

'That should have done it. I'll make you a sling so it is more comfortable and you must rest it for at least a week. If it is still painful at the end of that time then you should visit the hospital. Your ribs I can do nothing about. They will take time to heal if one is cracked, but provided you don't try lifting anything heavy the pain should lessen in a week or so. I'll call on you again when I'm next in the village. Tell me your name so I know who to ask for.'

'I'm Yiorgo.'

'Yiorgo who?'

'Yiorgo the roofer.'

Doctor Stavros made a note in his book. This could explain why the people were only listed by their baptismal name by Doctor

Kandakis. It was going to take him a considerable amount of time to have a comprehensive list of his patients.

He spent most of the morning in Shisma before he was able to travel on to Hamilo and repeat the process. By the time he had spoken to most of the inhabitants of Flamouriana it was too late to consider travelling on to Fioretzides and he rode his donkey wearily back to Aghios Nikolaos. The evening would be spent checking the names he had gleaned against those recorded in Doctor Kandakis's notebooks. If there was no one of that name still residing in the village it was more than likely they had died but he would have to speak to the villagers again to ensure that his assumption was correct.

When he arrived in Fioretzides the following day he saw a priest walking along the road and immediately stopped, introduced himself and asked the priest for his help. Sitting at a taverna with a glass of wine Father Vassilis was able to inform the doctor of the names of those who had died during the previous few years.

The priest was also willing to accompany him to visit the inhabitants of the village and the doctor then added them to his ever growing list. One elderly woman was suffering from a chest complaint and Doctor Stavros was able to reassure her daughter that giving her nourishing food and keeping her warm was the best way to effect a cure.

'Provided she is out of any draughts it will not hurt her to sit outside in the sunshine for an hour or two each day. Make sure she is well wrapped up and not in direct sunlight.'

'Will she be well enough to go to church on Sunday?'

'I see no reason why she shouldn't. I'm sure the priest will be pleased to see her there.'

Father Vassilis nodded agreement. Many of the villagers called in on a Sunday, said a quick prayer and returned to their work. To have another person sitting in the church and listening to his sermon would be a bonus. Before Doctor Stavros left Fioretzides he asked the priest to inform his parishioners that he would be calling regularly and anyone who needed his attention should leave his name at the church.

1932

Each time Doctor Stavros visited Spinalonga he observed the rudimentary treatment that was given to the sufferers, his own ministrations being little better due to lack of essential medicinal supplies. When he returned he wrote to the government again, becoming exasperated at their lack of response.

Taking his letter from the government that declared him responsible for the island he approached the hospital in Aghios Nikolaos and asked for medical supplies. The Matron shook her head.

'I have very little here. We only hold small quantities of medication for emergencies. Serious cases are transported to the hospital in Heraklion for treatment. I can place an order on your behalf but I have no idea how long it will be before anything is sent. I'm waiting for more cases of bandages. The priest took most of my supplies.'

'Who is this priest? Which church does he come from?'

'I believe he said his name was Father Minos, but he's not a local priest.'

'I'll be grateful for anything that you can spare me that cleanses or disinfects.'

'I have no disinfectant, but I can let you have some methylated spirit.'

'Thank you, that will be better than nothing.'

'I'll try to give you some supplies each week provided I can spare them. Come along and check with the caretaker.'

'I need to find that priest,' thought Doctor Stavros. 'He obviously has the ear of someone in the government if he was able to send a crate of bandages over.' The doctor slapped his knee; why hadn't he gone to the church and made enquiries there? He also needed to ask about the building materials that were being sent over. Was the priest expecting them to be used to build a church? It was too late in the afternoon to go the church now, but he would walk down to the port and speak to Manolis. It was possible he knew the priest's whereabouts.

There was no sign of Manolis in the harbour and he scanned the horizon. There were a number of small boats returning from their fishing trips, but too far away to discern the occupant. Two priests walked past, also looking out to sea. The younger of the two men shook his head and began to walk back towards the town whilst the older one sat on the harbour wall.

Doctor Stavros had overheard their conversation and decided to approach the priest. 'Would you be Father Minos?'

The priest nodded and Doctor Stavros smiled in relief. 'Are you waiting for Manolis, the young boat man?'

'I'm hoping he will be able to take me to Spinalonga with him tomorrow.'

Doctor Stavros held out his hand. 'I am so pleased to meet you. When you have made your arrangements with young Manolis would I be imposing on your time if I asked you to return to my house so we could talk? I have been asked to take over medical responsibility for the island.'

A broad smile spread across Father Minos's face. 'Believe it or not you are just the man I need to talk with.'

When Father Minos and Andreas landed on Spinalonga they were surprised that Flora was not sitting in her usual spot on the jetty. They walked up towards the main square and people began to call that Yannis was mixing cement a short way further up. They stood and waited until he had finished mixing and supervising the application of the rendering to the house.

'Come and see the other house we're working on and then you should visit Panicos. He's improved considerably since he's been having goat milk regularly.'

Dutifully they followed Yannis and whilst Father Minos was speaking to Panicos he took the opportunity of asking Andreas about his family.

'Your mother is much the same. Anna is wonderful with her.'

'And how is Babbis managing with a baby along with his little daughter? It must be hard for him. He loved Maria so much. I imagine his mother is mainly looking after them.'

'No, Anna has the baby living with her. Babbis said it would be too much for his mother. I think he blames the poor baby for the death of Maria and does not want to see him continually. It will take him some time to accept what has happened.'

'Poor Babbis and poor Anna. She must have enough to do with looking after our mother and running the house.'

'It will be easier for her when Stelios goes to school in Aghios Nikolaos. He's going to live with my parents, the same as you did. By the way, where is Flora? Manolis seemed surprised that she wasn't on the jetty. Has she given up asking for supplies now you have everything sent over?'

Yannis shook his head. 'She's very sick. Spiro is with her. The infection in her arm spread suddenly. We'll go up and ask him if she's showing any sign pf improvement.'

'The doctor. He could have some medicine for her. Why don't we ask Manolis to go over to the mainland and fetch him?'

'He's probably gone fishing by now.'

'I'll go and see.' Andreas ran down to the jetty where Manolis still had his boat moored, hoping that Flora would put in an appearance. He could see a small pile of stones that she had gathered in readiness for her counting lesson.

'Manolis, we need the doctor. You must get him. Tell him it's urgent.'

Manolis raised his hand in acknowledgement as he cast off and Andreas walked slowly back to the house where the sick girl lay.

'I'll bring you some fresh water,' said Phaedra.

Father Minos nodded and knelt down beside Flora, Andreas joining him. Yannis crossed himself and accompanied Phaedra down to the square.

'You know where I am if I'm wanted. I may as well continue down here as there's nothing I can do to help Flora.'

'I'll go up on the headland and look for Manolis. I'll call you when I see him return.'

It seemed a considerable time before Phaedra saw a boat coming and scrambled back down the hillside. As soon as she called to Yannis he handed his trowel over to a companion and hurried down to the quay. As they arrived Doctor Stavros was scrambling ashore.

'Who's my patient?' he called.

'Flora. Spiro says she's developed gangrene.'

'Flora! Why didn't you tell me?' Manolis finished mooring his boat and jumped ashore. 'Where is she?'

'You can't go to her,' Yannis warned him. 'You're not supposed to set foot on the island. She'll be alright now the doctor is here.'

'I'll take you,' said Phaedra. She pushed her way through the men and Manolis followed her gratefully.

'Tell me more about her,' said Doctor Stavros as he lifted his box containing the medication he had been able to procure from the hospital. 'She's the little girl who's always on the jetty, isn't she?'

Yannis nodded. 'Her arm's been getting steadily worse, then her temperature shot up a couple of days ago and this morning she was delirious.'

'You're sure it's gangrene?'

Yannis nodded. 'We all know the smell.'

'Why wasn't I asked to look at her arm before?'

'She seemed alright and never complained.' Yannis pointed to the house Flora shared with Phaedra. 'She's in there. Spiro's with her.'

'I expect Manolis is also with her by now,' observed the doctor as he removed his jacket and rolled up his sleeves. Spiro made way for the doctor beside Flora's mattress and continued to mop her forehead whilst the doctor unwrapped the bandage that was wound around her arm.

'It's too dark in here for me to see properly,' complained Doctor Stavros. 'You'll have to bring her outside.'

Yannis, Spiro and Manolis manoeuvred the mattress through the doorway and laid it on the ground outside. Doctor Stavros looked at Flora's arm. The blackness of the dead flesh had spread above her elbow and down to her wrist where the discolouration gave way to a greenish bruising streaked with red.

Doctor Stavros looked around helplessly. He had never been confronted with a situation like this. Amputation was the only answer and he was not sure if the girl was strong enough to survive such drastic surgery under such primitive conditions.

'I'll need hot water, plenty of it.'

'I'll get Ritsa to help me. It will take some time.'

Doctor Stavros opened the box he had collected from the hospital. There was insufficient morphine for the operation and the poor girl was going to suffer. He looked at the concerned faces watching him. 'Go and wash,' he ordered Yannis, Spiro and Andreas. 'I'll need some help.'

Already there were a small group of people gathering and the doctor turned to Father Minos. 'Take the people away from here and conduct a service; make sure Manolis is with you.'

Phaedra and Ritsa returned with more hot water and once the doctor declared there was sufficient they moved away; neither had any inclination to watch the operation taking place.

Doctor Stavros worked as speedily as possible, but by the

time he had severed the bone and had to remove the remainder of the decayed flesh the morphine had run out. 'Hold her tight,' he ordered and Andreas lay across her legs whilst Yannis pinned her shoulders to the ground and Spiro held her head. Flora screamed. Each time the doctor cut into her flesh her screams became louder and more anguished. Phaedra covered her ears and shuddered at the sound. Finally Flora's screams lessened, becoming sobs and moans until her amputated arm was finally bandaged and the doctor stood up.

'I've done my best,' Doctor Stavros said wearily as he rose from his knees. 'Phaedra, can you give her a wash and then we'll take her back inside the house.'

Phaedra sat beside Flora almost continually, giving her sips of water and holding her hand. At times Spiro would come and take her place and Ritsa had assured Phaedra that they could manage without her help when preparing and cooking a meal. Every day Manolis would sneak onto the island and walk openly up to Flora's house to see if she was recovering.

'She isn't running a temperature,' Phaedra assured him. 'Her arm doesn't feel hot to the touch, but more than that I cannot say. You'll have to ask Doctor Stavros.'

Manolis would sit in the little house for the remainder of the morning, holding Flora's hand and talking to her quietly whilst Phaedra took the opportunity to visit the storeroom and see what food there was that she could prepare for Flora that would be no effort for her to swallow.

When Doctor Stavros visited he declared himself pleased with Flora's progress and he was relieved that the amputation he had accomplished, under somewhat difficult and unorthodox circumstances, had been successful. Provided the girl did not develop an infection in her wound there should be no reason why she should not make a full recovery.

Once Flora regained full consciousness she complained that her arm hurt, but she still did not appear to realise that part of it was missing. Manolis continued to visit her, bringing her a small present each time and when he arrived with a bunch of wild flowers she was delighted and Manolis promised rashly to bring her flowers every week.

Spiro would call in each day to check on her progress, but he and Yannis had persuaded the men to help rebuild the old hospital before the winter set in. At first the men had appeared dubious and unwilling until Takkis had stepped forward, declared himself a builder, and offered to supervise the necessary work in exchange for a house of his own.

Father Minos had been haunted by his first visit to Spinalonga when he found Yannis living there and the destitute situation of all the occupants. He had visited Yannis's father and to his surprise the man had produced a considerable sum of money that he wanted spent to benefit everyone; Andreas's father had done likewise and Father Minos had used the money sparingly and wisely. He had purchased the necessary tools, sand, cement that was needed to repair the houses and give the occupants somewhere reasonably decent to live, along with new mattresses, blankets and clean bandages.

He did not feel he had done sufficient and approached the Church Authorities requesting permission to go to Spinalonga and live there himself. At first his application was refused, he was told he could visit, but it was not practical for him to live on the island.

Father Minos had visited the taverna where Yannis had lodged whilst in Heraklion earlier. His father had paid Yannis's expenses for the complete year, but when the boy left abruptly no money had been returned to his father. When Father Minos requested the repayment he was met with excuses by the girl who ran the establishment who claimed the money was rightfully hers as she was bringing up Yannis's daughter. The priest was not sure he believed her and when he mentioned the child Yannis claimed that her father was Yiorgo Pavlakis, the school teacher Louisa had married, and who was now a politician.

Father Minos approached Yiorgo Pavlakis hoping the politician would support his request to live on the island and be able to use his influence with the government. The man had been shocked to hear that Yannis, his former pupil, was now living on Spinalonga. Father Minos explained that he was trying to trace any money owing to the islanders from when they had entered the hospital in Heraklion and Pavlakis agreed to make some enquiries although he was doubtful that he would have any success. The hospital would no doubt claim that the money had been used to cover the expenses of their patients, and asked if a small extra allowance for Father Minos would be a help to purchase some luxuries for the islanders. Father Minos impressed upon the politician that he was not asking for anything for himself and it was necessities that the islanders needed, not luxuries.

Yiorgo Pavlakis considered the conversation he had had with the priest. There was an election in six months time and he very much wanted to be in charge of the prefecture. If he could present himself as a philanthropist the people were likely to vote in his favour. After careful deliberation on his part he slipped a note into the box beside Father Minos's door announcing that he would call that evening.

Hoping Pavlakis had managed to find money at the hospital that was owed to the former in patients Father Minos greeted him in eager anticipation. His hopes of financial help were dashed when Yiorgo Pavlakis declared that he needed information about the occupants of the island that he could put before the government and ask for their assistance in bringing the idea to fruition.

'Something that will always be remembered as having been donated by you?' Father Minos raised his eyebrows.

'Not at all,' Pavlakis hastened to assure him. 'I am talking about something that will be of benefit to all of them for ever more.'

'So many items come to mind. If you visited the island with

me you could then assess for yourself the conditions and decide on an item the government would consider most acceptable.'

Yiorgo Pavlakis hesitated. He had no wish to go to the island. 'I have a wife and daughter to consider.'

'Having spent a considerable amount of time in the company of Yannis I do not think there would be any great risk in visiting him on the island. You will not be expected to meet the people in their homes. A visit from you, a representative of the government, would make the people realise that they had not been forgotten by the authorities. It would have the added bonus of raising your esteem in the eyes of the local people as a man who cared about his fellows and could talk about their suffering with first hand experience.' Father Minos smiled at the man's discomfiture. 'Shall we make a definite date?'

When the day of the proposed visit arrived the day was overcast with rain in the air. By the time they arrived in Aghios Nikolaos it was raining steadily and a strong wind blowing. Yiorgo Pavlakis hoped it would be too rough to make the crossing and the priest would be willing to return to Heraklion.

Father Minos ignored the inclement weather and went from boat to boat looking for Manolis who he finally found playing cards with some companions. Manolis was more than willing to take them to Spinalonga and suggested they took the journey through the canal.

'It will not be so rough if we stay close to the shore and once we are through the canal and into the bay there will be no problem.' He flashed a confident smile at Yiorgo Pavlakis. 'You have no need to be concerned.'

As they arrived the island looked deserted and Father Minos led the way up the ramp to the main pathway. Once there he stood and called loudly and Ritsa appeared.

'I've brought a visitor for Yannis. Do you know where he is?'

'In his house I expect like everyone else on a day like this. You know your way, don't you?'

Father Minos nodded and Ritsa retreated back into the shelter of the house where she lived.

Seated on the mattress in Yannis's house Pavlakis began to explain that he wished to persuade the government to provide something of permanent benefit for everyone. Spiro listened to the proposals put forth by both Yannis and Pavlakis, Yannis wanted visits from his relatives and friends, but Pavlakis shook his head and said such an idea would not be acceptable. Books, paper and pencils appeared to be out of the question; not everyone could read or write.

'We could at least write to our relatives,' persisted Yannis. 'We could always write a letter for someone who was unable to write it for themselves.'

Spiro shook his head. 'That's not practical, Yannis. The letters would have to be taken ashore and posted. Who is going to pay for that? Some people may no longer have any relatives and others will have moved away from their original village due to the stigma attached to them.'

'New clothes, then?'

This time Yannis shook his head at the idea. 'We're all different sizes. We would never receive clothes that fitted all of us.'

'We could ask a boatman to buy them for us on the mainland,' suggested Spiro.

'Where would we get the money to buy them with? You know what it's like to get money back from the government.'

'Money.' Pavlakis suddenly seemed enthused by the idea. 'I'll ask the government for a sum of money for everyone.'

Yannis smiled derisively. 'Assuming the government agreed how much would they give us? Five drachmas each? That wouldn't last very long.'

'No, I'm talking about a small; regular amount every month that you could spend or save as you wished.'

'It sounds good,' said Yannis after he had considered the idea. 'How would you go about it?'

'I don't know,' admitted Yiorgo Pavlakis. 'I'll have to give it some thought and work out the details; I'll need to know exactly how many of you are living here.'

'We can start compiling a list. Let us know when you want it and we can send it with Manolis.'

'I can't promise anything,' Pavlakis warned them. 'I will do my best.' He stood up. 'I really think we should go. I don't want to be out on the sea when it's dark.'

'I'll find Manolis and tell him you are ready. I can show you the house I want to have as my own eventually.'

Yiorgo Pavlakis nodded. He was eager to leave the island and he was not interested in viewing the house Yannis had in mind to renovate for himself.

Having waved Yiorgo Pavlakis away Yannis turned to find Phaedra waiting by the steps for him. 'Who was that man?' she asked curiously.

'He was my old school teacher and when I went to Heraklion we shared a lodging. We were good friends then, but he doesn't seem interested in anything except politics now. He even seemed disinterested when I asked after his wife and child.'

'So what did he want?'

'I'm not sure. He said he wanted to help us, but I felt there was something he was not telling me.' Yannis placed his arm around Phaedra and gave her a squeeze. 'I used to think that one day I would be able to return to Heraklion and continue my studies and everything would be just as I remembered. Now I know it wouldn't be and I'm not sure I would want to return.'

Yannis read the letter from Yiorgo Pavlakis and frowned at the contents. 'I'm not prepared to give him all the information he asks for. He wants to know our names, ages, where we lived and the names of our relatives. It's a trick to enable the government to persecute our families.' Angrily Yannis tore the letter in half and threw it on the ground where Spiro picked up the pieces. 'I'm going for a walk.'

Yannis walked along the main pathway until he reached the

area where he stood each day looking for Anna to wave to him. He gazed sadly across to the farmhouse which had been his childhood home.

'What's wrong, Yannis?' Phaedra slipped her hand into his and looked at him in concern.

'I had a letter from that schoolmaster friend of mine. He's a politician now and wants to persuade the government to give us some money.'

'What would we do with it? asked Phaedra.

'We could buy whatever we wanted. If people on the mainland were willing to send goods out to us we could pay them.'

'You mean new things? Not the bundles of old clothes that arrive now? That would be wonderful.'

Yannis shook his head. 'In return he wants to know the name of everyone living here and also where their families live. That would mean the government could track them down and the whole village would know if a neighbour's relative was living over here. They could be driven out of the village.'

'Do you have to tell him? Suppose families have moved on and people don't know where they are living now? Why don't you speak to Orestis and ask his opinion. He was a lawyer before he came here so he might well be able to help.'

'Phaedra, you're wonderful. You always seem to know what to do.'

When Yiorgo Pavlakis received the reply to his letter that Orestis had compiled he was not amused. Orestis had pointed out that much of the information that had been requested was irrelevant and the only information the politician needed was the name of each islander. Pavlakis replied that he was willing to waive all the questions regarding relatives and former places of residence but a full list of the occupants of the island was essential.

When Doctor Stavros heard that a full list of the inhabitants of Spinalonga had to be made he was delighted. He walked up to Orestis's house and asked how he was going to complete the request made by the government.

'I'm going to sit outside and the people who are able will come up to me and give me their name. Once all the able bodied have seen me I'll visit the others.'

'Suppose some people refuse?'

'Then they won't be included in the list and won't be eligible to receive a pension.'

'And if someone comes a second time?'

Orestis chuckled. 'I know most of the people. If I think they are trying to cheat I'll tell them that Father Minos is going to check the lists. They respect the priest. They wouldn't lie to him.'

'Will you make a copy of the list before it is sent?'

'Of course. I don't want them to claim that it has been lost and I have to start all over again.'

'May I also have a copy?' asked Doctor Stavros eagerly. 'I only have the names of the people who were sent here from the local area. It would be helpful for me to have a list of everyone who lives here now; those sent from the other islands and mainland Greece.'

'Provided you are willing to copy it out. It will be a tedious job.'

Doctor Stavros nodded. He would certainly not have time to sit and copy the list of names and wondered if he could prevail on someone else to undertake the onerous task.

Doctor Stavros was pleased when Yannis finally handed him a copy of the list Orestis had made of the occupants of Spinalonga.

'It made a change from mixing cement. I quite enjoyed it,' smiled Yannis.

'This will be invaluable to me. I see Orestis listed the family name as well as the person's baptismal name.'

'It's as accurate as possible. The spelling may be incorrect as many of those over here can't read or write. Can you send the list Orestis has made on to Yiorgo Pavlakis for us?'

'Certainly. Would you be willing to undertake a further task for me?' asked Doctor Stavros.

Yannis eyed the doctor warily. 'That would depend upon what you wanted.'

'Doctor Kandakis only listed the villagers on the mainland by their baptismal names. I'm gradually getting my records updated but there are some people that I'm finding it impossible to trace. I think this could be because they have been sent over here and their relatives refuse to be associated with them. If you could ask everyone where they lived originally I might finally be able to get all my records up to date.'

Yannis shook his head. 'You have to remember that a number of people have been sent here from the hospitals. They could have lived anywhere on mainland Greece or one of the islands, not just Crete.'

'I realise that some of the information would be no use to me, but you came from the hospital although you had lived in Plaka.'

'If you found out where other people had lived would this mean you would want their families to be tested? The whole area would know.' Yannis shook his head. 'I couldn't be responsible for the authorities carrying out a witch hunt.'

'I certainly don't have that in mind. The information would be confidential to me. At the moment I have thirty five men named Mikaelis listed as living here and there are numerous entries of men with that name in the notebooks from Doctor Kandakis as living in the villages. At the moment I don't know if it is the same person he treated on a number of occasions or if the patient was sent here.'

'So how would it help if you knew where they came from?'

'If they had lived locally I could visit the village and check how many people with that name were still living there. If there is a discrepancy that cannot be accounted for it would be a fair assumption that they were over here and I could then check where someone of the same name had lived previously.'

Yannis frowned. 'Not everyone would be willing to disclose where they had come from if they knew I was passing the information on to you.'

'You don't have to tell them why you want to know. Just ask them whilst making general conversation. I ask them when I examine them and they have had no hesitation in telling me the name of their village, but I never have the time to speak to everyone whilst I'm over here.'

'I suppose I can try,' agreed Yannis reluctantly.

Doctor Stavros had finally managed to complete a comprehensive list of the people who lived in each of the villages that he was expected to visit. He checked them against the original list that Doctor Kandakis had given to him and made a note of any of the names that he did not have. He would have to ask if the person had moved away or subsequently died.

He now needed to turn his attention to the occupants of Spinalonga. The notes Doctor Kandakis had given him were useless. Having received a copy of the list of inhabitants that Orestis had sent to the government in Heraklion he had completely abandoned his original plan of working from Doctor Kandakis's notes and made some new notebooks for himself in which he recorded the date he had examined or treated a patient and the subsequent outcome.

The lists that Yannis had presented him with were helpful and he would have to find time to speak to the many Anna's, Maria's, Yiorgo's and Yannis's who were listed and ask if they had been diagnosed by Doctor Kandakis and if so the name of the village where they had lived. This could enable him to remove a number of people from the list of villagers that he was unable to trace at present.

He had been able to ascertain details of those, like Yannis, who had been sent from the hospital in Athens and also the people who had arrived on the island since. It was those who had been sent there when it first became a leper colony that he had scant and often conflicting details.

When he asked about various people he was told they had died, but he had no way of knowing for certain which of the twenty or more women named Anna or Maria that referred to. Ariadne thought she had spent eight or nine winters on the island, and Flora insisted that the old lady had been there when she arrived and Phaedra confirmed that she had also stayed in Ariadne's house upon her arrival. That would mean that Ariadne had been living there for at least ten years. Ritsa claimed to have arrived at virtually the same time which was why they were close friends.

The doctor leafed through Doctor Kandakis's notes on Spinalonga and finally found a brief reference to a woman named Ariadne who had given birth to a child that had subsequently been removed and sent to an orphanage on the mainland. Was this the same Ariadne as was living there now? Would Ariadne have confided in Ritsa and been comforted by her? The information about the child was irrelevant to him, but it could enable him to remove one of the three women named Ariadne from his outstanding list of untraceable villagers.

Now the inhabitants of Spinalonga had revealed where they had lived before being sent to the island Doctor Stavros was gradually able to cross someone off from Doctor Kandakis's list of villagers. At present he was searching for woman a named Maria who claimed she had lived in Lakkonia or close by. She thought her family name was Kortinis and this was the one she had given to Orestis, but it could quite well have been Kortakis or Kasatakis.

On a subsequent visit to Lakkonia he decided to ask if there was anyone of that name still in the village. A woman was sitting outside her door slicing beans whilst watching a small girl playing and he decided to approach her.

'Excuse me. May I ask you a question?'

'Certainly, Doctor. I'm only too happy to help you if I can. Is it a drink that you would like?'

'No, I'm enquiring about a woman called Maria Kortinis who may still live in the village.'

The woman shook her head. 'My mother in law was named Maria. She's been dead for years now. My little girl is named after her. There are two other women called Maria. Maybe it is one of them that you wish to speak with.'

Doctor Stavros consulted his notebook. 'I may have the family name incorrect. Do you know of a family called Kortakis or Kasatakis.'

Again the woman shook her head. 'My name, since I married, has been Kastanakis. Are you sure that isn't the name of the person you are looking for?'

'It's possible. Where can I find your husband so I can check his mother's name with him?'

The woman smiled in amusement. 'You'd do better to return this evening. He's somewhere down in the valley with the goats.'

Doctor Stavros nodded. 'I'll call on you on my return journey. I have no wish to go chasing a herd of goats.'

The doctor rode on, feeling convinced he had found the woman he was looking for. Provided the man was prepared to be honest with him when he returned it could be another name accounted for and crossed off his list.

'Maybe we could talk outside,' said Nikos with a wary glance over his shoulder. His wife had told him that the doctor wanted to check his mother's family name. 'Litsa is washing our daughter before serving up our meal.'

'Certainly. I'll not keep you long. I am enquiring about a lady whose name is Maria. I understand your mother had that name and lived in this village.'

Nikos nodded.' She died a long time ago now.'

Doctor Stavros cleared his throat. 'I have to ask you a very delicate question and no offence is intended. Is there a possibility that your mother was sent to a leprosarium?'

Nikos swallowed and seemed at a loss for words. 'What makes you think that?' he asked gruffly.

'I am also the doctor for the island of Spinalonga which is a leprosarium. Doctor Kandakis left very incomplete records of the patients both there and in the villages. I have a number of people I cannot account for and I believe their name may have been entered on the list for Spinalonga, but never removed from the list of villagers. Any information you are able to help me with will be entirely confidential.'

'You'll not tell my wife?'

'Certainly not. I only wish to have the information correct in my records.'

Nikos sniffed and seemed to be holding back his tears. 'She was admitted. My father said she had gone to another village to look after her invalid sister who had been widowed. The villagers asked after her for a while and then forgot her.'

'Thank you. I believe your mother was still trying to protect your good name when she told me three variations of her family name.'

'She's alive?' Nikos looked at the doctor in amazement.

'I regret to say that she is very sick as the infection has spread, but she is happy and cheerful. Would you like me to take her a message from you?'

'I light a candle and say a prayer for her every Sunday when we go to church.' Nikos looked at Doctor Stavros with misty eyes. 'Could you tell her that? I'd like her to know that I've not forgotten her and still love her dearly.'

'Certainly. I'm sure those words will comfort her more than any medicine I could give her.' Doctor Stavros held out his hand. 'I am truly grateful for your help.'

Doctor Stavros was encouraged by his success in finding Maria Kasatanakis's son. He would certainly try to trace some of the other relatives of those who lived on Spinalonga and had come from the villages he visited regularly.

The next time the doctor visited Spinalonga he went looking for Flora. Each week he checked her arm to ensure that no infection had started. He was surprised that she was not sitting on the jetty waiting for Manolis and finally found her down by the tunnel. The doctor unwrapped her arm and was pleased to see that it was healing well. He took the pin he always carried in his lapel and instructed her to look away as he touched her arm above the amputation and then her right hand lightly with the sharp point. Each time Flora reacted to the prick he gave her.

'I'm very pleased with you Flora. I'd like to have a quick look at your feet. Have you noticed any signs anywhere on your body?'

Flora shook her head. 'Nothing.'

Doctor Stavros nodded. 'I'll make time to give you a complete examination the next time I come over,' he promised. 'Whilst I'm here can I check something else with you?'

Flora eyed him warily.

'Have you any idea how long you have lived on Spinalonga?'

Flora shook her head. 'I've been here for a long time now.'

'Which village did you come from?'

'Vrouhas.'

'Were you found living on the hills?'

'No, I was in the shed outside the house. My father took me to the doctor.'

'Does he know you are here?'

Flora shrugged. 'I don't know. The doctor may have told him when he visited the village.'

Doctor Stavros entered the details into his notebook. When he next visited Vrouhas he would see if he could locate the girl's father. If the man was receptive he could at least tell him that his daughter was alive and well, despite her amputation.

Flora stayed where she was; every so often a tear would trickle down her face and as fast as she brushed it away another appeared. Phaedra found her still sitting there when she arrived at the fountain for some water.

'What's wrong, Flora? Manolis was asking where you were. He wanted to talk to you.'

'I don't want to talk to him.'

'Why not? Is it your arm? Did the doctor give you bad news?'

Flora shook her head. 'He said my arm is looking good.'

'Then what is it? Manolis seemed very worried and miserable.'

'It doesn't matter how well my arm heals; I'm still a leper.'

'Manolis doesn't take any notice of our illness.'

'He has to. Talk to him Phaedra. Make him understand that we are contagious.'

'He knows that. You and Manolis were good friends. What has happened between you?'

'He wants to marry me.' Flora's voice was almost a whisper.

'Oh, Flora.' Automatically Phaedra placed her arms around the girl. 'Do you love him?'

'Of course I do. That's why I'm avoiding him. What would people on the mainland say if they knew? They'd drive him away and I'd never see him again.'

'Have you told Manolis how you feel?'

'I've tried, but he won't listen. Tell him to forget me, Phaedra and to find some nice girl on the mainland to marry who can be a proper wife to him and give him healthy children.' Flora turned her tear streaked face towards Phaedra. 'Promise me, Phaedra.'

Manolis was surprised when he saw Phaedra waiting on the jetty to greet him and the doctor. 'Where's Flora?' he asked.

'She's somewhere around.'

Manolis scowled as he unloaded the boxes he had brought and helped the doctor ashore. Phaedra waited until the doctor had walked up through the arch and then she turned to Manolis..

'Flora has asked me to talk to you. She says you take no notice of whatever she says. She keeps telling you that you must forget her and find a girl on the mainland.'

'Phaedra, I love Flora. I know she has leprosy and only one arm but that makes no difference to me. I'm not prepared to go looking for any other girl. I've spoken to the doctor and he said I'm no more likely to catch leprosy from Flora than I am by talking to you.' Manolis did not admit that the doctor had said that having an intimate relationship with Flora could well increase his chances of developing the disease. 'If I catch it I will be able to come over here and live with you; until then I'll just come over every day and visit her.'

Phaedra shook her head helplessly and turned away. She had not expected Manolis to heed her words.

As soon as he had finished unloading Manolis walked up to Flora's house. She did not answer when he knocked on the door and he looked inside to see her cowering in a corner.

'Flora, please don't hide away from me. Come and sit down. I want to talk to you.'

'You mustn't come in, Manolis. You mustn't come near me.'

'Don't be silly, Flora. For the last two years I've visited you. When you were sick I held your hand and kissed your forehead. I haven't become sick and I have talked to Doctor Stavros. He says there is no more chance of me catching it from you than from anyone else on the island. I love you, Flora, and I want to marry you. Do you love me?'

Tears began to run down Flora's face and Manolis wiped them away with his fingers. 'Look, I've brought you a special present.' From his pocket he took an ornate gold cross inset with small purple and red glass stones.

Flora looked at the necklace in awe. 'Is that really for me?'

'Will you accept it in place of a wedding ring? It will be my promise to love you for ever.'

Flora turned the cross over and over in her hand. 'Does this mean we are properly married now?'

'As properly as possible. This is my promise to you, the same as if it was a wedding ring, but it will be our secret.'

Manolis took the cross from her and fastened the chain around her neck.

Yannis saw Father Minos arrive on the island and went to greet him, his pleasure turning to disbelief when the priest said he was now going to live permanently on the island.

'You can't. There's nowhere for you to live.'

'If I can store my belongings with you for a while it won't be any hardship to sleep outside. I'll take my turn and wait until a house is ready for me. I don't expect any special treatment.'

Yannis led the way up the hill to his tiny house. 'Put your belongings wherever you like. There's plenty of space now Spiro and Kyriakos are no longer here.'

'The hospital is finished then?'

'Takkis had it finished well before the worst of the weather last winter. Spiro insisted on moving up there to live. He says someone needs to be there in case of an emergency in the night. He persuaded Kyriakos to go into the hospital and I have to admit I was relieved. I don't enjoy tending to the sick the way Spiro seems to.'

'What was the outcome of Yiorgo Pavlakis's visit?'

'Pavlakis wrote and asked for a considerable amount of personal information which we refused to give him. Orestis replied and Pavlakis finally agreed that he only needed the names of everyone living over here. We've heard nothing since then.'

'Is that why you are so depressed?'

Yannis shrugged. 'Partly. I'm sick of living in this hovel. I was so proud of it when I first built it and now I hate it.'

'So repair one of the other houses and move there.'

'I made a promise to stay here until everyone was decently housed. I know which one I want eventually but it will take a lot of repair work.'

'I think part of your problem is that you are lonely.'

'I miss Spiro,' admitted Yannis.

Father Minos shook his head. 'It's more than just missing a friend. You should get married.'

'You're not allowed to get married if you're a leper,' answered Yannis bitterly.

'How many of the men and women who live together over here are legally married? None of them. No one condemns them for their commitment to each other.'

Yannis looked uncomfortable. 'Shall we go up to the hospital and tell Spiro that you're coming to live over here?'

Spiro looked at Father Minos in amazement. 'Is he really going to stay?' he asked as the priest began to make a round of the mattresses and speaking to the occupants.

'He's brought all his belongings and he's staying with me temporarily.'

'Good. He'll be company for you.'

'What makes you think I'm not happy living on my own?'

'You can't live like a monk for ever. Take a look around and see what's staring you in the face.'

Yannis frowned. This was the second time within an hour that his monastic existence had been criticised. 'How's it going up here?'

'Thranassis is failing fast. Ritsa sat with him last night; she was convinced he would go then. At least Father Minos is here now to give him the last rites. Do you think the Father will object to placing him in the tower?'

'There's no alternative. He knows that.'

'The man is mad to come here to live voluntarily, but he could be useful.'

'How do you mean?'

'He'll soon be bored living on an island with little to do and could be willing to help with the building. He could even encourage those who are too lazy to help themselves and expect to have a house provided for them. Once they see he is willing to do manual labour they could be shamed into joining him.'

Father Minos had no problem settling into a new life on the island. Each morning he would hold a short service for any who wished to join him and then he would change from his robes into a pair of old trousers and a shirt. He would find Yannis and ask where he could be of most use during the day, working alongside the other men to collect stones or hammer nails straight so they could be reused. To his surprise he was happy participating in the manual labour and fell into a deep and untroubled sleep each night.

The priest was elated when Manolis finally delivered a letter to him from Yiorgo Pavlakis saying that the government had agreed in principle to grant a pension to the inhabitants on the island.

'How much and when can we expect to receive it?'

Father Minos shook his head. 'He says the government have agreed to a sum of thirty drachmas a month for each person. You can read the letter for yourself. He doesn't give any details.'

Yannis read the brief letter and snorted in disgust. 'He says they need to discuss the details further and will let us know in due course when our pension will commence. That's just delaying tactics. They are relying on us all being dead within a few more years. We're never going to receive anything from them.'

'I plan to reply and urge them to make arrangements as rapidly as possible. I'll stress that you all need to purchase items that are not supplied by the medical authorities like new boots or cloaks. I'll have my letter ready for when Doctor Stavros visits next and ask him to post it on my behalf.'

'If you are allowed to write letters could you write one for me to go to my family?'

Father Minos shook his head. 'If I did that for you everyone would want me to write letters for them. I have permission to reply on this occasion, but I am bound by the same restrictions as everyone else. You can always ask Manolis to take a verbal message to your family as they are so close.'

1933

Yannis stood and looked across the expanse of water to the farm house where he had lived. It was not very far away. He had learnt how to swim close to the shore as a boy, but he certainly would not have the confidence or ability to swim across the bay.

He walked slowly down to the storeroom. Stacked in one corner were the wooden bath tubs that Doctor Stavros had insisted should be sent over so the people could fill them with heated rainwater and have a proper bath. Yannis examined one carefully. It was wooden and strapped together the same way as a barrel was constructed. Barrels held water and wine so they had to be water proof.

If the bath tubs did not let water penetrate into them they should be able to float on the sea without sinking. He knew he would be taking a risk. There were strong currents in the area and it would be no use asking Manolis about them as they often changed direction during the night. He would need help from Spiro and Takkis to take one of the heavy tubs down to the shore and hold it steady in the water whilst he climbed inside.

Yannis made his way back up to the walls of the Venetian fortress and looked across the bay to his home trying to assess exactly how long it would take him to float to the opposite shore.

'What is it that's troubling you, Yannis?' asked Phaedra as she suddenly appeared at his side.

'Just homesick. I'm trying to work out how long it would take to get from here to the mainland.'

'Yannis, no, you mustn't try to swim over. It's far too dangerous. You could be caught in the currents and swept out to sea or just find that you couldn't swim against the current and become exhausted. Please, Yannis, don't even consider it.' Phaedra looked at him fearfully, remembering how her brother had drowned.

'I'm not thinking of swimming over, but I could float over quite easily in one of the bath tubs. Provided I ended up reasonably close to the shore I would be able to swim the remaining distance. Once I'm there I just walk to my farmhouse and stay hidden until the family start their daily routine.'

'How will you get back?'

Yannis shrugged. 'I'm sure I'll find a way.'

'Can I come with you?'

Yannis looked at Phaedra in surprise. 'Why would you want to come with me? You've already told me you consider it dangerous. You know you are still frightened of the sea so if the tub did capsize you can't swim and would probably drown.'

Phaedra knew Yannis was right; she still did not venture past her knees if she went into the sea and when she bathed she sat on the very edge and poured the water over herself. 'How long will you be gone?'

'That depends where I land and how far I have to walk to Plaka. Probably at least three days.'

'I wish there was some way you could let me know that you were safe.'

'I'll ask Anna to wave her red scarf so you'll know I'm there. You'll have to look out for her tomorrow.'

'Tomorrow!'

Yannis nodded. 'I'm planning to leave tonight as there is no moon. I just need to find Spiro and Takkis and ask them to help me get the tub down to the beach and launched.'

Phaedra listened to Yannis telling Spiro and Takkis his plans. They were enthusiastic and more than willing to help him in his attempt.

'Couldn't you ask Manolis to take you over?' she suggested tentatively. 'It would be much safer.'

Yannis shook his head. 'If the authorities found out he had taken me across he would have his boat impounded. I can't put him in that position, besides he wouldn't be able to visit Flora.'

As darkness descended and the people retired inside their houses for the night Yannis, Takkis and Spiro made their way down to the storeroom with Phaedra following them. She watched as the men hauled the bath tub to the edge of the jetty and held it whilst Yannis climbed in. It rocked dangerously and Yannis clung to the sides until it had steadied. Takkis and Spiro pushed him away when he declared himself ready and he began to use the piece of wood he had picked up as a paddle to try to steer the tub out into the bay.

Phaedra watched him fearfully until he was swallowed up by the darkness. She made her way back up the path to the small house that she shared with Flora and laid on her pallet, hot tears stinging her eyes. Would she ever see Yannis again?

Sleep eluded her and as the sky began to lighten she rose quietly so as not to disturb Flora and walked up to the fortress wall where Yannis always stood to watch for Anna to wave to him. She wished he lived further inland and then he would not have embarked on his hazardous journey. If he was successful in visiting them on this occasion he would probably attempt the journey again and disaster could overtake him.

As the sun rose she saw the fishermen preparing the barrels of water to bring out to them. If Yannis had been swept out to sea it was possible that Manolis would see him as he made his way to the island and rescue him. It seemed an age before she saw two men leave the house and walk up onto the hillside and even longer before Anna appeared and waved a red scarf. Finally she was able to breathe a sigh of relief. At least Yannis had reached the shore safely. Phaedra continued to watch, waving back to Yannis's sister, until the woman turned abruptly and ran back towards the farm house. Still Phaedra stood there and saw two men carrying something that looked like a bath tub between them.

The boats bringing the water and food did not arrive. Flora sat dejectedly on the jetty looking for any sign of Manolis whilst the other villagers grumbled. There was no reason why the boats should not come out; it was a fine day, hardly any breeze and the sea was calm. Instead of sailing their boats all the men seemed intent on walking along the shore and peering into the crevices amongst the rocks.

Phaedra saw another figure walking up the hillside, but she was unable to discern if it was Yannis or one of his family, and shortly afterwards she saw a cart coming down the track and going towards Elounda. Phaedra continued to watch, but Anna did not return and finally she gave up her vigil.

The boats began to make their customary journeys across to the island to deliver the water and some scant supplies again but the boats from Aghios Nikolaos did not appear and there was no sign of Manolis until late in the afternoon.

To Phaedra's immense relief Yannis stepped ashore. People surged around him, asking if he managed to visit his family before being discovered by the authorities. Phaedra hung back until they had dispersed, their curiosity satisfied.

'Welcome back.'

Yannis smiled at her. 'It's good to be back. '

'How is your mother?'

'I was pleased to see that my mother was far better than I had expected. She can't walk without help or use one arm, but mentally she is as alert as evert. She pretends to be asleep and actually listens to everything that is being said. She is a naughty old lady.' Yannis shook his head. 'It's Anna I feel sorry for. She has no life of her own. She spends all her time looking after Mamma and the children.'

Phaedra shrugged. 'At least she has a family; not like us. Tell me about your trip over. Did you have to swim?'

'It was rather dark and frightening at first. I had no idea if I was going towards Plaka or drifting much further down the coast. I knew I hadn't been taken out to sea by the current, but I needed to get to the shore before daylight. I finally felt some rocks beneath my feet and swam the last few yards to the shore. I wasn't that far from the farmhouse so I went and knocked on the door. My brother didn't recognise me at first.' Yannis smiled at the memory of Yiorgo's reaction.

'I went into the kitchen and they gave me some food and dry clothes and then I bedded down with the donkey. They wouldn't let me see my mother until they had told her I was there. If I had suddenly appeared before her the shock could have been too great. Did you see Anna waving?'

Phaedra nodded. 'I'd been watching for hours.'

'I'm sorry. That was my fault. I was so excited to be with my family again that everything else went out of my head. It's thanks to Father Minos and my father that the food that is sent out to us is decent now and not going mouldy. Thank goodness I did finally remember to ask Anna to wave to you. She saw the men discover the bath tub and ran back to the house to warn me. I didn't want anyone to find me there so I went up to where my father and Yiorgo were working and my father made me get on the cart.'

'So it was you I saw walking up the hill.'

Yannis nodded. 'My father said that Yiorgo was to take me to Aghios Nikolaos but we were only a short way from Plaka when we were stopped.'

'They didn't find you?'

'My foot was showing. The man told Yiorgo to cover it up, but I insisted that I left the cart and walked. No one stopped me until I was almost the other side of Elounda and then I was noticed.'

'What happened?'

'I was escorted the remainder of the way to Aghios Nikolaos

by a rather unfriendly crowd. The boatmen there had been told they couldn't leave the port until I had been found. I think Manolis was as pleased to see me as I was to see him.'

'Flora had been anxious. We none of us knew why the boats hadn't arrived.'

'If they hadn't found the bath tub they wouldn't have known I was on the mainland. Next time I'll go when there's a moon and hide the tub.'

'Next time?'

'Why not? Now I know I can do it I can drift across again.'

'Suppose a storm blew up and you were wrecked?'

Yannis shrugged. 'That's a chance I would have to take. Everyone has to go some time.'

Phaedra shivered. 'Please don't talk like that. I'm going up to the church to give thanks for your safe return.' Phaedra began to scramble to her feet and Yannis caught at her skirt and pulled her back down beside him.

'Do I mean that much to you?' Yannis placed his arm around her and pulled her closer to him. 'I realised when Manolis was bringing me back that I care a good deal about you. You're very special to me and I wanted to be back here with you.'

Phaedra looked at him uncertainly; her heart was beating fast. 'Do you mean that, Yannis?'

Yannis pushed her back down on the grass and kissed her passionately. 'I certainly do. I'd like you to belong to me so we were a couple like many of the others who live over here.'

Phaedra lay very still. 'Where would we live?' she asked finally. 'There wouldn't be room in my house unless Flora was asked to leave. I couldn't do that to her.'

'I wouldn't contemplate it. Be patient for a short while. Now everyone is housed and the hospital is running efficiently I can finally think about rebuilding the house where I want to live, provided we don't suddenly receive a number of patients from the hospital again.' Yannis smiled at her. 'I've had my eye on the one down in the square ever since I arrived. Whenever it was suggested that we repaired that one I always found a reason to attend to another.'

'But that would be a big house, Yannis; much bigger than the other houses that have only two people living in them.'

Yannis nodded. 'I know, but I have plans. When someone new arrives on the island there is never a house available for them and they have to wait, often living in the tunnel. Even Father Minos had to share the shack I have on the hill until somewhere suitable was built for him. They would feel far more welcome if they were taken into a decent house for a few days or weeks and were then able to move into a house they could call their own.'

Phaedra considered Yannis's idea. 'I was grateful that Ariadne gave me some shelter when I first arrived.' She shuddered. 'I can't imagine what it would have been like if I'd had to sleep in a doorway or in the tunnel. I think it's a good idea, but suppose a group arrive? There wouldn't be enough space for all of them in your house.'

'Not at first,' admitted Yannis. 'It's going to take time. I'd like to replace the upper floor. It's large enough to be two separate rooms. Then we could have a number of people staying for a few days and accommodate men and women.'

'Wouldn't a wall built of stone up there be too heavy?'

'I'd ask Takkis to make a wooden partition. It would also mean that Flora could have her house to herself and Manolis could stay as long as he wanted.'

'I think they would appreciate that. I always leave when Manolis arrives and it makes her feel that she is turning me out.'

'That's settled then. I'll ask some of the men to start work on the house with me. Would you be willing to share my present shack with me for a few weeks until our new house is completed?' Yannis drew Phaedra close to him. 'I wanted to ask you long ago, but I also wanted to have a decent house to offer you.'

'I'll be happy to live anywhere with you, Yannis, but will Father Minos approve?'

'I'm sure he will give us a blessing the same as he has the other couples. We'll be able to wear the same woven bracelets he has given to them to confirm we are promised to each other.'

'What about Doctor Stavros?'

'It isn't up to him. He may say that everyone should be celibate but it isn't possible. We are all ordinary people and deserve to have a happy life with someone we have grown to love. I'll look for Takkis and he can come and tell me if we should repair the upper floor before we renew the roof.'

Phaedra enjoyed living with Yannis. She would ensure that when he rose each morning she had some water heating over their fire so he could wash his hands and face. She would then place a mug of coffee and some rusks before him. She would sit with him whilst he talked about his plans for the day and once he had left she tidied their bedding before going to the storeroom to collect ingredients for their evening meal. She tried to remember the variety of food she had helped her mother prepare and replicated the dishes as nearly as possible.

There was only one thing Phaedra wanted to make her happiness complete but when she had approached Yannis and suggested they had a child Yannis had been horrified.

'It's totally out of the question. We're both leprous and it could inherit the sickness from us. How would we feel about that? Condemning a child to have the same or worse deformities that we have.'

'It could be born perfectly healthy,' argued Phaedra.

'And then what would happen? It would be sent away to an orphanage somewhere on the mainland and we would never see or hear from it again.' Yannis shook his head. 'I'm sorry, Phaedra, but there is no way I would want to see you heartbroken. Better for you to forget the idea.'

'I could ask Doctor Stavros.'

'I know exactly what he would say. He is still against couples living together. He would certainly not approve of us having a child. Believe me, Phaedra, when I say I would love to have a child as much as you would, but we have to be sensible. If you persist in this idea I'll have to take to sleeping alone upstairs.'

'You wouldn't!' Phaedra was horrified at the idea. She enjoyed lying in Yannis's arms each night as she gradually drifted off to sleep.

'It would be the only solution; and I wouldn't enjoy it any more than you. Have you forgotten that my sister died when giving birth? I would never forgive myself if I caused your death. I would always blame myself and hate the child. I can understand why Babbis could not bear to have his son around.'

After Yannis left Phaedra cried miserable tears, but she knew in her heart that Yannis was right to refuse her.

Despite success in Lakkonia Doctor Stavros could find no trace of Flora's family in Vrouhas. She had declared that she could not remember her surname and Doctor Stavros believed her. Each time he visited Vrouhas he asked if anyone knew of any relatives for a young woman named Flora. His enquiries were met with a shake of the head until he despaired of finding anyone who remembered her and had to conclude that they had moved away or died.

It was months later when he was in Selles that a woman approached him.

'I've heard that you were asking about Flora when you were in Vrouhas.'

'That's correct. I would like to give her relatives some news of her, but no one seems to have any knowledge of her family.'

'I might be able to pass a message on for you.'

'I'm sure her family would be grateful to hear any news.'

Doctor Stavros watched as the woman appeared to be struggling to control her emotions. 'I can give you more details if you wish.'

The woman looked around warily. 'I wouldn't want my husband to know I had spoken with you.'

'As a doctor I am bound by confidentiality. I know Flora has two sisters. Would you be one of them?'

Sotiria bowed her head. 'She was only a little girl when my father took her to the doctor about her arm. We never saw her again and my father refused to speak her name.'

Doctor Stavros patted Sotiria's shoulder. 'I understand how difficult it must have been for all of you. I'm sure your father was worried that one of you would also suffer the same fate.'

'I understand. At least I can tell Olga about Flora. How is her arm? Any better?'

Doctor Stavros hesitated. 'Unfortunately she developed gangrene and I had to amputate.'

'Oh, no. You mean she's dead?' Sotiria looked at him in horror.

'Not at all. She made an excellent recovery from the operation. She is well and has a good life on Spinalonga. She has a relationship with a young man over there and is happy. Would you like me to take a message back to her from you?'

Sotiria shook her head. 'It's better that she continues to forget us. I'll pass the news on to my sister, but our husbands must not know.'

'What about your father? Surely he would be grateful to know that his daughter was safe and well?'

'Pappa is dead and I have no idea where our mother is. She left us all one day. I thought she no longer loved us.' A tear appeared in the corner of Sotiria's eye. 'Maybe she knew she was sick and hoped we would all stay healthy if she went away.'

'That sounds very likely. It must have been extremely difficult for her leaving all of you, whatever her reason.'

'Do you know where she is? I'd just like to tell her that we understand.'

Doctor Stavros shook his head. 'If you give me her name I will do my best to find out, but it is obviously some time ago.'

'It was Anna, Anna Petrakis.'

Doctor Stavros entered the name on the inside cover of his

notebook. 'I cannot promise anything, of course, but look out for me the next time I am in the village and if I have any information I will tell you.'

Sotiria turned away. At least she had asked this doctor who seemed kind and friendly. She had never felt she could approach Doctor Kandakis who she did not trust not to go immediately and tell her father that she had enquired after the whereabouts of her mother.

Doctor Stavros searched through the notes from Doctor Kandakis. He found the name Anna Petrakis and a few lines further down was the name Ariadne Manolakis. It was possible that she might be able to give him some information about Anna Petrakis. He was still searching for the brother and sister whom Despina had told him had been found in the hills above Kastelli. He would have to pay her another visit and see if she was able to remember their names.

Doctor Stavros spoke to Spiro and was told that Ariadne had finally been moved to the hospital. 'Her legs have become so painful and swollen that she could not leave the house and it was too much to expect the other occupants to cope.'

The doctor nodded. 'I'm pleased you're looking after her. Is she well enough for me to speak to? I believe she may be able to help me with a query I have about an earlier resident.'

'I can't guarantee she'll remember or be much help to you, but you're welcome to try.'

Doctor Stavros picked his way amongst the mattresses until he reached the area where Ariadne lay.

'Hello, Ariadne. I thought I'd give you a quick visit as you've been brought into the hospital.'

'I hope I'll not be here long being a nuisance to everyone.'

'You're not a nuisance. The hospital was meant for sufferers like yourself when living in a house became too difficult.'

Ariadne looked at him scornfully. 'I know I'll only leave here when I'm carried to the tower. The sooner that happens the better. I'm ready to go.'

'At least you know you will be kept comfortable and well looked after until that time comes, not like in the old days.'

Ariadne nodded. 'That was hard. Living in a house with people who knew they were dying and all we could do was give them a wash and a bit of food. The smell from some of them,' Ariadne shuddered. 'Worse than my legs when they're unwrapped and the bandages changed, but you became used to it.'

Doctor Stavros remembered the unsavoury aroma that had emanated from many of the houses when he had first arrived due to the disabled who were being cared for inside. It was no wonder that so many people had chosen to sit outside in the open air whenever possible.

'Do you remember the names of any of the people who lived with you at that time?'

'Of course I do. There's nothing wrong with my memory.'

'Do you remember Anna Petrakis?'

'Anna? She was with me for some years. Nice woman.'

'Did she have any family?'

'I'm sure she did, think they were girls, but I can't remember their names now. She spoke about them a good deal when she first arrived.'

'Do you remember when she died? How long ago?'

'Before we had the hospital; before you came.'

'Flora says that you were here when she arrived; that's fifteen years ago. Had Anna died by then?'

Ariadne gave a snort of disgust. 'Anna was one of the women she complained about when she stayed in my house, along with Agata and Sofia. There were three women who were nearing the end of their lives. Said she couldn't bear the smell and would go and live elsewhere. Took herself off and didn't mix with us again for a long time; not until Phaedra arrived and talked some sense into her. She's a nice, sensible girl.'

Doctor Stavros agreed with Ariadne's opinion of Phaedra but he felt very sad on Flora's behalf. Would she have been so unfeeling had she known that Anna was her mother? He would certainly not tell her, but the next time he was in Selles he would be able to tell Sotiria that her mother had died many years ago. He would also ask Sotiria if he could tell Flora that he had made contact with her sister and pass on the news that her father had died.

Doctor Stavros looked for Sotiria when he next visited Selles and could see no sign of her. He entered the small general store and asked if they could direct him to her house.

'I can, but there's little point in you going there today. She's visiting her sister.'

'Does she live in this village?'

The man shook his head. 'She lives in Loumas.'

'Oh, well, I'll see her when I'm this way next time. It's nothing urgent.'

'If you want to leave some medicine with me I'll make sure she gets it.'

'No, it was just a message I was asked to pass on.' Doctor Stavros looked at his watch. He would pass through Loumas on his return journey and could easily make enquiries for the woman whilst he was there. If Sotiria was with her sister he would be able to give both of them the news of their mother and Flora at the same time.

It took him longer to ride to Loumas than he had envisaged and he hoped Sotiria had not taken a short cut over the fields to walk back to Selles. At the first house he came to in the village he stopped and asked the woman if she knew Sotiria whom he believed to have a sister living in the village.

'Do you mean me? I have a sister Sotiria.'

'Is she visiting you today? If so, may I speak to her, please?'

'You'd best come in.' She opened the door wider and Doctor Stavros could see a woman sitting at the table. 'Sotiria, there's a man here looking for you. Are you up to something you wouldn't want Alecos to know about?'

Sotiria turned. 'Doctor Stavros,' she exclaimed. 'How did you know I was here?'

'The man in the general store told me you were visiting your sister in this village. Loumas is on my route back to Aghios Nikolaos so I thought I would see if I could find you.'

Sotiria turned to her sister. 'This is the doctor I was telling you about. Please, have a seat.' She pushed a plate of biscuits towards him. 'Would you like a coffee? Have you any news of our mother?'

Doctor Stavros smiled. 'It is no to the coffee, thank you, and yes regarding your mother. I have managed to find out that she was on Spinalonga, but I'm afraid she died a number of years ago. I can tell you no more than that as it happened before I took over responsibility for the island.'

'Oh!' Sotiria looked at Olga. 'We were hoping we might be able to send her a message.'

'That is obviously impossible, but if you wanted I could take a message to Flora for you. I thought I should have your permission before I told her that we had met.'

'Have you told her about mother? It won't distress her, will it?' asked Olga.

'I'm sure it won't. She has probably accepted that fact for a number of years. I have said nothing at all to her at present. I would prefer to be able to give her the good news that you are both keeping well before I tell her about her mother and father.'

Flora looked at Doctor Stavros in disbelief. 'You have found my sisters?'

Doctor Stavros nodded. 'They were very pleased to hear that you are safe and well.'

'Did you tell them about my arm?'

'Of course, and they were happy to know that you have made a complete recovery.'

'What about my father? What did he say?'

'I have to tell you that your father has died. I didn't press your sisters for details.'

Flora shrugged. 'How he died makes no difference. What about my mother?'

'She was sent here many years ago and subsequently died.'

'Is that why she left us all so suddenly?'

'I can only imagine that was the reason.'

A tear crept down Flora's cheek. 'Poor Mamma. I hope she was well looked after over here.'

'I'm sure she would have been.' Doctor Stavros wished to avoid the subject of Flora's mother. There was no need for the girl to know that her mother was living on the island when she had first arrived. 'Both your sisters are married. It took me a while to locate them as one lives in Selles and the other in Loumas. I could take a message back from you now I know them.'

Flora nodded. 'I'll have to think what I want to say. I must tell them about Manolis, of course.'

'Of course,' agreed Doctor Stavros. He would not tell her that her sisters already knew of her association with the boatman.

'Have they got any children?'

'I have to admit I didn't ask them.'

'It's not important. I'll never get to see them and it's better that they don't know they have an aunt over here. Thank you, Doctor,' Flora beamed at him. 'If you can bring good news like that to everyone here it would make them so happy.'

Doctor Stavros patted her hand. 'I will do my best.'

Flora could not wait to tell Manolis. 'I'm so excited. I never thought I would be able to tell my sisters that I am married the same as they are.'

Manolis placed his arm around her. 'If you're happy, then so am I. I'll bring a bottle of wine over with me tomorrow and we can celebrate properly.'

'I've never had a glass of wine. What does it taste like?'

'Very nice. It's made from grapes.'

'Then I'm sure to like it. Could you bring two bottles; then we could have one each?'

Manolis laughed and shook his head. 'If you drank a whole bottle you would have a bad headache and possibly be sick. I'll bring one bottle and you can have one mug when I arrive and another later before I leave. There will be sufficient for us to do the same the following day. I must not be accused by the doctor of making you drunk.'

Still excited, Flora went looking for Phaedra after Manolis had left. Phaedra listened to her, pleased that she had news of her family.

'I wonder if Doctor Stavros could find my relatives? I'd like to know about my parents and whether they have any more children. I might have lots of brothers and sisters.'

'Why don't you ask him?'

'I might. At least they would know I was well and happy, although he would have to tell them about Mikaelis.' It was the first time that Phaedra had mentioned her brother since spending her first day on Spinalonga looking unsuccessfully for him. She had accepted that he had drowned and blamed herself for his fate.

'Have they finally decided to send us thirty drachmas every month?' asked Yannis in disbelief.

Father Minos nodded. 'You will all have some money you can spend as you please.'

Yannis smiled ruefully. 'Where can we spend it? We're not allowed to go across to the mainland.'

'Father Andreas and I talked about this when he was given permission to take over my parish so I could come here. You make a list of the items you want to purchase and give it to Manolis. The money is held in the bank so the bills from the suppliers are taken to the bank by Manolis and they are repaid.'

Yannis frowned. 'How will we know when we have spent all our money? Many of the people over here cannot read or write, let alone count past ten.'.

Father Minos smiled triumphantly. 'We took that into account. A ledger will be made up that has everyone's name in it. Each month thirty drachmas will be credited against their name and whenever they make a purchase the amount will be deducted.'

Yannis nodded slowly. 'Sounds like a good system, but who is going to keep this ledger and the accounts?'

'Manolis.'

'Manolis! But he's a fisherman.'

'He also received a reasonably good education. He had wanted to be a grocer. It was only through the untimely death of his father that he became a fisherman. You or I should be able to help him if he has a problem'

'If Manolis is going to spend all his time shopping for us and keeping the accounts when will he go fishing? He'll end up without an income.'

'A small allowance for a book keeper has been included in the agreement. That should be sufficient for Manolis to live on, and besides, think how much more time he will be able to spend on the island with Flora. I'll reply to Pavlakis and say that we have accepted the government's generous offer and look forward to receiving it immediately.'

'It's not exactly generous,' remarked Yannis. 'Although paying us a pension has been agreed no doubt the government will drag their heels over the details. They probably hope we will all be dead before they have to pay us anything.'

The news that they were finally going to receive a monthly pension from the government spread through the community. Everyone had their own ideas of how they should spend the money. Father Minos listened to them arguing in consternation and approached Yannis.

'I think we need to hold a meeting. Tempers are becoming frayed. It isn't practical for twenty or so men to have the same occupation. We need to have some agreements and organisation.'

'Orestis would be the one to draw up any agreement. He could be paid and that would make it a legal document. Do you think talking to people individually would be beneficial?'

Father Minos shook his head. 'Better to have a general meeting, then everyone knows what was said and agreed. I'll spread the word and ask people to be down in the square where you can talk to them.'

'Me? Why me?'

'It was your idea initially and you know what the majority of the people over here need.'

Yannis sighed. The people would take far more notice of the priest than they would of him. 'You'll be there to back me up?'

'Of course. I'm sure everyone will be happy eventually.'

Yannis was surprised at the many ideas that were put forward by the community. Takkis had agreed to become the official builder on the island, whilst Antonis wanted to be recognised as the barber, claiming that as he had lived on the island longer than the other men who had wanted the same occupation he should have priority. Vassilis and Stathis were arguing about who should be allowed to open a taverna until it was agreed that there were sufficient people on the island to have at least two establishments.

Yannis and Father Minos addressed the meeting and asked each person to give their name and their proposed occupation to Orestis. Orestis promised to go through his notes and where there was duplication of ideas he would consult with them and decide if it was feasible to have a number of people offering the same services and he would then draw up an agreement.

Not everyone was happy, but Father Minos impressed upon them that if they argued and disagreed it was quite likely the government would withdraw the concession.

Doctor Stavros was both amazed and delighted at the change

that had come over the people on the island. Those who had claimed minor ailments and demanded his attention on each of his visits were now too occupied with their plans to make some money to supplement their pension. No longer did people sit around for most of the day doing nothing.

Manolis finally appeared on the island bearing a large ledger. Flora accompanied him up to her house and he explained his intentions.

'I'm going to sit outside your house every day and people can come and tell me what they would like me to buy for them. You're first in the queue. What would you like?'

'I can't think of anything.'

'What about a new skirt or blouse?'

'Maybe. There's usually a blouse or skirt sent over in the bundles of clothes. I don't really need to buy anything new.'

'So what is the point of you having money to spend if you don't use it?'

Flora shrugged. Everything she appeared to need was already provided for her on the island.

Manolis spent most of the day sitting outside Flora's house, but no one came near him. He was puzzled. He had expected a queue of people asking him to buy items for them from the mainland. Finally he went in search of Yannis.

'No one has been near me,' he complained. 'I expected to have more orders than I would be able to deal with.'

'You probably soon will have. We've spent a considerable amount of time talking about our ideas. We think we have it all worked out and Orestis has drawn up some official agreements for us. He'll ask you to deduct five drachmas from the account of the people he's drawn up an agreement for and credit his account. Once that is done people will soon have a list of goods they want you to bring over along with some money.'

'I don't know if the government will allow me to do that.'

'Then don't ask them. Once Orestis has been paid for drawing up the agreements the money is theirs to use as they please. Maria is going to be a seamstress and make blouses, skirts and trousers for anyone who wants them. She says she will charge them and that way she will be able to afford to buy more material. Vassilis and Stathis plan to open tavernas where the people can meet during the evening. They'll charge them for the wine and when they have sufficient money saved they'll ask for some tables and chairs to be made so it becomes a proper taverna. Andreas wants hens that lay eggs so he can sell them and buy more. Some of the men are going to ask for sacks of soil so they can make small gardens and grow vegetables. Those who live on the main street are going to turn the front of their houses into small shops. Even Father Minos wants to buy more candles so he can sell them and save up for a bell.'

'I didn't realise I would be expected to bring money over here,' frowned Manolis, 'You realise that once it is on the island it cannot be accepted back on the mainland?'

'I understand that and I've tried to impress that knowledge on the people. If you brought five drachmas for everyone that would give them some money in their pocket to start with. Provided the system works the money should just keep changing hands.

Manolis sighed. This appeared to be far more complicated than he had envisioned when originally asked to be the book keeper.

Despite Manolis's forebodings the system began to work well. He had talked for a considerable amount of time with Father Minos and finally agreed that he would withdraw cash from the bank and bring it over with him. He would only be responsible for purchases made on the mainland on their behalf. Whatever they did with their cash was their own business and he could bring more if necessary provided there was sufficient recorded against their name in his ledger.

'I'll add up the cost of the various purchases each week and draw cash from the bank to pay the shop keepers for those. I can always add a little more on if extra cash is needed over here. By the time anyone realises it will be too late to put a stop to the system.'

Father Minos smiled at Manolis's devious idea. The fisherman would have made a very crafty politician.

1934

Aristo arrived on Spinalonga and stood hesitantly on the jetty.

Yannis walked forward to greet him. 'I'm sure you are not here by choice, but I would like to assure you that we are all friends and you will be welcomed into the community.'

Aristo looked at the man before him doubtfully. 'Are you the island doctor?'

Yannis shook his head. 'No, that's Doctor Stavros. I'm Yannis. I'll make sure you are introduced to the doctor the next time he visits.'

'I thought I would have to go to the hospital and report my arrival to him.'

'Only the really sick or disabled people live in the hospital. I don't think you would qualify for a bed there. What's your name?'

'Aristo. So where do I go?'

'I'd like to invite you to stay with my wife and myself until there is a house ready for you. If you would like to come with me you can meet Phaedra and get settled in. We can have a meal and get to know each other.'

Looking thoroughly bemused Aristo followed Yannis up to the main path and down to the square where his house was situated. Yannis stopped and pointed out the drinking fountain, where, as usual, there were a queue of people.

'The boatmen bring us over water, but it's more suitable for washing than drinking. Please don't waste any you take from the fountain. It's our most precious commodity.'

'What happens if it runs dry?'

'It hasn't done so yet. If it did we would be reliant on the water from the mainland. Here we are, come inside and meet Phaedra and then I'll show you to your room.'

Aristo looked around the room curiously. He could be in any village house. In one corner against the back wall was a large mattress and two stools; before a fireplace were three upright chairs placed on a rag rug beneath a table. On one side of the fireplace there were some shelves that held a miscellaneous collection of papers and books and on the other was a trunk with a cupboard above. Just inside the door was a wooden staircase leading to an upper floor and beneath it stood two large boxes that he assumed held the couples clothes and other belongings. An archway led through to a small area at the back and he could hear someone moving around out there.

'Phaedra, come and be introduced to a new friend, Aristo. I've invited him to stay with us until Takkis has a house ready.'

Phaedra emerged from the kitchen area, wiping her hands on her apron. 'I'm pleased to meet you, Aristo. I'd just started preparing our evening meal and there will be plenty for three. Shall I ask Father Minos to join us later?'

'That's a good idea. Have a seat.' Yannis waved his hand towards a chair. 'Our living accommodation is not exactly luxurious but sufficient for our needs. Upstairs you will find that you only have a mattress and a chair, but you are welcome to come and sit down here with us. Tomorrow I'll take you round the island and introduce you to some of our neighbours.'

Aristo nodded. He was completely lost for words. This was not at all what he had expected.

'I'm sorry we have nothing more to offer you than coffee or water to drink. Now, tell me about yourself and how you come to be over here.'

Aristo shrugged. 'There's not much to tell. I'm a carpenter by trade. I lived in Neapoli. About a year ago I developed a nasty looking scab on my forehead. I thought I had scratched myself and then got some dirt in it so I didn't take a lot of notice. As you can see it has spread and is somewhat unsightly. People, even my friends, began to avoid me, and I decided I should go to the doctor and get it cleared up.' Aristo spread his hands. 'The doctor took a sample and I was diagnosed with leprosy. There was no way I could hide the lesions and continue to work so I asked to be admitted to the hospital for treatment. Here I am.'

Yannis shook his head. 'I hate to disappoint you, but the only treatment you will get here is the Chaulmoogra Oil capsules that Doctor Stavros brings over. They make you feel sick and most people refuse to take them.'

'Surely it's worth feeling nauseas if the tablets cure you?'

'There's no guarantee of a cure. They say the capsules stop the disease spreading, but there's no cure. Those who refuse them don't seem any worse off so the choice will be yours.'

'So why wasn't I sent to a proper hospital?'

Yannis smiled sympathetically at the man. 'I can assure you that you are far better off here than in any hospital. I spent some years in the Athens hospital and it was barbaric. We were prisoners in the ward and the conditions were disgusting. Here, once you've settled in, you'll find it little different from living in a village on the mainland.'

Aristo eyes Yannis dubiously.

'Our only hardship,' continued Yannis, 'is that we are not allowed to go over to the mainland or have visits from our family. Our food is sent over to us, but it's considerably better now than it was a few years ago. I'll introduce you to Orestis and ask him to draft a letter to the government asking for your name to be added to the list of occupants eligible to receive a pension the same as the rest of us.'

Phaedra entered the living room carrying three plates that she placed on the table. 'Our food is ready. If you wish to wash your hands, Aristo, there is some water available.'

Aristo nodded, his hands did not look dirty, but it would be churlish to refuse the offer.

'When we've eaten I'll go up and ask Father Minos to come down to meet you.'

'Father Minos? Is he a priest? Do you have a church?'

Yannis nodded. 'Yes, he's fully ordained. He gave up his parish to come over here and live with us. He holds services each Sunday and on all the Saints Days. He makes sure he's always available if one of us wishes to talk to him. He's made a considerable difference to our lives.'

Father Minos greeted Aristo warmly. 'I never wish anyone to be sick, but it's always refreshing to have a new face over here. I'll be interested to know any news you have from the mainland.'

'Aren't you allowed to go over?' asked Aristo.

Father Minos shook his head. 'When I applied to come here it was made quite clear to me that I could never return to the mainland. I was willing to accept that condition, but by the time any news reaches us it is usually well out of date.'

'I don't think I have any news,' frowned Aristo. 'There was a house fire in a village just outside Neapoli. No one was hurt, thankfully, but the building is just a shell. All their possessions were destroyed.'

'Very unfortunate and sad. At one time all our cooking fires were outside. Since the houses have been rebuilt they are now in the living room. Just be careful that sparks do not fly out and cause any damage.'

'I'll introduce you to Takkis tomorrow and ask him to make some accommodation for you a priority,' said Yannis. 'He'll impress upon you the need for all aspects of safety. If you notice a roof tile slipping let him know. No one wants to be hit by it should it fall.'

Aristo nodded. He had never taken much notice of the buildings in Neapoli. Life over here was going to be different.

Takkis escorted Aristo up the hill a short distance from the square where there were three houses completed and occupied and another under construction.

'We've had to start building up here,' he explained. 'There really was no more space down by the main road. We have the foundations in place, but it will take us a bit of time to build up the walls and put the roof on. I'm sure Yannis and Phaedra won't mind you staying with them for a couple of weeks. We'll work as fast as we can.'

'I'll be willing to help. I'm a carpenter so I know how to make a window frame and hang a door.'

Takkis smiled. 'In that case we will certainly call on you. Once your house is completed I hope you'll be willing to work on some of the others with us.'

'Where are you building those?'

'Up here. We never know when someone is going to arrive and we are trying to have somewhere they can move into within a day or two. We're a bit behind as we have to move the rocks and boulders out of the way before we can level the ground.'

'How many people are living up here?'

'When you join them it will make five of you.'

'How many houses do you envisage eventually?'

'Another five or six; possibly more. It really depends how many more people are sent over here. The current occupants won't want to return to the overcrowded conditions they were living in previously and have four or five more people in the house with them. A couple of the houses down in the main area will probably become vacant soon so people will be housed in those first.'

Aristo did not ask the reason why the houses would become vacant. He would be more than happy living in one that was newly constructed and just hoped his neighbours would be as welcoming and friendly as Yannis and Phaedra had been.

More men and women arrived on the island and each was invited to stay with Yannis and Phaedra until some suitable accommodation had been allocated to them. Most were grateful, except Matthias. He complained that it had been necessary to stay in the upper floor in Yannis and Phaedra's house for over two weeks, although Phaedra had heated water for him so he could wash and also cooked him a meal each evening. The house he had now been allocated he claimed was too small and he did not like his immediate neighbours or having to climb up a hill.

Takkis spoke to Father Minos who agreed to discuss Matthias's problems with him. After listening to the man's complaints sympathetically Father Minos agreed to speak with Takkis and ask if a larger house could be built elsewhere

'Once I build a larger house for one person they'll all want bigger rooms,' grumbled Takkis. 'I know I've had to make some of the houses up on the hill a little smaller, but I had to work within the confines of the old Venetian walls and it became far too steep further up. He should be grateful that he has somewhere and isn't sleeping in the tunnel.'

'Just do your best, Takkis. If he decides he's not happy with the next house you offer him then he must stay where he is.'

Takkis smiled to himself. The man would regret complaining. Takkis went up the steps from the square to an area above the Venetian fortress. He could build a house here for Matthias and he would have no neighbours to complain about or a hill to climb. He would ensure that the living room was larger than Matthias's current space, but he would make no dividing wall to separate off a rudimentary kitchen.

Once completed Takkis told Matthias that a new and more spacious house was now ready for him.

'Are you certain you want to move? There's someone waiting

for your house once you leave it so you won't be able to return.'

'Provided it's bigger than this box I'll be happy.'

'Would you like me to help you move your possessions?'

Matthias accepted the offer of help with alacrity and having gathered together his bedding, few culinary items and his clothes, loading Takkis with as much as possible, he followed him down to the square, along the main road and then up the steps.

Takkis opened the door and dumped Matthias's possessions on the floor. 'There you are. A living room almost twice as large as your old house. Satisfied?'

Matthias nodded.

'In that case I'll tell Achilles he can move in to your old house immediately.' Takkis closed the door and hurried back down the hill.

'Come on, Achilles. Move yourself and get settled in before Matthias decides he would rather return. He hasn't realised yet that he has exchanged a hill for steps and is further away from the toilets.'

Achilles looked around the bare room. 'I've no complaints. Yannis and Phaedra have been very good allowing me to stay with them, but I'll be pleased to have a place to call my own.'

At mid day Matthias went looking for Takkis. 'My new house isn't finished.'

Takkis frowned. 'What's wrong?'

'I don't have a separate area to prepare my food and there's no toilet.'

'I can't make a toilet up there as you're above the Venetian walls. The waste wouldn't soak away. You didn't mention a kitchen area. You said you wanted a larger living room. I've given you that.'

'If you don't come back and finish it properly I'll complain to Father Minos.'

Takkis shrugged. 'Very well. I'll come up tomorrow and you can tell me what you want, but a toilet is out of the question.'

Takkis knew that when he had erected the new wall demanded by Matthias the man would have a living area that was no larger than previously.

Phaedra placed a dish of vegetables and pasta on the table in front of Yannis. 'There was only rabbit available from the butcher and I've already given you rabbit twice this week,' she explained.

'I'm sure it will taste good. What have you done today?'

'You know what I've done. I see you around continually during the day.'

'I still like you to tell me.'

'Well, I tidied up the house as usual and then prepared the vegetables for our meal. When I went up to the hospital to visit Panicos Spiro told me that Elena had not arrived. I said I would go and get some vegetables for him. I saw Elena as I was returning and gave her the vegetables so she had no excuse not to go up and help Spiro.'

Yannis nodded and Phaedra continued. 'I visited Flora and stayed with her until Manolis arrived.'

'What did Manolis have to say?'

'Nothing important so I thought it best to leave them alone and went to find Father Minos. I lit a candle when I was in the church. I wish there were some pictures in there like there were in the church in my village.'

'I like it the way it is. What did you talk to Father Minos about?'

'We just talked generally. He said he wants to see Doctor Stavros the next time he visits. I hope he isn't ill.'

Yannis looked at Phaedra in alarm. 'I'll go and speak to him myself when I've eaten my supper.'

It was nearly dark when Yannis left their house and walked along the path to the church. There was no sign of the priest and Yannis walked up the turning that led to the house where Father Minos lived. Again the priest was not in evidence and Yannis decided he must have been called up to the hospital. When he asked Spiro if Father Minos was up there Spiro had shaken his head and said he had not seen the priest since that afternoon.

'He's probably been invited to join someone for his supper.'

Yannis nodded. It was more than likely and now he would have to go from house to house to see if he could locate him. No one appeared to have any idea where the priest was and Yannis was becoming concerned. Finally he walked through the tunnel and began to make his way up the hill where he almost bumped into the priest.

Yannis gave a sigh of relief. 'Thank goodness I've found you. I was beginning to get worried.'

'Does someone need me?' asked Father Minos anxiously.

'No, I just want to talk to you. Phaedra said you wanted to talk to Doctor Stavros when he came next. You're not ill are you?'

Father Minos shook his head. 'Not at all. Come with me. I've something to show you.' The priest led the way to the ruined church and lit an oil lamp that stood just inside. He held it up and showed Yannis that the roof was nearly completed. 'I thought this church could be used for burial services.'

'It is nearer the tower,' agreed Yannis.

'I don't want to use the tower. Just across from here there are a few feet of soil. I thought it could be made into a proper cemetery.'

Yannis considered the proposal. 'It's a good idea, but there is still so much that needs to be done for the living.'

'The dead deserve respect also. If you are placed in the tower you just become another pile of rotting flesh and bones. That's what I want to talk to Doctor Stavros about. He may say my idea is not possible.'

Yannis felt a lump come into his throat. It was the callous way that the dead had been disposed of in a sack without any burial rites that had caused the first fight in the Athens hospital.

'What about coffins? We can't just place people into the ground.'

'Phillipos was a carpenter and so is Aristo. Between them they should be able to make a coffin.'

'Where would they get the timber?' asked Yannis.

'We have our pensions so it can be bought from the mainland. People will pay to have a coffin made and it can be stored until it is needed. I'll speak to Doctor Stavros and if he is in agreement then I'll talk to Phillipos.'

Doctor Stavros greeted the idea with enthusiasm, but immediately recognised a problem. 'If everyone wanted a grave we would soon run out of space.'

'We would have to employ the same system as there is on the mainland,' said Father Minos. 'A grave would be occupied for three years and then exhumed, the bones washed and placed in a casket.'

'Suppose people haven't bought a casket? What happens to them then?' asked Yannis. 'We'd also run out of space for storing caskets anyway. They can't be just dumped out in a heap somewhere.'

'The only alternative would be to place them in the tower at the end of the three years.'

'What about the coffins?'

Doctor Stavros looked at Father Minos. 'My immediate reaction is to say they could be re-used, but I realise a number of people would not be happy with that idea. They could be used as firewood.'

'We'll speak to Phillipos,' sighed Father Minos. The idea of using a second hand coffin was repugnant to him, but so was the method of disposal of the deceased at the moment. It appeared that he would have to compromise.

When Doctor Stavros saw Phillipos's damaged hands he wondered if the man would be capable of doing any woodwork. 'We could ask Aristo to assist you if you found the work too tiring.'

Phillipos looked at the doctor scathingly. 'I may not be able to work as I used to, but I can still turn out a decent job. All I'll need is the timber.'

'We should ask the government to supply the timber,'

complained Yannis. 'Just because we've been granted a small pension they can't ignore our requests in the future.'

'What more do you want?' asked Phillipos. 'Conditions have improved dramatically since you arrived.'

Yannis sighed. 'They may have improved, but they are still not good enough. We need to enlarge the hospital and have a doctor on the island every day. We need electricity as well, like they have in the hospitals on the mainland now. No doctor could be expected to operate by the light of our oil lamps.'

'It could take years to get those things,' laughed Phillipos.

'So we start asking for them now. If we wait for them to be offered by the government it will never happen. We should also be allowed to send letters to our families and receive replies from them.'

Phaedra approached Manolis nervously and explained what she wanted him to purchase on her behalf and promise that he would not tell Yannis. 'How much do you want me to spend?'

'How much does a watch cost?'

'I'd need to ask at the jewellers.'

'You can spend as much money as there is recorded against my name in the ledger.'

'You have more than fifty drachmas available. I should be able to find something suitable.'

Phaedra nodded. The money meant nothing to her. 'I need it in three weeks' time. Is that possible?'

'I'm sure I'll be able to buy one for you by then. I'll tell you how much it will cost and when I've bought it I'll show you the bill. You have to sign that with your name and I can deduct the amount from your balance in the ledger.'

Phaedra looked at Manolis in consternation. 'I don't know how to write my name,' she admitted.

'You can place a cross on the bill and ask Yannis to sign to say that you put it there.'

Phaedra shook her head. 'I can't do that if I want to keep buying a watch a secret from him.'

'Then ask Yannis to show you how to write your name. It isn't difficult.'

Phaedra spoke cautiously to Yannis. 'I've heard that when you ask Manolis to buy anything you have to sign your name. I ought to know how to do that in case I ever need to buy anything.'

Yannis smiled gently at her. He knew Phaedra was illiterate. 'It isn't difficult. Would you like me to show you?'

Phaedra nodded eagerly.

Unbeknown to Phaedra, Yannis had approached Doctor Stavros and requested that he purchased a gold wedding ring that he could present to Phaedra on their anniversary.

'Just a plain gold band; nothing fancy. I just want her to have a ring the same as she would if we lived on the mainland. Give the receipt to Manolis and he will repay you from the balance held in my name.' Although Doctor Stavros did not approve of any of the villagers living together and being intimate he knew it was impossible to prevent the arrangement and acquiesced to Yannis's request.

The doctor presented Yannis with the bill for the gold wedding ring he had purchased. Yannis looked at it in delight and signed the bill with a flourish. 'Give that to Manolis. There's enough on my account to cover it.'

Phaedra accepted the watch from Manolis and laboriously signed her name on the bill.

'That's fine. There are many who cannot write as neatly as you.'

Phaedra hid the watch amongst the folds of her clean skirt and waited, hoping she would remember the correct day when Father Minos had blessed them and wished them a long and happy life together. Yannis said nothing until they had finished their evening meal before pulling a small box from his pocket and telling her it was an anniversary gift.

'Wait, Yannis. I have a gift for you.' She rummaged amongst the folds of her skirt and pulled out an oblong box.

Yannis slipped the ring on Phaedra's finger; relieved to find that it fitted.

'It's beautiful, Yannis. Open your gift now.'

Yannis removed the watch from the case and beamed in pleasure. He had wanted a watch for so long. The only way to tell the time was by the sun. He held it up to Phaedra's ear so she could hear the mechanism ticking and showed her how the hands could be moved. He could see by the bemused look on her face that she had no idea how one told the time.

'I wrote my name on the bill just the way you had shown me,' said Phaedra proudly. 'Manolis said I had done it right and that some of the other people cannot write their names. I was pleased you had taught me how to make the letters.'

'How many cannot write their names?'

Phaedra shrugged. 'I don't know.'

'I'll have a word with Father Minos and Manolis. 'That could be a little job for me; teaching them to read and write.'

1935

Fotini sat in her father's cart as he drove her towards Aghios Nikolaos in the darkness. She had said a tearful goodbye to her mother, sister and little nephew. Her sister had disobeyed her father and crept into her room that night where she was sobbing uncontrollably. Maria had cradled her in her arms, heedless of her own safety, and assured her sister that she would always love her. That was little consolation now as the town drew nearer.

'What will happen to me, Pappa?'

'I will leave you with the doctor. He has agreed to examine you, but you have to be prepared to be sent to the leprosarium. Remember, you are not to mention our names to him and you are to say that you have come from Kritsa. We do not want him up in the village examining all of us for no good reason.'

Fotini sniffed. She has spent three weeks shut away in her room as her father had ordered, but at least she had been able to speak to her mother and sister through the door. Now she would have no one. A short distance from where the doctor lived Alesandros stopped the cart, told Fotini to collect her sacks and to follow him. He rapped smartly on the doctor's door and as soon as Doctor Stavros answered he pushed Fotini inside.

'Here's the woman I told you about. I picked her up on the road to Kritsa.' Without a word to his daughter he closed the door and returned to the cart.

Fotini looked at the doctor nervously.

'There's nothing at all for you to worry about,' Doctor Stavros tried to reassure her. 'I'll take a small amount of blood and send it to the hospital in Heraklion to be tested. It will take a while before the results are back. In the meantime I will take a look at your arm and give you a quick test.' He took a pin from beneath the lapel of his jacket. 'Turn your head away and look out of the window. Tell me whenever you feel me prick your arm.'

Fotini stood there. She could feel nothing when the doctor placed the pin close to where her arm was infected. It was not until he touched her just above her elbow that she gave a little start.

'You felt that?'

Fotini nodded.

'You felt nothing before then?'

'No,' whispered Fotini.

'Then I am certain the diagnosis is correct and the result from the blood test will confirm that. I'll take you down to the waterfront and Manolis will take you over to Spinalonga. There's nothing for you to be concerned about. You'll find living in the village there far better than living rough in the hills.'

Fotini was about to say that she had not been living in the hills when she remembered her father's instructions that she was not to mention Kastelli.

Doctor Stavros smiled kindly at her. 'Give me your name and tell me the village where you lived originally.'

Fotini but her lip. Her father had forbidden her to give her family name.'

'I've always been known just as Fotini. I lived in the hills behind Kritsa.'

Doctor Stavros entered the details on the pad in front of him. 'Collect your belongings and follow me.'

Silently Fotini picked up her sacks. The doctor was now going to take her to the hospital and she did not know what to expect upon her arrival. To her surprise he led the way down to the waterfront and called to a fisherman who was sitting in his boat.

'I have a passenger for you, Manolis.'

Manolis took the sacks from Fotini and helped her into his boat where she sat nervously clutching at the wooden seat as the boat was rocked by their movement.

'There's nothing for you to worry about,' he assured her cheerfully. 'It's a nice calm morning so you won't feel ill.'

Once away from the shore Manolis raised the sail and the boat increased in speed. As they approached a wooden bridge across the canal Manolis lowered the sail and steered carefully through the narrow waterway.

'Please take me back,' pleaded Fotini.

Manolis shook his head. 'I have to obey the doctor and take you to Spinalonga. I'm not allowed to take you anywhere else. Besides, where would you go? Sooner or later a search party would be sent out for you and you'd find yourself back on my boat making the journey again. Flora will be waiting to greet you. She'll take you to meet the other people over there and you'll soon feel at home.'

Fotini bowed her head. She did not want the boatman to see that she was crying. She wanted to be back home with her mother and sister, not arriving at an unknown destination and meeting strangers.

'There's Flora,' said Manolis and Fotini raised her head to see a diminutive figure waving to them. 'I'll ask her to take you to meet Yannis and Phaedra. I'm sure they will ask you to stay with them until a house is ready for you.'

Manolis threw a rope deftly over a bollard and secured the craft. He helped Fotini ashore and then began to unload the goods he had brought along with Fotini's possessions.

Flora held out her hand to Fotini. 'Hello, I'm Flora. Welcome to Spinalonga. What's your name?'

'Fotini.'

'Come with me and we'll see if Yannis and Phaedra are around.

Manolis will bring your belongings up to my house. They'll be perfectly safe. Where have you come from?'

Fotini was about to say Kastelli when she remembered her father's instructions. 'Kritsa.'

Flora led the way from the storeroom up to the main road and down to the square where she knocked and opened the door to Yannis's house. There was no answer when she called their names.

'We'll sit and wait for one of them to appear. The water fountain is over there if you want a drink.'

Fotini shook her head. Flora began to ask questions about the work she had done in her village and Fotini seemed perplexed and hesitant in her answers. Finally Flora gave up.

'I might as well show you around rather than sit here waiting for them. Yannis could be teaching and Phaedra has probably gone up to the hospital.'

Fotini followed Flora back along the main road where Flora stopped at one of the shops and bought some courgettes which she gave to Fotini to carry. They stopped at the church and Fotini was welcomed by Father Minos before they continued up to Flora's house where Manolis was sitting outside with a queue of people.

'Why are all those people waiting to speak to the boatman?'

Flora shrugged. 'They've either come to ask him for some money or to sign for the goods he has bought for them. He'll be quite a while.'

'I haven't any money with me.' Fotini's lip trembled. 'I was expecting to be admitted to the hospital and didn't know I would need any money.'

'Didn't you do any work in your village and earn money?'

Fotini shook her head. 'I just helped with the cooking and cleaning. I also know how to weave and knit.'

Flora gave her a quizzical look. The girl should have been paid for cooking and cleaning. 'Well you don't need to have any money with you. We'll ask Manolis to add your name to the ledger and Doctor Stavros will inform the government that you've arrived so you'll receive the same pension as the rest of us. It's about seven drachmas a week and you can buy anything that's here on the island or save it up. If there's something you want from the mainland Manolis will buy it for you and then you pay him.'

'What about my food? You bought some vegetables from one of the shops.'

'The boats bring over most of our basic supplies and you just help yourself from the storeroom. I'll make a meal for us whilst we wait for Yannis. You can help me and there'll be enough for three.'

She collected some pans and plates from the house and took them back outside where she sliced the courgettes and Fotini peeled and chopped the onions, until Flora finally spotted Yannis in the queue.

'I'll ask Yannis to come over and talk to you. He'll know where you can live.'

Yannis shook his head. 'Give me a few minutes to see Manolis. I don't want to lose my place in the queue.' Finally Yannis joined them outside Flora's house. 'I'm going up to the hospital to have lunch with Phaedra and you are welcome to join us, Fotini. There's always plenty cooked.'

'That's very kind of you, sir, but Flora has asked me to share the meal we have prepared.' Flora felt it would be churlish to refuse the offer Flora had made, but she did not want to offend this strange man.

Yannis smiled. 'You don't have to call me "sir". I'm Yannis.' He rose to his feet. 'I'll see you again when we have both had something to eat.'

Fotini entered Yannis's house. It was smaller than she had imagined when she had seen it from outside. Yannis carried one of her sacks up the wooden stairs and placed it beside the mattress.

'This is your room. There is no one staying next door at present. I'll bring up your other sack and then leave you to get organised. Your welcome to come back downstairs whenever you're ready.'

'I'd quite like to have a rest.'

'Whatever you want. We'll be meeting up with some of the other residents of the island this evening and it would be a good opportunity for you to get to know them. Phaedra will be around this afternoon and she'll be able to answer any questions you have.'

Doctor Stavros informed Fotini that the blood test he had taken had confirmed his initial diagnosis.

'That means I have to stay here?'

'I'm afraid so. You'll very soon become used to the idea and find the people friendly and helpful.'

Fotini accepted the news with tears in her eyes. She would never see her family again.

'Where will I live?' she asked.

'Yannis will make sure you have a little house somewhere and until then you can stay with him and Phaedra. They'll look after you.'

After a short stay with Yannis and Phaedra Fotini moved into one of the small houses up the hill. Her new neighbours had made her feel welcome. She was invited in to have a meal with Christos and Eleni that evening and after they had eaten Aristo joined them for a glass of wine. He assured Fotini that if there was anything he was able to help her with she only had to ask.

Her only furniture consisted of one of the mattresses that was sent over to the island regularly and a chair that Father Minos had lent her. Having assessed her immediate needs she asked Manolis to buy some plates, dishes and cooking utensils for her She could sit with her dishes on her lap whilst she ate. Her next priority would be to ask Manolis to bring her some knitting wool so she could make herself a blanket. Although she slept in her clothes with her cloak over her she was beginning to feel the cold.

Doctor Stavros entered the information that Ariadne had died into his notebook. He had updated the notes Doctor Kandakis had given him about the villagers regularly and he searched for the page where Ariadne was named to update the details. It was useful to have a cross reference. He slapped his hand on the table as he once again saw Phaedra's name and was reminded that she had lived in Kastelli. She had arrived on Spinalonga when only a teenager. Could she be one of the children Despina had mentioned and if so where was her brother? He had been intending to visit Despina in Kastelli for well over year. His only excuse was pressure of work; every village appeared to have someone either ill or injured and this left him no time to make enquiries. He hoped Despina would remember the name of the brother and sister who had been sent away. He would couch his questions carefully and be discreet.

He could hear Despina working on her loom from outside the door and waited for a break before he knocked.

'I'm sorry to disturb you, but I am visiting the village today and thought I would just call in to ask after your daughter.'

'There's no change in her, but you're welcome to come in and see for yourself..'

Doctor Stavros stood before Eleni's pallet. She muttered something then opened her eyes and looked at the doctor. Immediately a maniacal scream came from her and she began to rock herself to and fro.

The doctor moved away. 'I'm sorry. I appear to have upset her.'

'A new face often has that effect. You mustn't blame yourself.'

Doctor Stavros wondered just how many people visited Despina and tolerated her daughter's bizarre behaviour.

'I won't upset her further by asking to examine her. Is she keeping physically well?'

'Had a cold a few weeks ago, but nothing to cause concern. Most of the villagers seemed to have it and I expect her father caught it from a customer and gave it to me and I passed it on.'

'It didn't go to her chest? She had no difficulty in breathing?'

'Not that I noticed. She seemed no different from usual.'

'Very sad that she suffered such an injury. You told me it was caused by a woman in the village whose children had been taken away. You wouldn't remember their names, I suppose?'

'I've not thought about them for a long time. Yiorgo, their grandfather insisted that there had been a mistake and they would soon return, but as their parents had left the village how would they have known where to go?'

'They would probably have come here. I understand their grandfather keeps the taverna. He may have news of them.'

'Their other grandfather, Andreas, Elias's father, is a farmer. He still lives locally. They returned the cart to him so he may well know where his son and daughter in law are living now.'

'Very likely. It would help if I could ask after them by name. Both men could have a number of other grandchildren by now.'

'Not likely. I attended Maria on a number of occasions. The first two children were born healthy, but after that she either miscarried or the child died within a day or so of being born. She began to blame me, saying it was my fault and I was too old, and asked that Theophalia attended her. I know she was expecting again when they left the village. She may have had more success that time.'

'I would hope so. Another child would be some consolation to her for losing her oldest. Do you remember their names?' persisted Doctor Stavros.

'Mikaelis was the boy and I think the girl was called Phaedra.'

'Has anyone else from the village suffered from the same illness?'

Despina shook her head. 'Not that I've heard. Their grandfather could be right and it was a mistake to take them. If so I hope they were able to be reunited with their parents.'

Doctor Stavros smiled at her. 'I hope their grandfather will be able to confirm that for me. I'll leave you now to continue with your weaving. Thank you for your time. If you have any concerns about Eleni's health contact me and I will make her a priority visit.'

Doctor Stavros finally found Andreas turning the earth in one of his fields prior to planting courgettes.

'May I interrupt you?' asked the doctor.

'Who asked you to visit me? I'm not sick, never have been. A life in the open air helps you to stay healthy.'

'I thoroughly agree with you. I just wanted to ask if you knew where your son and daughter in law are living now?'

'Why? So you can go and hound them and haul them off for tests?'

'Not at all. I think they would be pleased to know that their daughter, her name is Phaedra, I believe, is as well as can be expected and is happily married.'

'Married? She's not allowed to marry.'

'Regulations are different on Spinalonga.'

Andreas passed a grimy hand over his forehead. 'Is that where they are?'

'It is where Phaedra lives. I have no news of your grandson, Mikaelis.'

'Who told you Phaedra was my granddaughter? Was it that Eleni's mother?'

'I have Doctor Kandakis's notes and I have been locating any people who lived locally and have been sent away. I treat every disclosure confidentially and they are usually pleased to have news of their loved ones.'

Andreas gave a deep sigh. 'It was my fault. I said she should be hidden away and not taken to the doctor.'

'The outcome would have been the same.'

'There was nothing wrong with Mikaelis. He should not have been taken.'

'Then he could well be living with his parents.'

Andreas shook his head. 'They've not heard from him any more than I have.'

'I'll continue to try to trace the boy. Perhaps Yiorgo at the taverna has some news of him. He is also their grandfather.'

'He would have told me.' Andreas picked up his hoe.

'When you next see your son please give him the news about his daughter. That was the only reason I was searching for them.'

Andreas nodded sullenly. He was certainly not going to disclose the whereabouts of Elias and Maria to the doctor.

Doctor Stavros returned to the village and entered the taverna, wondering what kind of reception he would receive from the man when he mentioned Phaedra.

'Do you want some food?' asked Yiorgo. If the doctor called in at the taverna it usually meant he was hungry.

'A bowl of soup and some bread would be sufficient if that is no trouble.'

Yiorgo shrugged and called the order through the doorway to his wife.

'I really wanted to speak to you about your grandchildren; the ones who were taken away.'

'That's in the past. Over and forgotten by now.'

Doctor Stavros continued regardless of the man's disinterest. 'Surely you would like to know how they have fared? I have news of Phaedra. She is living on Spinalonga, happily married and keeping well. I am afraid I have no knowledge of the whereabouts of Mikaelis. I was wondering if you could help me. Have you heard anything from him?'

'No,' answered Yiorgo shortly.

'I think Phaedra would be grateful for any news about her brother.'

Yiorgo glared at Doctor Stavros. 'I've told you; I don't know where he is. If that's all you came in here for then you can leave now.'

'I would like a bowl of soup, but if it troubles you I can go elsewhere.'

Yiorgo did not reply. He walked through to the back room and moments later returned with a bowl of soup and plate of bread. 'Five drachmas.'

The price was extortionate, but the doctor did not argue. He would not eat at the taverna again as he was obviously unwelcome.

Doctor Stavros found Phaedra at the hospital with the other women. 'I'd like to talk to you, Phaedra. Maybe we could go somewhere a little more private?'

'Is it Yannis?' she asked anxiously.

'Nothing at all to do with Yannis,' Doctor Stavros assured her. 'I just want to ask you a couple of questions.'

Phaedra accompanied the doctor to the far side of the hospital. 'What's wrong?' she asked.

'You come from Kastelli, don't you?'

Phaedra nodded and the doctor continued.

'I believe I have met both your grandfathers. I gave them news of you and they were pleased to hear that you are well and happy.'

'Did you tell my parents also?'

'I was unable to do that. They moved away from the village and they are not living in any of those that I visit. I was given the impression that your grandfather, the one who is a farmer, might know where they are and pass the news on to them. I understand that your brother was taken at the same time as yourself but they were unable to give me any news of him.'

Phaedra buried her head in her hands and sobbed. 'It was terrible. So terrible that I try never to think about it now.'

Doctor Stavros patted her shoulder. 'Can you tell me? I could at least let your grandfathers know his whereabouts.'

'He wasn't sick,' insisted Phaedra as she tried to control her emotion. 'He was just visiting me when the men came.'

'Did the doctor examine him?'

Phaedra shook her head. 'The doctor put us on a boat and sent us here. We had to walk down a piece of wood to get onto the jetty and Mikaelis fell off into the sea. He couldn't swim and the boatmen refused to help him. I tried to reach him, but he was too far away. His head went under.'

Doctor Stavros looked at Phaedra sympathetically. 'What a terrible experience for you. I am not surprised that you have tried to forget it.'

'It was getting too dark to look for him that night but I spent all the next day looking for him. Flora came with me, but there was no sign of him. I always hoped that somehow he had managed to get back to the mainland.'

'Neither of your grandfathers had any news of him so I think that was unlikely, I'm afraid.'

Phaedra gave a deep sigh. 'Ariadne said he had probably been washed out to sea or else he would have been washed up on the rocks and not survived. In my heart I knew that was true, but I held on to the hope that he had returned home.'

'I would like to tell your grandfathers. I think they would be grateful to know the truth about your brother, and also your parents if they can be contacted.'

Phaedra nodded. 'They have a right to know.'

Whenever the wind blew the window frames of Fotini's house rattled, the unaccustomed noise frightening and keeping her awake at night. When she mentioned this to Aristo he had immediately rectified the problem by shaping some wedges and inserting them between her window frames and the walls.

Fotini offered to pay him, but he refused. 'It took me no more than a few minutes to shape them and it was from some odd pieces of wood that I had lying around from where I had made my table. I'd be grateful if you'd cook me a meal sometime. That would be payment enough.'

'Of course,' agreed Fotini, 'but you will have to eat it in your house. I only have one chair.'

'You would be welcome to join me in my house or I could bring a chair in here.' He looked around her bare room. 'I could easily make you another chair and also a table.'

Fotini looked at him doubtfully. 'I've just bought some wool to make a blanket for myself. I'm planning to knit shawls and blankets and hope I can sell them. Until I have some more pension money I don't think I could afford furniture.'

Aristo smiled at her. 'All you would have to pay for would be the timber. You could always cook me another meal when I've made them.'

'I don't think a meal would be sufficient payment. Would you like me to make you a blanket?'

Aristo nodded. 'That sounds like a good arrangement. I'll ask Manolis to buy me some timber and you could repay me when you have enough saved on your account.'

'I would be grateful. It isn't very comfortable living here at the moment.'

'Once I've done that I could make you some shelves for your belongings. By this time next year you should have a proper home.'

'I'll pay you for everything,' Fotini assured him. 'As soon as I have enough money on my account you must give me your bill for the timber and I'll ask Manolis to transfer the amount to you.'

'I trust you, Fotini. I also know that you are not going to run away,' he smiled.

Fotini asked Manolis how much money she had on her account. 'I need more knitting wool,' she explained, 'and I owe Aristo some money.'

'You've plenty there for knitting wool. Why don't I ask your young man in Aghios Nikolaos to settle Aristo's account?'

Fotini shook her head. 'I don't know anyone in Aghios Nikolaos.'

'A young man was asking after you. He said his name was Yiorgo and he works at the shipping office.'

Fotini flushed. It could only be her brother in law who was making enquiries.

Manolis winked. 'He seemed very anxious about you. Would you like me to deliver a message to him?'

Fotini flushed even more deeply. 'Would you be willing to take a letter to him?'

'I'm not supposed to, but if you were willing to make it worth my while I could probably manage a discreet delivery.'

'How much?'

'One drachma.'

Fotini nodded. 'I'll need some writing paper. Can you bring me some tomorrow and an envelope?'

'As well as the knitting wool?'

'Provided there is enough on my account.'

Fotini could hardy wait for Manolis to arrive the following day so she could make a start on a letter to her sister.

The letter Fotini had commenced writing for Manolis to deliver to Yiorgo became longer and longer as she described her life on the island in minute detail. She wrote more than a page describing how there were shops on the island and if they did not have something that you wanted you could ask Manolis to buy it from the mainland and pay for it from the pension the government gave them.

She had insisted that Manolis bought her china plates as she refused to eat off tin plates like a peasant in the fields. She had bought wool and made a new shawl for herself and a blanket. Although she hoped she would be able to sell the shawls and blankets she made to the villagers she could not afford to buy any more wool at present as she needed many things for her house.

Fotini went on to describe how there was often a small gathering in the square in front of Yannis and Phaedra's house and music would be played and those who were able would dance. If people did not want to join in they could go to the taverna and spend the evening there or buy a bottle of wine and take it to share with their friends. Although Fotini missed her family she found life on the island far more social than when she had lived in Kastelli and only been allowed to join in with the villagers' celebrations if her father gave his permission.

Interspersed with her descriptions were frequent references to Aristo and what a good, kind man he was; how he had helped to fix her windows, made her a chair and was making her a table.

Fotini waited anxiously for a reply and could not believe it when Manolis delivered her a sack. Carefully she carried it back to her house and unpacked the contents, hardly able to believe her eyes when she saw that along with a new skirt and blouse she had also been sent a new pair of boots. The candles would mean that she could have some light during the evening and needles, cotton, and a quantity of knitting wool were an additional bonus.

She composed a long and grateful letter back and paid Manolis to take it to Aghios Nikolaos and deliver it to Yiorgo.

Phaedra watched the friendship between Aristo and Fotini growing. During the morning Fotini would join her up at the hospital, helping Spiro by mopping mattresses clean and placing them outside in the open air to dry before sitting with Elena and Ritsa preparing vegetables and meat that would be made into a meal for those who lived permanently in the hospital. Aristo would go wherever Takkis asked to help with repairs or to make a new window frame or door, but as soon as Takkis called a halt to the day's work he would hurry back to his house where Fotini would be sitting next door knitting and looking for his return.

'We have a romance on our hands,' Phaedra said to Flora. 'Fotini and Aristo are planning to get married with Father Minos's blessing.'

'They're a nice couple. Did Yannis organise houses next door to each other with that in mind?'

Phaedra shook her head. 'I don't think so. It was just the next house that was finished so she could move in. I enjoy having new arrivals to stay, but I'm always pleased when they can move out and we have our house back to ourselves for a few days.'

Flora told Manolis about the proposed wedding between Fotini and Aristo and he looked at her with concern. 'Can you ask Aristo to come and speak to me? I ought to pass some information on to him.'

'He'll be working somewhere with Takkis. Is there a problem with something he has asked you to buy?'

Manolis shook his head. 'No, I just need to speak to him. It could be important.'

Flora was used to going to find people on the island to tell them that Manolis had brought the goods they had ordered. She walked down to the square and up the steps that led to the area above the tunnel of the Venetian fortress. There she saw Aristo hanging a door on one of the new houses that had been built up there.

'I'm sorry to interrupt you, Aristo, but Manolis says he needs to speak to you.'

Aristo nodded without looking up. 'I'll have to finish hanging this door first.'

Flora watched as Aristo continued to screw the hinges into place and then swung the door closed. 'Fits perfectly,' he announced with a satisfied smile. He collected together the tools he had been using. 'I'll just take these back to Takkis and then I'll come up.'

Aristo strolled up to where Manolis sat outside Flora's house. 'I understand you wanted to see me. I was planning to check with you how much money I have on my account. I'm getting married and I understand that I will be expected to provide a wedding feast for my friends.'

Manolis shook his head. 'No, it's something personal. Do you know that Fotini is writing to a man on the mainland and receiving replies?'

Aristo looked at Manolis in disbelief. 'Are you sure? She's never mentioned anyone to me.'

'Who do you think sent her gifts? Ask her if you don't believe me. I've been taking letters back and forth between them for months now.'

Aristo turned away. He could not believe that Fotini was so

deceitful. If she cared for a man on the mainland their proposed marriage was doomed and he would tell Father Minos to cancel the arrangements. He spent the remainder of the day turning the information over in his mind. He would have to ask Fotini to tell him the truth, however much it might hurt him.

Aristo looked at Fotini accusingly. 'I hear that you are writing to a man in Aghios Nikolaos. Who is he? Are you already married or betrothed?'

Fotini shook her head. 'Certainly not. He's my sister's husband.' Tears gathered in Fotini's eyes. 'Yiorgo has been taking letters to my sister for me. My father said I wasn't to give my family name or give anyone any information about them.'

Aristo raised his eyebrows. 'Why ever not?'

'He didn't want it known in the village that I was over here. My father is an important government official. If it became known that I was sick he might be dismissed.'

Aristo sighed. 'I think you need to disobey your father on this occasion. If we are to be married there should be no secrets between us.'

'You'll not tell anyone? Not even Father Minos or Doctor Stavros?'

'There is no need for either of them to know.'

'I'm Fotini Danniakis,' she said finally. 'I don't come from Kritsa, I come from Kastelli.'

Aristo took her in his arms. 'It wouldn't matter how cross your father might be with you for telling me. He can't come over here and punish you and I'll always be here to look after you.'

Fotini wrote a long letter to her sister, explaining about the misunderstanding there had been between her and Aristo earlier. "I had to tell Aristo the truth. He has promised to keep the information to himself. I trust him, as you trust Yiorgo, as he is now my husband." She continued to describe her wedding day and how happy she was with Aristo.

1936

A generator was delivered to the island and workmen appeared. They were watched as they strung wires between the houses, connecting them with china fitments and finally placing light bulbs in the houses and connecting them to a switch. It was a novelty and many of the residents left their living room light switched on all day and at night the whole island would be lit up. Spiro was the most grateful.

'At last I will be able to see what I'm doing. Carrying an oil lamp around between the mattresses is not safe. If I tripped a fire would start and I would never be able to get everyone out before it took hold.'

Yannis considered the installation. The workmen from the mainland had spent weeks on the island. If they were able to come over there was no reason why they should not have their relatives visit. Father Minos agreed to support Yannis in his petition to the government and Phaedra could not believe it when Yannis told them that they had finally been granted permission to have visitors.

'Visitors? You mean proper visitors from the mainland like family and friends?'

Yannis nodded. 'They'll have to be disinfected when they arrive and also before they leave like the workmen were,' he explained. 'I'm quite pleased about that. We don't want them bringing us any germs from the mainland and we certainly do not want to infect them.'

'What germs would they bring us?' asked Phaedra.

'Could be anything. If a child in their village has measles or chicken pox they could bring that over to us.'

'Will your sister come over to visit you?'

'She's bound to. I can't wait to introduce you to her.'

'Do you think Doctor Stavros would tell my grandfathers that we are allowed to have visitors?'

'I'm sure he'll make the knowledge known in every village he visits. He could tell the priest and ask him to tell everyone when they go to church on Sunday. That way no one would be singled out.'

'Will they be able to come over whenever they please or only on certain days?'

'I don't see why they should be restricted to certain days,' frowned Yannis. 'That could be difficult for some people. The boatmen come over every day so they only have to ask for a ride.'

'Fotini would be pleased if her sister and brother in law visited, but she doesn't think her father will allow them.'

'Her brother in law had enough initiative to seek out Manolis so letters could go backwards and forwards between them. I'm sure he'll think of a way to bring her sister over.'

Doctor Stavros was not best pleased when he heard the news. 'I agree that you should be allowed visits from your family provided they are healthy. Even a common cold germ could be fatal to some of the residents here. They often don't know they have a cold until they begin to cough and sneeze but they will have been carrying the germs for some days beforehand. That could make them susceptible for picking up germs from here. I can't give all of them a medical check.'

'We'll just have to rely on them being honest and if they think they are going down with a cold or anything else they use their common sense and avoid us. We've waited this long. A few more days for some of us will make no difference.'

'I'll just have to insist they go through the disinfection process,' answered the doctor morosely.

'I imagine they will be more than happy to do that. They'll none of them want to return home and find they will be joining us permanently over here.'

Doctor Stavros hoped fervently that would not happen. He checked and re-checked his notebooks. He was sure he had managed to notify any villager if their relative had died since he had become the doctor in charge of the island, but there could be others that he had been unable to trace. He would not want them to arrive expecting to meet someone who was no longer alive.

'I think we should make a definite date for when visits can commence,' said Doctor Stavros. 'It will take me a month to visit all the villages and ask the priest to spread the news. It could cause trouble if some people were able to come before others.'

'Is it only relatives who are allowed to visit?' asked Yannis. 'I'm thinking of those who have come here from mainland Greece. It's unlikely any of their relatives would be able to visit and they'll feel very left out and isolated.'

'As far as I am aware there are no restrictions, but I can't think why anyone would want to visit unless they have a relative here.'

'If a mother or father was too old or infirm to make the journey it would mean news could be taken back to them,' answered Yannis reasonably. 'My mother couldn't possibly make the journey but I know she'll be pleased at whatever news my sister takes back about me.'

'Do you think Maria and Yiorgo will visit us before I have the baby?' Fotini asked Aristo excitedly.

'How do I know?' answered Aristo gently. 'Your father may not permit them to come over here.'

'He's certain to say they cannot come, but I'm sure they'll find a way to visit without asking him.'

'I hope they will, but don't sit looking for them every day. You know Father Minos said it would take some time before the doctor had visited all the villages and spread the news.'

'Yannis thinks his sister will come as soon as she knows.'

'She probably will. He's one of the lucky few who have a relative close by. For many people it will be a day's journey to reach the coast.'

Fotini's face fell. 'I hadn't thought about that. Maria and Yiorgo probably won't be able to come then.'

'Just be patient and wait and see what happens. You have our baby to look forward to, even if you cannot see your sister.'

Yannis was correct in his prediction that Anna would arrive on Spinalonga as soon as she heard that the visiting restrictions had been lifted. Flora greeted her as she stepped out of the disinfection room.

'Hello, who have you come to visit?'

Anna smiled. This must be the girl that Yannis had told them about who had endured the amputation of her arm with hardly any anaesthetic.

'You must be Flora. I've come to see Yannis Christoforakis. He's my brother.'

A broad smile crossed Flora's face. 'He'll be thrilled to see you. He's been waiting for this day ever since we were told we could have visitors.'

'I only heard yesterday.'

'Anna! Anna, it is you. I was sure it was you I could see sitting in the boat.' Yannis rushed towards his sister and stopped a short distance away. 'I'd love to hug and kiss you, but I wouldn't want to make you ill.'

Anna shrugged. 'I doubt that you would. The winter before you were diagnosed we all lived together and you shared a bed with Yiorgo. That would have been the time to become infected.'

'You're probably right, but I wouldn't want to take the chance. Come with me and I'll show you where I live and then we'll find Phaedra.'

'I'll go,' offered Flora. 'She's bound to be up at the hospital.

You don't want to go up there.' Before Yannis could answer her she had set off running up the path.

Yannis opened the door to his house and ushered Anna inside. 'You've no idea how good it is to see you. How's Mamma? And Pappa and Yiorgo and Stelios? What about the children? Are you still looking after the baby?'

'Slow down, Yannis. Mamma is much the same, Pappa and Yiorgo are well and Stelios is in Heraklion at the University. The baby, assuming you mean little Yannis, is now six years old and Marisa is nearly nine. I've left them with Eleni and I will need to get back to attend to Mamma. She wished she could come with me, but it's impossible. I persuaded Davros to bring me over today when he made his first journey with the water barrels. I can't stay long as he has agreed to take me back after his next delivery.'

'What about Babbis?'

'He's still very melancholy. I don't think he will ever get over losing Maria. He alternately blames himself and then little Yannis. I was just thinking he was getting better when he lost his mother and that made him very depressed again.' Anna sighed. 'I wish he'd meet a local girl and get married again.' She smiled sadly. 'Of course, if that happened he would take the children away from me. I think of them as my own now. Yannis even calls me "Mamma Anna".'

Yannis looked at Anna and was going to make a suggestion that would solve the problem when Anna interrupted him. 'Show me the electricity, Yannis, and tell me how it works. I was so frightened when I saw the lights all over the island. I thought everywhere was on fire.'

Yannis pointed to the naked bulb that hung down from his ceiling.' Go over by the door and put the switch down.'

Cautiously Anna obeyed him and gasped as the bulb was illuminated. 'It's like having an oil lamp hanging there.'

'It's better than that,' Yannis assured her. 'You don't have to put oil in it and when it becomes dark the room is as bright as if the sun was shining.'

Anna pressed the switch up and down, marvelling at the way the bulb lit up each time, when Phaedra opened the door.

'Hello, you must be Anna. Flora was so excited when she told me you were here she could hardly stand still. Spiro insisted I left the mattresses and came down here to meet you immediately.'

'I'm very pleased to meet you at last, Phaedra. When Yannis came over in his bath tub he kept talking about you and we were delighted when we heard you were married.' Anna looked at Phaedra's face. There was a large discolouration mark on one side that reached up to her hair line and down to her ear. The other side of her face was unblemished and showed that she would have been a pretty woman had the ravishes of the disease not taken its toll, making her look considerably older than her years.

'I was so worried that he would sink or might decide to stay over there with you hidden in the hills.'

'My brother might do some silly things, but he's not stupid. It was one thing taking a chance on making a visit but he knew it would be impossible to stay hidden for very long. I had the impression that he wanted to return here to be with you.'

'That was what he told me.' Phaedra blushed. 'I must make you some coffee. Have a seat. I'll stay with you for a while and then I ought to return to help Spiro and you two will have much to talk about together.'

Yannis turned to Anna as Phaedra went into their kitchen area. 'Well?' he asked quietly.

'Well what?'

'What do you think of my wife?'

'She's lovely, Yannis. Mamma said she thought you would have chosen the loveliest girl on the island and I'll be able to tell her that she was right.'

'You really like her?' asked Yannis anxiously.

'Yes, I do. I'm sure that if you lived in the village we would become friends.'

Yannis smiled in relief. 'I was worried that you might find her disfigurement distasteful.'

Anna shrugged. 'I've seen worse. Angelika tipped a bowl of boiling water over her face. Her scars are far worse that Phaedra's blemishes.'

Phaedra returned, instead of bringing coffee she had a bottle of wine along with a plate of biscuits. 'I'm sorry we have to drink from tin mugs but I thought we really should have a glass of wine to celebrate. You are our very first visitor.'

'I hope I will be the first of many. I'll come over every week to visit you – if I may,' she added.

'You will always be welcome, along with Yiorgo and Pappa and anyone else who is prepared to come.'

The visit that Flora finally received from her sisters was not so successful. She did not recognise either of them when they stepped ashore and asked who they had come to visit.

Sotiria looked Flora up and down. 'I imagine it must be you as you have only one arm.'

Flora looked at her in surprise. No one had mentioned her amputation in a long time. 'Me?'

'You're Flora, aren't you? I'm Sotiria and this is Olga.'

Flora felt embarrassed. 'I'm sorry. I didn't recognise you. I was only a little girl when I last saw you. Come up to my house and we can sit and talk. I'd like to hear all your news. I'll introduce you to Manolis when he arrives.'

Silently the two women followed Flora up to her house, averting their eyes from anyone they met on the way. The island looked very little different from their villages but the inhabitants made them feel uncomfortable, so many people had bandages on their limbs or were using a stick to aid them as they walked.

'Is everyone sick?' asked Sotiria eventually.

'Of course, everyone except Father Minos and Manolis. Father Minos decided to come and live here with us. Once there were enough houses for everyone we cleaned the church and he holds regular services. Takkis supervises the building of the houses for the people who are sent over here, but Yiorgo does most of the physical work since Takkis fell off a ladder and broke his leg. It was Yannis who insisted that we should all have a home to call our own rather than having to live crammed in together. Oh, here comes Manolis. He'll be up here all day as people will be coming up to settle their accounts or ask him for money, so you won't have to worry about missing the boat to take you back to Aghios Nikolaos.'

'We need to return to Plaka. We were told there would be a boat available during the morning.'

Flora nodded. 'They always bring the water first and then some others come over with food.'

'We mustn't miss a boat. We have to walk home from Plaka.' Olga looked around. People were gathering close by and she felt uncomfortable. 'We won't be able to see them from here.'

'Would you prefer to go and sit down by the jetty?'

Both Olga and Sotiria nodded firmly. 'That would be more practical.'

No more than two hours later the sisters left Spinalonga, assuring Flora they would visit her again when they had time.

Flora returned to where Manolis sat outside her house. She shook her head sadly. 'I'm sure they only came to see me out of a sense of duty. We hadn't seen each other for so long that we didn't know what to talk about. I didn't even recognise them when they arrived.'

Manolis shrugged and placed his arm around her. 'You don't need them. They have their lives. Your family are over here now and you always have me.'

Fotini could not believe it when she saw her sister and Yiorgo waiting outside the church on Spinalonga. She and Maria fell into each others arms crying tears of happiness.

'I hoped you would come, but I never thought Pappa would give you permission.'

'Pappa doesn't know we are here. Yiorgo told him he had to go to Heraklion on business and wanted me to go with him. Mamma agreed to look after Alexandros so here we are.'

'I would like to see Mamma and Pappa again.'

'I'm sure they will come one day. Can we see your house, Fo, and meet Aristo?'

'I'll take you up to my house and then I'll go and find Aristo. He'll be expecting to find me up at the hospital and will be worried if I am not there. Look, this is our main street where the shops are. We can buy almost anything we want and if it isn't available we ask Manolis to bring it over for us.'

Fotini took a side turning and walked up the rough road slowly, her hand supporting her stomach.

'Are you alright, Fo?' asked Maria anxiously.

'I'm fine. It just helps me walk if I hold the baby up. Roula says the baby is in the right place to be born and it could be any time soon.'

'Not today, I hope,' said Yiorgo.

'I would love it to be born today,' replied Maria. 'That would be so exciting.' She then remembered the difficult birth she had experienced with Alexandros. 'Provided it all goes well, of course.'

'There's no reason why it shouldn't. Doctor Stavros says I'm fit and well. Here we are.' Fotini opened the door of the house she shared with Aristo. 'I used to live next door, but I moved in with Aristo after we were married. His living room was larger than mine. Sit down and I'll go and tell Aristo you are here.'

Maria and Yiorgo looked around the room, noting the curtains and rag rug that Fotini had made. In one corner stood a wooden cradle and Yiorgo inspected it, running his hands over the smooth wood.

'Aristo is a clever man if he makes items of this quality. We could do with a carpenter like him in Kastelli.'

Fotini returned and smiled happily at them. 'Aristo is going up to the hospital and will bring back a bowl of vegetable stew. He said it would be quicker and easier for me to heat up than cooking the dolmades that I had made earlier and no one will go short. We always make more than enough food for the patients and the workers. Now tell me all the news from Kastelli.'

Maria shrugged. 'Mamma is well, Pappa says his arthritis is troubling him. Alexandros is a joy. He is beginning to chatter away and keeps us amused all day. Eva has had another baby.'

'Another!' exclaimed Fotini.

Maria nodded. 'That will be five now. She keeps saying they will not have any more and before you know it she is pregnant again. They have no money. I gave her some of Alexandros's clothes that he had outgrown and she was so grateful. I have made some new nightdresses for your baby and I will make some more clothes when we know if it is a boy or a girl.'

'I have made some, but I am not as clever with my needle as you. '

As they talked Aristo arrived and Maria was struck by his good looks; without the unsightly blemish on his forehead he would have been a handsome man. He shook hands with Yiorgo and Maria and welcomed them to his house.

'I am sorry that we do not have more than two chairs. I can take the table outside and I am sure Christos will lend me his chairs.'

'There's no need,' Yiorgo assured him. 'I'll be happy to sit on the ground.'

'We can all sit on the ground,' said Fotini. 'We can picnic as we used to when we picked the olives or apples.'

Aristo shook his head. 'You cannot sit on the ground, Fotini. You will never get up. You and Maria must sit at the table and Yiorgo and I will sit on the ground. I'll go to the taverna and get a bottle of wine. We need to celebrate.'

Yiorgo went to take some money from his pocket but Aristo shook his head.

'I wish we had some proper glasses to drink from,' complained Fotini. 'I was going to buy some, but when we knew I was having a baby I thought we should save our money. We can drink from enamel mugs for a while longer without coming to any harm. When we have eaten we'll take you on a tour of our island and then you will know exactly where I'm talking about when I write to you.'

'We've already seen the shops.'

'I'll take you up to the hospital and you can meet Spiro. I'll show you where we go to do our washing and where the water tanks are. I'm sure Father Minos would appreciate you making a visit to the church.'

'I would like to see inside.'

Aristo returned and placed the bottle he had purchased on the table. 'I will open it when Fotini says our food is ready.'

'The thing I want to see most is the wooden seat you have made in the outhouse. I'm not as clever as you, but if you tell me how to make it I'm sure I'll manage.'

'I want to see the electricity,' said Maria. 'Where is it?'

Aristo smiled. 'Up there.' He pointed to the bulb that hung down from the ceiling.'

'How do you reach it?'

'You don't have to touch it. Look.' Aristo stood by the door and pushed a switch down; immediately the bulb glowed. 'When it's dark the bulb shines more brightly. Fotini can see to sit and sew or knit by the light.'

Maria looked at it in amazement. 'How does it work?'

'Electricity comes through wires from a generator.'

Maria looked at him sceptically. She did not understand what a generator was or how anything the size of the bulb could pass through a wire. She would have to ask Yiorgo later rather than show her ignorance. 'Very clever. I wish we had that in Kastelli. Pappa doesn't like us to have more than one oil lamp lit at a time as he says it's a waste of money.'

Fotini smiled understandingly; their father had never been one for spending money unnecessarily.

Between them Aristo and Yiorgo carried the table outside and returned for the chairs. Maria insisted that she carried out the pot of vegetable stew whilst Fotini brought out the plates and mugs. Aristo poured a generous measure into each mug and held his up.

'I would like to welcome you both to our home and say how much your visit means to both of us. I hope you will come again.'

Having eaten the vegetable stew, which they declared was as good as any Sofia made, Fotini and Aristo walked back down to the main area with them. They pointed out Yannis's house, the baker, the tavernas and the washing troughs before entering the church, received a blessing from Father Minos and lit a candle before continuing up to where Manolis was sitting outside Flora's house.

'What time do we have to leave?' asked Yiorgo.

Manolis shrugged. 'There's no rush. You go back to Fotini's house and I'll ask Flora to run down and tell you when the doctor has finished his work over here. He's asked the government to provide beds for the people in the hospital so he doesn't have to spend all his time kneeling down when he treats them. He and Spiro are working out how many beds will fit in or if they will have to ask Takkis and Yiorgo to build on two extra rooms and how large they will have to be. He's supposed to be having some equipment coming over that will help him if he has to operate and space will be needed to accommodate that.'

'I don't see why he needs special equipment to operate,' said Flora. 'He did a wonderful operation on my arm and that was in the open air.'

'It would have been less painful for you if the hospital had been up and running by then,' Manolis reminded her. 'The doctor would have had sufficient morphine with him and you would have felt nothing.'

'The pain is forgotten now. He was successful and that's all that matters.' Flora smiled at Manolis. 'I'm just so grateful that I am alive and able to enjoy my life.'

Yiorgo and Maria exchanged glances. So far everyone they had met appeared to be happy living on Spinalonga.

As Manolis rowed away from the jetty he pointed up at the ramparts of the Venetian fortress where Aristo and Fotini could be seen waving farewell to them. Clutching Yiorgo's hand and with tears in her eyes Maria waved back.

'We can come again, can't we, Yiorgo? I want to see Fo's baby when it is born.'

Yiorgo squeezed her hand. 'I'm sure we'll manage to come again.'

Phaedra returned from the shops, the butcher had some chicken and she had sniffed at it suspiciously before deciding it was still fresh enough to be used for their evening meal. She had added some onions, tomatoes and peppers from the greengrocer and collected some rice from the storeroom. She would prepare kebabs and cook rice to go with them, along with a tomato and onion salad. Once home she realised she did not have enough vinegar for the salad she proposed to make. She would have to make another visit to the storeroom on her return from the hospital.

'Phaedra, are you there?' Flora opened her door and stood there smiling at her. 'I hoped you would still be at home. I've brought a visitor for you.'

'A visitor? For me?' Phaedra tried to peer around Flora. 'Who is it?'

'He says he's your grandfather.'

Phaedra was unable to move. 'My grandfather?' she said in disbelief. 'Which one?'

Andreas stood hesitantly on the threshold. 'Grandfather Andreas; your Pappa's father.'

'Can he come in?' asked Flora. 'I'll tell Spiro you have a visitor and can't come up this morning.'

Phaedra cast a quick glance around the living room. The bed was made and everywhere was tidy. 'Of course,' she managed to say.

Andreas walked inside and stopped. 'I'm so sorry, Phaedra.'

'Sorry? Why are you sorry? Come and sit down, Grandpa. I'll make you some coffee.'

'There's no need to go to any trouble.'

'It's no trouble. I'm delighted to see you. Do you have news of Mamma and Pappa? Let me make the coffee and then we can sit and talk.'

Andreas sat at the table and waited whilst Phaedra made coffee and brought some water through from the kitchen. It had been a difficult decision for him to make to visit his granddaughter and now he was here he would have to tell her about her mother.

'The doctor told me about Mikaelis,' he said gruffly to break their silence.

Tears came into Phaedra's eyes. 'I couldn't save him. I tried and I couldn't reach him. The water was too deep.'

'You're not to blame. It was my fault. I should never have suggested that you went up to live in a cave. I should have insisted that your Pappa took you to the doctor so you went to the hospital.'

Phaedra shook her head. 'This is the hospital, Grandpa. I just wish Mikaelis hadn't been with me when the men came. I kept telling them there was nothing wrong with him and I told the doctor. He wouldn't listen; he just sent us here. You mustn't feel guilty, Grandpa. If I had not been brought here I would not have met Yannis.'

'The doctor said you were married. Is that so?'

Phaedra held out her hand to show off her wedding ring. 'Yannis and I have been married for some years now. I'm very happy with him. Tell me about Mamma and Pappa. Have I any brothers or sisters?'

Andreas shook his head. 'They no longer live in Kastelli. She lost the baby she was carrying. Your mother isn't well.'

'What's wrong with her? I didn't infect her, did I?'

'No, nothing like that. It's in her head. She blames a woman in Kastelli for her loss. She carries a doll around with her and calls it her baby. She talks to it all the time, pretends it needs to be fed and put to bed.'

'Poor Mamma. Why should she blame someone in the village?'

'There was bad feeling between the two of them. It went back a long time; to before you were born. Somehow this woman found out you were living in the hills and told the doctor.'

'Is that why they moved away?'

'Your mother confronted the woman, actually beat her almost to death. I insisted that Elias took everything they could and leave that night before the villagers turned on them and drove them away. I think the fight and the shock of losing you and Mikaelis caused her to lose the baby and turned her mind.'

'That's terrible. Why didn't anyone try to stop them?'

'Your father tried, but your mother was out of control' Andreas shook his head again. 'Your poor father has a good deal to put up with. The villagers where they live now shun him as he has a deranged wife. Apart from her obsession with the doll she functions normally.' Andreas did not go into the details of the life that Maria inflicted on her husband; insisting that he waited for his meal until she had satisfied herself that her substitute baby was fed and asleep; then he had to talk quietly so as not to wake it; nor did he add that she called the doll either Phaedra or Mikaelis.

'Can nothing be done to help her? If she knew I was alive and well it might help her to get better. She could even come and visit me and see for herself.'

'I'll mention it to Elias when I see him next, but I don't know if he'll agree.'

'Why don't they return to Kastelli? After all this time the incident must be forgotten.'

'The woman your mother attacked is a helpless imbecile. It will never be forgotten whilst she is alive.'

'Oh, Grandpa. What an awful lot of trouble I have caused.'

'You didn't get sick deliberately.' He reached across the table and patted her hand. 'Tell me what you find to do with yourself over here.'

'There's plenty to do. I usually help up at the hospital in the morning, then there is our washing and I have to prepare a meal ready for Yannis.'

'This Yannis is the man you say you are married to?'

Phaedra nodded. 'He's very clever. He has taught many of the people over here how to read and write. He taught me and I can even read the newspaper now provided the words are not too long. Then I have to ask him what they mean.'

'He's good to you?'

'I couldn't wish to be married to anyone better.'

'You've no children?'

'It wouldn't be sensible. The doctor says they could be born infected.'.

'Provided you don't become like your mother.'

'I'm sure I won't. I haven't had children taken away or miscarried frequently. I don't know what it's like to be a mother.'

'Best keep it that way. I'll tell your father that I've seen you and leave it to him to decide whether to tell your mother.' Andreas rose. 'I'll be on my way and let you get about your business.'

'You don't have to go. You can stay until Manolis leaves. I'd like you to meet Yannis. He's teaching at the moment and he doesn't like to be disturbed then.'

Andreas shook his head. 'I'll not hang around. I'll catch the next boat that's going back to the mainland. I can always walk to Aghios Nikolaos and collect the donkey. I've done what I came for.'

Phaedra walked back down to the jetty with her grandfather. She was not sure how she felt about his visit. She would have preferred not to know about her mother and the sad mental state she was suffering from.

1937 – 1941

Manolis took the news to Yiorgo that Fotini had given birth to a healthy baby girl and Yiorgo had passed the news on to Maria and her mother.

'When can we go to see her?' asked Maria eagerly.

'Not until the weather is better. Snow is in the air and the roads could be slippery. You'd end up chilled to the bone riding the donkey to Aghios Nikolaos and Manolis would not be able to go out to the island if the weather was bad.'

Maria was disappointed but she knew Yiorgo's caution about making the journey prudent. She busied herself with making little dresses ready for her new niece whilst her mother made a new blouse and skirt for Fotini.

'If we make up a sack and you gave it to Manolis could he deliver it before Christmas?'

'Bound to be able to do so. I'll buy some wood working tools in Aghios Nikolaos for Aristo. I'm sure he would appreciate those more than a new shirt.'

Anna visited Spinalonga taking little Yannis and Marisa with her. 'I thought they should get to know their uncle,' she said to Yannis. 'Babbis didn't mind me bringing them.'

'As you look after them all the time he should have no objection to anything you do with them.' Anna looked at the two children who were sitting demurely at the table eating the biscuits that Phaedra had provided.

'Would Phaedra be willing to keep an eye on them for a few minutes whilst we went outside and talked?' she asked Yannis.

Phaedra nodded. 'I'm happy to look after them. Take as long as you like.'

Intrigued Yannis led Anna outside and through the tunnel. 'We should be undisturbed here. What do you want to talk to me about? Is it Mamma?'

Anna shook her head. 'No, Mamma is keeping well. She can get out of her bed and spend the day sitting in her chair provided I am there to help her. I sit with her and talk to her as much as I can during the day. When Pappa and Yiorgo come home they sit and tell her what they have been doing up in the fields.'

'Is Stelios giving cause for concern?'

'No, he's gone to Athens, working for the army I believe.'

'So what's worrying you, Anna?'

'Babbis has asked me to marry him.'

'About time too. You didn't need to ask for my approval.'

Anna shook her head. 'I refused him.'

'Why?' Yannis looked at his sister in puzzlement.

'I don't love Babbis and he made it clear to me that he will only ever love our sister. It would have been a marriage of convenience – his convenience. He suggested I moved up into his farmhouse. That would be impossible as I have to look after Mamma and there isn't room for him with us. Have I done the right thing, Yannis?'

Yannis nodded slowly. 'Provided he doesn't threaten to take the children away from you if you don't' marry him.'

'He wouldn't do that. He's a decent, honourable man, besides, he wouldn't be able to look after the children himself. I think he truly believed it was a solution so he could become a proper father to them and not just a visitor. Yannis adores him and is never happier than when he is up in the fields with him.'

'Then I think the present arrangements should stand.'

Anna gave a smile of relief. 'I hoped you would say that and not tell me I should marry him. I'm perfectly happy as I am.'

'I'm pleased to hear that. I'm sorry for Babbis, but he cannot destroy your life for his convenience. It's to be hoped that he will meet someone else whom he can love one day, maybe when the children are older and can understand.'

'There's not a lot of choice in the village.'

'Then he must look further afield. Is that all you wanted to talk about? If so we ought to go back to Phaedra. I have something exciting to tell you and an invitation to give you.'

'Is someone over here getting married?'

'No nothing like that. Do you remember that I said a new man had arrived, name of Remoundakis? We've had some long talks together and he's full of ideas.'

'More than you?' asked Anna with a sly smile.

'Many more. He wants to start an association, a group of men and women who represent everyone on the island. To let everyone know about it he's asked Manolis to bring him a printing press over and we'll have our own newspaper. The paper will be taken around to every house and if the people cannot read he'll read it to them. They'll have no excuse to say they don't know what is going on and they'll be able to agree or disagree with any proposals.'

'It sounds like a good idea,' agreed Anna, knowing that her brother would expect that response from her. A newspaper would appear in the village occasionally, but she never tried to read it.

'The other news is that Remoundakis has arranged for us to hire a projector and a film reel. He says that everyone in Heraklion goes to a cinema and watches films and we should be able to do the same over here.'

Anna had no idea what Yannis was talking about but she nodded dutifully.

'When we know when it will happen I want to invite you to come over in the evening to watch.'

'Why in the evening?'

'It has to be dark apparently or you cannot see the pictures.'

'What will the film be about?'

'I don't know, but I'm sure Remoundakis will choose something that everyone will enjoy. You will come, won't you, Anna?'

Anna hesitated. 'I wouldn't have to stay the night?'

'You could if you wished. Phaedra would welcome you.'

'I'm thinking of Mamma and the children. Provided I could return the same evening I would love to come.' Anna was not at all sure what a film was but was not prepared to hurt her brother's feelings by refusing. If she did not enjoy the visit, particularly the journey back in the darkness, she would make an excuse if invited to come again.

Phaedra visited Fotini frequently, enjoying nursing the tiny baby, and wishing once again that she and Yannis had a child. She kept her feelings in check. She would not become obsessed with the idea as her mother appeared to be. Maybe it was better that she and Yannis had never attempted to have a family. She could have been as unfortunate as her mother and had numerous miscarriages.

Already Fotini was making plans for her daughter. 'I'll ask Yannis to teach her to read and write as soon as she is old enough. She'll then be able to go over to the mainland, find work and get married. I don't want her to spend all her life living here.'

Phaedra listened to Fotini's ambitions for her child. Doctor Stavros had not yet taken a blood test to see if the child was carrying leprosy germs. If that was the case she would be staying on the island along with her parents. Should she be declared healthy it was likely that she would be taken to the mainland and sent to an orphanage. Phaedra did not mention either possibility to Fotini. She and Aristo were so happy that it would be cruel to put such worries into their minds.

Anna arrived on Spinalonga having arranged that Davros would take her over and collect her two hours later as Yannis had said that the proposed film should be finished within an hour. As she walked from the jetty up to the square she appreciated that she was able to see her way without having to rely on the light of the moon. At intervals there were electric lights that prevented her from stumbling or tripping.

Unsure what to expect she sat on a chair between Yannis and Phaedra looking at the tunnel entrance. A large white sheet had been fixed across the entrance and beneath a thick wire could be seen snaking its way across the ground to something on a wooden stand that Yannis told her was called a projector. There were ripples of excitement and anticipation amongst the spectators as more people arrived and jostled for a position that would give them a good view of the proceedings.

Anna sat entranced by the antics of Charlie Chaplin and clapped wildly as the film finished. 'There was only one problem,' she admitted to Yannis. 'I couldn't hear what they were saying.'

Yannis smiled at her. 'Remoundakis was only able to hire some of the old films that the cinemas no longer show. A technique has been developed where the talking can be heard and he hopes to be able to get some of those later.'

'I still enjoyed it,' Anna assured him. 'When you have a film next time may I ask Eleni to come with me?'

'Of course. Next week Remoundakis has arranged for us to have a puppet show. That will take place in the late afternoon so you could bring the children.'

'I certainly will. Life is far more exciting over here than in Plaka.'

Anna became a regular visitor whenever Yannis told her there was a film show taking place and most times Eleni accompanied her. The women would sit together, laughing until the tears rolled down their faces. Marisa complained that she was getting too old to be taken to the puppet shows and begged to be allowed to accompany her aunt and Eleni to a film until Anna finally gave in to her demands. Marisa spent the whole of the next day telling her younger brother about the event and he was envious.

'Why should Marisa be allowed to go with you and not me? She says the films are funny and I would like to see them. Ourania is going to ask her mother if she can go over and if she is allowed I should be able to go with you.' Yannis set his mouth in an obstinate line. If his aunt refused him he would appeal to his father and ask him to persuade her.

The only reason Anna was reluctant to take her nephew with her was due to the dark boat ride. If anything should happen she would be unable to save both children from the sea. When Eleni agreed to take Ourania Anna realised that she must overcome her fear of a disaster and take Yannis as well as his sister.

Tassos arrived on Spinalonga. As Yannis came forwards to greet him he moved a step back.

'Please don't come too near me. I haven't got leprosy.'

Yannis looked at the man in surprise. 'So why have you been sent here?'

'I lost a finger in an accident some years ago. The doctor decided it had been amputated because I was leprous. He wouldn't listen to me,' he ended bitterly.

Yannis nodded sympathetically, but not really believing the new arrival. 'I'd like to invite you to my house. We can accommodate you there whilst I ask Takkis if there is a house available for you.'

Tassos looked at Yannis. 'No offence, I appreciate the offer, but I don't want to be inside a house with anyone. I'd rather sleep out in the open.'

Yannis shrugged. 'You'll come to no harm sleeping outside for a day or so, but I'd like to offer you hospitality. My wife will be happy to make you a meal and then I can show you around our island.'

Tassos shook his head. 'I know you mean well, but I cannot

accept food or drink from anyone. I do not want to find that I have become infected.'

'Well, you still have to eat. This is the storeroom. The food that the boatmen bring over is kept in there and you can help yourself to whatever you want or buy meat, vegetables and bread from the shops. There's a drinking fountain up in the square or you can buy a bottle of wine from the taverna. At least leave your belongings at my house. You don't want to be carrying those around with you all the time.'

'Will it be safe if I leave it outside? I have my tools in there.'

'No one will take it. What kind of tools have you brought with you?'

'I'm a cobbler. I was told to bring them as I would be able to work over here.'

'Everyone who is able works in some way. I'm sure you'll be in demand if you can patch people's boots up so they will see them through another winter.'

Although Yannis offered Tassos a bed for the night a second time he was met with a refusal. He collected his sack and walked up the hill towards the summit of the island. There he sat down and looked across the sea. He needed to leave as soon as possible before he became contaminated by these people, however friendly they might be.

Phaedra spoke to Yannis. 'This new man, Tassos is very strange. He insists he hasn't got leprosy. If he isn't sick he shouldn't have been sent here. I took my boots to him yesterday and asked him to patch them up for me. He won't let anyone inside his house and sits outside to do repairs. Manolis says he spends all his money each week on cobblers materials.' Phaedra shrugged. 'Everyone is grateful to have had their boots patched up but he will run out of customers soon and then he will have wasted his money on leather and thread.'

Yannis frowned. 'I haven't seen him in the taverna. How does he spend his time in the evenings?'

'I don't know. Fotini and Aristo invited him in for a glass of wine when he first arrived. Fotini wanted to show off the new glasses that Aristo had given her for Christmas. He agreed to join them provided they stayed outside and he could use his own mug to drink from and wouldn't touch any of the food Fotini had prepared. It was the same when Eleni and Christos invited him. He seems to think that if he stays out in the open air he won't become sick. He could be right, of course.'

'I'll go and have a word with him. He won't be able to sit outside to work when it gets cold. His fingers will go numb.'

Tassos was happy to sit outside and talk to Yannis.

'Will you be coming down to watch the film that is being shown tonight?' asked Yannis and Tassos shook his head.

'I don't like being amongst a crowd of people.'

'You could sit at the side.'

Again Tassos shook his head. 'I'd like to ask you a question. I understand you floated across to the mainland in a bathtub. How long did it take you?'

Yannis shrugged. 'I don't know. It was dark when I left here and dark when I arrived, but my family were still up.'

'About a couple of hours then?'

'Probably, but I don't recommend it. The current could take you and you'd be swept out to sea.'

'You weren't.'

'I'd lived across from here so I was pretty familiar with the currents. I was still taking a chance. Are you thinking of trying to make the journey?'

'When I'm ready.'

Yannis nodded. 'It would be wrong of me to encourage you, but let me know if you want any help.'

'You'll not try to stop me?'

'What you decide to do with your life is not my business. If you do attempt the crossing I will wish you a safe journey. There are some caves up in the hills. You might be able to hide out up there for a few days and then move on.'

Tassos shook his head. 'I have other plans. I'm not going to spend the remainder of my life hiding in a cave.'

However hard Yannis tried to press the man about his ideas for staying undiscovered on the mainland Tassos refused to be more forthcoming.

Fotini and Aristo looked at Doctor Stavros in disbelief. 'You can't,' said Fotini. 'She's our little girl, You can't take her away.'

Doctor Stavros looked at the distraught couple before him. 'It is for her own good. The second blood test showed that she is free from leprosy. It distresses me as much as it does you, but you cannot condemn her to living here on this island with people who are sick and maimed.'

'Where will she go? What will happen to her?' asked Aristo, his face grim. He held Fotini's hand tightly feeling her trembling.

'I cannot tell you that at present, but arrangements will be made so she is well cared for. She is young enough to forget you quite quickly and settle into her new surroundings.'

'Forget us?' Fotini's voice rose in a shrill scream. 'She is our daughter. We do not want her to forget us. You cannot take her away. We won't let you.'

'It will not happen for a few months. You will have time to get used to the idea.'

'Never,' screamed Fotini. 'She is our child, not yours to be disposed of as you think fit.'

Fotini collapsed into Aristo's arms, sobbing uncontrollably. Aristo felt helpless. Surely there was something they could do to stop Vivi being taken away.

'I'll speak to Remoundakis. He knows the law. There must be something he can do to stop this happening.'

Doctor Stavros shook his head sadly. 'I have to obey the medical authorities.'

'Stay here,' Aristo commanded Fotini. 'Play with Vivi. Do not let her see how upset we are, it would only make her unhappy. I'll be back in a short while.'

Remoundakis shook his head when Aristo composed himself sufficiently to explain that Doctor Stavros had told them their daughter was to be taken away from Spinalonga.

'I can write to the government, but I fear it would be of little use. Even if they decided to change the law it could be years before it came into effect.'

Disappointed in Remoundakis's response Aristo walked to the other side of the island and sat beside the church of Aghios Yiorgos where he cursed and railed against an uncaring God, pouring out his anger and grief. Still shaking he returned to the main road and a feeling of guilt overcame him. He entered the church of Aghios Panteleimon. He must say a prayer for his previous irreligious ranting.

Father Minos found him there a short while later and was full of concern when Aristo told him the cause of his distress.

'No one told us this could happen,' he ended miserably.

'No one talks about the children who have been taken away. The memories are too painful for them. Doctor Stavros has to abide by the law. If he left Vivi here, knowing that she was healthy, he could be dismissed. We might not be sent another doctor to take his place.'

Aristo shrugged and walked from the church, leaving Father Minos looking after him sadly. He would give the man time to return home and then visit the couple and see if he was able to give them some comfort in prayer.

'I cannot give up my child,' sobbed Fotini. 'When I held Alexandros in my arms I knew how much I would like a child of my own. Once I was sent here I never thought it would be possible and then there was the miracle of Vivi.'

'Who is Alexandros?'

Through her tears Fotini explained that he was her nephew.

Father Minos looked thoughtful. 'I can promise nothing, but I will speak to Doctor Stavros. It is possible there is a solution.'

Phaedra went up to play with Vivi as she did most afternoons and found Fotini with tears still running down her face and Aristo sitting with his head in his hands.

'What's wrong?' she asked anxiously. 'Is Vivi ill?'

'I wish she was,' said Aristo bitterly. 'If she was sick she would be able to stay here with us.'

'What do you mean?'

'Doctor Stavros has said she has to leave us and go into an orphanage on the mainland.'

'Oh, that's terrible.' Phaedra felt tears coming into her eyes. 'No wonder you are both so upset. Is there nothing that can be done? Have you spoken to Remoundakis?'

'He said he would write to the government. Even if they did agree to change the law it could take years. It would be too late for Vivi then.'

'What about Father Minos? Could he plead on your behalf?'

'He said he would speak to Doctor Stavros, but if it is the law there will be nothing anyone can do,' Aristo spoke resignedly.

Phaedra was still shaking from the news when she returned home. Would Fotini become like her mother and start to carry a doll around pretending it was a baby?

'Yannis, have you heard? Vivi is being taken away.'

Yannis frowned. 'I hadn't heard. When is she going?'

'They don't know. Doctor Stavros only told them this morning. Poor Fotini is almost out of her mind with grief and Aristo is little better.'

Yannis took Phaedra in his arms. 'Now you understand why I refused your request for a child. I could not bear to see you go through so much pain and heartache. Even if a mother over here had died whilst giving birth I would have objected to you caring for the child. You may have had to give it up if it was healthy and you would have been distressed if it was ill and you watched the disease developing.'

Phaedra pulled herself away. 'I do understand, Yannis, but now I am grieving for Fotini and Aristo as well as Vivi.'

That Sunday Father Minos asked his congregation to pray that Fotini and Aristo would be given the strength and courage to relinquish their daughter. They stood together, Vivi in her father's arms, whilst Fotini continually wiped the tears from her eyes. He had not mentioned his conversation with Doctor Stavros to them. It would be cruel to raise their hopes.

Maria and Yiorgo arrived with Manolis and immediately made their way up to Fotini and Aristo's house. Maria was shocked by Fotini's appearance. Her sister had neglected both herself and her house, the bed was unmade, dirty dishes sat on the table and the fire had not been lit. Maria knelt down before her sister and took her hands.

'They're taking Vivi away. Our Vivi. Taking her to an orphanage.' Tears flowed down Fotini's cheeks.

Maria tried to comfort her. 'We won't let that happen. We want to adopt Vivi. She will become a sister for Alexandros.'

'They're taking Vivi,' Fotini said again, not comprehending Maria's words.

'Find Aristo,' Maria said to her husband. 'We need him here. Fo is unable to think straight.'

Yiorgo left the house and called on the neighbours, but they were unable to tell him where Aristo was that morning. He searched the faces of people as he walked along the main street towards the church. He found Aristo inside on his knees, but the man did not even acknowledge him. In despair Yiorgo returned outside and after waiting a while in the hope that Father Minos would appear he began to ask passers by for help in locating the priest.

By the time Father Minos appeared Yiorgo was cold where he had been sitting outside the church waiting. He rose to his feet.

'Father, please help us. Aristo is inside the church and will not listen to me. Maria is with her sister and she seems unable to understand what we are saying to her. Doctor Stavros visited us and we have told him we are happy to adopt Vivi.'

A smile of relief crossed Father Minos's face. 'My prayers have been answered. Return to the house and I will talk to Aristo and persuade him to accompany me home. It may take me a while as both he and Fotini are still in a state of shock.'

When Aristo arrived back at the house he looked old and careworn. He sat down beside Fotini. 'Listen to me, Fotini. The prayers that Father Minos has delivered up have been answered. Maria and Yiorgo will take Vivi to live with them.'

Fotini looked from one to the other of us in disbelief. 'Is that true? She won't have to go to an orphanage?'

'That is what I have been trying to tell you, Fo. I promise you we will treat her as our own child. Yiorgo gave me a camera at Christmas and I will be able to send you photos of her and write to you regularly to tell you everything she has done and said.'

Phaedra relayed Fotini's news to Yannis. 'I am so relieved. They are unhappy that they have to part with Vivi but at least they will know where she is and receive news of her. I'm going up to the church to say a prayer and also to thank Father Minos.'

The winter gave way to spring and Tassos eyed the water between the island and the mainland. Manolis had pointed out to him the way the water rippled to show the direction the current flowed and explained that later in the year the wind died down and the currents were easier to see from higher up on the fortress wall.

Satisfied that he had sufficient cobblers' tools and materials he then began to ask Manolis to buy buttons, needles, sewing cotton, crochet hooks, embroidery silks, nails and screws. He would only be able to take items that he could carry easily with him. Finally he packed his sack carefully with all his possessions and approached Yannis.

'I need your help. I'm planning to leave tomorrow night.'

Yannis looked at the man in surprise. 'Once your bath tub is found there will be a full scale search for you.'

'I'll either sink it or hide it amongst the rocks. As a last resort I can tip it over so only the base shows.'

'Where are you going? Up into the hills?'

Tassos shook his head. 'I'm going to walk around openly in the villages selling my goods. I'm planning to be a pedlar and no one will take any notice of me.'

Yannis smiled admiringly at the man's audacity. 'Spiro and I will help you with the bath tub. All I can do is wish you a safe journey.'

Yannis told Phaedra the reason he was leaving their house that evening and she looked at him in concern.

'You're not planning to go with him, are you, Yannis?' she asked anxiously.

Yannis shook his head. 'I wouldn't want to worry you like that again. I have no need to go over now we are allowed visitors, although I would like to see my mother,' he admitted.

Phaedra believed her husband's words but she still waited in an agony of apprehension until he returned that evening.

Yannis was concerned. The newspaper that Manolis had brought over from the mainland had an account of fighting taking place in Europe. Having read the article he delivered the paper to Remoundakis.

'Sorry I'm a bit late with this today, but I wanted to read an account of the war.'

Remoundakis nodded. 'I'll print a report in our newspaper although I think very few will be interested. It's too far away to affect us.'

'It will give them something to talk about. Everyone will have their own opinion of the outcome. I hope it is soon over and done with. The newspaper says that hundreds have been killed.'

'Unfortunately that always happens.'

'It's not just the soldiers who have died. It says they are dropping bombs on the cities and destroying buildings. Many of the people who are dead are said to be ordinary workers and their families.'

Remoundakis frowned. 'Let me read it for myself and I'll decide what I should print. We don't want those who have a family on mainland Greece to be concerned, although it's unlikely to spread down that far before an agreement is reached.'

'I just hope you're right.'

Despite Remoundakis's optimism the fighting increased. Having taken Poland and Austria, the Germans continued their relentless march through Europe. France, Belgium, Luxembourg and The Netherlands had all capitulated and now the German troops were in Romania. Yugoslavia and Albania were supporting the German army in the hopes of avoiding occupation. Now Italy had joined forces with Germany and requested safe passage through Greece to have easy access to the territories the Germans had conquered in Africa. When Greece refused Remoundakis printed the news in the paper and said that was a victory for common sense. The refusal was ignored and the Greek people began to suffer the consequences.

Yiorgo Pavlakis, now the Mayor of Heraklion and leader of the government was also concerned. The fighting was getting closer daily and there was no guarantee that it would not spread to Crete. British troops were stationed on the island and it was hoped that they would be able to keep any invading army at bay. To ensure the safety of his wife and child he decided to send them down to Aghios Nikolaos. If by any chance the British were unable to prevent the Germans landing on Crete once they had taken Chania and Heraklion they were unlikely to have any further interest in the country.

Louisa was not happy about her husband's decision but he

would brook no argument from her 'You'll be safe down there and as soon as everything has calmed down I'll send for you to return.'

Louisa did not enjoy being in Aghios Nikolaos. Many tavernas were closed or were charging a high price for a meal. After a few weeks she had spent most of the money that Yiorgo had given her for food and lodgings and decided to return to Heraklion, leaving her daughter behind. She had given Anna a little money and promised her that she would be back within a few days.

Anna wandered miserably through the streets of Aghios Nikolaos. She had spent almost the last of the money her mother had left with her on a roll two nights before and now had only a few lepta remaining. She had managed to steal various pieces of fruit that she had eaten when well away from the shop, but she really needed money to pay the rent. As she bought an apple she was able to snatch a few coins from the box where the greengrocer kept his change.

She counted out the little money she had and went into the baker. 'May I have a roll, please?'

Her hand dipped into his box of takings but this time she was not so fortunate. The baker's wife caught hold of her arm and made her drop the coins and note she was holding. Anna kicked and wriggled, but there was no way she could escape from the grip the woman had on her.

Anna tried to explain that she had only taken the money because she was hungry; that her mother would be returning to the town soon and bring money with her.

'Let her go,' said the baker. 'She's only a child.'

Momentarily the baker's wife relaxed her grip and Anna made another attempt to escape. The woman grabbed her by the hair and held her tight, exposing the birthmark on her neck.

'You're coming with me,' she announced.

Holding Anna tightly she dragged the girl to the police station and pushed her inside.

'She's a thief. Caught her helping herself to the money in the shop. I want her locked up.'

The policeman looked at Anna kindly. 'Now, let's all calm down for a minute. Sit down there, child, and tell me who you are and where you have come from.'

Anna explained that she had been brought down to Aghios Nikolaos by her mother and left to fend for herself whilst her mother returned to the town to ask her husband for some more money. 'We owe rent to the lady where we've been lodging. That's why I tried to take the money. If she turns me out I have nowhere to go and my mother won't know where I am.'

'Maybe you could shelter her for a few days until her mother returns,' suggested the policeman.

The baker's wife shook her head and pulled back Anna's hair. 'She should be sent away. I'll not have her.'

The policeman looked at the red birthmark on Anna's neck. 'I need to go to speak to someone. Whilst I'm gone I want you to wait in there.' He pushed Anna gently through a door and locked it behind her. Immediately Anna began to scream and bang on the door.

'Stay with her. See if you can calm her down. I'm going to ask Doctor Stavros to come and look at her.'

Doctor Stavros was nowhere to be found and in desperation the policeman asked Doctor Kandakis to come and look at the mark on Anna's neck. Anna was huddled in a miserable heap in the corner when they arrived.

'Come here, girl, and show me your neck,' demanded Doctor Kandakis.

Anna did not move.

'Confirmed. I'll send you my bill.'

The policeman looked after the doctor in puzzlement. He would not have been able to see the mark on Anna's neck from the door of the cell.

'I'm off. I've wasted enough time here. You deal with her as you think fit, but I don't want to see her around.' The baker's wife pulled her shawl over her head and left.

Throughout the afternoon the policeman sat outside the cell and finally managed to persuade Anna to eat the rolls his wife had prepared for him for lunch. He continually looked at his watch and finally rose.

'I'm going to find a friend of mine. He'll probably have another doctor with him. I'll ask him to have a look at your neck and I'm sure he'll say it's nothing to worry about. Then as soon as I am off duty here I'll take you back to my house and the wife and I will look after you until your mother returns. How does that sound?'

Anna nodded dully.

To the policeman's consternation Doctor Stavros was not with Manolis when he arrived back at the port.

'Had an emergency in Elounda,' he explained. 'What's the problem?'

'Well, I've a young girl in the cells. Picked up thieving. She says her mother has returned to Heraklion to get some money. Could be perfectly true, of course, but she has a mark on her neck that Doctor Kandakis says is leprosy. If so it's likely that her mother has abandoned her here. I can't leave her locked up in the cells all night and I can't take her home with me. Can you take her over to the island now?'

Manolis sighed. 'I suppose so. Bring her down.'

Anna sat silently in the stern of the boat. She had no idea where she was being taken and if she would ever see her mother and father again.

As they drew into the jetty Manolis called to Flora. 'Find Yannis for me.' He helped Anna from the boat and stood and waited until Yannis finally appeared.

'I've brought a visitor for you. Take her up to your house Flora and make her feel at home whilst I speak to Yannis.

'What's this all about?' asked Yannis.

'I'm not sure. The policeman at Aghios Nikolaos was waiting

for me and asked me to bring the girl over. She was picked up stealing and tells some story about her mother bringing her down here. There's a nasty looking mark on her neck that she claims is a birth mark, but Doctor Kandakis says it's leprosy.'

'What did Doctor Stavros say?'

'He hasn't seen it. I had to take him over to Elounda this morning. He said he would make his own way back. If the girl is telling the truth he'll confirm that it's a birthmark and the policeman says he and his wife will take her in and look after her until her mother returns.'

'Where's she going to stay? My upstairs floor has the six new men staying. I can't put her up there with them.'

'I thought Flora could look after her.'

'You know that isn't possible. She has the two women sleeping in her house. I'll talk to Phaedra. She may be willing for the girl to have a mattress in the corner of our living room.'

Manolis smiled. 'I knew you wouldn't let me down.'

Phaedra fussed over Anna, insisting that she ate some breakfast before Doctor Stavros arrived.

'What will he do to me?' asked Anna anxiously.

'Nothing. He will only look at your neck and then he will probably take you back to Aghios Nikolaos.' They sat outside on the step an Anna looked curiously at the people as they passed by and called out a greeting.

'Where are they going?' she asked.

'To work, the same as the people on the mainland do. Some have small gardens where they grow vegetables or keep chickens, others help Spiro up in the hospital.'

'What does Yannis do?'

'He's a teacher. Some people were unable to go to school when they were children and he shows them how to write their names and read words.'

'My Pappa is a teacher. He's also the Mayor of Heraklion.'

'Really?'

Anna nodded. 'He's a very important man.'

Phaedra rose and took Anna's hand. 'I think we should go and find Yannis and tell him what an important man your Pappa is.'

Yannis was reluctant to finish teaching early and Phaedra walked back to their house to await the arrival of Doctor Stavros. As soon as she saw him she asked him to come and examine Anna.

'Manolis was telling me about her on the way over. I understand Doctor Kandakis diagnosed. Come here, Anna, and let me look at your neck.'

Anna submitted to his scrutiny. 'Who's looking after you over here?'

'Yannis and Phaedra. I stayed in their house last night.'

'Then I think I should speak to them next. I believe you when you say you have a birth mark. You have absolutely nothing to worry about, Anna.'

'So I can go back to my Mamma and Pappa?'

Doctor Stavros smiled kindly at her. 'I'm sure we will be able to arrange that very soon. Manolis told me that your Mamma had returned to Heraklion to ask your Pappa for some money.'

Anna nodded. 'My Pappa's a very important person and I'm sure they'll be looking for me soon.'

'She says he's the Mayor of Heraklion,' Phaedra informed him.

'I need to speak to Yannis,' said Doctor Stavros abruptly. 'Where is he?'

'Teaching. I spoke to him a while ago and he said he would soon be finished.'

'I'll go and find him.'

Doctor Stavros insisted that Yannis ended his lesson immediately as he needed to speak to him urgently. 'We need to be somewhere private.'

Yannis led the way to the far side of the island and both men sat on a granite rock. 'What's so important. Is it Phaedra? Is she ill?'

'Have you heard the news from the mainland?'

Yannis shook his head. 'We've heard rumours, but there have been no newspapers.'

'Heraklion fell last week. The citizens tried to fight them off, but it was impossible. Once inside they killed all the government officials.'

'All of them?' exclaimed Yannis in horror. 'What about Yiorgo Pavlakis?'

'Who was he?'

'The Mayor and my old school teacher. He was the man who managed to get our pensions granted.'

'That brings me to another problem. The child who has been sent over here. Do you know who she is?'

'She was caught stealing in Aghios Nikolaos. Her mother had left her there whilst she returned to Heraklion.'

Doctor Stavros took a deep breath. 'She says she's the daughter of Yiorgo Pavlakis.'

'What!' Yannis gasped and grabbed the doctor by his shirt. 'Tell me that isn't true. It would be too cruel.'

'You knew Yiorgo Pavlakis, you must know if the child is his.'

Abruptly Yannis rose from the rock and hurried back through the tunnel. Phaedra was at the drinking fountain with Anna and he went over to her, trying to smile and speak gently.

'I've been told that your Pappa is the Mayor of Heraklion. What's his name?'

'Yiorgo Pavlakis.'

'And your Mamma's name is Louisa and you live in a taverna?' Anna nodded. 'Pappa is a teacher too.'

'He was my teacher.' said Yannis sadly and turned away. He must speak to Father Minos. The girl could be his daughter.

Father Minos sat and explained to Anna that her father had been killed when the Germans entered Heraklion.

'Why was he fighting?' she asked.

'Everyone was fighting to defend the city.' Father Minos did not tell her that her father had been ignominiously marched from the council chambers and shot. 'Your Mamma won't be able to come down to Aghios Nikolaos and look for you for a while as the doctor says the buses are not running.'

'What's going to happen to me?' asked Anna fearfully.

'You can stay with Phaedra and Yannis. They'll look after you until your Mamma comes.'

Yannis listened to the German as he spoke to the crowd who had gathered on the jetty. In no uncertain terms the commander had made it clear that he did not care if the people on the island lived or died. He was not prepared to tolerate a seat of resistance on the island and to prevent this from happening they would no longer receive any supplies of food or water from the mainland. Yannis trembled as Father Minos tried to appeal to the commander on their behalf and in reply a gun shot had narrowly missed him. Anna slipped her hand into Yannis's.

'I don't like that man. I didn't like him when Uncle Pavlos brought him to the taverna and he took our photographs.'

'Are you sure he visited you, Anna?'

Anna nodded vehemently. 'I know it was Mr Dubois as he has that funny white mark on his face.'

Yannis walked slowly back to his house. It sounded as though Yiorgo had unknowingly entertained a German who had been sent to Crete to gather information.

'What are we going to do?' asked Phaedra.

'There's nothing we can do. I'm going to talk to Father Minos and see what he suggests. We just have to hope that the war is over quickly.'

1942 - 1944

Anna was not unhappy living with Yannis and Phaedra. She had her own bedroom on the upper floor and Phaedra had made her some new blouses and a skirt. Provided she sat at the table and did her lessons with Yannis each day she was allowed to do much as she pleased. On occasion she felt uncomfortable at the way Yannis looked at her, but he never did more than pat her head when he wished her goodnight.

The occupation she enjoyed most was drawing. She had drawn Flora on a number of occasions and now she sat at the table drawing Phaedra, making sure it was the unblemished side of her face that she reproduced. As she was adding some shading Yannis arrived. He looked at the sketch and picked it up.

'Where did you learn to draw, Anna?'

'I just can,' she answered.

'May I see any others you have completed?'

Anna went up to her room and returned with a number of drawings. Yannis examined them, sucking in his breath.

'I'd like to show these to Father Minos, Anna.'

'He can keep them if he wants. I can do some more.'

Yannis had confronted Father Minos with the drawings Anna had produced and also two he had treasured that had been completed by his sister, Maria.

'The style, the confident pencil stokes, they could have been done by the same person.'

Father Minos examined the work. In his heart he felt that Yannis was correct. Louisa had spoken truly when she claimed that Yannis was the father of her child. He shook his head.

'A few pictures prove nothing, Yannis. You have to remember that the child has lost her father. How would she feel if you suddenly told her that Yiorgo Pavlakis was not her father and you claimed her as your daughter? No, Yannis. You must forget this wild idea.'

The first effects felt by the blockade of the island was the lack of water. The boats no longer arrived every morning with supplies and the residents were reliant on the drinking fountain and the stagnant water stored in the tanks. Father Minos impressed upon them frequently the necessity of using the fresh water sparingly.

'On no account must the fountain run dry. It must only be used as drinking water. The water from the tanks must be used for washing. We don't want to have to resort to having to boil that to make it safe to drink.'

The people grumbled, but they understood that the restrictions were for their own good.

Flora sat on the jetty each day, watching and hoping that Manolis would appear. Although food was no longer delivered from Plaka, Elounda or Aghios Nikolaos the people were not hungry during the first year. There was a plentiful supply of vegetables in the shops and occasionally a boat would come from Plaka with an Italian soldier on board and a sack of vegetables would be thrown ashore. Spiro was given all the eggs and also the milk for the patients in the hospital. They no longer had fires in every house as there were no boxes arriving that could be broken up and used as kindling. For every ten people one fire was built and the food was cooked as a communal meal as it had been in the past.

It was a different situation in the second year; wooden fixtures in the houses were dismantled to provide fire wood; there were few vegetables available in the shops as no seed had been delivered. The chickens no longer laid as no grain was delivered for them and people ate their vegetable scraps rather than throwing them away. One by one the chickens were slaughtered, even the bones being saved to give some flavour to the water. The goats were so underfed that they were unable to give milk and they gradually met the same fate as the chickens.

The storeroom was empty; no longer were the people able to help themselves to rice, pasta, lentils or coffee to supplement their diet. The baker no longer produced any bread as there was no flour and certainly not sufficient fuel to keep his oven alight. Once carefully tended gardens and vegetable plots were now overgrown with weeds and grass. The only plants that seemed to flourish were the geraniums that Manolis had brought over for Flora. At least the flowers were edible, but it would have been more useful if they could have eaten the profusion of green leaves.

The church bell tolled daily, signifying another death had taken place. The villagers would gather together and form a procession up to Aghios Yiorgos church, the men carrying the coffin. No one had the strength to dig a grave and they also realised that the graveyard would soon be full and unable to accommodate any more bodies. As Father Minos intoned a prayer the deceased was tipped unceremoniously into the tower and the empty coffin taken away to be used again.

No building or repairs to the houses took place; there were plenty of empty houses. During the day those who were able would scour the shore and rocks for any edible sea food they could find to flavour the water that was their only source of sustenance. Those who were already in the hospital succumbed first, making way for others to take their place. However arduously Spiro attended to them he was unable to keep them alive.

Anna still waved from the shore at Plaka but Yannis only had the strength to raise his arm in a brief acknowledgement. As the effects of starvation took hold more and more people died and the bell tolled many times during the day as the weak congregation struggled to the church of Aghios Yiorgos to say a final farewell to loved ones or even those they hardly knew.

Phaedra insisted that any food available to them was always given to Anna and Yannis, often telling them that she had already eaten. Now she lay on her mattress. She had no strength left to fight. She was so tired, so weak. Anna had drawn her a picture of Yannis to help her feel better and she held it loosely between her fingers. She felt Yannis kiss her gently and she tried to smile as she closed her eyes, drew her last breath and the sheet of paper fluttered to the ground.

If you have enjoyed reading Phaedra, you will be pleased to know that the next book is planned for publication in June 2019.

Read on for a 'taster' of what is to come......

January 2015

Vasi answered his mobile 'phone, knowing that it was his father calling.

'What's wrong, Pappa?'

'Nothing. I wanted to know if you had looked at that house in Elounda that Monika mentioned.'

Vasi shook his head. He had completely forgotten. 'I'm sorry, Pappa, I've been rather busy with 'The Imperia'. I'll go down this afternoon and see if I can find out who owns it.'

'Ask if they are willing to sell.'

'You don't want to commit yourself to anything until you and Cathy have seen it. You could decide that it isn't suitable.'

'It may have to be.'

'What do you mean?'

'I have a prospective buyer for the "Central". If we come to an agreement he wants to buy the apartment in Heraklion as well.'

Vasi whistled through his teeth. 'Has he won the lottery like you did?'

Vasi heard his father chuckle. 'Not that I know of. He's a business man.'

'What business is he in?'

'Shipping.'

'You mean he has a fleet of ships?'

'I don't think so. He said he was a 'middle man' and arranged transport for goods being sent around the world. He's probably talking about shipping by air.'

'Is he Greek?'

'Partly.'

'What's the other part?' asked Vasi suspiciously.

'Russian.'

'Russian! Why are you thinking of selling to a Russian?'

'Now I've made up my mind to sell I want to do so as quickly as possible. "The Central" is a large hotel in a prime position. I want to sell it as a going concern and with the present state of the economy I don't think any Greek could afford it. The banks have clamped down on loans or else the interest rate is extortionate. This man has shown an interest and appears willing to pay me the asking price. He assures me he has the finance available. You go and look at that house. If you can gain access from the owner take Saffron with you and then drive up to Heraklion tomorrow. You can tell me if you think it will be suitable and Saffron can talk to Cathy. Arrange to stay over and you can also meet Mr Kuzmichov.'

Vasi ran a hand over his head. 'I'm opening "The Imperia" next week. I have stock arriving tomorrow. Couldn't I come up in a week or so?'

'I'm sure Yiorgo is capable of dealing with that. You said you plan to make him the manager. If Mr Kuzmichov is seriously interested I want to close this deal as quickly as possible.'

'Does Mr Kuzmichov speak Greek and have you consulted a lawyer? He may have the money available but will he be allowed to transfer it from Russia? There could be all sorts of international restrictions. You don't want to sign the hotel over to him and then find you cannot access the money. I'd like to meet him and discuss this further with you, Pappa, before you make a decision.'

'Then come up tomorrow. We will have the morning to iron out any problems you envisage. I'll arrange for my lawyer to come in the afternoon and I'm sure he'll know the legal position regarding money transfers. I already have an appointment with Mr Kuzmichov for the following day so you can meet him and we can talk again after he leaves. I'm sure we can solve any of the problems you envisage between us.'

Vasi sighed. His father was not going to accept any excuses.

'Once you're satisfied that the sale to Mr Kuzmichov is feasible, and if you both think the house in Elounda is suitable for Cathy we can drive back with you and have a look for ourselves.'

'I suppose so.'

'You don't sound very happy about the arrangement.'

'It will mean changing my plans and also asking Saffron to get the bedroom ready for you. Will Cathy be able to manage the stairs?'

'If she takes it slowly and I help her. Tell Saffron she only needs to make up the bed. We'll see you tomorrow.'

Vasi closed his 'phone and shook his head at Saffron. 'There are times when my father is impossible. I have to go and look at that house today, find the owner and then ask you to come with me to look inside. Then tomorrow he wants us to drive up to Heraklion and stay with them. He has a meeting arranged with his lawyer for the afternoon and the following day he wants me to meet a prospective buyer for "The Central".'

'Why does he want me to go with you?' asked Saffron.

'So you can talk to Cathy about the house in Elounda and he probably thinks you would be company for her whilst we are having business discussions.'

'I'm happy to spend some time with Cathy, but I wouldn't want to make a decision on her behalf about the house. She would need to see it for herself. I know Monika said the front door would be wide enough for a wheelchair but the other doorways inside could be too narrow; even a few centimetres could make access impossible.'

'That's the other thing. My father wants to return to Elounda with us so Cathy can see the house for herself. Are you able to get the bedroom ready for them? He says they'll stay over. I really could do without this. I've already advertised that "The Imperia" will be opening next week.'

'Stop stressing, Vasi. You know Yiorgo will deal with everything there. You contact the owner of that house and arrange when we can visit. Call me and I'll come straight down.'